The Archers

THE AMBRIDGE CHRONICLES

The Archers

THE AMBRIDGE CHRONICLES
PART TWO

Looking for Love

1968-1986

JOANNA TOYE

BBC

For Mary Cutler, with love, to mark her twenty years on the writing team.

This book is published to accompany
the BBC Radio 4 serial entitled *The Archers*.
The Editor of *The Archers* is Vanessa Whitburn.

Published by BBC Worldwide Ltd,
Woodlands, 80 Wood Lane, London W12 0TT

First published 1999
Copyright © Joanna Toye 1999
The moral right of the author has been asserted.

ISBN 0 563 55125 9

Commissioning Editor: Anna Ottewill
Project Editor: Lara Speicher
Designed by Tim Higgins
Text set in Adobe Plantin and New Caledonia Semi Bold Italic
by Keystroke, Jacaranda Lodge, Wolverhampton
Printed and bound in Great Britain by Butler & Tanner Ltd,
Frome and London
Jacket printed by Lawrence-Allen Ltd, Weston-super-Mare

Contents

Contents

Acknowledgements

As ever, thanks are due to many people without whom I could not have begun to contemplate writing this book.

On the production team of *The Archers*, the Editor, Vanessa Whitburn, has given me her unstinting support. Keri Davies read the manuscript and Camilla Fisher again helped me hugely with my endless continuity queries.

At BBC Worldwide, Lara Speicher worked tirelessly as Project Editor, and Commissioning Editor Anna Ottewill enthused in all the right places, while at the BBC's Written Archives Centre in Reading, Neil Somerville and James Codd helped me to access past script material by Alan Bower, Debbie Cook, Mary Cutler, Tessa Diamond, Dave Dixon, Simon Frith, Graham Harvey, Brian Hayles, Helen Leadbeater, Edward J. Mason, Keith Miles, Bruno Milna, Margaret Phelan, James Robson and William Smethurst.

In the years that this book covers, Tony Shryane retired after nearly 30 years as Producer and William Smethurst took over as Editor. I worked for them both and each, in their way, developed and encouraged my ambitions.

Finally, I have to thank Roger Florey, without whom I wouldn't have had a desk at which to write, and Rob Hutchings, for lunch.

Joanna Toye
August 1999

The Archers

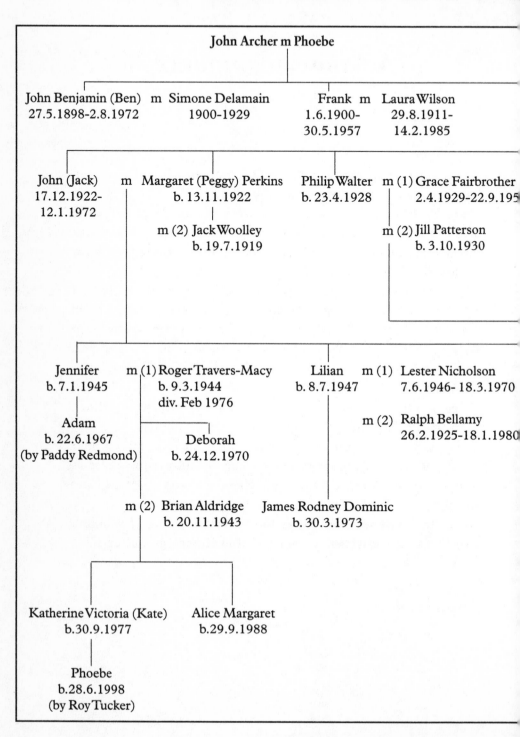

John Archer m Phoebe

John Benjamin (Ben) m Simone Delamain
27.5.1898-2.8.1972   1900-1929

Frank m Laura Wilson
1.6.1900-   29.8.1911-
30.5.1957   14.2.1985

John (Jack) m Margaret (Peggy) Perkins
17.12.1922-   b. 13.11.1922
12.1.1972

Philip Walter m (1) Grace Fairbrother
b. 23.4.1928   2.4.1929-22.9.195

m (2) Jack Woolley
b. 19.7.1919

m (2) Jill Patterson
b. 3.10.1930

Jennifer   m (1) Roger Travers-Macy
b. 7.1.1945   b. 9.3.1944
                   div. Feb 1976

Lilian   m (1) Lester Nicholson
b. 8.7.1947   7.6.1946- 18.3.1970

m (2) Ralph Bellamy
26.2.1925-18.1.1980

Adam
b. 22.6.1967   Deborah
(by Paddy Redmond)   b. 24.12.1970

m (2) Brian Aldridge
b. 20.11.1943

James Rodney Dominic
b. 30.3.1973

Katherine Victoria (Kate)   Alice Margaret
b.30.9.1977   b.29.9.1988

Phoebe
b.28.6.1998
(by Roy Tucker)

Family Tree

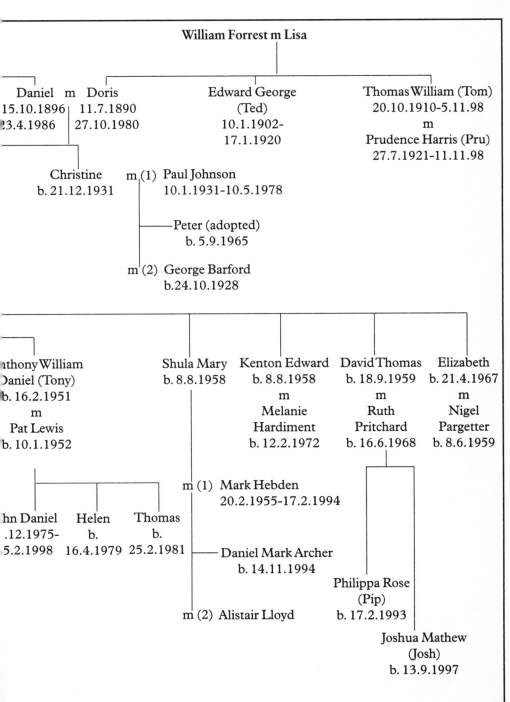

William Forrest m Lisa

Daniel m Doris
15.10.1896 | 11.7.1890
23.4.1986 | 27.10.1980

Edward George
(Ted)
10.1.1902-
17.1.1920

Thomas William (Tom)
20.10.1910-5.11.98
m
Prudence Harris (Pru)
27.7.1921-11.11.98

Christine
b. 21.12.1931

m (1) Paul Johnson
10.1.1931-10.5.1978

————— Peter (adopted)
b. 5.9.1965

m (2) George Barford
b. 24.10.1928

Anthony William
Daniel (Tony)
b. 16.2.1951
m
Pat Lewis
b. 10.1.1952

Shula Mary
b. 8.8.1958

Kenton Edward
b. 8.8.1958
m
Melanie
Hardiment
b. 12.2.1972

David Thomas
b. 18.9.1959
m
Ruth
Pritchard
b. 16.6.1968

Elizabeth
b. 21.4.1967
m
Nigel
Pargetter
b. 8.6.1959

John Daniel
.12.1975-
5.2.1998

Helen
b.
16.4.1979

Thomas
b.
25.2.1981

m (1) Mark Hebden
20.2.1955-17.2.1994

————— Daniel Mark Archer
b. 14.11.1994

m (2) Alistair Lloyd

Philippa Rose
(Pip)
b. 17.2.1993

Joshua Mathew
(Josh)
b. 13.9.1997

PROLOGUE 1967

Lost and Found

'Mum, you're having me on. That sort of thing doesn't happen in Ambridge!'

In the hallway of the converted Victorian house where she'd finally found a landlady prepared to consider a single mother with a small baby – in most places she'd tried the attitudes were as Victorian as the houses – Jennifer Archer shifted her son from one hip to the other. Adam grabbed greedily at the frayed telephone cord and attempted to wrap it round his neck. Jennifer tried to untangle it as her mother, Peggy, protested that the news was, unfortunately, true. The Borchester mail van had been held up and robbed just outside the village while the inhabitants of Ambridge were tucked up in their beds.

'I had to ring you, dear, before you heard it on the wireless. I knew you'd be shocked.'

'Shocked! That's the least of it!'

'And there's the first shoot of the season up at Grey Gables today,' her mother worried, 'so once the guests start arriving, that'll confuse the issue. Assuming they get through the police road-blocks.'

Adam was beginning to fret, lunging dangerously towards the wall lamp with its fringed parchment shade. Jennifer tried to interest him in a length of ribbon she found in her housecoat pocket. He threw it contemptuously to the floor, a tiny tyrant with an unconsidered bauble.

'I'll have to go, Mum,' she apologized. 'You must let me know what happens. How's Dad, by the way?'

'Oh, the same as ever.'

Still spending all his spare time at the casino in Borchester, then, thought Jennifer.

Peggy cursed the day that Nelson Gabriel had opened the Monte Carlo Casino, but her husband Jack was in his element. Peggy only ever heard about Jack's winnings – a staggering £840 on one occasion – and that was after he'd paid his bar bill. But it didn't take her long to realize that no news was bad news, and there were far more mornings after the night before when Jack said nothing than when he exultantly waved fistfuls of fivers in her face.

As time went on and Jack had become a more and more frequent fixture there, Peggy had cursed more than the casino. She'd cursed Nelson Gabriel himself, especially when, the previous year, he'd treated his father, Walter, to a lavish Mediterranean cruise.

'Flaunting his ill-gotten gains!' she'd fulminated to Doris, Jack's mother, who knew only too well her son's weaknesses – and not just for cards.

Peggy had been even more furious when Walter had returned with souvenirs of Maltese lace and Spanish leather, which he pressed on members of the Archer family. Putting aside the hand-tooled and gilt-embossed address book that he'd brought her, Peggy had asked him crisply where Nelson was.

'He's stayed on. He's got business to do out there,' explained Walter proudly. 'Property and what not. He's a rare h'entrepreneur, my Nelson.'

Peggy assumed one of her more vinegary faces.

'Funded by the customers he fleeces at the casino,' she remarked acidly. 'Well, I'm sorry, Uncle Walter,' she continued, as she took in Walter's wounded look. 'But how do you expect me to feel? I just hope Nelson can live with himself, that's all.'

'H'I'm going to forget you said that, Peggy me love,' said Walter with dignity. 'My Nelson's just trying to make an honest living.'

Walter might have tried to forget, but Peggy had remembered – and regretted – her words six months later when news had reached the village of a terrible tragedy. Nelson had been on his way home when the private plane he was travelling in had come down in Kent.

The pilot had baled out but his passenger had been killed outright. Nelson, Walter Gabriel's adored only son, was dead.

The casino, however, had lived on, its Grecian portico on Market Street a Utopia for Jennifer's father and a Nemesis for her mother.

'I'd better let you go, Jennifer, you'll be late for work. And I've got six breakfasts to do for Detective Superintendent King and his men. They're using The Bull as a sort of headquarters.'

'Thanks for letting me know, Mum. Love to you and Dad. And Lilian and Tony, of course.'

'Bye, Jennifer dear. And give little Adam a big hug from his grandma.'

'I will. Bye.'

Jennifer replaced the receiver with relief and scuttled towards her room. Lance, who lived on the floor above, would be leaving for work soon and she didn't want him seeing her in her baby-doll pyjamas. He was a customs officer at the docks. He'd come knocking on her door within hours of her moving in, ostensibly selling raffle tickets for the Merchant Seamen's Association and, hearing Bob Dylan playing on her transistor, had enquired what music she liked before asking her to a Val Doonican concert. Jennifer, who'd told him she liked the Stones, the Kinks, Bob Dylan and Donovan, had been somewhat confused by the offer.

'I'm sorry,' she said firmly. 'My boyfriend wouldn't like it.'

'Boyfriend?' Jennifer had had the satisfaction of seeing Lance's leer waver momentarily. 'Where is he, then?'

'He – he works away a lot. But he'll be coming to visit me. Soon.'

Lance gave her a speculative look which made her spine tingle in a way that definitely did not signify sexual attraction.

'Another time,' he'd shrugged. 'What the eye doesn't see, eh?'

It seemed a rather curious maxim for a member of Her Majesty's Customs.

Jennifer's mornings were a triumph of lateral thinking over logistics. She was up at seven, to get herself and Adam into the bathroom before the other tenants started thumping on the door. Then she got

13

him dressed while his bottle and the milk for his baby rice heated on the gas ring in the corner of her room. (The landlady called it a flat, but that was just because of the flimsy partition that screened her bed and Adam's cot from the old moquette settee and the yellow Formica table which constituted her living room.)

With Adam fed, she'd prop him up in his cot while she got dressed, and he'd burble away to her as he rocked backwards and forwards and banged his rattle against the bars. Jennifer would talk back to him, telling him what a beautiful baby he was, and how clever, and how much she loved him. Every day, as he became more aware and responsive, it was harder and harder not to stand there barefoot in her slip, holding him close, smelling his intoxicating, innocent, baby smell, feeling his tiny starfish hands clutch at her breast or tug her hair. She couldn't let herself linger, for if she had, she could have played with him all day, and already the bedside clock was telling her it was time to leave, to take him to the woman she'd found to mind him while Jennifer taught a class of seven-year-olds at a run-down school near the docks.

The post had arrived just before she left that morning, and Jennifer read her sister's letter in the staff-room at break-time, as she munched her stale digestive and drank the watery coffee that the school provided.

'Much to tell!' Lilian wrote in her loopy, sloping script. 'I've passed my driving test! First time!' Lilian was a great friend of the exclamation mark. 'It must be all those lessons Roger gave me.'

Roger Travers-Macy had come to the village a couple of years before. He'd called himself Roger Patillo then because he'd fallen out with his rather autocratic upper-class family. He hadn't wanted anything to do with them, but now they were back on speaking terms, he was using his family name again. Jennifer could still remember her delighted surprise when, soon after he arrived, Roger had struck up a conversation with her in her parents' pub and told her that his favourite book was *Cyrano de Bergerac*.

'Triangular situations are always so interesting, don't you think?' he'd speculated.

Jennifer, who was then at teacher-training college, had been intrigued. A good-looking guy, her own age, articulate and well-read, in Ambridge? It was too much to hope for.

She and Roger had been out a few times, and something might have come of it, but, newly arrived, he was the focus of attention for every female in the vicinity – and he clearly enjoyed it. At around the same time, Jennifer had fallen for Paddy, Adam's father, and that, as far as she was concerned, put an end to her and Roger. After a while, Roger and Lilian had begun going out together, and Lilian, Jennifer thought, seemed pretty keen. She'd be mad not to be.

She returned to Lilian's letter, written on paper with an eye-bending op art border.

'If Dad'll lend me the car, Roger's suggested we come and see you – it'd do me good to try a longer drive. Let me know some dates.'

Jennifer sighed as she stirred her coffee. She wasn't at all sure that she wanted Lilian or anyone else to see how she was living in Bristol. The flat she was in now was infinitely preferable to the damp bedsit she'd first rented, but it was still hardly luxurious. She didn't want Lilian to have to lie on her behalf back in Ambridge in order to keep Peggy happy; and keeping Peggy happy, when she had worries enough with their father, was high on both girls' agenda.

The trouble was, Jennifer had left Ambridge in such a hurry that there'd been no time, really, to think.

All through her pregnancy, and even now, she'd told no one the identity of Adam's father. When Adam had been born with his shock of red hair, she'd thought that everyone would immediately make the connection between him and her Uncle Phil's copper-haired cowman, Paddy Redmond, but no one had said anything. Paddy had known she was pregnant, but he'd never asked if he was the father and she'd never told him. He knew she'd been seeing other people – Roger, for one, as well as Henry King, an assistant at the bookshop Roger managed – even Nelson Gabriel on a couple of occasions, and, she concluded, he conveniently assumed that one of them was the lucky man.

But Paddy was the only one of them she had been in love with – and the only one to whom she had made love. For her, it had been the real thing. Then, out of the blue, Paddy had returned from a holiday in Ireland with a fiancée in tow – his childhood sweetheart who, to add insult to injury, found work as a barmaid at The Bull. There Jennifer had to listen to Nora McAuley's alternating paeans of praise and catalogues of injustices about 'Red', as she called him, while Paddy's baby kicked inside Jennifer against the unfairness of it all. But in the spring before Adam was born, Paddy had fallen out with both his employer and his fiancée and had found himself a new job in the south of England where, as her Uncle Phil had recounted, he felt he would be 'better appreciated'.

He'd left without a word to Jennifer, which was hardly surprising, but which had made his letter, when it came at the end of August, all the more staggering. He'd heard about Adam, he wrote, and he knew from what he'd heard that the baby was his spitting image. If he and Nora were reconciled, would Jennifer consider giving Adam up for them to adopt? Jennifer didn't stop to think, let alone consider. She didn't stop to think that Nora might be as outraged, or feel as used, by Paddy's preposterous suggestion as she did.

She had a friend in Bristol from her college days. Jennifer phoned her in a panic and she agreed that Jennifer could stay with her while she found somewhere suitable to live. So, in the thick heat of an August Bank Holiday weekend, when the Flower Children had taken over Woburn Abbey for three days of love, peace and dope-smoking, Jennifer found herself, feeling anything but peaceful, struggling on to a train with her baby and a bulging suitcase, only wanting to put Ambridge and Paddy far behind her.

In one frantic, fraught week, she somehow managed to sort herself out. She found herself a job in Bristol, a place to live and some-one to take care of Adam. Her peace of mind, though, would take longer to restore. Two months later, she still looked behind her as she wheeled Adam home from his babyminder. She still drew her curtains long before it got dark in case Paddy should be out there among the rhododendrons and she'd had a door chain fitted. It would be a long time – if ever – before she felt safe from Paddy Redmond.

. . .

When she opened the door that misty Saturday morning, Jennifer was so astonished to see him that she took an involuntary step backwards.

'What are you doing here?'

'What a charming welcome.'

Jennifer shook her head. She smiled despite herself.

'I'm sorry. Come in. I was surprised, that's all.'

Roger Travers-Macy followed her in and Jennifer tried to see her flat through his eyes. Though she'd spent all half term and, it seemed to her, nearly half a term's salary, on doing the place up, she still felt it looked both crowded and tawdry. Roger didn't seem to think so. He went straight over to the mantelpiece and picked up a papier-mâché bird which she'd found in a curious little shop near the university. Then he moved along the mantelpiece, fingering all her other bits and pieces, the joss sticks, the brass candlesticks (nothing ethnic there, they'd belonged to her grandmother), the photograph of her parents outside The Bull. Then he turned and took in the rest of her décor – the striped blanket that she'd thrown over the itchy moquette of the settee, the poster of Che Guevara that covered a damp patch on the wallpaper and – she followed his look – her mini-skirts and dresses hanging from the picture rail.

'No room for a wardrobe,' she explained, embarrassed. 'Only a chest of drawers.'

'It looks great,' he said warmly. 'You might start a trend.'

It was funny seeing him standing there, so tall and dark and – well, male, in this room which hadn't even had a visitor before.

'Where's Adam?' he enquired.

'Having a nap,' Jennifer replied. 'But you haven't answered my question. What *are* you doing here? Lilian rang last night to say you couldn't make it.'

'Ah well,' Roger grinned. 'Just because Miss Lilian's decided she's too busy, it doesn't stop me from coming.'

'Obviously not,' smiled Jennifer, suddenly realizing how pleased she was to see him. 'Well, now you're here, what shall we do?'

They went to the seaside. All right, it was November and everything would be closed, but the weather was mild, if damp, and five-month-old Adam had never seen the sea.

'He'll be lucky to see it at Weston,' commented Roger as he pulled the car up on the seafront and they were confronted by a flat expanse of wormcasts which met the dazzling white horizon.

'It really doesn't matter.' Jennifer was doing her best to hold a wriggling Adam on the front seat of Roger's Hillman Imp. 'I just want to smell it. I want to feel the sand under my feet instead of pavements. And I want to feel a wind that's blowing in the prospect of escape, not bits of grit and the exhaust fumes of buses.'

He turned round and smiled at her.

'Very poetic,' he said. 'You're an unusual girl, Jennifer.'

They walked for miles along the beach, taking it in turns to carry Adam, who windmilled his arms at the seagulls and imitated their calls. Roger told her all the news of Ambridge which hadn't reached her yet. He brought her the latest bulletin on her grandmother, who'd been attacked by burglars at Brookfield, leaving her with a broken wrist. And he told her that her Uncle Phil had won a competition with his essay 'Farming in the Future' and that he'd soon be setting off on a three-month round-the-world trip as his prize.

'Who knows, perhaps he'll run across Nelson Gabriel somewhere,' Roger speculated, as they sheltered from a shower in an ornate wrought-iron pavilion on the promenade.

Incredibly, there was a warrant out for Nelson's arrest in connection with the Borchester mail van robbery. Jennifer didn't know what was worse: Nelson's supposed implication in the crime, or the fact that he had calculatedly staged his own death six months before it, presumably to preclude any suggestion of his involvement. If it were true, Jennifer couldn't fathom how the Nelson she knew could have staged such a heartless and elaborate trick on his own father.

'Poor, *poor* Uncle Walter,' fretted Jennifer. 'First he thinks his son's dead, now he's got to live with the fact that he's on the run. And if

18

Nelson is ever found and brought back to this country, he could spend the rest of his life in jail.'

'Don't try saying that to Walter. He's adamant that his Nelson's "h'innocent".'

Jennifer sighed and kissed the top of Adam's head.

'I hope this little one never gives me as much to worry about.'

'I hope you've done all your worrying, Jennifer,' said Roger simply, his dark eyes holding hers. 'If you ask me, you've had a lifetime's share already.'

It was dark when they got home: they'd had fish and chips and given Adam his bottle in a café.

To Jennifer's horror, as she was about to put her key in the front door, it opened to reveal Lance, in his off-duty gear of a Bri-nylon polo-neck and mustard-coloured car coat. Lance took in the scene – Jennifer, tousled and pink-cheeked, with Roger behind her holding an angelically sleeping Adam, worn out by all the fresh air.

'So this is the boyfriend,' he sneered. 'Nice to meet you, squire. Funny, the baby doesn't look anything like you.'

'He doesn't look like either of us, does he?' said Roger smoothly. 'But then, *your* parents were probably quite presentable.'

'Eh?'

Leaving Lance to puzzle it out, Jennifer opened the door to her flat and collapsed against the wall, laughing. She took off her black wet-look mac and hung it on the back of the door.

'That was a bit snide. I have to live with him, you know.'

She held out her arms for Adam and Roger handed him over.

'Not literally, I hope.'

With a smile, Jennifer laid her sleeping son against her shoulder.

'I'll put him in his cot just as he is.'

She went to move away but found that she couldn't: she and Roger were somehow bound together. When she looked down, she saw that Adam's crocheted blanket had got caught round one of the buttons on Roger's jacket.

'Oops.'

With her free hand, she tried to disentangle it. They were so close she could feel the rise and fall of his chest. She could see the dark hairs that writhed at the open neck of his shirt. His hand moved towards hers. She thought he was going to help her but instead he caught her fingers.

'I'd like to come and see you again.'

Jennifer bit her lip and looked up at him. Lilian's boyfriend.

'I can't stop you,' she said softly.

'You can. Just say no.'

Jennifer said nothing. Adam stirred in his sleep. Roger smiled. Her sister's boyfriend.

'I'll be in touch,' he promised.

•1•

Sisterly Love

'Jennifer . . . how lovely . . .'

'Hello, Mum . . . and Lilian.' Jennifer kissed her sister warmly. 'It's so good to see you.'

'Same here.'

It was four days before Christmas and Jennifer had come home.

She'd been agonizing over the decision for weeks. It had taken time, but her immediate family – even her grandmother, Doris – had come to accept her unmarried status with love and a defiant sort of pride. Her younger brother, Tony, was still giving her the cold shoulder, but he'd always, Jennifer thought, had a self-righteous streak. Anyway, she wouldn't have stayed away for Tony. It was her maternal grandmother, Mrs P, who was the problem. Although she was now married to Arthur, her second husband, and living in London, she'd been invited to Ambridge for Christmas. But she'd made it plain that if Jennifer was there, she didn't feel that *she* could be, so Jennifer felt she had no option but to stay away. It was Roger, that day at Weston, who'd persuaded her that she had every right to spend Christmas at home.

'This is the 1960s, even in Ambridge! If they refuse to come, it's because of their own blinkered prejudice,' he'd declared as they'd balanced Adam on the railing of the promenade and watched the sea creep gradually towards them under the furrowed afternoon clouds.

'But I'll have spoilt Christmas for them.'

He shook his head in exasperation.

'They're quite prepared to spoil it for you by making you feel guilty. Put yourself first for once, Jennifer. Do what *you* want.'

'I'm not sure what I want,' she said helplessly, supporting Adam's little fists with her forefingers. She'd tested her family's loyalty already: she'd put them through so much. Now she only wanted to do what was best. On top of it all, she was rather alarmed by Roger's vehemence. She hadn't expected him to have quite such strong opinions about it. 'Anyway, forget it. Why should you get involved in my problems?'

He kicked a shell back on to the sand.

'Haven't you worked it out yet? I thought you were the clever one.' He glanced at her quickly, then looked away again to the wet Welsh coast. 'I care about you, Jennifer. Your happiness matters to me.'

The wind whipped her hair into her eyes. She looked at him furtively as she hooked it behind her ears.

'I still don't know what to do about Christmas.'

He turned towards her and spoke more gently.

'Come home,' he said. '*I'd* like you to. I'd like to see you in Ambridge.'

So she'd come, only to discover that Arthur Perkins, who had a heart condition, wasn't well enough to make the journey from London anyway, and Roger himself was away, spending Christmas with his stuffy family. In their ancestral hall, no doubt, with a piper piping in roast swan for Christmas dinner, thought Jennifer bitterly, as she peeled an Everest of potatoes for her mother on Christmas morning. Then she checked herself. Maybe it was a good thing he wasn't around.

Roger hadn't, in fact, come to see her again after that day by the sea in November. He'd written to say that it was such a busy time at the bookshop in the run-up to Christmas that he'd had to forgo his alternate Saturdays off. He said how sorry he was, and how much he'd enjoyed their day together. Jennifer wasn't sure whether to believe him or not. She didn't think he was lying about being busy, but was it a convenient excuse? Was he backing off?

On Christmas afternoon, she tried to ask Lilian casually about her relationship with Roger, but she didn't get much sense out of her.

'He's a great bloke and of course I like him, who wouldn't?' Lilian said, pouring them each a crème de menthe to fortify them for the washing-up, which made the earlier mountain of potatoes look like a mere foothill. 'But I just take it as it comes. I'm working hard, he's working hard . . .'

Jennifer nodded understandingly. It was true that Lilian had recently set up on her own, running a riding school and stables. It was what she'd always wanted to do and she was determined to make it work.

But deep down Jennifer knew that, if she had been the one working hard, she would still have made time for Roger. She wouldn't have been able to stop herself. What she had to stop, and stop very firmly, was the idea that there could ever be anything between the two of them. However casual their relationship, Roger was Lilian's. Jennifer had disgraced herself once in front of her family and was still paying the price. She was not going to add to her overdraft.

In the days between Christmas and New Year, she took a firm line with herself. She told herself – and almost believed it – that she'd imagined everything between them. Roger was concerned about her, yes, but as Lilian's sister, who'd made an unfortunate mess of her life and was reaping the consequences. The more she thought about it, the more she convinced herself that the idea of any relationship with Roger would be ludicrous. Why, after all, when he could have Lilian or any girl like her, would he want to take on a woman who had a past and who brought with her, like the free plastic rose with Peggy's soap powder, someone else's child? And in what moment of arrogance had she ever, for one instant, thought that she might deserve him?

Jennifer worked it all out as she bounced Adam's pram fiercely down the rutted December lanes beneath the mocking rooks. So when Roger came back from his family Christmas, how exactly did she come to agree to go out to dinner with him?

• • •

After a long day at the riding school, whose pupils were still enjoying their Christmas holidays, Lilian had announced that she was absolutely worn out and was going to bed early. Peggy was delighted to

23

look after Adam so that Jennifer could, so she told her mother, go and see a girl she'd used to teach with at Penny Hassett. Roger and Jennifer would probably have been quite safe in Borchester. But he still drove her all the way to Felpersham, even though it was sleeting. He took her to an expensive-looking Italian restaurant near the cathedral, and when she protested, told her to think of it as her birthday treat a few days early. Jennifer tried her hardest, but she still felt guilty. Guilty yet exhilarated.

It was impossibly romantic. The waiter showed them to their corner table and lit the candle with a Latin flick of the wrist. A soulful guitarist serenaded them with 'O Sole Mio' and 'The Isle of Capri'. But mostly it was him. It was sitting opposite him, watching his slim hands with their dusting of dark hairs snap a breadstick; it was sitting back and watching him as he bantered with the waiter, and the way he consulted her so seriously about the merits of sautéed versus straw potatoes. True, he kept topping up her glass, but that wasn't what was intoxicating. It was him.

As they ate, they talked about anything and everything – everything except what they were feeling. Finally, she could bear it no longer.

'Roger . . .' she began when the waiter had brought them two black, bitter espressos. By now they were the only customers left.

'Yes?'

'I'm going back to Bristol tomorrow. First train.'

'You can't.' The way he said things so simply and irrefutably enchanted her.

'I've got a job to keep.'

'You mustn't.'

He was doing it again. Jennifer stared into the dark depths of her cup, as if the liquid might part and there would be her future, written in the coffee grounds. She raised her head and looked at him. A strand of hair caught in the corner of her mouth and she flicked it away.

'I think we both know what would happen if I stayed.'

'It's already happened, hasn't it.'

It wasn't a question, it was a statement. Jennifer's bobbed blonde hair swung forward again as she inclined her head. She couldn't argue with what he was saying. But she had to argue against what she was feeling.

'We've got to stop. Before it's too late.'

'Jennifer.' He leant towards her pleadingly.

'It's just emotion . . .' she improvised. 'Once I've gone back it'll be quite different. Difficult. But it'll pass.'

'It won't. Not for me.'

'It's got to. I'm serious, Roger. No phone calls, no visits, no letters. Please.'

• • •

She tried, she really did try. When Roger sent her some books for her birthday, beautiful books, just what she would have chosen herself, she parcelled them up with a pair of Lilian's jeans she'd mistakenly brought back with her to Bristol and returned them, pretending she'd ordered them and asking her mother to pass them on because they were unsuitable. When he sent her a postcard of a Botticelli angel, she left it unanswered, and when Lance told her he was on the phone, she told him to say she was out. Lance had looked smug but Jennifer didn't care. She was doing what was right. Although she couldn't enjoy the feeling of virtue it gave her because she felt so miserable.

When her mother rang, Jennifer asked – not too pointedly, she hoped – about Lilian. She wasn't working too hard, was she? Surely she was having some kind of social life? Her mother told her happily that Lilian was out with Roger and that she really seemed a one-man girl. Jennifer bravely told her mother to send Lilian her love. Then she went and cried into her pillow as the jaunty rhythms of Russ Conway's 'Piano Party' filtered down from Lance's room above.

She couldn't see why things should change. She couldn't see why she shouldn't have to go on like this for ever, day after day, taking Adam to his childminder, rushing to school, dashing to collect him, coming home in the dark, wet, winter afternoons, lighting the fire, folding the washing, feeding Adam his scrambled egg and stewed apple, playing with him exhaustedly, bathing him and putting him to bed. And then, usually, collapsing on to her bed herself, in her clothes – but forcing herself to get up, heat a tin of soup and then begin cutting templates for the next day's art lesson. She wouldn't let herself think about Roger – how if he were there he might take her out to a folk club near the university, how she'd make them spaghetti when they got back but how, most importantly, he'd take her in his arms and smooth her day – and all the other awful days – away.

Then, one afternoon, when the country was still struggling with February's finger-nipping cold, she bought an *Evening Post* on her way home and tucked it under the pram cover with the bananas and the small loaf and only remembered it when Adam had gone to bed.

And there it was, at the bottom of the front page, underneath the inevitable news about inflation and the rallying call to the 'I'm Backing Britain' campaign. 'Man Apprehended for Mail Van Robbery', it said. It was accompanied by a photograph that, however small and fuzzy, could only be of Nelson Gabriel.

'Oh, my God,' Jennifer whispered to herself. 'Uncle Walter must be beside himself.'

• • •

'Gingerbread, Walter? Or another scone?'

Doris stood in front of Walter's armchair with the two-tier cake stand. It had taken her days to persuade him to come to Brookfield for Sunday tea. He hadn't left his cottage since the news about Nelson had broken. But Walter shook his head.

'I'm sorry, Doris me love. I don't seem to have much h'appetite.'

Doris clucked and returned the stand to the tea trolley.

'Here, what about your old man? Don't I get any?' Dan protested. 'I've still got the afternoon milking to do.'

'You can help yourself,' said Doris dismissively. She sat down by the fire. 'Now, listen to me, Walter. This has got to stop. You'll be getting yourself into a decline.'

'Well, what would you do,' cried Walter piteously, 'if it was your

Jack or young Phil clapped in prison with a serious charge hanging over his head? My Nelson's been framed, Doris. He must have been.'

'What about the evidence, Walter?' put in Dan, helping himself to a jam tart.

Walter folded his arms.

'If my Nelson says he wasn't in Ambridge when it happened, then that's God's honest truth.'

'So what about the whisky bottle?' probed Dan gently, wondering which God Nelson Gabriel might pay obeisance to. Mammon, perhaps? 'The one with Nelson's fingerprints on it that they found at Paunton Farm?'

'There's been a mistake,' said Walter defiantly, sticking out his bottom lip. 'There must have been. The inky prints must have got mixed up at the labotomory.'

'Laboratory,' corrected Doris.

'That's what I said! Anyway,' Walter snorted contemptuously, 'the whole idea's cock-eyed! Can you see my Nelson on a pig farm?'

'Not really,' admitted Dan. The idea of the foppish Nelson wading through pig muck was truly ridiculous. 'But if the police reckon it was his hideout hereabouts . . .'

'I thought you were me pals!' Walter knocked the small table at his elbow in his agitation and his teacup rattled alarmingly in its saucer. 'You'm sounding just like the police! My Nelson's a respectable businessman. And they're trying to make out he's a h'international criminal!'

'Well, it'll all come out in court, won't it?' said Doris sensibly. 'Look what happened to our Tom a few years back with that man-slaughter charge. He got off.'

There was one big difference, thought Dan, but he didn't say it. There had been no doubt in anyone's mind that Doris's brother Tom had been innocent.

• • •

'So they've found Nelson's fingerprints at the farm? I wish you'd keep me up to date.'

It was the same Sunday afternoon and Jennifer was making her weekly phone call home. Normally her mother was waiting for it and pounced on the phone, but this time Lilian had answered. She sounded subdued.

'I'm sorry. We've had one or two problems of our own to deal with.'

'Lilian?' Jennifer could tell from her tone that she didn't mean that the drayman had been late with the brown ale or that the pork scratchings had run out. 'What is it? Where's Mum? She's not ill, is she?'

'*She's* not, no.'

Jennifer knew with a sickening thump of her heart that it must be their father.

'What's happened?'

Lilian explained. How Peggy had gone upstairs on Thursday morning and asked Jack if he wanted any breakfast. How he'd refused, though that in itself was nothing unusual. He rarely had the stomach for it these days, not when he'd been out drinking. So she'd left him and gone back down again to cook Tony's bacon and eggs. But when she'd gone back up half an hour later to get dressed, there he was, unconscious in bed, with an empty whisky bottle by his side.

'He won't go into a clinic,' Lilian explained. 'Won't hear of it. Says he's going to do it by himself. He's giving up alcohol for Lent.'

'Well, we've heard that before.'

Since they were tiny, Jennifer, Lilian and Tony had grown up in the shadow of Jack's drinking. Jennifer could remember periods of normality – happiness, even. One spring, a robin had built its nest under the bonnet of Jack's car, and, to the children's delight, he'd refused to drive it until all the eggs were hatched. Once he'd had a bumper crop of redcurrants at the market garden he managed: the owner, Carol Grey, had given him a rise and he'd taken them all to the circus to celebrate. But as the family grew up, his drinking bouts had got worse. Jennifer knew that his outbursts against her 'beatnik' appearance and her college friends, and his reaction to her pregnancy, had been all the more extreme because of drink. And she knew poor Lilian would never forget the time she'd come back triumphant with a cup from the Horse of the Year show to find Jack slumped across the kitchen table in a haze of whisky fumes. Instead of being able to enjoy her moment of triumph, she'd had to make her father black coffee, splash his face with cold water and heave him up the stairs. At the other end of the phone, Lilian sighed and Jennifer knew she was remembering it too.

'I'm coming home.'

'Don't be silly, Jennifer. There's nothing you can do.'

'I can take a bit of the strain off you and Mum. It's half term next week. I can come straight away.'

'Look, I can't pretend it wouldn't be great to have you here. But we can't meet you from the train or anything – I'm frantic at the stables . . .'

Jennifer could hear her sister's voice rising as she sensed more pressure, not less.

'Lilian, don't worry. I'll sort myself out.'

• • •

Jennifer settled herself in the car and held out her arms for Adam but his eyes were fixed on the lollipop that Roger had produced from his pocket.

'You'll rot his teeth!'

'He's only got three.'

'You'll rot the ones that haven't come through yet!'

'Listen to your mummy, Adam, doesn't she talk a lot of nonsense?'

With a grin, Roger handed Adam into the car, lollipop and all. Jennifer unwrapped it to the accompaniment of Adam's excited shrieks.

As Roger slid behind the wheel, she turned and smiled at him gratefully. She didn't want him to get the wrong idea.

'I hope you didn't mind me ringing you. I knew I just had to get home and there was no one else I could turn to.'

Roger stopped in the middle of firing the engine.

'Do you know how I felt when you phoned?' he asked. 'I couldn't have been happier if – if –'

'If you heard they were bringing *Hair* to Borchester Little Theatre?' teased Jennifer, desperate to keep things light.

'I was going to say, if the USA pulled out of Vietnam tomorrow – but you get the picture.'

'Well, thanks for meeting me from the train, anyway.'

She stroked Adam's hair and saw Roger watching her.

'I thought when you sent back the books – when you didn't reply to my cards or my calls . . .' He glanced away from her, beyond the empty railway tracks to the frozen February fields. Then he turned back and she felt the intensity of his longing surge towards her. 'I didn't realize how strong you were.'

'I didn't feel very strong.'

So much for her good intentions. So much for keeping it on a friendly footing. And she'd only been back five minutes.

'So why did you do it?'

'Oh, Roger,' she despaired, 'you know why. I can't get involved with you because of Lilian.'

'Jennifer,' he implored her, 'if you'd let me explain instead of putting up this wall of silence, I'd have told you. I think about it all the time. I don't feel for Lilian what I feel for you. And she doesn't feel it for me.'

'Have you asked her? How can you be so sure?'

'I don't have to ask her. If you'd ever seen us together, you'd recognize it straight away. We're more like . . . I don't know, brother and sister.'

'You're wrong,' insisted Jennifer. 'From what I've heard Lilian's very struck on you. Oh, she may not show it, but – well, as Mum put it to me once, she's a one-man woman.'

Roger fiddled with the indicator switch on the steering column.

'If that's the case, I'm sorry. Those aren't the vibes I get from her. And anyway, I just don't feel the same.'

'That hardly makes what we're doing right.'

'So you've decided we can't fall in love? It's that easy, is it?'

Of course it wasn't easy. It was downright impossible. For the five days she was at home she saw Roger every moment that she could without anyone suspecting. Fortunately, Lilian was run off her feet at the stables, and her mother was occupied in keeping a watchful eye on Jack. But Peggy was only too delighted to mind her grandson for a couple of hours each day, leaving Jennifer, under the pretext of doing the shopping, free to meet Roger at the bookshop. He kissed her in the stock-room when his assistant was at lunch and gave her books of poetry – Elizabeth Barrett Browning, of course, and Byron, and e.e.cummings. In the evenings, once Adam was settled, all Jennifer had to do was to invent an old schoolfriend whom she'd promised to look up and, borrowing Jack's car, meet Roger at his cottage. By the time she went back to Bristol at the end of the week she knew that the unthinkable had happened. She was in love with her sister's boyfriend and he was with her.

Now Jennifer didn't ignore Roger's telephone calls and letters, she lived for them. He was short-staffed at the bookshop but he would tear down to Bristol on his rare days off to see her after school, leaving at midnight for the dark drive back to Ambridge.

'What are we going to do about Lilian?' she asked him, her head resting in the curve of his shoulder as they sat snuggled up on the sofa. He'd brought her a new LP by a group called Pink Floyd. Roger said that when people woke up to them they were going to be very big indeed.

'It's awful. I feel awful. I'll tell her I can't see her any more.'

'Oh, I don't know,' sighed Jennifer. 'I feel I should tell her. I'm her sister, after all.'

'Whatever you like.' He kissed the top of her head. 'But let's do it soon. I just want to be with you. Openly.'

• • •

It wasn't long before Jennifer was home again, this time for Easter. Ironically, every time the school holidays liberated her, they meant more work for Lilian: a daily stream of would-be three-day eventers.

It meant that Jennifer and Roger had plenty of opportunity to meet, and each time they did, Jennifer felt worse and worse.

She'd been doing a lot of thinking. Adam was nine months old. He was already crawling: soon he'd be staggering around. He had an extensive vocabulary of coughs, gurgles and chuckles and would soon be forming his first proper words. When he'd been tiny, Jennifer had convinced herself that any kind person who fed him and changed him was doing as good a job as she, his mother, could do. Now he was older, she was not so sure. He was cheerful enough when she left him with his minder in the mornings, but at night his joy on seeing her was unconfined, and she felt more and more anguished by every parting.

What with her guilt about Roger and her guilt about Adam, she'd been distracted at school, and it wasn't long before she was feeling guilty about neglecting her work as well. She could see that every aspect of her life was going to demand more and more of her attention and she couldn't see where the time or the energy was going to come from. In the end, she knew that something would have to go. It obviously couldn't be Adam. And she didn't want it to be Roger. So before she broke up for Easter she handed in her notice.

Her mother was ecstatic at the news, delighted to think she'd have Jennifer and her grandson home. But Jennifer knew that she was just exchanging one set of problems for another and, after days of agonizing, rehearsing what she had to say to her sister to a puzzled Adam as she played with him in the pub garden or pushed him along the budding banks of the Am, she went and found Lilian at the stables.

'Don't tell me you've come to ride?' Lilian demanded as they emerged from the tack room into the thin spring sunshine.

'You must be joking. I thought we could watch some of your star pupils.'

Lilian scrutinized the half-dozen girls on ponies being led round the paddock by one of her helpers. 'Not very many rivals for the Elizabeth Taylor role in *National Velvet*, I'm afraid. But don't tell them I said so.'

She hoisted herself up to sit on the paddock railings. Jennifer leant with her arms on the top rail, her chin lowered to her forearms.

'Georgina! Straight back, please! Amanda! Give him some rein! More! That's better!' Lilian shouted. Then she turned to her sister and, as if commenting on the weather, said evenly, 'I suppose this is about Roger.'

Jennifer, who'd been nerving herself to speak, was so taken aback that she almost swallowed her tongue.

'Has he said something?'

Lilian laughed.

'Oh, sis, he doesn't have to. I've seen the looks when he comes in the pub. And you should have heard him these past few weeks. The times he drops your name into the conversation. Do I think Jennifer's seen such and such a film? Isn't it nice for Jennifer that Granny Perkins has finally come round? And so on and so on.'

'I didn't realize.'

'He's got it bad, hasn't he?' Lilian asked. Jennifer said nothing. 'And I take it you feel the same?'

'Oh, Lilian, I'm so sorry,' Jennifer burst out. 'I didn't mean it to happen. I struggled against it, I really did! You must hate me for it, and you're right to.'

'Oh, for heaven's sake, Jennifer, tune in and turn on, isn't that what they say?' Lilian broke off to bellow across the paddock. 'Georgina! I don't want to tell you again!'

'Tune in . . . ? How do you mean?'

Lilian casually flicked a lump of mud from her boots. A pony, passing close by, sneezed and snorted.

'Roger and I have been going off the boil for months. It may be to do with you, it may not. Personally, I think it would have happened anyway. He's hardly my type.'

After all her weeks of worry, Jennifer was incredulous.

'When did you find that out? No one would ever have known.'

'It's obvious. I'm the outdoor, horsey type, he's indoor and bookish. Much more your can of Coke, really.'

'I don't believe it!' exclaimed Jennifer. 'I've been tying myself in knots about telling you. I thought you'd shout and scream and call me all the names under the sun and now you're telling me you really don't mind.'

'Better than that.' Lilian was smiling. 'I wish you all the luck in the world. Oh, here he comes.'

'Who, Roger?' Jennifer spun round.

'No, silly, my new client.'

Over the brow of the hill a rider was cantering towards them on a glistening black horse.

'What new client?' asked Jennifer.

'The one who brought me a bunch of roses this morning,' said Lilian smugly. 'The one who turned up ten minutes early just to talk to me. The one who's an officer in the Canadian Air Force, over here on a course, who's stationed nearby and who wants to get in some riding two or three times a week . . .'

'Lilian! Has he got a name?'

'He's called Lester Nicholson. But his friends call him Nick.'

'And I suppose that includes you? How long has this been going on?' Jennifer demanded.

'Well, that's choice, coming from you,' retorted Lilian.

'Ooh, if you weren't my sister . . .'

'It's because I'm your sister that I'm like I am! Let's face it, Jennifer, we're both as bad as each other!' Turning towards the approaching rider, Lilian waved and called. 'Nick! Over here!' Then she swivelled back to Jennifer and added, 'And keep your hands off this one. I saw him first!'

·2·

The Next Generation

'Sausage roll, Mrs P, ma'am? Or how about one of them volleyvents?'

Walter indicated the buffet table laid out in the function room of Duke's Hotel in Borchester, where the wedding party had gathered after the register office ceremony. Mrs P shook her head.

'I've had quite sufficient, thank you, Mr Gabriel. And you could do with laying off the pastry yourself, what with your sugar problem.'

'Doh.'

Walter's disappointment reverberated round his tonsils. He had recently been diagnosed with sugar diabetes and his friends, more careful of his health than he was, wouldn't let him forget it. Jack kept a selection of bottled 'specials' for him at The Bull, and Doris made him cakes with grated carrot instead of sugar, which she said took her back to the war.

Defiantly helping himself to a piece of cheese and pineapple on a stick, which was protruding from an upturned grapefruit half, Walter sat down next to Mrs P. She had discarded her usual black duster coat in favour of a jacquard Crimplene suit – after all, it was her granddaughter's wedding. It was a pity it couldn't have been a church service, of course. Roger's father had stayed away and it had been all his stuck-up mother could do to pass the time of day with the Archers, but there it was. A girl in Jennifer's position was lucky to find any young man to take her on.

'It's been a very pleasant day,' she observed. 'But there's no need to over-indulge yourself.'

'Oh, ar, very pleasant,' agreed Walter in a melancholy way. 'But it's the last wedding I shall be h'attending.'

'What ever for? You can't have taken against Roger. If you ask me, Jennifer's done very well for herself.'

She looked over to where Jennifer in her short cream dress and Roger in his velvet suit were talking to young Tony.

'It's nothing to do with that,' said Walter sadly. 'They just puts me in mind of weddings that have been – and weddings that ain't.'

Mrs Perkins looked at him sideways from under the brim of her hat. She knew how devastated he'd been when she'd married her second Perkins, Arthur – even more so when they'd moved away from the village to Arthur's home in London. She was fonder of Walter Gabriel than he would ever know, but she wouldn't dream of showing it.

'If that's a dig at me, Mr Gabriel, it's in very poor taste, with my Arthur on his sickbed.'

Arthur's health had been declining for the past year. He had a failing heart and the doctor said he hadn't got long to live.

'The mill can't grind with water that has passed, Mrs P, ma'am,' Walter declared philosophically, and Mrs P added, under her breath, as Walter said it out loud, 'As my old granny used to say. If you want to know,' he went on, 'I was thinking more of me and my Annie,' – he named his late wife – 'and, of course, my Nelson.'

Mrs P's thin lips almost disappeared in disapproval. There was nothing guaranteed to raise her blood pressure more than the mention of Walter's wayward son. Despite what had seemed the overwhelming evidence against him, Nelson had been found not guilty of robbing the Borchester mail van. He'd urged his father not to attend the trial and Walter had obediently stayed away, confident of Nelson's innocence and expecting the prodigal home when the verdict had been announced. But all he'd received from Nelson had been a message to say he was going abroad and would be in touch. You didn't have to be Miss Marple, thought Mrs Perkins, to jump to the conclusion that he'd hopped on a plane to wherever the loot was stashed and was leading the life of Riley, drinking cocktails on marble terraces overlooking the Mediterranean, while his old dad went on living in his cottage with its patchy thatch and outside toilet, reading and re-reading Nelson's intermittent postcards.

'Have you heard from him lately? What's he up to nowadays?' she demanded.

'He's getting into property again,' announced Walter proudly.

Other people's, no doubt, thought Mrs P.

'In Spain. Villas and that,' Walter added.

'Villas? Whatever next?' Mrs P sniffed. 'After that piece of news, I'll have another half a glass of that white wine, if you please. The sweet one, not that sour stuff.'

'One vintage white Burgundy for mademoiselle,' said Lester Nicholson, handing the glass to Lilian. 'They had some Sauternes, but I don't suppose they'll have many takers for that.'

Lilian sipped her pale wine.

'This is perfect. Thank you.'

Nick raised his glass of beer.

'Here's looking at you.'

'And you.'

He took her free hand in his and nodded his head in the direction of the bride and groom, who had broken away from their guests and were gazing into one another's eyes.

'We're next, you know.'

'You keep saying that. I never know if you're serious.'

'Oh, you think I took this new job to get away from you, right?'

Nick had left the Canadian Air Force in early September when, to everyone's surprise and his horror, he'd failed a routine medical. The ear trouble they'd diagnosed meant he didn't meet the rigorous standards of the air force, but it wouldn't stop him flying. He'd walked straight into a job as private pilot to a millionaire businessman whose interests took him all over the world.

'Well, didn't you?' Lilian teased. 'I know how you hate us horsey types with our chapped hands and big bottoms.'

'Nonsense,' replied Nick. '"Shall I compare thee to a summer's day? Thou art more lovely and more temperate,"' he quoted, straight-faced, taking her hand.

'Temperate?' smiled Lilian. 'I can tell you haven't spent too many summers in England. Why is it,' she went on, 'that foreigners appreciate our literature so much more than we do?'

'I appreciate *you*,' said Nick simply. 'That's all.'

Lilian looked at him lovingly. He wasn't tall – but then, neither was she – and he looked so handsome in his aubergine suit and daring floral tie.

'And for the record,' he went on, his honeyed Canadian accent pouring over her, 'I took this job because it's well paid. I can practically live on my expenses. I'm saving nearly all my salary – then we can get married as quick as you like.'

'That's what worries me,' fretted Lilian. 'If it's so well paid, it must be dangerous. What are you going to do if you come down in the jungle surrounded by unfriendly natives?'

'Suggest they pickle me in alcohol before eating me.' Nick drained his glass. 'You're being ridiculous, sweetie. It's not going to happen. *We* are going to happen. Believe me.'

And she did.

'They look so happy, don't they?'

Christine, who'd been standing near a pillar by herself, turned to find the mother of the bride at her shoulder.

'Jennifer and Roger?' she hazarded. 'Oh, yes.'

'Well, they do, of course,' replied Peggy. 'But I was thinking of Nick and Lilian.'

The dancing had just started. Nick and Lilian were draped over each other, swaying gently while the band played 'What a Wonderful World'.

'Well, what do you expect,' Chris said lightly, 'when they met through horses? It's the only way to find true love.'

'You should know. It worked for you and Paul.'

'Yes, it did, didn't it?'

Christine wondered if Peggy would detect the restraint in her tone, but Peggy had other considerations. She undid the top button of her ruffled blouse.

'Goodness, it's hot in here. Where is Paul, by the way?'

'Oh, who knows?' Christine had long ago given up trying to keep track of her husband on these occasions. 'Off with your Jack, probably. Telling him about his latest wheeze.'

'Or hearing about Jack's. What shall we do with them, Chris?'

Before Christine had time to reply – though she was not sure that there *was* an answer – Peggy was gone, whirled on to the dance floor by her new son-in-law, leaving Christine alone again. What *could* she do with Paul? Put up and shut up, as the Americans said, seemed to be the only answer, or the only one Chris could think of.

The more weddings she attended, the more cynical she felt she became. Today's had been just the same. Instead of feeling thrilled and excited for the young couple, she'd found herself wondering how long the gloss would last before it was rubbed down to the bare, everyday woodwork. No one deserved this second chance more than Jennifer, and Chris really hoped it would work out for her, but she'd felt a chill during the speeches, when John Tregorran, Roger's partner at the bookshop, had said such glowing things about the pair of them and Roger's brother, George, had toasted their health. And the chill had begun to feel like positive pneumonia when Roger had stood up to reply.

'This is a perfect ending,' he'd said. 'We've had our problems . . . and I daresay we'll have them in the years ahead. But Jennifer and I have nothing but the greatest faith in our future and we know that, with the friends we've got – and by we, I mean me, Jennifer and little Adam – we're going to have a wonderfully happy life together.'

Everyone had clapped and cheered and Chris had noticed Phil give Jill a loving look. Her dad had squeezed her mum's hand as Doris had searched for a dry bit of hanky to dab at her eyes. Even Jack had given Peggy a quick kiss. And Paul? Paul had lit up another cigarette and said something to Tony, which had made him hiccup his champagne and smother a laugh.

All the other married couples Chris knew seemed to regard weddings as a chance to renew and reinforce their own vows. She and Paul, though, seemed to move through them like – she searched for a comparison and one which seemed at first unlikely, then appropriate, came to mind. Like satellites in separate orbits, cold and hard, mechanical, recording what they saw, but removed from it, and untouched.

• • •

'Where's it all going, Paul?' she asked him one evening a few months later. It was the middle of January, that most depressing time of year when there was nothing to look forward to and, it seemed, never would be.

'It's a temporary thing, that's all,' he insisted. He squatted in front of the fire and added a few more lumps of coal. 'It'll pass.'

The coal was damp. Smoke began to snake up the chimney.

'But the profits at the garage are down nearly twenty per cent on the same time last year. Why?'

'I don't know,' he replied tetchily. He prodded at the fire. 'I'm not doing anything different.'

'Well, maybe that's the problem. Maybe you should. I don't know, put on some special offers or something.'

'Oh, you're an expert in the motor trade now, are you?' Paul wiped his hands on his trousers and sat down again.

'No, of course I'm not,' said Chris wearily. Neither was Paul, really. His background was in agricultural machinery, but he hadn't been able to resist buying the garage in Ambridge when it had come up for sale about eighteen months ago. 'I'm trying to compare it with what I do know. All the shops have sales, don't they, at this time of year. Maybe –'

'Look, Chris,' he snapped, 'will you just leave it alone. Don't interfere in what you don't understand.'

'Mummy?' Their son Peter stood in the doorway in his pyjamas. 'My bed's wet.'

'Oh, darling, not again.' Chris stood up. Peter was proving difficult to train at night and Chris was finding it hard to keep up with the washing. 'That means your pyjamas are wet, doesn't it?'

Peter nodded.

'Come on, let's get you upstairs before you get cold,' she said briskly. 'And get those sheets changed.'

Paul said nothing but she could see by the look on his face that he felt he'd been let off the hook.

'Night night, Petey old chap,' he said cheerfully, picking up the newspaper. 'See you in the morning.'

'Night night, Daddy.' Peter idolized his father. What did he know? He was only three.

If Chris had been more histrionic, she might have said she'd never felt so miserable, but she was too truthful for that. She knew she'd felt just as miserable, and more, in the past, when Paul had met up with an old flame in Paris, for example, and then again, before they'd adopted Peter, when she and Paul had seemed to drift so far apart.

In the beginning, every time she'd analysed her marriage, Chris had placed the blame for its deficiencies squarely on the fact that they had no children. When they'd finally decided to adopt, Paul had seemed besotted with the baby, and Chris had really believed that this was what they should have done years ago, and that everything would change.

But in the end, Peter's arrival made no lasting difference. Paul the family man was soon back to being the thrusting executive. Despite a succession of cool, rainy summers, which depressed farm incomes and made farmers cautious with their cash, he'd pushed to expand his agricultural machinery business which dealt in sales and repairs. Then, confident that a development scheme for Ambridge would get council approval, he'd planned to add a coffee bar to the garage and to make it a focus for youngsters in the village. Sid Perks, the young Brummie who worked as his forecourt attendant, had been keen, and Paul had spent money on an extension – only for the scheme to be thrown out. Now trade at the garage was down and, Chris found when she stole a sneaky look at the accounts one evening when Paul was out, even the work Paul had done and billed remained unpaid.

By the time Paul told her a month later that his accountant had advised him to sell up or go under, there were bad debts amounting to thousands of pounds.

She was outside, putting the toast crusts and bacon rind from breakfast on the bird-table. A robin who favoured their garden was being pursued by a persistent female and Chris wanted to encourage them to nest. She'd thought Paul had left for work but he came and found her, incongruous on the slippery grass in his camelhair coat and black brogues.

'I wanted to tell you over breakfast,' he said defensively when she pointed out how muddy his shoes would get, 'but you were prattling on about Nick and Lilian's wedding date and all that.'

Oh, so it was *her* fault.

'What does it mean, Paul? Bankruptcy?'

'It may not come to that. I might find a buyer.'

Chris wiped her greasy fingers on her apron.

'Who? Who's going to buy if business is no good?'

She moved away from the bird-table, back towards the house, to give the birds a chance. Paul followed her.

'There's always some opportunist around who'll snap up a business at a knock-down price.'

'Not less than you bought it for?'

'Needs must, darling.'

How could he be so blasé about it all? She was a full-time mother now, she was bringing in no income. What were they going to live on? Scraps, like the birds?

The female robin was back, flitting persistently into the male's territory from a low hazel bough. She wanted the male to notice her. Chris knew how she felt. The male flew at the hazel in a rage. Paul watched her, watching the robins.

'I suppose you're thinking "Why does she bother? She'd be better off without him",' he observed. 'Like you'd be better off without me.'

'Paul! I never said that! I never would –'

'It's true, though, isn't it? When you look at the people you could have married.' He gave a harsh laugh. 'Perhaps you should have stuck with your old beau Nelson Gabriel. He's got a million quid stashed away somewhere. You'd never have to worry about money again. And they say crime doesn't pay!'

'I'd rather be married to someone who stays the right side of the law, thank you.'

'And on the right side of the bank manager?'

Chris said nothing. Still the female robin fluttered about, chased from the hazel but dipping down from the hawthorn hedge. The male was still attacking, defending his territory, but his flurries seemed more half-hearted now. Paul put out a hand and touched her arm.

'I'll sort it out, love. But you'd rather I told you, surely . . .'

'Of course. Of course.'

But there was no one *she* could tell. Chris knew that she would have to get through this one alone.

She would normally have confided in Jill, calm, serene Jill with her great good sense and infectious laugh. But Jill was busy enough keeping the peace between her husband and his father. Ever since Phil had returned from his round-the-world trip he'd been restless. He'd always worked reasonably well alongside Dan, but now he found his father wasn't 'progressive' enough for him. Phil complained about being left behind in the great white heat of the technological revolution, which was coming as surely to farming, he maintained, as it had come to industry. But, true to form, Dan dug in his heels and there was no shifting him. They'd had trouble drilling the crops in a wet autumn and a wet spring and now Dan had developed bronchitis. Chris knew her mother was worried sick about him, so she couldn't confide in Doris, either. And at The Bull, after a period of remission, Jack was drinking more than ever. How, Chris wondered, did Peggy put up with him?

But Chris didn't have long to keep Paul's secret to herself. The opportunist Paul had spoken of was indeed awaiting his moment. One night, when she was reading Peter his favourite 'Thomas the

Tank Engine' story, she heard the front door bang and Paul whistling in the hall. She tucked Peter in, listened to him say his prayers and went to find out what had made her husband so unusually cheery.

Paul was singing under his breath as she entered the lounge. He turned from the gilt trolley where they kept the drinks and gave her a gin and bitter lemon and a smacking kiss.

'Ralph Bellamy?' she said, incredulous, after he'd told her. 'What does he want with the garage?'

'Since he took over his father's estate, he's the biggest landowner for miles,' explained Paul reasonably. 'He'll save a fortune on maintaining his own machinery, apart from anything else. Anyway, who cares? He's offering a fair price, all things considered.'

To Chris, it sounded providential. And Paul, she hazarded, could get a salaried job again.

'God, Chris, no! I couldn't work for anyone else. That's the terrific thing about not having to declare myself bankrupt.' Paul crunched on a cheese football from the tin on the trolley. 'I can set myself up again in another company tomorrow. I've already got my eye on the one I want to buy.'

Christine looked down. No, the ice-cubes Paul had placed there were still in her drink. So why did she feel as if she'd swallowed them? Whole? She put her glass gingerly on a side table and sat down. The garage wasn't the first time Paul had got his fingers burnt in business. Surely he could see the sense – the security – of working for someone else, even if only temporarily? But before she could protest he had launched into an explanation of his plans: something to do with motor parts.

'I'll get the money for research out of some big motor manufacturer,' Paul was pronouncing blithely. 'I tell you, love, I should have done this ages ago instead of fiddle-faddling around with little old ladies and their Morris Minors.'

Chris put her head on one side and looked at him. There was so much she could have said, so much she wanted to say – like where did she and Peter come in all this, did they have any say in their own future? And couldn't he do something for them for a change, instead of for himself? She knew she wouldn't say any of it. And she didn't have a chance to.

'Mummy!' Peter's voice travelled thinly from upstairs. 'My bed's wet!'

Wet, wet and more wet, thought Chris, as the sodden spring refused to break. It was a good thing, in a way, that Nick and Lilian had had to postpone the date of their wedding owing to his work – on the original date they'd chosen it had poured and poured. Now they had a new date – Spring Bank Holiday Monday – and everyone was praying for sunshine.

When the late spring finally did arrive, the clouds in Chris's life seemed to be clearing too. There was even the faintest shimmer of a silver lining, as she told her mother when she called round for a cup of tea and to hear how her parents had got on in Torquay, where Ralph Bellamy had lent them his house for Dan's convalescence from his bronchitis.

Doris offered her a plate of flapjacks. With coconut, she said. A new recipe, given to her by Mrs Blossom, old Brigadier Winstanley's housekeeper. Chris helped herself to the smallest – still the size of a pack of cards – and chewed.

'You know how it's been, Mum, ever since Paul set up on his own as an engineer again,' she began hesitantly.

'Not easy, I should imagine . . .' Her mother pushed the sugar bowl towards her. 'Have some sugar in that tea, Chris. You're too thin these days. You worry me.'

Chris helped herself. She preferred her tea without sugar, but it wasn't worth the fight. She began to explain about Paul's latest breakthrough and as she explained it to her mother, it was as if she was explaining it to herself. And understanding why she had to support him.

'You know how Paul is, Mum. Very ambitious. Driven, almost. And he's always wanted to make his mark in life. Well, up to now in this new business of his, he's been doing small-scale work for the motor trade, but all the time, he's been working on a project of his own.'

Doris picked a sticky clump of flapjack from the sleeve of her cardigan and popped it in her mouth.

'How d'you mean, Chris? An invention?'

'More a development really,' explained Chris. 'A refinement of something that's been done before. Don't ask me what it does – it's electrical or transistorized or something and to do with the transmission –'

'You've lost me there!' chuckled Doris.

'Exactly. Just like Paul loses me when he tries to explain. But the important thing is, he's got a firm interested in the prototype. They took it away for testing. And the report's just come back.'

'And?'

'They think it's marvellous! So now we just have to see what sort of deal they're going to offer him. Isn't that wonderful?'

'Well . . .'

Doris wasn't sure what to say. She'd never felt comfortable with her son-in-law. Ever since he'd swept Chris off her feet with that flashing – and flashy – family ring of his, and his mother had been so hoity-toity about the wedding, as if Chris weren't good enough, Doris had viewed Paul with suspicion. And though Chris had never said a word, her mother knew that, aside from the sad business of them not being able to have kiddies of their own, which would have put a strain on any couple, there were things that were just not right in the marriage. Chris was looking at her, waiting for her reply.

'It'll be wonderful, love,' she improvised. 'If it happens.'

'*When* it happens,' Chris emphasized.

How Chris managed to maintain her faith in Paul after all the blows he'd dealt her, Doris simply didn't know.

'If and when,' repeated Doris. 'But I don't want you being disappointed, love. So remember what I always used to tell you – before exams and such.'

Chris laughed. When her mum put it like that, she could still see herself that summer of her School Certificate, hot and bothered at the kitchen table with her books spread around her. Old Simon

Cooper coming in to get his flask filled up before going back out to the fields. Lass the sheepdog panting on the quarry-tiled floor, her mother making lemonade and piles of sandwiches for the hay-makers.

'Hope for the best – expect the worst – and take what comes,' she smiled.

'It's something folk usually learn the hard way,' said Doris perceptively. 'Especially someone as good-natured as you, Chris.'

And Chris knew she wasn't talking about exams any more.

• • •

'So you've passed with a distinction, have you?'

It was August in Ambridge. Ralph Bellamy leaned back against the sun-warmed wall of the cow byre and regarded the young man who stood in front of him. Tony Archer grinned sheepishly.

'Makes me sound a swot, doesn't it, when students in Paris have been on the streets rioting.'

'Not those from farm institutes, I don't think,' the older man smiled. 'Must be something to do with the early mornings.'

'Oh, I don't mind those.'

'Even after a late night?'

Only the previous evening, calling at The Bull for a scotch and soda, Ralph had seen young Tony setting off on his scooter with Tessa Latimer, the vicar's daughter, riding pillion. Peggy had told him that they were off to a party in somebody's cellar in Borchester.

'Not at all.'

Ralph stroked his beard thoughtfully. His wider business interests – property development and the recently acquired garage – were taking up more and more of his time and he was certainly in the market for a bright young man to work with his dairy herd. And the reasons Tony had given him for not going in with his uncle and grandfather at Brookfield were not designed, he felt, just to flatter him. Tony had stressed that he wanted to work for someone who was a modernizer, in a place that embraced all the new developments – insecticides, pesticides, organo-phosphates. And – he hadn't been

47

too shy to say – a place that would give him the freedom to use his own ideas.

Ralph could see the lad's point of view. He himself had nothing but respect for Dan Archer: he had a lifetime's experience of the land. But Ralph knew that Phil increasingly chafed against his father's wishes and he could imagine it would be even worse for a youngster.

'Well, the job's yours if you want it,' he said, smiling broadly. 'Start as soon as you like.'

'That's fantastic! Thank you!' Tony grabbed his hand and pumped it up and down. 'You won't regret it. Mum and Dad'll be thrilled – coming on top of Lilian's wedding and everything.'

'Of course. How are the newlyweds?'

Ralph Bellamy hadn't been invited to the wedding, and he hadn't expected to be. That was the trouble with his position. He owned thousands of acres in Ambridge and beyond but he was an anachronism: who wanted a village squire in this day and age?

He'd been passing the church in his Jaguar, though, on the day of the wedding, as Lilian had arrived. He'd often seen her out riding and now he couldn't resist slowing down. He'd seen her get out of the bridal car with her bouquet of rosebuds. The wind had lifted her veil and he'd thought how pretty she looked. And she had a good seat on a horse.

'Nick and Lilian? Oh, you know,' said Tony dismissively. 'All gooey.'

Ralph nodded benignly. He'd seen Nick around the village in the months leading up to the wedding. He was a handsome chap, this Canadian she'd married. It was obviously a real love match.

'And what's your father up to these days?' he enquired. 'Has he still got a share in that cabin cruiser on the River Severn? He's a card, isn't he?'

• • •

If Phil thought he had problems with Dan, and Chris with Paul, they were nothing compared to Peggy's with Jack. Predictable only in his unpredictability, he could spend months doing nothing but drinking and gambling. Then, one day, he'd shake off his stupor and arrive down for breakfast with some new-fangled idea that Peggy was supposed to welcome with whoops of delight and help him put into place. She always meant to fight him, she really did, but in the end, what could she do but go along with him? How could she refuse him when she blamed herself for his drinking bouts because, simply by coping, she'd made him feel superfluous at the pub?

'Close the restaurant and open a coffee bar?' she protested weakly, cutting Adam's toast into soldiers. It was the lazy, late-summery end of September and Jennifer and Roger were having a weekend away to celebrate their first anniversary. 'Surely it'll attract all the wrong sort?'

But Jack had been talking to Paul. Paul dated all his troubles at the garage from his missed opportunity with the coffee bar. If he'd gone ahead, he reckoned, it would have been the making of the place. And Jack believed him.

'There's a gap in the market, Peg,' he insisted. 'Nowhere round here for the youngsters to go.'

'But do we want them here?' Peggy worried. 'Mods and Rockers, those funny anoraks, scooters and motorbikes churning up the village green . . .'

Jack wasn't listening. He flipped open a glossy brochure.

'Look at that,' he enthused. 'Isn't it beautiful?'

Peggy looked, puzzled, at a shiny machine swarming with buttons and handles.

'What is it?'

'A Gaggia, Peg. The latest Italian coffee machine. And we'll have milk shakes in tall glasses with long spoons and sandwiches and savouries and cakes and pastries . . . and fruit machines. And a juke box, of course, the youngsters'll want that.'

'But Jack, isn't this a young person's game?'

'You're as old as you feel, Peg. And I feel eighteen again!'

'So I see.'

Eighteen or eighty, he'd never have the sense he was born with.

• • •

'Espresso, Grandad? That's the little black coffee. Or what about a frothy one, made with hot milk with chocolate sprinkled on the top?'

Jennifer tried to interest her grandfather in the new Playbar menu without success. It was the opening night – Hallowe'en, as it happened, and the place was decorated with jack o'lanterns and skulls that glowed green in the gloom. Dan studied the list of beverages as best he could in the available light. Peggy had told him they were keeping things deliberately dim as the alterations weren't quite finished. Luckily, the eerie theme concealed this rather well.

'I don't suppose you can get such a thing as a cup of tea?' he asked helplessly.

'You're hopeless!' Jennifer smiled. 'I'll see what I can do.'

She sashayed off in her bell-bottomed trousers and peaked cap. Dan couldn't understand why she wanted to dress like the second mate off *Mutiny on the Bounty*, but there were a lot of things, he felt, he didn't understand these days.

He'd had another row with Phil before he'd come out. At the end of last year, claiming that Dan was a 'dinosaur' (charming!), Phil had gone ahead and bought some land of his own, saying that if they weren't welcome at Brookfield, he'd try out his ideas there. Now, of course, Dan felt that Phil was putting too much time into his own enterprise at the expense of getting the autumn seedbeds prepared and the barley drilled. But when Dan had pointed this out, Phil had given him a mouthful about how he'd 'carried' the farm last spring when Dan had been ill and how he was sick of being held back. Dan sighed heavily as Doris came to sit beside him.

'Cheer up, love,' she chided him. 'It's Jack and Peggy's big night.'

'I don't know why they wanted to inflict it on us.' Dan raised his voice as he spoke. The music had started up again. 'What in the world is Tony doing?'

Tony had dragged Tessa Latimer into a space between the tables where they were prancing about to something which seemed to have words about honky-tonk women and their honky-tonk blues. As Dan and Doris watched, Lilian and Nick, then Jennifer and Roger, joined them. Sid Perks from the garage and his wife Polly, who ran the shop and Post Office, were next, writhing around, Dan thought, like a couple of sheep scratching themselves on a gatepost. And there were Greg Salt, Dan's dairyman, and his wife Nora, who'd once been engaged to Paddy Redmond, at this honky-tonk lark, too! Dan thought Greg would have had more sense. Time was when a farm worker liked a mug of cider and a spot of morris dancing, but not now. Dan shook his head in amazement. He should have realized things were changing ten years ago when his apprentice, Jimmy Grange, had taken up with a skiffle band. And now look at the state of things! When Phil and Jill's eldest three, Shula, Kenton and David, who'd been allowed to stay up late for the occasion, squashed on to the impromptu dance floor as well, Dan stood up and held out a hand to Doris.

'No, Dan, we couldn't! You'll put your back out!'

'We're not dancing, Doris, ' he said. 'We're going. Come on, get your coat.'

'Well, you were a right misery,' Doris scolded as she placed a cup of cocoa at his elbow when they were safely home. 'I don't know what's got into you. Must be your age.'

'Must be,' he said shortly.

'Dan?' Doris perched on the arm of his chair and took his hand. 'What is it?'

'It's no good, love,' he sighed. 'I've got to face it. What's the point of going on, rowing with Phil over every little thing, ruining the perfectly good relationship we've had up to now. You saw it tonight, Doris. It's a young person's world. My hanging on at Brookfield is like trying to turn back the tide.'

Doris held her breath. She hardly dared hope.

'What exactly are you saying, Dan?'

'What I'm saying, love, is that it's time I went. Handed over the reins to our Phil. I'm going to retire.'

·3·

Making Room

It was what Doris had always wanted. She'd first begun to dream about Dan's retirement years back, when Simon Cooper, their farm hand, had retired in the mid-1950s. A couple of years later, Lettie Lawson-Hope, the Squire's wife, for whom Doris had worked as a lady's maid before she married Dan, had died and left her Glebe Cottage. It had seemed like a gift from the gods. Now she and Dan would have somewhere to go when they left Brookfield and her hints had become heavier – almost as heavy as her heart when Dan met her requests with a gruff 'Are you writing me off?' When Ned Larkin, Simon's successor, had retired too and been replaced by his son, Jethro, Doris's longing for her and Dan to pack up and move to Glebe Cottage had been almost too much to bear.

'When I leave Brookfield it'll be in my box,' he'd declared robustly only the previous year, despite a badly bruised shoulder. The cows had got loose and while he was trying to rescue one which was sinking into the slurry pit, another had fallen on him.

'You'll get your wish, the way you're going,' Doris had retorted, rubbing in the embrocation that Walter had assured her was his old granny's great-granny's own concoction and which had cured the aches and pains of the Gabriels since one of them had been injured in the Napoleonic Wars.

Now, twelve years after she had first mentioned the idea, and at the age of seventy-four, Dan had finally bowed to the inevitable.

In truth, the last few years hadn't been happy ones at Brookfield. There'd been all the arguments between Phil and Dan, five rainy summers in a row *and* the problems of inflation and interest rates.

But now they had the prospect of moving. It was with delight that Doris gave Hugo Barnaby, a cousin of John Tregorran's who'd been renting Glebe Cottage, notice that she and Dan would be requiring it from Lady Day. Phil would take over as Chairman of Ambridge Farmers Limited, the cooperative he and Dan had set up some years back, on Midsummer's Day and at the same time, he, Jill and the children would move into Brookfield.

But if Doris had thought Dan's retirement was an end, she was to find out that the announcement was just the beginning. Jill offered to help her turn her usual spring clean into a mammoth clear-out but Doris refused any help. She wasn't feeling very pleased with Jill, who'd announced that there'd have to be alterations to Brookfield and they couldn't possibly move in before Michaelmas.

'I've brought up three children here perfectly well,' Doris objected to Mrs Perkins when Peggy's mother called in for tea, 'but these young girls today have to have all mod cons, as they call them. Jill wants a fitted bathroom and they're even talking about knocking the scullery through into the kitchen. No scullery! Can you imagine!'

Mrs P could not, but then she and Doris were of the same generation. The twin-tub and the frozen fish finger were anathema to them.

With the date for their move set for late March, only a couple of months away, Doris thought she should perhaps begin her spring cleaning early. Ambitiously, she decided to start with the kitchen dresser, whose bulging drawers were the repository for bottle-openers, bits of string, cuphooks, safety pins and everything else that needed a home.

'I've been looking for that darning mushroom everywhere!' she exclaimed to Dan. It was a Sunday afternoon in the middle of January, and a hard-hearted wind was driving the rain diagonally across the window panes. 'Did you put it in there?'

'What would I do that for? The only sort of mushroom I'm interested in is the one I find in my steak and kidney pie,' retorted Dan.

Galvanized by Doris's determination, he'd brought a couple of box files through from the farm office to sort out on the kitchen table in the warm.

'Knitting patterns, recipe for mock cream – can't think why I ever wanted that with a herd of milkers outside – programme from the village fête – goodness, the year Gilbert Harding opened it and . . . ooh look! A cake box from Phil and Grace's wedding!'

Doris came across to the table with her handful of treasures and spread them out in front of her. 'This cardigan in blackberry stitch . . . I made it for our Chris when she was about twelve.'

'I can't think why you've kept all that rubbish,' remarked Dan, heaving a pile of papers out on to the kitchen table. Doris reached across and took a couple off the top.

'Receipt from the Imperial Hotel, Borchester,' she read. 'Dressed poultry, fifty birds received with thanks . . . 24 December 1952! Newspaper cutting from the *Borchester Echo*, 27 August – 1952 again – and you talk about me!'

'1952? That was the summer that RAF plane crashed into the Five Acre,' mourned Dan. 'Best crop of winter wheat I never had.'

'It's a nice picture of you, though,' conceded Doris. 'And listen: "Mr Thomas Forrest, a local gamekeeper, who was patrolling nearby at the time of the incident, said, 'It was like the war all over again. I thought I was a goner.'" I'll have to show that to Tom.' She sat down opposite, intrigued. 'What else have you got there?'

'What haven't I got?' Dan dealt the papers one by one on to the table, like a pack of tattered cards. 'Brochure on bulk milk tanks, Ministry hand-out on warble fly eradication programme, postcard from Phil . . . good Lord, from that trip he made to Holland with Grenville and Carol Grey. When was that?'

Doris was delving in the pile.

'Amber's rosette when she won Best of Breeds at the Borchester Show, third prize certificate for a plate of broad beans from the Flower and Produce Show – only third? – oh, Dan, doesn't it bring it all back?'

Dan nodded and rubbed his chin.

'Aye, love, it does.'

'Where are we going to start? I don't think I can bear to part with it all. It's our lives.'

But it had to be done. Slowly and regretfully, then, as time went on, more remorselessly, Dan and Doris began throwing things out. In consultation with the family, who earmarked the pieces they wanted, the bigger items of furniture were sent for auction. David was thrilled with Phil's old toy fort which they found in the loft, but Chris said a polite 'no, thank you' to Muffin, the stuffed donkey on wheels which had kept her amused for hours when she'd been a girl. Shula declared that some of the old frocks, which Doris had planned to give young Elizabeth to dress up in, were 'groovy' and was soon to be seen parading round the village in a 1930s tea gown and feather boa. Apparently a shop called Biba had opened in London selling the self-same things and was doing very well. But Jill shook her head when Doris offered her some of her old preserving pans, saying she had stainless steel now: scientists said that aluminium was bad for you. The old meat-safe, which had remained for years in the outhouse, had to go, but John Tregorran had a contact in the antiques trade who was only too happy to take the mangle and the old dolly for a couple of pounds each.

Bit by bit, Doris felt that they were making progress and by the time the spring came, she had made her peace with Jill and conceded that it would be useful to have some help in cleaning the place. But then something happened that made everything else seem trivial and unimportant. Lester Nicholson – Lilian's beloved Nick – suddenly died.

For someone so young and apparently vigorous, Nick had not truly been well since he and Lilian had married. The ear trouble which had seen him invalided out of the Canadian Air Force had returned and he'd had to undergo treatment in London. At Brookfield at Christmas he'd still been under the weather. He and Lilian had come to the big family lunch, but then Tony had driven them back to The Bull so that Nick could rest, and they'd reappeared for only a short time in the evening to play Kim's Game and charades. Early in the New Year, understandably, though his health hadn't much improved and everyone worried about how he'd cope with the long flight, Nick started to talk about going back to Canada to see his folks. As well as his parents, it seemed he had legions of aunts and uncles he hadn't seen since he'd been posted to England nearly two years previously. He especially wanted Lilian to meet his Aunt Dorothy, who lived in Avonlea, a village in rural Saskatchewan. It was the nearest thing in Canada, he said, to Ambridge. Lilian, whose favourite book had always been *Anne of Avonlea*, was thrilled by the coincidence and keen to go. And her enthusiasm for the trip increased when it emerged that there was a prominent consultant over there who might be able to do something for Nick's troublesome ear condition.

In early March they'd set off, full of hope. Nick was booked into hospital for some exploratory tests, but by the end of the month he planned to be free of doctors for good.

'If this guy can't clear up the problem, nobody can,' he told Peggy when she and Jack drove them to London Airport. 'And then I can start to give your daughter all the good things in life she deserves.'

'There was no need to say that, Nick. I've got everything I want with you,' Lilian told him later as they waited for their flight to be called.

Nick put down the aviation magazine he'd been reading and kissed the tip of her nose.

'Maybe. But isn't it great to know things are going to get even better?'

But a couple of weeks later, the phone had rung at Brookfield at 10.30 at night.

'Who on earth would be calling at this time?' Doris had clucked. She'd been about to boil the kettle for their hot-water bottles.

'Probably a wrong number.'

Dan unhooked two mugs for their cocoa as Doris picked up the receiver. At first she couldn't even make out who it was. Peggy's voice was clotted with tears.

'Oh, Mum,' she sobbed. 'Something terrible's happened. It's Nick.'

Nick had somehow fallen down a flight of stairs in the hospital where he'd been receiving treatment – and had been making such an improvement. He'd died instantaneously.

Doris couldn't believe it. Goodness knew, she'd sat in this kitchen and heard news of some deaths over the years, from Walter's poor wife Annie to the Squire's wife, her old employer, Lettie Lawson-Hope. But sorry as she'd been, and much as she'd suffered for those left behind, the truth was that they'd had their lives. But for Nick to die in a stupid accident, just when he was getting better, just as he and Lilian had their whole lives in front of them – it was so pointless. And such a terrible waste.

'Oh, Mum,' sobbed Peggy, 'You've been through this with Phil. Tell me what to say to Lilian when she rings again.'

Dan, realizing something was wrong, had come and put his arm round his wife. Doris had mouthed to him what had happened and now, unable to carry on without breaking down herself, she passed him the receiver. Peggy repeated her plea.

'Peggy, love, there's nothing you can say,' he advised. 'It's more important that you give her the chance to talk to *you*. If she wants to.'

'It'll break her, Dad,' whispered Peggy. 'They were so much in love.'

But when Lilian came home, having endured the funeral with Nick's grieving parents, her own family were surprised. She was a tougher character, it seemed, than they'd given her credit for. She didn't want any fuss, she said. She didn't want to talk about Nick and she didn't want anyone to talk about him to her.

'I couldn't take it,' she said emptily. 'I know you all mean well and I daresay you think it'd be better for me if I did talk about it, but I just can't.'

Instead, a week after her arrival back in Ambridge, a widow at the age of twenty-two after nine months of marriage, she announced she was going back to work at the stables.

Lilian had thought it would be a good idea. Didn't everyone say that work was the one thing that got you through times like this? Hadn't her Uncle Phil – she could remember her grandmother tut-tutting about it – done the very same thing when his first wife, Grace, had died? But the stables were the last place Lilian could forget about Nick.

She could still remember that first day nearly two years ago when he'd turned up for a ride: he'd phoned the previous evening to book. He'd come up behind her when she'd been mucking out a stall and asked where he could find the boss. An easy mistake to make, he'd sallied smoothly when she'd told him *she* was the boss, because she looked far too young and pretty to be running the place. She'd looked at him warily, not sure whether this was merely the same transatlantic charm she'd seen on cinema screens and which he might have used automatically on any female under the age of sixty, or whether it was for her alone.

Even more than that, she was intrigued to find that from his voice on the phone she'd pictured him entirely wrong.

She'd imagined him tall, lean and dark, rather like Roger Travers-Macy. Instead he was short and stocky, his curly brown hair glinting bronze in the April sun.

'You're not in uniform!' she'd exclaimed, disappointed, and he'd laughed, his green eyes smiling at her.

'I'm off duty.' He pronounced it 'dooty', of course. 'Else I wouldn't be here.'

So she'd apologized for being silly and had led Ebony out into the yard for him – Ebony, the first horse she'd bought for the stables with £375 of Aunt Laura's money and still her favourite. After that first day Ebony had been Nick's regular mount, and before long Nick and Lilian had begun riding out together, when she could spare the time, galloping over Heydon Berrow with the gorse vivid around them and the rabbits transfixed by the flashing hooves.

One morning in early May, when she'd been back in Ambridge just over a month, Lilian awoke early. The room was already light and the dawn chorus was deafening. She lay in bed for a moment, genuinely puzzled by the angle of the eave and the crooked dormer window, before realizing she was back in her old room over the lounge bar at

The Bull, with her rosettes from gymkhanas taped to the wall and her Pat Smythe books on the shelf. In that brief time, before she realized where she was, she had a moment of pure peace as she anticipated the day ahead. Then she remembered what had happened and why she was there and all the weariness, undiminished however much sleep she had, enveloped her again. But Lilian was determined not to give in to it. She pushed back the covers and swung her legs out of bed. In the pearly light she scrambled into jodhpurs and a shirt. Then she crept downstairs and let herself out of the back door.

Nick wasn't here to ride with her any more, but at the stables Lilian saddled up Ebony anyway. He snickered and stamped, excited to be going out so early with a rider he knew rather than waiting for Roberta, Lilian's assistant, to come and give him his bran mash, then lead him out for a lesson.

They trotted down the drive under the horse chestnuts, leaving hoofprints in the dew, then for a short way along the lane, before turning on to a bridle path that led to the bluebell wood on the Estate. Starlings and sparrows twittered in the trees on either side of the track and fieldmice scuffled in the hedge-bottoms. Lilian couldn't help noticing that the oak buds were just breaking. She ought to look for an ash tree to check her Uncle Tom's annual prediction: 'Oak before ash, you're in for a splash, Ash before oak, you're in for a soak.'

The ash trees had been in leaf before the oak in the past few years, he maintained, and the summers had been excessively rainy. Perhaps there was something in it.

Seeing it all, yet taking no notice, Lilian rode along, leaving the horse in charge, thinking of nothing except the warm feel of Ebony's flanks and the light reins between her fingers.

'Hoy! I thought it was you!'

The shout from the field startled her and she pulled the horse up short. She hadn't been paying attention. Perhaps Ebony had wandered from the path and she was trespassing. But it was her brother, Tony. He'd obviously come to get Bellamy's cows in for milking: they stood at the gate at the far side of the field, udders bulging. Tony tramped across the wet grass, swinging his stick.

'I've been yelling at you for ages!'

'Sorry. I was . . . you know.'

'Right.'

She hadn't seen much of Tony since she'd got back, though they were living under the same roof. It was a busy time on the land, her mother had explained – weren't they all – and Tony didn't want to blot his copybook with Bellamy. And he was out a lot in the evenings with Tessa: by the time he got back Lilian had long gone to bed.

'Had some good news yesterday,' he volunteered when Lilian said nothing more. 'Bellamy's going in for computers. Wants me to use them to keep an eye on herd performance, that sort of thing. And he wants me to enrol on a management course at Borchester Tech.'

'Good for you.'

'Yes. And, look, he . . . um . . . he's been asking me to give you his . . . condolences, you know.'

'That's kind of him.'

Lilian looked at her brother. A cowlick of hair fell over his eyes. When he'd been little her mother had called it a kiss curl. He'd hated that.

It was funny to think of Tony being kissed by a girlfriend, but then to her he'd always be her kid brother, the one she and Jennifer had used to tie up in their games of cops and robbers and imprison in the shed with the spiders. Suddenly, shamefully, she remembered, too, how one afternoon she'd forced him to be her pony and take part in a gymkhana in the pub garden. It wouldn't have been so bad had Jennifer not torn up a handful of grass and insisted that he behave like a proper pony and eat it.

'Hello, you two!'

As if conjured up by Lilian's reminiscence, there was Jennifer, coming towards them along the track. Adam, who'd be three next month, walked beside her clutching a posy of daisies and dandelions.

'I'll have to leave you to it,' said Tony, with some relief. 'Got to get a move on.'

He'd never been any good at feelings. It had taken him over a year to come round to the idea of Jennifer having Adam and he ducked

61

out of any discussion about their father's erratic moods, which this year had become worse than ever. Thinking about it, it struck Lilian for the first time how like their father Tony was when it came to avoiding the realities of life.

'You're out early,' said Lilian as Jennifer drew level. 'Couldn't sleep?'

'It's this little monkey!' Jennifer waggled Adam's hand. 'Up at five every day. Obviously a farmer in the making.'

Adam looked pretty perky on it, Lilian thought, but Jennifer looked exhausted. Terribly pale.

'Good ride?' Jennifer continued as Tony chivvied his cows through the gate. Adam tried to slither from her grasp to see what was going on and to distract him Jennifer picked him up to pat the horse.

'I can't say I've noticed,' Lilian sighed. 'Oh, it's a beautiful time of year – but it just seems to . . . slide over me somehow.'

'Oh, Lilian.' Jennifer bit her lip. 'I wish there was something I could say.'

Lilian glanced away. She didn't think she could stand any more sympathy. Seeing her, a blackbird froze on a branch as if playing a game of musical statues and fixed her with an unblinking – but at least not a pitying – eye.

'I understand, you know.' Lilian felt Jennifer's fingers on hers. 'I know what it's like to lose someone you love. When Adam's father –'

'That's hardly the same!'

'No, but –'

'Oh, forget it, Jennifer. Please. It's no good.'

No one understood what she was going through. No one.

'Ebony and I have got to go now, sweet,' Lilian said gently to Adam. 'Sorry.'

Adam protested feebly as Jennifer lowered him to the ground.

'Let's wave,' she urged. 'Wave to the horsey.'

'Walk on,' Lilian instructed Ebony. 'Bye, Jennifer.'

Jennifer looked after her sadly. Lilian was right. What *could* she say? That if Lilian had married Roger, none of this would have happened? But it was Jennifer who'd married Roger and it was Jennifer who, before the end of the year, would be presenting him with a son or daughter of his own. That was why she was waking early, nauseous, and why, she knew, she looked so ghastly. She hadn't even told Roger the news yet and how she would tell Lilian she couldn't begin to imagine – when everything was going so right for her and so disastrously wrong for her sister.

In the end, Jennifer didn't have to tell Lilian about her pregnancy. Lilian had guessed from her pallor the morning she'd met her out walking.

'You looked even grimmer than I felt!' she'd said, once Jennifer had told the family. 'Tell me it gets better.'

'It gets better after three months,' Jennifer had replied wanly. All she'd managed to keep down that day was half a digestive biscuit and a few sips of soda water. 'Then you have three months of feeling reasonable and eating like a horse. And then you're so huge you can't eat anything anyway.'

'Well, it's lovely news,' said Lilian warmly. 'Stand by for a very indulgent auntie.'

'It's lovely of you to take it like this,' replied Jennifer. 'I felt so . . . guilty, somehow.'

'Don't be like that.' Lilian gave a rueful smile. 'In a way, it sort of helps me to accept Nick's death more. It's funny how it works out, isn't it?' she said thoughtfully. 'A new life for one that's gone. Almost as if God was making room.'

·4·

Ring in the New

Rather to her surprise, as the summer passed, Lilian found that she was, slowly, feeling a little better. Granny Perkins had asserted that she'd have to 'go round the clock' before she'd feel anything like herself again – meaning that a full year would have to pass. She'd have to get through all the important dates by herself – first their wedding anniversary at the end of May; then Nick's birthday at the beginning of June and her own at the beginning of July. Then, thankfully, there was a respite until Christmas, which she was not expecting to enjoy.

The thing that probably helped most was moving out of The Bull to lodge with Aunt Laura. Lilian's own grief was hard enough to bear, and to see her mother suffering for her as well had only added to her pain. Aunt Laura, wrapped up in the Ambridge Protection Society, the WI and the Over Sixties Club, didn't have the time or the inclination to sit around moping with her.

'There's 300 envelopes to address tonight!' she'd announce after their spartan supper. 'Find yourself a pen!'

As long as Lilian could escape to her room some evenings to listen to Radio Luxemburg, she didn't mind. She wasn't moping, she told herself. It was quite understandable that her favourite pop song that summer should be 'The Wonder of You'.

• • •

'He's done *what?*' squeaked Jennifer.

It was early September – a quiet time at the bookshop. The only customer – a middle-aged woman in tweeds furtively leafing through *Women in Love* – raised her head sharply.

'Sorry,' Jennifer mouthed. Roger had left her in charge while he attended a book fair.

Lilian moved a pile of Germaine Greer's *The Female Eunuch* to one side and perched on the corner of a display table.

'He's asked me to hostess a dinner party for him. Tomorrow night.'

'*Ralph Bellamy*? I thought he had a thing going with Lady Isabel.'

Ralph Bellamy would have been astonished to learn that, no sooner had Brigadier Winstanley's niece, Lady Isabel Lander, arrived in the village than bets were being laid in The Bull on the date of their wedding. But, it seemed, it was not to be.

'They've had a terrific bust-up, apparently, and she flounced off to dinner with Hugo Barnaby.'

'So he's asked you to take her place?'

'Well, not in the romantic sense, obviously.' Lilian smiled, remembering how the worldly Ralph Bellamy had blushed when he'd realized she might think he was propositioning her. 'He was very proper about it.'

'Are you going to do it?'

'I told him I'd think about it. I wanted to ask you what you thought.'

'Oh, Lilian!' Jennifer squeezed her sister's arm. 'What do you want to do?'

'I'm tempted. It'd be a night out, wouldn't it? Make a change from watching the telly with Aunt Laura.'

'Well, if you ask me,' said Jennifer, 'it's no more than you deserve. We've all been nervous of trying to force you to go out, but if you want to have some fun at last then I'm all for it.'

'Who said anything about fun? It's only a dinner for his food-processing and horse-racing chums!' Lilian hopped off her perch on the table. 'Anyway, I'm going to do it. The real reason I'm telling you is I haven't a thing to wear. I wondered what you could lend me – it's not as if you can squeeze into them any more.'

Lilian was surprised by how excited she felt about the dinner party. She knew she was no real replacement for Lady Isabel Lander, who had a family tiara and had been to finishing school in Switzerland. She hardly knew Ralph Bellamy, except for the fact that he was her brother's boss and she'd seen him at horse shows and point-to-points. But it didn't matter. It was just nice to have something to look forward to. Jennifer had lent her a long dress in dusty pink crêpe, which she said was by Ossie Clark. Lilian, who was happier in jeans or jodhpurs, thought the neckline was a bit low, but Ralph Bellamy didn't seem to share her doubts.

'You look absolutely beautiful,' he exclaimed, taking her hands as she was shown into the sitting room on the stroke of seven, half an hour before his guests were due to arrive. 'I hope you're going to enjoy yourself this evening.'

Lilian did. Ralph introduced her tactfully as 'Lilian Nicholson – the best horsewoman in the district', without mentioning either her marital status or her relationship with him. Lilian had been prepared to be asked and had worked out a careful speech about Nick, one she could say without her voice cracking, but in the end, nobody enquired and she had to smile.

She'd thought she'd be the centre of interest, the plucky little widow, but these were people with bigger lives than those she met in Ambridge. They'd come from outside the area, they had wider concerns, and they were too well-bred to probe.

Instead the talk was of racing stables and stud farms, which Lilian could contribute to, or of their boxes at the opera and summers on the Riviera, which she couldn't. Yet she hadn't felt left out. Ralph had brought her into the conversation at every opportunity – but in a natural sort of way – and when she'd had to confess that she'd never been to an opera, he'd said that that was something they must put right very soon.

It was another world. And she was only a tiny bit disappointed when, after a chaste kiss on the cheek, Ralph sent for the car and his chauffeur drove her home. It wasn't that she wanted him to seduce her – she wasn't sure how she'd feel about any other man's arms round her, after Nick – but that she felt it was, ironically, almost ungallant of him not to have tried.

'So you didn't feel like Ambridge's answer to Christine Keeler, then?' Tony asked her the next day. He'd bumped into her in the yard at Sawyer's Farm where Bellamy's main herd was kept. She'd popped up to thank Ralph for the bouquet of tiger lilies he'd sent her as a thank you.

'What, trying to get the secret of tasty tinned peas out of Sidney Goodman? Hardly.'

'Would you do it again?'

'Ralph's got to ask me first.'

'Hm.' Tony considered. 'Well, as a route to the top it's not quite Joe Lampton. But if Ralph hasn't got a daughter for me to marry, then I suppose him marrying my sister is the next best thing.'

Ralph came round the corner just as she was giving Tony a hefty thwack for his presumption. Luckily, he laughed.

• • •

'So Peggy's all worked up about it.'

In the sitting room at Brookfield, lit by low table lamps and a crackling fire, Jill, Phil and the children were decorating the Christmas tree. The radio was relaying the Service of Nine Lessons and Carols, but it was the only restful thing about the scene.

They were terribly late in getting the decorations up. Phil had been claiming for the past fortnight that he hadn't got a minute to dig up the tree – and none of the men could possibly be spared. Ploughing was well ahead but, even with Dan's retirement turning out to be more of a semi-retirement, Jill had to admit that Phil had had his hands full on the farm. Then Doris had been laid low with a nasty bout of flu, and what with looking after her and cooking for Dan, Jill hadn't had too much time to think about Christmas either.

She helped three-year-old Elizabeth to hang a bauble she'd made out of scrunched-up crêpe paper on a low branch. Shula was busy arranging holly along the mantelpiece. The boys were supposed to be winding tinsel round the banisters, but by the sound of the fake machine-gun fire, they had reverted to type and were playing *The*

Man from U.N.C.L.E. in the hall. Phil was kneeling by the piano stool sorting out his organ music for the Christmas service.

'What, because Lilian's skipping the family New Year's Eve party at The Bull?' he asked. 'Look, after all she's been through this year, if the girl wants to be on her own with her memories . . .'

'Do you ever listen? She's not going to the family party because she's spending New Year's Eve with Ralph Bellamy.'

'Is she? What does she want to do that for?'

'I've just told you, he seems to have quite a thing about her . . . Oh, I give up.'

In the hall, there was an ominous thud, then silence, then scuffling and stifled giggles. Jill went to the doorway and in those few steps her tone changed from silver to steel.

'Kenton! David! If anything gets broken – apart from your heads, which deserve it – you're going up to your rooms and you won't come down till Boxing Day.'

'Oh, Mum . . .' wheedled David.

'He started it . . .' Kenton put in smartly.

'This is our first Christmas at Brookfield,' said Jill with saintly severity. 'I've got all the family for lunch tomorrow and I don't want to spend the whole day explaining to Gran why the fanlight's broken and there's a big tear in the wallpaper.'

'Yes, cut it out, you two.'

Phil came to lend Jill moral support, standing behind her in the doorway. Muttering, the boys returned to their tinsel-winding duties.

'What d'you think, Mum?' Shula sucked a finger which a holly prickle had pierced and surveyed the effect. 'I've never seen so many berries, have you?'

'Lovely, darling. Very artistic. Oh, Elizabeth, be careful.'

The whole tree was tilting as Elizabeth pulled a branch towards her, hoping to balance a moulting robin on it. It was an old cake decoration of Jill's that Elizabeth claimed had flown in among the Christmas baubles to build its nest. By next year, she confidently told them, it would have three babies to go on the tree as well, called Kevin, Heather and Ringo.

'Can we put the star on now, Mum?' Shula was holding out the battered silver star that Phil and Jill had bought for their very first tree, thirteen years and two homes ago.

'Me, me!' shrieked Elizabeth.

'I've promised her, I'm afraid,' Jill confessed, but, prepared for Shula's disappointment – the star had been her job ever since she'd been three – added, 'Daddy's rigged the lights up. You can switch them on, hm?'

Shula went to take her place by the switch as Jill extinguished the lamps. The afternoon sky, which hadn't seemed particularly gloomy, suddenly deepened, indigo over the tops of the trees in the orchard.

'Shall I call the boys?' asked Phil.

'Leave them, it's nicer without,' pleaded Shula.

'All right,' agreed her mother. 'Come on Elizabeth, I'll lift you up.'

She picked the toddler up and helped her to secure the star to the topmost branch, which was bent back against the low ceiling.

'Ready?' Shula asked.

Jill sat down and lifted Elizabeth on to her lap. Shula pressed the switch and the tree glowed into life.

'Pretty!' cried Elizabeth.

Shula moved to stand beside her father, one knee up on the piano stool, her arm round his waist. Phil looked at Jill. Lozenges of coloured light from the Christmas tree fell on her face. He looked round the low, beamed room. All their things which had looked so lost when they'd moved in, even with the furniture which Dan and Doris had left behind, seemed to belong here now. Jill smiled, knowing what he was thinking. Their first Christmas at Brookfield. The start of a whole new era.

The phone shrilled in the hall. Both boys shouted at once:

'I'll get it!'

'Leave it! I'm coming!'

Jill stood up to avert the inevitable fight. She arrived in time to see Kenton shove David out of the way and pick up the phone.

'Hello?'

David grabbed the receiver and added: 'Brookfield Farm.'

Jill silenced them both with a look and took the phone. It was Peggy.

'I had to let you know,' she began excitedly. 'Roger's just phoned. Jennifer's had the baby!'

'What timing!' cried Jill. 'Phil! Jennifer's had the baby!'

'Baby Jesus!' squealed Elizabeth, running out into the hall and attaching herself to Jill's skirt.

'He couldn't remember the weight or anything,' explained Peggy. 'Typical man! But I phoned the hospital back and they told me. Six and a half pounds. Dark curly hair. And they're calling her Deborah!'

The radio was still playing in the sitting room, and the angelic voices of the choir of King's College Chapel streamed out: 'The cattle are lowing, the baby awakes, But little Lord Jesus, no crying he makes . . .'

Jill felt Elizabeth's cheek pressed against her thigh and she hugged her own small daughter.

'Oh, Peggy! I'm so happy for you. After the year you've had – with Lilian and with Jack – what a lovely Christmas present!'

• • •

From the way her family had reacted, Lilian thought, it was as if she'd told them she was going to be spending New Year's Eve in bed with Ralph Bellamy, not just at his house. She was at pains to explain that New Year's Eve would be like the other evenings she'd spent with him since that first dinner party: a gathering of his friends with interests in growing and food-processing or horse-racing and breeding.

'And what's your role in all this?' Jennifer had enquired when Lilian had visited the hospital to admire her new niece.

Lilian, who was holding Deborah, touched her soft skull, awed. She looked at her sister, at Jennifer's look of dazed exhaustion but utter happiness. She wondered if she'd ever experience it.

'To tell you the truth, I don't know any more,' she confessed.

'When Ralph first asked me to dinner, I thought I was just there to be on show and make up the numbers. And I think that's what he thought, too. But now I've got to know him better – well, he's awfully nice, and very good to me and . . . I like him.'

'And he likes you, obviously.'

'It's a bit more than that. He hasn't said anything but – I can tell he's pretty fond of me.'

'He's in love with you, you mean,' said Jennifer shrewdly. 'And you don't feel the same.'

Lilian tucked the baby's tiny foot back under her shawl.

'Oh, Jennifer, how can I? It's not a year since Nick died. I'm still in love with him. I never expected to be in this position,' she went on. 'I wasn't looking to meet anybody. I didn't want anybody else, ever. But I like knowing that Ralph cares about me. I mean, I know you all care about me,' she added hastily, 'but it's not the same.'

'Well.' Jennifer shifted in her chair. She'd had stitches this time, and they were painful. 'It looks as if the New Year might be ringing in a lot of changes, doesn't it?'

Given her conversation with her sister, Lilian was not entirely surprised when, at ten minutes to midnight, Ralph came and found her. Mercedes, Sidney Goodman's Spanish wife, had just been telling her how they usually celebrated New Year with fireworks on Las Ramblas in Barcelona, but Ralph linked Lilian's arm in his and explained that they had things to discuss. Then he led her out through the French windows on to the terrace.

It was a startlingly clear night, the sky freckled with stars. Lilian shivered and Ralph, apologizing for dragging her out of the warmth, draped his dinner jacket round her shoulders. He led her over to a stone bench. She sat down and he sat beside her, bulky in his stiff white shirt.

'Lilian,' he began. 'I want to talk to you. About the future.'

'Oh, I was listening at dinner,' she said flippantly, terrified of what was coming. 'You're going to reduce the ewes by half but double the beef cattle, increase the potato acreage and –'

'Not that sort of future,' he said impatiently. 'Our future.'

Lilian took a breath. She had a good idea what he was going to say but she still had no idea what she would say in reply.

'It's the start of a year, Lilian,' he began pompously, 'that could see great changes. For both of us.'

Lilian stifled a smile and Ralph sighed crossly at his own inarticulacy.

'You know what I'm trying to say, don't you?' he appealed. 'I'm asking you to be my – oh, Lilian, I want us to be together.'

It was endearing to see him, usually so confident, being so tentative.

'Ralph, you must understand it's not an easy decision,' said Lilian, feeling awkward and ungenerous. Her reaction was hardly romantic but Ralph didn't seem put out.

'No,' he agreed. 'I know that.'

With relief, Lilian realized that he wasn't expecting an answer then and there.

'Unless . . . you're ready to decide now?' he added hopefully.

'No,' admitted Lilian. 'I don't think I am. I'm sorry.'

Bellamy nodded understandingly.

'That's all right. It's more than I've a right to expect. And at least,' he gave a self-conscious laugh, 'you haven't said no.'

'I haven't, have I?' she said evenly.

He took her hand and held it very gently in both of his.

'But don't spend too long thinking about it,' he appealed. 'Please. I'd rather you told me straight out, if I'm . . . not wanted,' he went on brusquely. 'I want you to be honest with me.'

'Ralph, I couldn't be anything else!' She placed her free hand on top of his. 'But I don't want to hurt you by saying one thing now and then having second thoughts. I know you're serious and I'm taking you seriously. But I won't be rushed.'

'I'm sorry.' He was immediately contrite. 'It's just that our relationship's so important to me. But I won't rush you, I promise.'

The church clock began to strike twelve. Lilian got up and held out her hands to him.

'Come on,' she said gently, 'your guests will be wondering where you are.'

For someone not rushing her, Ralph Bellamy had a funny way of doing things. Barely a fortnight later, he turned up at the stables in the middle of the morning when she was struggling with the accounts and told her he had something to show her.

'Not the first consignment of Brussels sprout plants, I hope,' she joked as she climbed down from his brand new Range Rover in the stable yard at his house, Ambridge Court. Another part of his reorganization of the Estate was replacing the spring barley with sprouts. Tony had been sent to Cambridgeshire on a recce over Christmas and had come back enthused.

'Better than that,' Ralph replied, leading her towards the end loose box. He opened the stable door. 'Take a look inside.'

Lilian gasped. Inside the stable was the most beautiful chestnut gelding, a good sixteen hands high.

'Aren't you a beauty,' she said, patting the horse. 'What's his name?'

'Red Knight,' answered Ralph.

The horse dipped his head and tried to nuzzle in her pocket, where she kept her mints and sugar lumps.

Bellamy laughed. 'He likes you all right.'

'I like him. What's his temperament like?'

'As good as his pedigree,' confirmed Ralph. 'He's by Red Arrow out of a very good mare of Tom Stevens.'

'Class,' conceded Lilian, offering the horse a mint. 'So. What are your plans for him?'

'Well,' confessed Ralph, 'this is where you come in. I want to enter him for the local point-to-point. And I want you to ride him.'

Lilian had to admit Ralph was clever. Oh, she wasn't saying that he approached his wooing of her as if it were just another business deal – far from it. She never doubted the sincerity or depth of his feelings for her. It was just that, after all his years in business, he was incapable of letting things take their course. Ralph was a man of action. He was used to making things happen, calling the shots. She didn't believe for a moment that he thought so little of her that he imagined she could be swayed in her decision by the chance to ride a beautiful horse, the like of which she could never afford. But with the point-to-point in April, Ralph had guaranteed that for the next couple of months, they would be spending a lot of time together as she got used to Red Knight and he to her. And he had certainly strengthened the common bond between them – their great love of horses.

The South Borsetshire Point-to-Point, traditionally held on Easter Tuesday, was a fixture in the Ambridge calendar. Dan and Doris had hardly missed one since they were married, and this year was no exception. Doris was up at eight, packing the creaking picnic hamper with hot soup, iced lemonade (you never knew what the weather was going to throw at you in April) and enough food to feed a family of six for a day – or her husband for one meal, plus mid-morning and afternoon snacks. They arrived in time to get a good pitch for the car, from where, seated at the picnic table, they'd be able to see a lot of the action both on and off the course. Part of the fun of the point-to-point was simply seeing who was there.

'Takes you back, though,' observed Dan as he enjoyed his first cup of coffee of the day, 'having one of the favourite riders in the family. Remember when our Chris was a regular at these?'

'My heart used to be in my mouth,' remembered Doris. 'How many times did she break her collar-bone? Was it two, or three?'

'Ralph Bellamy seems pretty certain Lilian's in with a good chance,' Dan reflected. 'Perhaps I should put a fiver on her to win.'

'You leave that betting lark to Walter Gabriel, thank you,' said Doris crisply. 'He's coming with Mrs Lily, I believe.'

'And it's a safe bet Mrs P isn't very impressed about that,' chuckled Dan.

Last year, Walter had proposed to Mrs P, now widowed, but had been turned down. She had another admirer, Henry Cobb, the cellar-man at The Bull, who tried to better everything Walter did for her.

When Walter had given Mrs P a budgerigar for her birthday, Henry had given her a mynah bird, and finally Walter had turned his attentions to Martha Lily, a widow from Penny Hassett who was the new forecourt attendant at the garage.

'Mum! Dad!'

It was Chris, calling them from the far side of the paddock. Dan waved back and she shouted that she'd come across and see them later: she and Paul were going to walk the course.

Doris sniffed. It was quite something these days to see Paul and Chris out as a couple: horses might have brought them together, but they weren't enough to keep them together. Paul's engineering business was doing all right, apparently, though his 'invention' hadn't turned out to be the money-spinner he'd hoped. But Doris couldn't help feeling that Chris was merely making the best of things with her marriage and though, in a sense, she was only following Doris's advice to 'take what comes', Doris grieved for her. Chris had been such a lovely, vivacious girl. She'd had such a lot about her. She could have married anyone. But she'd had to pick Paul, who seemed to have squashed all the life out of her, somehow.

'Aye, aye, here they come.'

Dan nodded in the direction of the paddock. Ralph was leading out Red Knight. Lilian, in her royal blue and white colours, was seated very straight in the saddle. She looked scared stiff.

'I hope she knows what she's doing,' worried Doris, not thinking just about Lilian's getting round the course.

Lilian had popped round to see her gran the week before to talk to her about Ralph. It wasn't the first time she'd done so. When Jennifer had told Doris she was pregnant with Adam, Doris felt she'd judged the girl too harshly. She was gentler with her grandchildren these days, or maybe nothing that her family got up to could surprise her any more. To tell the truth, she was flattered that a youngster like Lilian would want her opinion, and she gave it when prompted. Mostly, though, she poured the tea and offered cake, and let Lilian talk. That way she answered her questions for herself.

'It'd be something, wouldn't it,' said Dan, watching Lilian bend down to confer with Ralph about something, and his smile of pride and pleasure. 'All these years our Jack's had a bee in his bonnet about Phil carving himself a bigger piece of Brookfield, and Jack being left out, and now, the way things are going, Jack's daughter could be the lady of the manor, presiding over the whole bloomin' Estate!'

'Language!' scolded Doris.

'And then there's the question of Brigadier Winstanley's estate.' Dan carried on regardless, taking the second cup of coffee, which Doris had sugared and stirred for him. 'Thank you, love.'

Poor Brigadier Winstanley had died in a hunting accident at the beginning of the month. He'd bequeathed his estate while he was still living to his niece, Lady Isabel Lander, who'd been running it with the help of consultants, but she'd already declared her intention of selling up. After all, as the village sages pondered in The Bull, when you already had a house in Sussex and a flat in Belgravia, what did you need 1000 acres and a dower house in Ambridge for? It would have been surprising, Dan thought, if Bellamy and Jack Woolley, the Brummie businessman who owned Grey Gables Country Club, didn't buy up the land between them: the Dower House could always be sold off with a couple of acres as a country retreat for some townie, a development that Dan didn't approve of, but which seemed more and more common these days.

'I don't think I can do this.'

With the start of her race looming, Lilian felt as if she were drowning in wave after wave of panic.

'Of course you can. Look how well you rode him when you tried out the course.'

'That was different. Can't you ride him?'

'Don't be ridiculous!' laughed Bellamy. 'We've had the weigh-in now. And there's a few stone between you and me. Anyway,' he went on, 'Red Knight's used to you. You move beautifully together.'

'I don't want to let you down, Ralph,' pleaded Lilian.

'You never could,' Ralph told her. 'Now come on, you'd better get in position.'

As she lined up for the start with all the other riders, Lilian tried to work out quite why she was so nervous. She'd ridden in point-to-points before, she'd ridden at three-day events, she'd even ridden at the Horse of the Year Show. She knew all her family were there, but that didn't put her off, she was used to it. She knew that they'd be shouting their lungs out for her. It was Ralph who made the difference. She knew he'd be watching her through his binoculars, straining every muscle, as she would be, willing her to win. And willing something else as well.

He'd already told her that, win or lose, he'd booked them a table at Redgate Manor, an exclusive country hotel, for dinner that evening. And she had a feeling that he would be using the occasion to repeat the question he'd asked her at New Year and that he would expect her to have come to a decision. And she still didn't know what to say.

Ralph had planned everything down to the last detail. When they got to Redgate Manor, Lilian found that he hadn't just booked a table, but a private room, with a roaring log fire and a table laid for two. Ralph placed the trophy from the point-to-point – she'd won her race, but that seemed almost incidental – on the mantelpiece, where it was reflected in a huge mirror and sent shafts of scintillating light out into the candlelit room. He took her hand and led her to the table. He pulled out her chair and she sat down. She'd borrowed another dress from Jennifer and she had to stuff the full skirt under the table. That was just one thing that bothered her about a future with Ralph. She didn't have the wardrobe for it. Still, she supposed he'd provide all that.

He sat down heavily opposite her. Now, she noticed, *he* looked nervous. His sleeve caught his knife and it clattered on his plate. It didn't help Lilian's nerves, either.

A waiter who'd been hovering came forward at Ralph's gesture and began to peel off the gold foil from the bottle of champagne that was waiting in the ice-bucket. Lilian watched with rapt attention as he untwisted the wire from around the cork – anything rather than look at Ralph, whom she knew was looking at her. The waiter rotated the bottle with slow precision and suddenly the cork popped out, smoking. He deftly upended the bottle first into Lilian's glass, then Ralph's, and when both were full, produced menus from a side table with a magician's flourish. Then he left them alone.

Lilian gave a nervous gasp and raised her glass.

'Well, cheers! Quite a day!'

'I hope so,' said Ralph cryptically.

'At least I won. Otherwise I wouldn't have deserved your going to all this trouble.'

'The result wouldn't have made any difference. I was going to give you this anyway.'

Out of his pocket he took a small leather box. A ring box.

Lilian put her fingers to her lips but he took her other hand and closed it around the box.

'Open it,' he said.

She did as she was told. Inside was the biggest solitaire diamond she'd ever seen.

'Try it on,' Ralph urged.

Lilian knew she shouldn't. That to do so was – without saying anything for definite – at least implying something. But she couldn't resist.

She looked down at her hands. Until today she'd always worn her wedding and engagement rings from Nick – nothing as opulent as this, just a plain gold band and a tiny diamond cluster. But she'd taken them off before the race so they wouldn't chafe against the reins. She'd given them to Chris and she suddenly realized with a lurch of her heart that she hadn't got them back. Her wedding finger was free.

Ralph saw her hesitate. He took the ring from the box. Tenderly he picked up her left hand and eased the ring over the knuckle. It sat there, winking at her, dazzling her.

'How does it feel?' he asked.

'Fabulous,' she admitted. 'But Ralph – haven't you forgotten something? Isn't there a certain question . . . ?'

'Oh,' said Ralph bashfully. 'But I'm so bad at making speeches.'

'Even so . . .' said Lilian, struggling with the ring. Now they'd got this far she wasn't going to be done out of a proper proposal. 'Oh!' she exclaimed impatiently, 'I can't get it off! It won't come past my knuckle!'

'Then it'll have to stay where it is, won't it?' smirked Ralph.

This wouldn't do. He had to ask her properly, even if she still needed to play for time before giving him her answer.

'No, Ralph, you've got to do it properly,' she insisted, as he burst out laughing. 'Get me some butter or something. Stop laughing – and help me get it off!'

The fiasco over the ring helped, in the end. Whatever Ralph might say about fate – more a *fait accompli*, Lilian thought – it took the awkwardness out of a situation where she was still, to her amazement, undecided about what to say.

She had thought she'd made up her mind. She knew she wasn't in love with Ralph. What she felt for him when she saw him was nothing like the head-spinning euphoria she'd felt with Nick. She didn't think about Ralph all the time or live for their next meeting. She felt fond of him, of course, she'd told him so, and she knew that she'd warmed to him more and more over the six months they'd been seeing one another and that possibly the warmth she felt might yet grow into something else. Not love exactly, but something a bit closer to it.

Objectively – but should she have been able to be objective? – she could see that Ralph was a terribly good catch: he had a beautiful house, a position in the community, and more money than he knew what to do with. She was sure that some girls would have found that more than enough. But in marrying Ralph, Lilian felt as if she would be selling herself short, somehow. And, obscurely, as if Ralph would be selling himself short in marrying her, too.

She must have been undecided because she'd even talked it over with her family. They were no help, of course.

'He's asked you already? That was quick!' Tony exclaimed, and her parents were so overwhelmed that they just muttered things about 'only wanting her to be happy' and told her that whatever decision she made, they'd back her up. Very useful.

At the end of the evening at Redgate Manor, she'd asked Ralph for a week to make up her mind. She'd been holding him off since the New Year and to spin it out would only have been prolonging the agony. And though she might claim to feel disappointed that her parents had not given her more of a sense of direction, instinctively Lilian knew that the decision, as Ralph had said in the first place, was hers and hers alone. It had to be that way.

She found herself going on lots of long rides. As she and Ebony plunged through the bracken on Heydon Berrow, she thought about Ralph. And she thought about Nick.

She never expected to feel again what she had felt for Nick. She could either spend the rest of her life missing it, or trying to find it again. Or she could settle for what some might say was second best – though the biggest landowner in the area was a funny sort of consolation prize – and marry someone who clearly adored her, who would look after her, and with whom she had a lot in common. It wasn't as if she was pretending to Ralph that he was the love of her life. She'd told him all along the truth about her feelings for him. If he still wanted her to marry him, knowing that, what was stopping her?

Pulling Ebony to a halt, she looked down over Ambridge. She could easily pick out Ralph's house, Ambridge Court, with its tall red-brick chimneys. And there was the Dower House, with its carp pool and that beautiful wisteria round the front door, the house which had been Brigadier Winstanley's and which, Ralph said, if she accepted him, he would buy and where they would make their home together. And there was The Bull, with its cramped back kitchen and the persistent smell of ashtrays and spilt beer. Ebony whinnied and shook his head. He wanted to be galloping again. He wanted to move on. So did Lilian. And suddenly, with blinding clarity, marrying Ralph seemed the only way to do it.

·5·

Rites of Passage

Lilian's parents were delighted, though on her father's part, that might have had something to do with the bottle of twelve-year-old malt that Ralph brought round when he came to ask them formally for her hand. The wedding date was set for 3 September. Lilian had chosen it specially – a year to the day since he'd asked her to act as hostess at that first dinner party. Ralph was charmed.

'You're a sentimental little thing really, aren't you?' he smiled.

Planning for the wedding began immediately. Ralph had tactfully said he'd like to make a contribution – something else which was music to Jack's ears – and soon the postman was busy, bringing to The Bull sample menus from caterers and brochures for hire cars. Jennifer was enlisted as matron of honour. Peggy and Lilian scoured first Borchester, then Birmingham, and finally London for the perfect dress. The invitations were printed. ('Tell them to charge it to my account,' said Ralph grandly). The photographer was booked, and the florist. ('Get them to send me the bill,' said Ralph again.) And, so that he didn't feel left out, the cake was entrusted to an old army pal of Jack's from the Catering Corps.

'"That's a lovely drop of cake, Stan!" we always used to say,' grinned Jack. 'He steeps the fruit for weeks, y'know.'

Peggy had tutted and said something about there being a breathalyser nowadays, in case he hadn't noticed, but in the end, Jack's poor liver wasn't required to take any more punishment from an innocent-looking slice of wedding cake.

In July, he collapsed at home. He never had any colour these days, and he had gone to skin and bone. The local GP, Dr MacLaren, had him admitted to Borchester General immediately. There they ran tests and the doctors told Peggy that his liver was barely functioning. Unless Jack submitted to a course of treatment in a clinic – a drying-out clinic, though they didn't say as much – they couldn't hold out much hope for him. Too weak to resist, Jack agreed to go to a specialist clinic in Scotland and that's where he was, staring into space with a rug tucked round his knees, on the first Friday in September when Lilian and Ralph were married 300 miles away in Ambridge.

Right up to the morning of the wedding, Lilian was having doubts.

'Tell me I'm doing the right thing!' she implored Jennifer as her sister helped her into her peasant-style dress with its bands of cream lace. Ralph had wanted her to go to a dress designer, Clare Madison, who was an old girlfriend, but Lilian had insisted on choosing – and paying for – the dress herself.

'Lilian, stop torturing yourself,' Jennifer replied. 'It's too late to do anything about it now.'

At that moment Roger tapped on the door and called that the photographer had arrived to take pictures of the bride at home: was Lilian ready? Lilian didn't think so, but Jennifer plonked the cream, floppy-brimmed hat on her sister's head, teased her hair out beneath it and declared that she looked stunning. Roger, when he saw her, agreed, and so did her mum and Tony, who looked in his morning suit like a small boy in his new school uniform.

'You're shaking!' Lilian said to him as they arrived at the church and she took his arm. 'You're supposed to be propping me up as we go down the aisle, not the other way round.'

'It's a bit nerve-racking, isn't it?' Tony peered inside the gloom of the church. 'All these people.'

All the tenants and workers on the Bellamy Estate had been invited. Lilian could see Bobby Waters, who worked with Tony in Ralph's dairy unit, and his wife Jessie, as well as the greasy suit which could belong only to Joe Grundy from Grange Farm. He was a tenant Ralph had inherited when he'd bought the Brigadier's land, and what with the shambolic state of his farm, and Joe's lateness with the rent, Ralph had already given him notice to quit.

'Treat it as a rehearsal,' whispered Lilian to her brother. Somehow, Tony's nervousness was helping her feel more confident. 'After all, you're the only one of us left now.'

'Thanks a bunch. I hope I've got a few years of freedom yet!'

Certainly, none of Tony's romances so far – with Tessa Latimer, with Roberta, Lilian's assistant at the stables, or with Michèle Gravençin, Jill and Phil's au pair – had looked as though they would lead to marriage.

Lilian's Uncle Tom, as church warden and chief usher, was approaching them.

'All set?' he asked. 'I think Mr Bellamy's getting a bit restless.'

Poor Ralph. One way and another, she'd kept him waiting long enough.

Lilian tightened her grip on Tony's arm and nodded. Tom gave the pre-arranged signal to Phil, who was playing the organ, and the first bars of the 'Trumpet Voluntary' – without the trumpet, of course – vibrated through the church.

Lilian took her first tentative step down the aisle, her first step towards her new life. Deep down, though she could hardly believe it when she'd stalled for so long, she was still wondering if she was doing the right thing.

But as she drew closer to the altar, to Ralph's broad back straining the seams of his morning suit, her heart, which had been in her mouth, slowly sank back to its usual place. As the music crashed to a stop and the final notes reverberated through the air, the sun, which had been coming and going all morning, flashed into life outside the church. It streamed through the windows and Lilian looked instinctively towards her favourite, the one the Fairbrothers had installed in memory of Grace a few years after her death. The stained glass depicted the lion lying down with the lamb. A metaphor for her and Ralph, perhaps? But who had tamed whom? Ralph had told her he'd believed he was a confirmed bachelor until he'd met her; she hadn't been contemplating another attachment, ever. Yet here they were, a year later, about to be joined to one another for life.

Lilian looked at Ralph for the first time. He looked back at her adoringly.

'You look beautiful. I simply don't believe my luck,' he whispered.

Lilian smiled, more to herself than at him.

All in all, she thought she was the lucky one.

In an awful way, which didn't make her very proud of herself, Lilian was almost glad her father wasn't there to spoil her day. She'd seen enough of him at family weddings over the years, sneaking an extra glass of sherry behind a curtain for later, making friends with the waitress so she'd make sure and refill his wineglass, and always the first to the bar when the speeches were over. He hadn't made a speech at Jennifer's wedding – lucky Jennifer – but at hers to Nick he'd rambled on and on about why shouldn't he say a few words since he was paying for it all, when the Nicholsons had bought them a brand-new Ford Capri which must have cost a lot more.

When she'd first realized that her father wouldn't be there at her wedding, she'd asked her grandfather to give her away, but he'd suggested Tony. Lilian had been surprised, and a little hurt, but then it occurred to her that Dan, wise as ever, was grooming Tony for something. He thought it wouldn't be long before Tony would have to take over as man of the house. He didn't think Jack was ever coming home.

Maybe Jack knew he hadn't got long. Unlike Lilian, he'd never been particularly sentimental about anniversaries – he couldn't remember them if he was fuddled with drink, could he? But on 17 December, Dan and Doris's golden wedding day and his own birthday, Lilian and Tony between them persuaded him to phone Peggy before she went to the village hall which had been booked for Dan and Doris's anniversary party.

'Oh, Jack! It's wonderful to hear you again!'

Eavesdropping from the kitchen, Lilian squeezed Tony's arm. They could write, but they weren't able to contact Jack by phone at the clinic. The call had to come from him. And this was the first time he'd spoken to his wife in almost five months.

It wasn't a long conversation – what had the poor fellow got to say, except that the nurses were very nice and it made a change to be waited on hand, foot and finger – joke, Peg! But it made Peggy's day, and it made her Christmas when he sent her a soft mohair stole, which he'd asked one of the nurses to buy on his behalf.

'I know you always say there's a draught from the bedroom window,' he wrote. The writing was very shaky. 'I never fixed the sash, Peg, and I'm sorry. Hope this'll keep you warm. It comes with all my love. Your Jack.'

Hopeful that the phone call and the parcel might mean that Jack had turned a corner, Peggy waited until New Year was over, with all the increased trade it meant for the pub, then contacted the clinic to ask if Jack would be up to a visit. The Matron said guardedly that he had made some slight improvement but that she would have to consult the doctors. Peggy was ecstatic when she phoned back and said that they could see no reason why not.

The following Sunday, Ralph and Lilian took Peggy to the airport and promised to collect her on her return.

'Give Dad our love, won't you?' said Lilian as she kissed her mother goodbye. She didn't say anything about hoping to see him home soon. Privately she had come to share her grandfather's unspoken view of the situation, but Peggy remained optimistic and she didn't want to dampen her spirits. 'And let us know the time of your flight home.'

She and Ralph drove back to Ambridge through the empty countryside: it was the chauffeur's day off. The Jaguar was an automatic and as it hummed down the new stretch of motorway, Ralph twined his fingers through hers.

'I'm so sorry about your father,' he said. 'It must be agony for you all.'

'We can't say we didn't see it coming,' replied Lilian.

Ralph squeezed her hand.

'But apart from that . . . well, we've been married a few months now. Perhaps it's vanity, Lilian, but I have to ask – am I making you happy?'

Lilian turned her head lazily against the headrest and stretched her feet out on the thick carpet, admiring the glossy patent boots Ralph had bought her on their last shopping spree in London. When they got home tonight, she reflected, she'd got to look at the plans he'd had drawn up for creating an en-suite bathroom off the master bedroom at the Dower House and for extending the kitchen. Mrs Blossom, the Brigadier's housekeeper, whom they'd retained, had promised them venison for supper, followed by pears poached in red wine. Lilian smiled her secretive, cat-like smile.

'Very,' she said, and she meant it.

Three days later, having heard nothing from her mother about her return flight, Lilian phoned the clinic in Scotland. But quietly Peggy told her that she wouldn't be coming home as arranged. When she'd got there, she explained, she'd found Jack far worse than she'd expected. He'd rallied a bit when he'd seen her, but last night he'd taken a turn for the worse and that morning, he'd died in his sleep with Peggy at his bedside.

'I'm all right, love.' Her mother sounded frighteningly composed. 'You mustn't worry. I've had a little think . . . and I'm all right. I'm just so glad I was here when it happened. You know . . . he looked so – rested . . . yes, that's it, rested. And happy, Lilian. At last.'

It was a hard time for the family. Jack had left specific instructions that there was to be no funeral: instead he'd requested that his body be given for medical research.

'I hope they're not interested in his liver. Can't see as there'd be much of it left,' quipped one wag *sotto voce* in The Bull when this surprising news leaked out.

But in general, the village was more shocked than surprised by Jack's sudden death. Everyone had known that he was an alcoholic, everyone had known about his admission to the clinic, but everyone had expected him to return.

Dan took the loss stoically. He'd long ago got the measure of his elder son. Way back in the 1950s, when Jack had scrounged money for the coal bill or had sold up the smallholding on a whim to move the family to Cornwall, Dan had paid Jack's dues, fobbed off questions in the pub, and kept his own counsel. Privately, he concluded that in Jack there was something of Dan's own younger brother, Ben, the black sheep of the family, who'd had the nerve to pay court to Doris while she and Dan were engaged and who'd finally emigrated to Canada under a cloud. Jack had never been a womanizer, not seriously, but he'd had his own areas of weakness, which in the end had brought him down. Dan had grieved for Jack when he'd heard the news, but he knew he'd actually lost him years before when he'd given up hope that Jack might make something of his life. Dan's thoughts now were with Peggy and the children. Better, in some ways, he thought, a quick, clean death after a messy life than a long drawn-out period of suffering for everyone.

But no mother ever anticipates her child dying before her and Doris was shattered. Without even the ritual of a funeral to help her say goodbye and begin to come to terms with the death of her son, she clung to Dan and wept.

'Do you think he knew?' she gulped. 'That we *did* love him, I mean? All I can remember, Dan, all his life, is either telling him off or worrying about him. There must have been good times too?'

'Of course there were.' Dan rubbed her back awkwardly, the rough skin on his palms catching on her cardigan. 'What about when Walter paid him threepence for scaring crows with a tin can and a stick? He was cock-a-hoop. And don't you remember our Jack's face when he brought home the first rabbit he'd shot? He must have been all of twelve – Tom took him out.'

Doris dabbed her eyes with the back of her hand.

'Yes, I remember. But I mean more recently than that. I always feel Jack had so many disappointments in life.'

'Most of them were of his own making, you know, love,' said Dan gently. He had never let sentiment get in the way of his assessment of Jack and he wasn't going to start now. 'And he managed to wangle his own way quite a lot of the time. Look how Peggy had to give in over the Playbar.'

'I suppose so.'

Doris sniffed and tried to get a grip on herself. Carol Tregorran had said she'd drop by later for a word about the WI and Doris didn't want to greet her with puffy eyes and blotched cheeks.

'I know you'd have preferred a funeral,' Dan went on. 'It's only natural. But there's this memorial service Peggy's organizing. That'll make sure folk don't forget him.'

The memorial service was just one of the things on Peggy's mind. There'd been a temporary manager, Dick Corbey, at The Bull since Jack had been taken ill, and Peggy was just wavering over whether to keep him on or not when Jack Woolley put a proposition to her.

'You're standing at a crossroads, Peggy,' he told her in his grating Birmingham accent, which, despite his pretensions to the life of a country squire, gave away his roots every time. It was barely a quarter to twelve – too early even for the hardened lunch-time drinkers – and they had the bar to themselves. 'You could carry on here, but however well things go, it'll never be the same.'

'No,' smiled Peggy, pushing his whisky across the bar to him, 'it'll be harder. Oh, I know having Jack around was like having another child half the time, but he was someone to discuss things with. Now I'm on my own. And maybe it'll be good for me, a change of pace. With Jennifer and Lilian married and Tony striking out on his own –'

Woolley, who'd been taking a sip of his drink, gulped it down and interrupted her.

'Peggy, with respect, it isn't a change of pace you need. It's a change of direction. Why not give up The Bull and come to Grey Gables as my assistant. Something fresh. A new life, almost.'

'You think that's what I need?' asked Peggy doubtfully.

The book on bereavement which Jennifer had got out of the mobile library for her said that you shouldn't make any major decisions about changing your life for at least a year. Jack Woolley, though, was not assailed by any such doubts.

'Personally,' he asserted, 'I think it's the only decision you can make. If you stay as you are, nothing'll change much, except by comparison with the past, and that's not healthy, now, is it?'

Say what you liked about Jack Woolley, and people said the most dreadful things behind his back, he wasn't afraid of speaking his mind. In some ways it was nice, thought Peggy, to have someone come out and tell her what they thought she should do instead of telling her that they were sure she'd do what was best. And though Jack's motives were clearly not just philanthropic – Peggy was a devil for work and she knew the licensed trade backwards – she was flattered that he'd obviously thought about her predicament and where she would go from here. Nonetheless, she told him only that she'd think it over.

The date for Jack's memorial service was set for Saturday 30 January and the night before, fortified by a schooner of sherry, she telephoned Jack Woolley and told him that, subject to Dick Corbey being willing to stay on for another three months, she would accept the position on a trial basis. Now all she had to do was to find the right moment to break the news to the family.

Barely two weeks later, it was Tony's twenty-first birthday. Though it would not have been appropriate to have held the usual big family party, Peggy didn't see why Tony should be done out of some sort of celebration. She was quietly planning a family supper at The Bull when Lilian, who seemed, Peggy couldn't help noting wryly, to have slipped very easily into her Lady Bountiful role, phoned and made a suggestion.

'It's too much trouble for you, Mum. Ralph and I'll host it at the Dower House,' she offered. 'There's more room, for a start, and dear old Mrs Blossom loves having a party to cook for.'

Peggy prevaricated, but not for long. The thought of Mrs Blossom having to worry about studding the ham with cloves and getting the aspic to set over the salmon instead of having to bother herself was just too tempting. There was talk of a miners' strike over a pay claim, of three-day weeks and electricity cuts and households being allowed to heat only one room. Peggy certainly didn't fancy decorating the trifle by the light of a paraffin lamp.

In the end, the evening was as good as they could have hoped for under the circumstances. Ralph and Lilian gave Tony one of the new semi-portable stereo record players he'd been wanting and Jennifer and Roger gave him a silver-plated tankard which could, they said, be kept ready and waiting for him over the bar at The Bull. Peggy was able to tell him that probate had been granted on his father's will and that Jack's shares in Ambridge Farmers Limited would soon be coming Tony's way. And, most importantly, the £2000 that Jack had put in trust for him from Aunt Laura's generous £25,000 gift nearly ten years previously was Tony's to spend as he liked. So in a way, it felt as if Jack really had contributed to his son's twenty-first birthday after all.

As Tony drove her home, enthusing about the sports car he hoped to buy with his inheritance, Peggy was quiet. At the memorial service, David Latimer, the vicar, had emphasized that they should concentrate on the Jack Archer they'd all known, not the Jack that they'd lost. That they should be grateful for the time they'd had with him, not be miserable at missing him. And the vicar had unerringly latched on to the most important thing about Jack, which Peggy knew to be true – sometimes maddeningly so. Whatever adversity faced him, the vicar had said, Jack had always remained cheerful. You can say that again, Peggy had thought, remembering the times when he'd forgotten to re-order the mixers (somehow, he never forgot the spirits) and how, when she'd berated him, he'd always reply, with that boyish grin, 'Don't fret, Peg! Worse things happen at sea!' How when, years ago, at the market garden, they'd lost a whole crop of cabbages to slugs and Jack had quipped, 'Never mind, let them eat kale!' And suddenly, surging back, there came another memory, which wasn't maddening, but moving, and made her want to smile and cry at the same time. How on the night that Tony had been born, Jack had come up to see her when it was all over. How he'd hovered in the doorway, shyly, and how his hand, when he'd reached out to stroke the baby's head, had been trembling. And how he'd looked at her and said, as if he couldn't quite believe it, 'The first Archer grandson, eh? Aren't we clever, Peg, you and me?'

·6·

The Boy Wonder

But if Tony had officially reached the age of majority, he was still in many respects a long way from adulthood. A group called Chicory Tip had a record called 'Son of My Father' in the charts for weeks around the time of Tony's birthday and Lilian could never hear it without thinking that never a truer word had been said – or sung. In his stubborn mulishness, Tony was so like their father, though sadly lacking in Jack's occasionally redeeming bonhomie. And when, in the summer, he had a terrible falling-out with Ralph, Lilian could only stand by and watch with a dreadful feeling that was both foreboding and déjà vu.

It all started with a girl, of course. It always did with Tony. This one was called Jane Petrie. She'd been employed by Hugo Barnaby to run the arts and crafts summer school at Arkwright Hall, a field studies centre in the village which was owned by Jack Woolley. She'd only been in Ambridge five minutes when Walter, plying her with Dubonnet and lemonade in The Bull, established that she was fresh from a doomed love affair, which had resulted in her being cited in a divorce case.

'Don't tell me – she's come to Ambridge "to forget",' mocked Lilian when Walter recounted Jane's sad story.

'That's right! How did you know?' marvelled the credulous Walter.

But Lilian had come across Jane's type before – Clare Madison, Ralph's ex-girlfriend, was another. They portrayed themselves as the victim of some unscrupulous male, but it wasn't long before they'd got a victim of their own hanging on their every word, who lasted as long as they were useful and who was then swiftly dispatched in favour of a newer, more dashing model.

If you'd listened to Tony, he'd have had you believe that he was a real ladykiller, and now he had his red MG Midget, he seemed to think that any girl was within his reach. Anyone could have told him that Jane was trouble, but naturally he didn't stop to ask. Captivated more by her liberal use of kohl eye pencil and her floaty Indian print skirts than her skill at the potter's wheel, he might as well have enrolled on her course for all the time he spent up at Arkwright Hall that summer.

Gently, Lilian, who knew how Ralph would take it if he found out, tried to reason with her brother. Two-hour lunch breaks might have been acceptable for a dairyman in the depths of winter, once the milk records and the movement book had been brought up to date, but not in the height of summer, with the cows in-calf and out in the fields, where they were exposed to any number of hazards, from picnickers' litter to being scared by a low-flying jet. They say love is blind: Tony was deaf to her pleas and, as Lilian could have predicted, it ended the only way it could.

One day there was a sudden, isolated thunderstorm. Lilian had been gardening – well, dead-heading the climbing rose on the terrace: they had a gardener for all the heavy work. She'd noticed the breeze building, making the willow toss its trailing branches, bending the geraniums in their pots, but she'd worked on.

She was bored at home. A couple of weeks back she'd taken a tumble from a new horse, landing hard on her behind. Ralph had been nagging her about having an X-ray but Lilian had her own reasons for refusing, reasons which she didn't want to share with Ralph, not yet anyway. Impatient at her intransigence, in his quaint old Victorian way he'd forbidden her from riding until she'd seen a consultant, even though Dr MacLaren had said it was merely a bruised coccyx – painful, but no bones broken, cracked or even compressed. Lilian could have defied Ralph and gone riding, but until she was sure in her own mind about what her body was trying to tell her, she preferred not to. And so she had resorted to gardening.

But when the rain came, huge drops the size of half crowns splashing on the stone flags, she abandoned her trug and was driven indoors. From there she watched the sky split sulphur yellow by the lightning and heard the terrific rending sound which she knew at once wasn't thunder but something that had been struck – something very close to home.

'It was an act of God, Ralph, that's what any insurer would say,' she reasoned later when Ralph came in, livid.

'They'd better not try it with me!' He let her take his thornproof jacket, from which water was streaming on to the hall carpet. 'Anyway, it was an act of idleness, more like, on the part of your brother! I've been telling him since last Wednesday to get that fence fixed!'

Bit by bit, Lilian pieced together what had happened. Tony had failed to mend a fence and the cows had strayed out of their pasture into the neighbouring field. When the storm had started they'd taken shelter, poor foolish things, under an oak tree and when the tree had been split by the storm, it had toppled directly on to one of the cattle, killing it outright.

'That's a couple of hundred quid your brother's cost me! And where is he? Nowhere to be found!' Ralph continued as Lilian made soothing noises and poured him a cup of his favourite lapsang souchong. Though she was always nagging him to watch his weight, she piled a scone with jam and cream and handed it to him on a plate.

She certainly wasn't going to let on that she knew exactly where Tony was. He'd told her excitedly that morning that he was going up to Arkwright Hall later on: Jane Petrie had invited him, he'd winked, for a 'private view' of her exhibition. All very nice for Tony, but now Lilian was the one who would have to calm Ralph down.

None of this would have been so bad, as Lilian said to Peggy, if Tony really had been in love with Jane, as he certainly thought he was, or she with him. But she was at best cool, at worst downright bitchy to him, or so Hugo had told Carol Tregorran, who'd told Lilian.

'How can I defend him to Ralph when he's making a complete fool of himself?' Lilian complained to her mother. 'Jane's not interested in Tony, is she, with all her arty friends in Chelsea to choose from.'

Peggy sighed. It was hard to know what to do. Tony was too old and too stubborn to take advice from the females in his family – not that he'd ever taken it well. Now, if Jack had been around to speak to him, it might have been different.

'It's so difficult,' Peggy fretted. 'I had hoped Ralph would be a sort of father figure to him, but if Tony goes on behaving like this . . .'

'Ralph won't put up with it,' Lilian warned. 'He won't be made to look a fool. Someone's got to talk to Tony.'

But before anyone could, Tony was in trouble again. It was now the end of August and Jane's stay at the summer school was over. Ever since he'd known the date of her departure, Tony had been offering to take her to her train, but Jane had always refused, saying that all her stuff wouldn't fit in his car. On the day she was due to leave, however, he simply turned up in a Land Rover from the farm and told her that he'd solved the problem. Despite her continuing protests, he insisted on taking her to Hollerton Junction.

The train was already in when they got there, steaming gently in the shimmering heat. Staggering under the weight of her easel and suitcase, Tony found Jane a seat and began stowing her things on the rack.

'You really needn't have bothered,' she said petulantly, hoping that the rather good-looking young man sitting opposite, deep in a Solzhenitsyn novel, wouldn't think that Tony was her boyfriend. 'I could easily have got a cab.'

'You don't get away from me as easily as that, you know!' quipped Tony gaily, though his heart was heavy.

'Let's go out into the corridor, shall we?' said Jane menacingly.

God! He was so irritating. When he'd first started hanging around her with such dog-like devotion, she'd been vaguely amused, but that had been when she'd first come to Ambridge and she'd assumed there'd be someone more exciting in prospect. Then she'd found out what a dump it was, average age 103 and absolutely no eligible men at all. But instead of making her feel warmer towards Tony, this had only fuelled her resentment – resentment against herself, mainly, for her own poor judgement. How could she ever have thought that getting out of London into the middle of nowhere was going to solve anything?

Now, in the stuffy corridor, sweat running down her back, the more Tony pleaded, the stonier her face became, and when he placed his hand hotly on her arm and told her that he loved her, it was all she could do not to laugh.

'Tony,' she said as patiently as she could. 'You're very young. And very immature.'

She wished she could have added 'And very sweet', but she didn't think he was. Pathetic, more like, making those big cow's eyes at her. Come to that, he could have taught his cattle a thing or two about being bovine.

He sighed heavily, his breath misting the window pane.

'I've sacrificed so much for you, Jane,' he declared solemnly. 'I've got myself into trouble. A valuable cow killed in a storm . . .'

'Oh, for goodness' sake!' Jane exploded in laughter. She couldn't help it. She simply didn't care any more. 'Is this your idea of seduction? Talking about the cows?'

'I'm just trying to explain . . .'

The guard blew his whistle. Jane could have jumped for joy.

'You'll have to get off now,' she said with relief. 'You're not coming with me.'

'Why not? I would, you know.'

She didn't disbelieve him, but what a ghastly thought! Roughly she took his arm and bundled him towards the door.

'Sorry, Tony, time to go.'

He was still protesting as she shoved him down the step and on to the platform. He stood there, watching her goofily, though she'd immersed herself in her magazine, tapping on the window at intervals and mouthing, asking if she'd write.

When, finally, the train pulled out, Jane put down her magazine and stretched. Her foot bumped that of the young man sitting opposite. He looked up from his book and smiled. Jane smiled back. Perhaps all was not lost. Something might yet be salvaged of her weeks in Ambridge.

She took her cigarettes out of her bag.

'I don't suppose,' she said, 'you've got a light?'

He produced a box of matches and struck one for her. Jane Petrie leaned into the flame and Tony Archer was forgotten.

'Don't you worry, Jessie. Tell him to go back to bed and look after himself. We'll manage! Bye, now.' Ralph slammed the receiver back on its cradle and swore colourfully – he always blamed his language on the influence of his father's naval career.

'What's the matter now?' It was the same afternoon and Lilian wandered in from the garden, where she'd been sunning herself on the terrace.

'Bobby Waters has gone sick. He's been dragging himself round trying to find Tony and now he's in bed with a temperature of over a hundred!'

'How inconsiderate of him,' said Lilian mildly. 'Stockmen shouldn't get ill.'

'It's your brother who's inconsiderate!' raged Ralph. 'Where is he this time, I'd like to know? Passing Miss Petrie her pastels? Cleaning her brushes?'

'Now, now, darling, remember your blood pressure.' Lilian crossed the room. She stood in front of Ralph and laced his arms round her waist where the flesh was bare in her bikini and warm from the sun. 'Anyway, she leaves today.'

'That's it, then! He'll be penning her a poem before she goes! In *my* time!'

'There's not much you can do about it if he is,' Lilian pointed out. 'Not till he turns up. Now why don't I ring for some nice iced lemonade?'

'I haven't got time for that.' Ralph moved away from her, fretful. 'May Queen looks as though she might calve. Bobby wasn't happy about her yesterday. And she's weeks before her time.' May Queen was one of the in-calf heifers Ralph had bought earlier in the year. She was a beauty – and she'd had a price to match. 'I'd better get down to the milking unit and see what's going on.' Ralph kissed the top of Lilian's head. 'Oh, sorry, darling, didn't you say after lunch you'd got something to tell me?'

Lilian's mouth twisted.

'Well, I did have – I do. But business must come first. Anyway, this hardly seems to be the right moment.'

She was beginning to wonder when the time would be right to tell Ralph she was pregnant. She'd suspected at the end of July, about the time she'd had the fall from her horse. She'd held out so determinedly against having an X-ray because she knew the damage they might cause, in the early weeks at least, but a few days ago, when she'd gone back to Dr MacLaren for a check-up on her injury, she'd asked him at the same time if he'd send off a pregnancy test for her. When she'd rung the surgery that morning they'd confirmed that the result was positive.

She knew Ralph would be thrilled. Practically from the day they were married, he'd been dropping hints about having a son to pass the Estate on to – always a son, Lilian noted; so much for bra-burning feminism. She hadn't been too sure about a baby at first, saying she needed to adjust to her new life, but Ralph was so pitifully doting with Adam and Debbie whenever he saw them, and since Lilian wasn't actively against the idea, she gradually came round to feeling that the sooner, the better. Ralph was nearly fifty, after all: if he was going to enjoy his child, they really should get on with it.

When Ralph came in an hour later, in a slightly better mood now that he'd found Tony and given him a roasting, she judged that this was as good a time as any.

'You're not!' He seized her hands, his eyes bright with tears.

'Ask the doctor.'

'Oh, Lilian. Thank God!'

'What a funny thing to say!' She cuddled close to him on the sofa. She'd put on a big printed shirt over her bikini but her feet were still bare and she hooked her legs over his knees. 'We're the ones who did it.'

'I suppose we did.'

'We're in this together. And I want you there at the birth,' she warned him. 'I don't intend to be like poor old May Queen having to go through it on her own. Oh, no!' She clapped her hand to her mouth. 'I've reminded you about that wretched cow.'

'No, you haven't, darling. Right now I'm going to concentrate on you. And for the next nine months I'm going to spoil you within an inch of your life.'

'Oh, Ralph.' Lilian smiled at him indulgently. 'As if you don't already.'

Ralph could afford to forget about May Queen simply because he'd told Tony in no uncertain terms that he was to stay at her side till she calved.

'I don't care if it takes all night!' he'd thundered. 'I don't care if it takes all weekend! I want a nice live calf and I'm holding you responsible!'

Tony had nodded glumly. He didn't really mind if he did spend all weekend in the warm, sweetly sour-smelling barn with a calving cow. At least he'd have all the time in the world to think about Jane. And about the possibilities open to him. The Foreign Legion was beginning to look appealing.

But when Ralph had gone, he'd begun to feel uneasy. He'd delivered hundreds of calves in his time but he had to admit he didn't like the look of this set-up. May Queen was standing up, anxious and alert. She knew something was different, but she didn't know what and she didn't like it. Tony did his best to soothe her, but she jerked her head away. He'd never been so relieved to hear his grandad's voice, even if he didn't like what he said.

'Not very happy, is she?'

Dan was already putting on a smock which was hanging by the door.

'You've come to stay?'

'One of the lads from the Estate was saying in the pub that you'd had words with Ralph and you were up here on your own. Thought I'd look in and see how things were.'

'It's her first. And she's weeks early.'

'Hey up.' May Queen's sides were starting to heave in rhythm. Dan washed his hands rapidly at the tap. 'Looks like something's happening.'

Tony moved to the cow's back end and lifted her tail. The calf was definitely on its way.

In the end it was a very easy birth. A couple of surprised bellows from May Queen, half a dozen spasms and a blood-smeared calf thudded on to the floor of the pen. Hugely relieved, Tony squatted down to clean it up with some straw and get it on its feet. But when he got close, he knew things had gone wrong. The calf wasn't fully formed.

'It's an abortion, isn't it?' he said in a low voice.

His grandfather nodded. They both knew the implications. It wasn't just the loss of the calf, it was the reason for the abortion that was worrying. Tony read his grandfather's mind.

'It can't be brucellosis,' he insisted. 'She's from an accredited herd.'

'Well, sommat's wrong,' said Dan. He was at May Queen's head, trying to reassure her. 'The vet's going to need a sample. You'd better clear the afterbirth, lad – and careful you don't touch it with your hands.'

Tony cursed under his breath and pulled on a long pair of rubber gloves.

'I bought this cow in. From Lancashire. I've got the paperwork. She's clear!'

'You've got nothing to worry about, then. But with this brucellosis scare on, you've got to ask the question. At least Bobby Waters had the sense to isolate her.'

But Tony refused to be dazzled by the prospect of bright sides and silver linings.

'If it is brucellosis,' he panicked, 'the whole herd's at risk! Thirty thousand quid's worth – all the milking stock. We wouldn't be clear for another nine months – a whole new pregnancy period!'

'You're running on a bit, aren't you?' replied Dan. 'Anyway, Ralph'll be insured.'

'That's just it.' Tony was still delving deep in the slippery insides of the cow while Dan held her head. 'We haven't completed the blood tests. They're not going to pay the full amount.'

Logically, Tony knew that it wasn't his fault: he'd bought the animal in good faith from an accredited herd. But when, the following week, both May Queen and her calf tested positive for brucellosis and she was sent off unceremoniously for slaughter, none of the venom that Ralph directed at him could make him feel any worse than he did already. When Ralph told him that he was fired, Tony didn't even protest. He simply collected his flask and his sandwich box, hung his overall on its peg for the last time, said goodbye to the cows, and left.

· · ·

'Hello, Mum?'

'Lilian, love, this is a surprise.' Peggy tucked the receiver between ear and shoulder. She perched on the arm of the sofa in the flat at Grey Gables, which Jack Woolley had thrown in with the job when she'd agreed to become his permanent assistant back in October. Sid and Polly Perks had moved from the shop to take over the licence of The Bull.

'Well, Ralph had to go out . . . just a sec.'

'Lilian?'

The other end of the phone line had gone quiet.

'It's all right, I'm back now.'

'Lilian, what is it . . . oh, you haven't started with the baby, have you?'

'Uh-huh, I rather think I have.'

There was a sharp intake of breath.

Peggy stood up, feeling under the sofa for her shoes and trying to sound calmer than she felt.

'Just take it easy. I'll be with you in about ten minutes. You make a pot of tea for when I arrive.' She'd only just had a cup, but it'd give Lilian something to think about. 'Where did you say Ralph was?'

Lilian swallowed hard, obviously dealing with another twinge, and puffed out a breath.

'He's at the solicitor's in Borchester.'

'I know the one. They're Mr Woolley's solicitors too. Lilian, just do as I've told you. Leave everything else to me.'

'I wouldn't mind,' panted Lilian as Peggy held her hand in the delivery room, 'but I told Ralph from the start he'd got to be here at the birth! It's all Martha Woodford's fault. She told me in the shop on Tuesday that by looking at me, she could tell the baby wouldn't come till the middle of next week!'

She broke off to clamp the mask over her face so that the gas could help her deal with another contraction.

'Mind you,' she admitted when she surfaced, 'she also said it would be twins.'

'That'll teach you to take any notice of her,' said Peggy tartly. The former Martha Lily had married one of Ralph's foresters, Joby Woodford, at Christmas, after a summer fending off the joint attentions of Joby and Joe Grundy. She was a good soul, but her interest in everyone else's business verged on the voyeuristic and most of the gossip she passed on in the name of 'just takin' a neighbourly interest, m'dear' was often more fiction than fact. Added to which, her clairvoyant and midwifery skills were obviously non-existent. Still, she'd served a purpose, distracting Lilian momentarily from the fact that Ralph still hadn't arrived.

In the event, they heard him before they saw him, out in the corridor, demanding to know why he hadn't been told at once that his wife was in labour and telling the sister just to take him to Lilian.

'You'll have to scrub up first, please, Mr Bellamy, we can't risk infection . . .' the sister began.

'I haven't got time for that, woman!' They heard Ralph's agitated footsteps coming towards the door of the delivery suite. 'I've been held up in a traffic jam, thought I was never going to get here . . .'

'Mr Bellamy.' The sister's tone was determined. 'You scrub up or you don't go in.'

'Listen to him,' said Lilian wearily. 'He has to know best. Go and tell him to do as they say, Mum.'

By the time Ralph had conceded and garbed himself in a long robe and face mask, Lilian was nearing the end of the second stage.

'Oh, Ralph! Just hold my hand!'

Lilian screwed her face up against the pain. She couldn't be bothered messing with the gas and air any more and they'd told her it was too late to give her an injection. The head was already out and with one fierce, final push she felt the baby shoot out into the midwife's hands.

'There's a good girl!' The midwife congratulated her as she and the doctor set about doing unspeakable and luckily largely unseeable things with scissors and clamps and a needle the size of a crochet hook. Lilian lay back, sweaty and exhausted. Ralph embraced her, tearful.

'Darling. Darling. Our baby.'

Lilian pushed him off and struggled up.

'I haven't heard it cry . . . is it . . . is everything all right?'

In answer there was an outraged wail as the baby's airways were cleared and it was welcomed into the world with a couple of swift slaps on the back.

'Happy now?' asked Ralph.

'No,' said Lilian. 'Is it . . . is it a boy?'

The nurse brought the baby to her, its eyes screwed up against the bright light of the world after the darkness of the womb. She placed the snug bundle in her arms and nodded.

'Mr and Mrs Bellamy, say hello to your son,' she said.

·7·

Working It Out

It was a blustery Saturday night in October. In the bedroom at Willow Farm, Tony Archer stood in a bath towel in front of his wardrobe. Working clothes presented him with no problem – a checked shirt and overalls were his daily uniform – but going-out clothes were a different matter. Jeans were frowned on at Young Farmers' Club dances, but should he wear his suit, last seen at the christening of his nephew, James Bellamy, or should he go for the pale blue Simon shirt and Farah trousers? His deliberations didn't last long. If he wore his suit, he'd have to iron a shirt – and find a tie – and he was supposed to be picking up Neil Carter, his uncle Phil's new apprentice, in fifteen minutes.

He sprayed himself liberally with Brut deodorant, scrambled into his clothes and slicked down his hair. He picked up his car keys from the dressing-table and, as he paused to turn out the light, caught sight of the bottle of Hai Karate aftershave that his mother had given him for his birthday. When the bloke in the television advert wore it, it had the power to summon up a doe-eyed beauty who promptly put him in an arm-lock and wrestled him to the floor. Tony realized that this might be setting his sights a little high for a disco in Waterley Cross, but he daubed some on nevertheless. You never knew what life might have up its sleeve.

After all, he reflected as he drove to collect Neil, he wasn't a bad catch. Losing his job at the Estate following the business with May Queen had been the best thing that could have happened. First, he'd spent a year working for his grandad and uncle Phil at Brookfield – he was a shareholder in Ambridge Farmers Limited now and he wasn't going to let them forget it the way his dad had done. Then Tony had heard that Haydn Evans, a Welshman who'd bought Willow Farm to work with his son, Gwyn, was on the look-out for a new partner. Gwyn was heading off to Canada, but the old boy didn't want to sell up in Ambridge. He wanted someone to put in a bit of capital and take over the day-to-day running of the farm while he helped out from time to time.

Tony had only moved into Willow Farm at Michaelmas, and a month on he was starting to get to grips with running his own place. He realized it would take time. The stock work was the same, of course – cows needed milking morning and evening whether they were yours or someone else's – but what terrified him most was the amount of paperwork. He knew he was guilty of letting it pile up, and as he stopped the car in front of April Cottage, where Neil lodged with Martha and Joby Woodford, he resolved to spend at least part of the next day trying to clear his desk.

The village hall at Waterley Cross was little more than a Nissen hut, but someone had attempted to make it look festive with a few balloons and a glitter ball. Thankfully, they'd got a licence for the evening, and Tony and Neil were soon propping up the wall with pints of scrumpy in their hands.

'What d'you reckon to the talent?' asked Neil.

Tony looked sideways at him. He hoped Neil wasn't going to try this 'man about town' act all night. Neil was only sixteen: he shouldn't even have been drinking and Tony knew for a fact that his experience of girls was limited to a collection of Suzi Quatro posters and a vivid imagination.

'Nothing very exciting, is there?'

In the middle of the hall, four girls were dancing round their handbags to an over-amplified number by The Sweet.

'I could go for that one in the purple hot-pants.'

'Neil, even without her platforms, she's got three inches on you.'

'So?'

Tony sighed heavily. Gordon Armstrong, Jack Woolley's under-keeper, had already pinned the only decent-looking girl in the room to the wall near where they were standing and was busy giving her a love-bite that would probably disfigure her for life. Disillusioned, Tony took another swig of his cider.

'Excuse me.'

'Sorry?'

Surely the blonde girl standing in front of him in a short skirt and wet-look boots wasn't talking to him?

'Fancy a dance?'

Tony looked from side to side. She couldn't be talking to Neil and there was no way she was going to attract Gordon's attention.

'What, me? With you?'

'Well, you don't have to,' she said huffily.

Tony looked at her again. She had feathered blonde hair and rather fat legs, but heck, at least she was interested. And she could always diet: Neil's chosen partner would have to saw three inches off her legs before he stood a chance.

'No, no, wait. I'm sorry . . .' blundered Tony. 'I just – didn't think you were talking to me, that's all.'

'I'll dance with your brother if you can't be bothered,' said the girl.

'Brother? Oh, you mean Neil. You don't want to dance with him. Two left feet.'

He shoved his glass towards Neil. 'Hold that for me, mate. And don't drink it.'

Tony might have known he wouldn't get away with it. Once he'd recovered from his colossal hangover, Neil didn't seem to have wasted any time in putting it round the village that Tony had been propositioned by some girl at the dance and had spent the rest of the night snogging her in a corner. Or at least, that's how Tony heard it back from Jennifer.

'Thanks a lot, mate,' he protested to Neil when he ran him to ground eating his sandwiches in the tractor shed at Brookfield early the following week.

'I never said a word!' said Neil indignantly. 'Martha asked me how we got on Saturday night, that's all.'

'Oh, well, if you told her, I'm not surprised. It's a wonder that old crone hasn't got me married off to Mary by now!'

'Oh, her name's Mary, is it? Are you going to see her again?' asked Neil slyly, offering Tony a sandwich. Tony took one and munched. Crab paste.

'I might,' he shrugged. 'Got any crisps?'

He didn't want to tell Neil that there was just one snag. He'd enjoyed dancing with Mary and the bits of shouted conversation they'd been able to have during the breaks in the music. He hadn't been that surprised when he'd asked her to go outside with him – which meant a serious snogging session – and she'd refused: he'd been pushing his luck, really, for a first meeting. But as a result, he'd acted all casually dismissive for the rest of the evening, when really he was feeling unsure of himself. Fearing another rebuff, he hadn't had the nerve to ask for her phone number and she hadn't offered it. As a result, he had no way of contacting her.

'Is that Ambridge 2121?'

'Eh?'

It was a terribly bad connection. It sounded as if someone were frying eggs on the line, which was, ironically, what Tony was doing himself. He'd just finished the milking and had come in to cook his breakfast. He glanced worriedly at the stove where a pan of fat crackled malevolently.

'Is that Ambridge 2121?'

'Ambridge 2121,' repeated Tony.

'Well, you might have said so before.' The voice at the other end sounded puzzlingly familiar. 'This is Ridgeways Secretarial Services. You booked a travelling farm secretary? I was going to suggest two o'clock today.'

'Two o'clock?'

'Are you going to repeat everything I say?' said the voice.

'No, no, that's fine.'

Tony groaned inwardly. He'd have to spend the whole morning sorting out his desk so that this secretary-person could even make a start. And there was a whole stack of stuff from the ministry that he hadn't even opened yet.

'Good. Well, I'll look forward to seeing you again, Mr Archer. Bye for now.'

The dialling tone buzzed in his ear and Tony replaced the receiver.

How could she see him *again* when he'd never used the secretarial agency before? Shaking his head, he went back to the stove. The sausages had welded themselves to the pan and the eggs had lacy brown edges. Still, it would probably taste all right . . .

It was two minutes to two and Tony had just finished three days' worth of washing-up – this blasted secretary had better be worth all the trouble – when there was a knock on the back door.

'Come in!' he yelled, and turned from the sink to find the door being opened. Too late he realized he was wearing the joke apron Roger and Jennifer had given him last Christmas – a woman's body in frilly underwear printed on PVC. As the suds dripped on to his socks from the mug he was holding, he found himself face to face with the girl from the dance.

'How did you know it was me?' he asked Mary later that afternoon when they sat over tea and crumpets at the kitchen table.

Mary sipped her tea and looked at him over the rim of her cup.

'It had to be. I knew your name was Tony Archer and you lived in Ambridge. There can't be that many Archers in the village.'

'You'd be surprised,' grinned Tony. 'But I'm not complaining. It's – well – it's great to see you again. *And* you've sorted out my paperwork!'

'Oh, I've hardly started,' said Mary, then added flirtatiously, 'I can see I'm going to have to pay you a lot more visits.'

'Do they – um – do they all have to be work-related?' Tony busied himself spreading honey on a crumpet. 'I mean – would you consider spending an evening with me in your own time?'

And that was how they started going out.

'It must be serious,' chortled Jennifer when she and Lilian met on the village green late one afternoon. 'I caught him mopping the kitchen floor!'

'And he's been seen in a shirt that doesn't come from the farmers' cash-and-carry,' added Lilian. 'When are we going to meet her, d'you think?'

It was early December. Fairy lights and artificial snow twinkled in the window of the village shop, which was now run by Martha Woodford for Jack Woolley. Eight-month-old James waved his arms at them from the warmth of his pram, while Adam and Debbie, six and nearly three, ran about puffing their breath out in front of them and pretending to be dragons.

'Well, it's nearly Christmas,' speculated Jennifer. 'Time for a happy family get-together, I think.'

Jennifer, it turned out, wasn't the only one who was thinking about Christmas and, as a result, the prospect of meeting Tony's new girl-friend paled into insignificance. One afternoon, when she got back to the flat above the bookshop after collecting Adam from school, Roger had a message for her. His mother had been on the phone.

'She wants us to go and spend Christmas with them this year,' he began tentatively. 'Now I know what you're going to say, but you must admit, your mother gets the lion's share of the children all year –'

Jennifer thumped the breadboard down and began preparing the children's tea.

'It's not about the children, though, is it?' she demanded, swiping a knife through the butter. 'Your mother's not a bit interested in them – well, not Adam, anyway.'

Mrs Travers-Macy had always behaved as though Jennifer had had Adam deliberately to offend her sensibilities.

'That's hardly fair –'

'I'm not feeling very fair! Face it, Roger, it's you she wants to see.'

'Well, what's wrong with that?'

Jennifer knew she was being unreasonable. Roger had been estranged from his parents for most of his adolescence and he'd still hardly been speaking to them when he'd first come to Ambridge. When his father had had a mild heart attack and had subsequently retired, they'd become close again, but Mrs Travers-Macy had never bothered to contain her displeasure at Roger's choice of wife and Jennifer always found visits to their beautiful Queen Anne rectory in Hampshire excruciating. The idea of spending Christmas cooped up there, worrying about the children's sticky fingers on the Chippendale, was more than she could bear.

'The fact of it is,' she said, deftly slicing cheese, 'that I don't know how much time I'll be able to take off over Christmas, anyway.'

Since the autumn she'd been working at Grey Gables to help her mother out. Jack Woolley wanted to build up the Country Park into a proper conservation area and Jennifer had taken on the project. It fitted into her life very well: Adam was at school now, and Debbie went to the playgroup that Christine Johnson ran in the village.

'You'll have to come up with a better excuse than that, darling,' replied Roger, rather sardonically, Jennifer thought. 'Gordon Armstrong will be far too busy with the Boxing Day shoot to talk to you about stoats or whatever.'

'You've never taken this job of mine seriously, have you?' Jennifer cut the sandwiches viciously into quarters and put them on a plate. 'You didn't mind me working in the bookshop where I was at your beck and call, but now –'

'I'll call the children.' Roger moved to the doorway, bringing the conversation smoothly to a close. 'We'll talk about it another time, shall we?'

It was always the same. Roger had said when he first met her that he'd been attracted by her intelligence, but whenever she tried to utilize it, he didn't seem to like it. Jennifer had read *The Female Eunuch* and had thought it went a bit far, for Borsetshire at least, but she didn't really see how having a part-time job that fitted round the children constituted a threat to the male hegemony.

'So what *are* you doing for Christmas?' Christine asked her a few days later as they stuck tinsel to cardboard angel wings in preparation for the church nativity play. Earlier in the week Jennifer had already had to flee to Christine's with the children when the dreaded Mrs Travers-Macy had descended unexpectedly on the bookshop. She too had started berating Jennifer about neglecting her duties as a wife and mother.

'Oh, don't ask me,' Jennifer sighed. 'At this rate, Roger will go to his mother and I'll go to Mum. Perhaps the break would do us good. He's certainly very restless at the moment.'

Chris gave a short laugh.

'You have my sympathy. I think restless is Paul's middle name.'

'What exactly is Paul doing these days? Gran said something about a permanent exhibition site in Germany.'

'For the horseboxes, yes. That's where the market is, so he says.'

Paul had given up on his inventions. A little while back he'd decided that selling horseboxes, principally on the Continent, was something he could do very well. It certainly combined all his interests – horses, motors . . . and being away from home, as Christine had caustically noted at the time.

'So he'll be away a lot more?'

'It looks like it.' Christine banged her fist down on a stubborn piece of tinsel to make it stick. 'I used to think all this travelling would make him appreciate home more. Now I'm not so sure.'

Jennifer said nothing. She was wondering whether to confide in Chris that Roger, too, had come up with a plan for working away. He was fed up with the bookshop, he said. It was too tying. He'd had the offer of a job as a buyer for a firm of antiquarian book-dealers and he said he was tempted to take it.

Jennifer wasn't sure of the implications. Roger insisted that it was a new challenge he was looking for, not a separation from her and the children.

'I didn't hold you back, did I,' he'd reasoned, 'when you wanted to take the job at Grey Gables?'

He hadn't, that was true, but he wasn't exactly helpful either. When Adam had had to have a day off school with a sore throat, Roger hadn't offered to mind him, although he could have sat quietly colouring in the back office at the bookshop. It was Jennifer who'd had to phone Jack Woolley and explain that she'd have to put off her meeting with the conservation expert as she was needed at home. And when Jennifer tapped away at her portable typewriter in the evenings, writing her nature articles for the *Borchester Echo*, Roger complained about the noise of the keys and the 'ting' of the carriage return, until she took to writing them out in longhand and typing them up at Grey Gables in her lunch hour.

In the end, she didn't tell Chris that day, but on the afternoon of the nativity play, as she secured one of her grandmother's tea towels on Adam's head – shepherding seemed to run in the family – she found herself blurting it out. How night after night she and Roger had discussed his job offer and what it meant for them, and how they'd decided that the bookshop would be easier to sell or let if they could throw in the flat over it as well. And how she'd finally realized that he was determined to take the job, no matter what she thought.

'So who knows,' she joked hollowly, 'come the New Year you could find me, Adam and Debbie asking if there's any room at the inn and being glad of the use of your stable!'

'Well, why not?' said Christine at once. 'Move in with me. Oh, Jennifer, it'd be perfect! Adam and Peter are such good friends that they're more like brothers. You know, Castor and Pollux, David and Jonathan –'

'Bill and Ben?'

'You know what I mean. I'm serious, Jennifer. You will think about it, won't you? We'd love to have you.'

After a miserable Christmas with their respective families, which she'd had a lot of trouble explaining to people, not least the children, Jennifer and Roger did actually spend New Year's Eve together at the flat. Jennifer had started the evening with high hopes. She cooked beef stroganoff and cheesecake, even though money was tight. She couldn't afford champagne, so she put a bottle of sparkling wine to chill in the fridge. But Roger fell asleep in front of *The White Heather Show* and, in the end, poor Jennifer slunk off to bed on her own.

New Year's Day was now an official bank holiday and Jennifer had hoped they might take the children out, but Roger told her that was impossible: he'd accepted the job, he was starting the next day and he needed to pack. Why didn't she take the children over to her mother's, he suggested, if she wanted a change of scene? He'd be perfectly all right on his own. That's not the point, Jennifer wanted to scream – or perhaps it was. He simply didn't seem to want her around.

She took the children out to the park in the still of the grey afternoon, smiling emptily at their antics. When she got back, Roger himself was out. He'd apparently gone to have a farewell drink with John Tregorran, his former partner in the bookshop. 'Back late,' said his note, 'don't wait up.'

The next day, Roger kissed Jennifer and the children goodbye and set off cheerily for a house sale in the Borders, where, he said, he'd had a tip-off that a large collection of books on the plant life of Papua New Guinea would come under the hammer. He wasn't sure when he'd be back: after that it was Yorkshire, then Surrey. He'd give her a ring.

Jennifer was left with all the arrangements: placing the flat and the bookshop with an agent, packing up the children's clothes and toys and trying to push down her own feelings of panic and insecurity. All the time she was trying not to believe that, different of course and yet startlingly the same, this was Paddy all over again.

'Happy birthday, dear Mummy, happy birthday to you,' the children sang a week later, clashing their mugs of Ribena together and shrieking with laughter. Jennifer smiled wanly. Roger had phoned that morning and told her he was loving being out on the road, and what a good deal he'd struck on a first edition of *Ivanhoe*. But he hadn't told her he loved her till she'd said it first, and he wasn't sure if he'd be back at the weekend or not.

'Happy birthday, Jennifer,' she toasted herself when the children had gone to bed. She sipped her wine. She was twenty-nine today. She had two children by two different fathers, neither of them present. She'd put on a brave face for her mother, telling her that she and Roger loved each other as much as ever and that being separated from him was a sacrifice she was prepared to make for the sake of his career.

'It's not a separation in the legal sense of the word,' she'd insisted. 'We're just – well, living apart, that's all.'

Her mother looked at her suspiciously.

'Chris and Paul haven't lived in each other's pockets all these years and they're all right, aren't they?' Jennifer went on.

Peggy said nothing. She shared Doris's view that Christine and Paul's marriage left a lot to be desired. And it saddened her to see Jennifer, the next generation, doing exactly what Chris had done all these years – covering up for her husband and hiding her hurt. Jennifer seemed such a modern girl – she had two children and two jobs and she coped with it all heroically. But the success of anything she took on still depended on her husband supporting her in it. And Roger, like many men, Peggy reflected, though willing to endorse a working wife in principle, still had trouble with it in practice.

Peggy had always envied her daughters their wider opportunities. Lilian had certainly done all right for herself. But in the end, it didn't look as if her opportunities had brought Jennifer enormous benefits.

·8·

Choices

It had hardly been the happiest Christmas of Jennifer's life but for Tony, the festive season brought with it an unaccustomed feeling of goodwill which was due entirely to Mary.

After his sorry experience with Jane Petrie, he'd been determined not to reveal his feelings quite so naively again. But Tony wore his heart not so much on his sleeve as in his mouth and he'd only been seeing Mary for a couple of weeks when he found himself telling her how much she meant to him.

At first she seemed shyly alarmed.

'This is all moving a bit fast for me.'

They'd been into Borchester to see *The Sting*. Tony had driven all the way to Churcham, on the far side of Hollerton, to collect her, even though, thanks to the Arab sheiks increasing the price of crude oil, petrol was rationed. Now he'd driven her home and they were sitting in the car in the yard.

'I don't want to rush you.' Tony began back-pedalling furiously. He wasn't sure himself why he always felt this frantic need to plunge in headlong, but in this case he felt it was justified. Mary was different. He didn't want to lose her.

He'd been in love with Jane Petrie, he was sure of it, but even he couldn't translate the feeling into reality. He couldn't imagine Jane standing at the stove cooking his breakfast or soothing his brow when he toiled over the farm accounts. Jane would have wanted the fertilizer store for her pottery kiln and she would have replaced, he was sure, the print of *The Hay Wain* on the landing with one of her arty hangings. But Mary understood about farming. She was a farmer's daughter, so she must do. She would know, like his gran, that a casserole was a better bet for dinner than chops because a farmer could never be sure when he'd be in. She would understand that you took your holiday at the back end of July, in the gap between hay-making and harvest, or not at all, and she wouldn't moan about mud on the kitchen floor.

'I'll have to go in,' she said. 'It's nearly midnight. They'll be wondering what we're doing.'

Tony glanced up at the dark shape of the farmhouse. A couple of days ago, the Chancellor had unveiled a pre-Christmas crisis budget in response to the industrial disputes that were crippling industry. The miners were still on an overtime ban and a three-day week was predicted for the New Year. Even television was having to close down at 10.30 and without it, Mary's parents had obviously got bored of waiting up for her.

Tony manoeuvred himself round awkwardly behind the steering wheel, his leather jacket creaking as he put his arm round her and pulled her towards him.

'You like me a bit, don't you, Mary?' he wheedled.

But she went all brisk and secretarial on him, as she had a habit of doing. She kissed him firmly on the lips then scrabbled for the door handle.

'I'll ring you tomorrow,' she promised, then, as the clock on her village church struck midnight, 'or should I say today.'

But bit by bit, as Christmas approached, she'd relented, until Tony got her to admit that she did care for him. But, she said, she was wary. Tony was her first proper boyfriend and, as her boss was always telling her: 'Never get married in the morning. You don't know who you might meet in the afternoon.'

'What's that supposed to mean? And what's it got to do with him?' demanded Tony.

But he was mollified when Mary invited him to spend Christmas with her and her parents, and when she said she'd spend Boxing Day with him at Willow Farm. By early in the New Year, after she'd been through the ordeal of meeting all the Archer clan at the traditional

New Year's Eve get-together, Tony was sure she was the one. Even his mother had liked her.

'She seems a nice girl,' Peggy conceded. 'Sensible, got her head screwed on the right way.'

Jennifer, who'd met Mary on Boxing Day, liked her too. Lilian didn't seem so sure and had made a catty comment about some curtains with a rather bold red design that Mary had put up at the farmhouse. But when had Tony ever bothered about what Lilian thought? He asked Mary to marry him. With a deep blush which Tony found delightful, she agreed. Together they chose a tiny diamond, which was all he could afford, and they set a date in July.

One afternoon in mid-May, Tony went up to Grey Gables to see Jennifer. The visitor centre in the country park had opened at Easter but she was still busy adding the finishing touches to Jack Woolley's vision of a sort of wilderness where visitors could wander at will without disturbing the wildlife. The latest issue of *Farmer's Weekly* had a supplement about conservation, which he thought she might find useful. She seemed unusually pleased to see him.

'Let's get out for ten minutes,' she suggested, putting the cover over her typewriter. 'It's such a lovely day. I'll show you how the nature trail's coming on.'

She pulled on a crocheted waistcoat over her summer dress and they stepped out through the French windows. Sculptured lawns fell away to shrubberies, but they struck off round the side of the building to where the woods began.

'How's Mary?' Jennifer began brightly as they crunched along on the gravel. 'I heard she found her engagement ring.'

'In the pocket of her best suit.'

The ring had been lost for almost a month: Mary had slipped it into the pocket of her suit when she'd been washing up and had forgotten – forgotten! – all about it.

'Looking forward to the wedding? You'll have to send the invitations out soon.'

'Don't remind me. Every time I go to her place Mary's mother pins me in a corner and tries to talk to me about cakes or place cards or something.'

Jennifer smiled thinly.

'I remember,' she said quietly. They'd reached the edge of the woods now and bluebells glimmered all around them. 'The excitement when you're planning a wedding. There's nothing like it.'

She'd been pleased to see Tony because she had something to tell him. She had to start telling people because only then would she start to believe it. Roger had come back at the weekend and told her bluntly that he didn't think they would ever live together again. Their marriage had run its course, he said. There was no one else, but he didn't feel he loved her any more.

In the months that Roger had been working away and she and the children had been living at Christine's, Jennifer had been through every possible emotion.

For the first few weeks, she'd maintained her jolly outward pretence that everything was fine. Roger wouldn't have this travelling job for ever, or if he did keep it, they would eventually have to be based somewhere. Even if it meant a move from Borsetshire, they would be together again.

But gradually Jennifer had grown wary. When Roger did come back, he felt like a visitor. It was difficult for them to have any privacy at Christine's, but that seemed to suit him: the last thing he appeared to want was time alone with her. Worst of all, for Jennifer, he'd refused to enter into any discussion about their marriage, citing Chris and Paul as an example of a couple who lived mostly apart and seemed perfectly happy. But Jennifer had sat up late too often that winter with Christine to be deluded by that. Huddled round the stove in the kitchen – the three-day week was now in force and there were frequent power cuts – Jennifer had learnt about the compromises that Christine had made for the sake of her marriage and how, sometimes, she wished she'd done things differently.

'You're not me, though, Jennifer, and I'm not you,' Chris had said. 'You'll make up your own mind about what you want to do and that's the only way it can be. But make sure it is what you want to do. Don't do anything you're not happy with and don't for good-ness' sake feel you have to do anything because it's what's expected of you.'

Jennifer knew Christine spoke from experience and she was sure it was good advice. The trouble was, she didn't know what she wanted to do. She was sure that she still loved Roger. She would have done anything she could to make the marriage work, and not just for the children's sake. But she couldn't do it on her own and she couldn't make him feel what he clearly didn't feel any more. She was begin-ning to realize that he had, as they would have said in the book trade, simply withdrawn his goodwill.

She didn't accept it lightly. She didn't want to turn every phone call with Roger into resentment and recriminations but it was hard to bandy banalities when night after night she lay awake puzzling over the collapse of her marriage. Had she done something wrong? What had she not done right? Had she failed Roger or had he failed her? And night after night she wept – out of loneliness, humiliation and sheer physical emptiness.

'Christine keeps telling me to do what I want, but parting from Roger's not what I want and yet it's what's going to happen,' she said sadly to Lilian when she went round to the Dower House to tell her. 'I just keep wondering if there was any more I could have done.'

'That's right, take all the blame on yourself,' replied her sister, handing her a gin and tonic. 'That's typical of you, Jennifer.' Lilian sat down and tucked her legs under her. 'You've gone all the distance and more to make things work. I don't suppose Roger's sitting in some commercial hotel right now pondering what else he could have done.'

Jennifer knew she was right. She knew she had to shake herself out of her despondency and out of her desire to assume all the blame. But . . . first Paddy had left her, now Roger. And she was the common factor. It did seem depressingly like a pattern.

• • •

'It'll never happen to us, will it?' Tony said to Mary a few weeks later. They'd gone out one Sunday afternoon strawberry-picking at one of the local pick-your-own places: Mary had said she'd like to have a go at making jam.

'End up like Jennifer and Roger?' Mary popped a strawberry in her mouth. 'Hardly.'

'Mary – you are – you are quite sure you want to get married, aren't you?'

Tony felt ridiculous asking the question, and he certainly felt ridiculous asking it here, stooped among the strawberry runners, but he was starting to wonder. Despite what seemed to Tony like the military precision of her mother's plans, Mary had told him that they couldn't possibly have everything ready for July and that the wedding would have to be postponed. She picked a couple more strawberries before she replied.

'Silly, of course I do,' she said firmly. 'Have you heard from the travel agents yet about those provisional honeymoon dates for September?'

'I'll chase them tomorrow,' he promised. 'I'm sorry. I've been so busy with the silage and then the hay –'

'You give me a date and I'll be at the church,' she reassured him. She leaned over and gave him a brief, strawberry-tasting kiss. 'But, Tony –'

'Yes?'

'I've been thinking. I don't think I can wait till September for a holiday.'

Puzzled and surprised, Tony sat back on his haunches.

'Well, I'm sorry, love, it's practically harvest. I don't see how I can get away.'

'Oh, it's all right,' said Mary. 'My parents want to book for a fortnight in Majorca at the beginning of August. I thought I'd go with them.'

Tony felt he had no right to refuse. He justified it to himself, saying Mary was perfectly entitled to a holiday, but he couldn't help but feel resentful. If they could just set a date for a wedding in September, it was only a few more weeks to wait. But Mary still didn't want to book anything definite: she said she'd think about it while she was away.

Once they were married, Tony hoped she'd be a bit more understanding about the pressures on him during the summer months. He didn't like the idea of her taking off on holiday with her parents every year. And he was disappointed that she didn't seem able to comprehend his life in the way that he'd hoped and assumed she would.

Tony wasn't the only one who was uncomfortable about the arrangements.

'You must admit it's odd.' Lilian swept the brush briskly over Ebony's shining rump. 'Wedding postponed. No new date. And now Mary's off on holiday all on her lonesome.'

'With her parents.' Christine, who had returned to work with Lilian in the riding school, placed a bucket of water at the horse's head. 'Nothing wrong with that.' Ebony lowered his muzzle to drink.

'Maybe not.' Lilian stopped her brushing and flexed her arm. 'You know, timing's a funny thing in our family,' she observed. 'First Jennifer pinches Roger off me –'

'Did she?' asked Christine.

'Well, maybe not, but that's what it felt like,' admitted Lilian. 'But then I met Nick and it couldn't have mattered less. But then I lost Nick, and Jennifer was, oh – mind-blowingly happy, expecting Debbie and everything. And I had to be brave about it. And then I met Ralph. And now, just when Tony's on the threshold of marital bliss, there's Jennifer and Roger splitting up.'

'And what about you?' asked Christine. 'Are you the mind-blowingly happy one?'

Lilian pursed her lips.

'I don't know about mind-blowingly,' she mused. 'But I'm comfortable, Chris. I'm content. And when I look round the rest of the family, I'm jolly grateful for it.'

'Yes,' agreed Christine feelingly. Paul was spending more and more time in Germany and showed no signs of wanting to come home. 'So you should be.'

'Hello!'

Tony cursed. All he needed now, with the grease-gun playing up and spraying more of its contents over him than into the tractor engine, was a visitor. He'd had a bad enough day already. There'd been no bread for breakfast, so he'd had to go down to the shop, where Walter Gabriel had quizzed him about Mary's unexpected holiday plans. When he got back there was a phone call from the dairy complaining about the low butterfat content of the milk, and he had a nasty feeling that one of the heifers was coming down with New Forest disease. He gave the grease-gun a last hopeless squirt and looked up.

Standing in front of him, wearing a loose yellow shirt and a look of amusement, was a girl he had never seen before.

'Uncle Haydn's popped over to have a look at the cows,' she explained. 'I'm his niece, Pat Lewis.'

'Sorry.' Tony dropped the grease-gun and wiped his hands on a bit of rag. 'Haydn did mention you were coming to visit.' He hadn't mentioned how pretty she was, with her short dark hair and dark eyes. 'So, um – what do you think of Ambridge so far?'

Her dark eyes sparkled.

'Oh, I'm liking it better all the time,' she said. 'I've already met someone called – Jill Archer. Your aunt, I think. She seemed awfully nice.'

'Oh, yes,' agreed Tony. 'You'll find the natives very friendly.' And, quite forgetting that he was way behind schedule in his preparations for harvest, added, 'You've got time for a coffee, haven't you?'

She smiled and nodded, and Tony congratulated himself. Thanks to his early morning shopping trip, he even had chocolate biscuits to offer her.

Pat, he established, was pretty knowledgeable about farming. She looked after a herd of pedigree Welsh Blacks in a valley beyond the Black Mountains which she described lyrically as being full of buttercups. To his surprise, Tony found himself confiding in her about the struggle he'd had at Willow Farm so far, how the milk yields had been low because he'd relied too much on silage rather than fork out for expensive concentrates and how two of his best cows had become blown through eating clover. She'd nodded sympathetically, and when they'd walked round the cows, she'd advised him to get the vet out quickly to the suspected New Forest disease, before it spread, which is what he'd known anyway. If anyone else, even Haydn, had tried telling him what to do or giving him unasked-for advice, he wouldn't have liked it, but somehow it was acceptable from Pat, when she delivered it with her wide smile.

He was sorry to hear that her visit was going to last only a few days.

'You'll have to come and visit me!' she said when he came out into the yard to wave her and her uncle goodbye. 'See some real cows!'

The way she spoke to him was cheeky, almost, but felt so natural. It was the way his sisters spoke to him – when they were in a good mood, anyway – a tolerant, indulgent sort of jokiness that made him feel totally at ease. He couldn't imagine that you'd ever wonder what a girl like Pat was thinking or feeling because she'd tell you, straight out. After Mary's inscrutability, the prospect seemed appealing and very refreshing. But – Mary was his fiancée, even if the wedding date still wasn't settled, and that was all there was to it.

Not that she was being a particularly attentive fiancée. Her fortnight away was nearly over before Tony received, in the same post, a postcard and a letter. Jennifer was with him when they came: he'd asked her to call round to warn her that tongues were wagging over the fact that she'd been out ten-pin bowling with Gordon Armstrong. Jennifer retorted that that was typical of the village. Gordon had merely been giving her advice about clay-pigeon shooting because, to take her mind off the separation from Roger, she'd turned to writing again and was trying to plot a thriller set on a country estate. But both she and Tony knew that that wouldn't wash with Martha Woodford and her cronies from the WI.

When he'd seen Jennifer out, Tony came back into the cool of the kitchen and poured himself another cup of tea. He'd just take ten minutes, he reasoned, to read his letter from Mary. By then, the dew would be off Bank Field and, if Gerry Goodway, his contractor, didn't let him down, it looked as though they could make a start on cutting it today. He slit the envelope and drew out a couple of sheets of air mail paper.

'Dear Tony,' Mary had written. 'Hope you got my postcard. I'm having a brilliant time. The hotel is fabulous, two pools and the food's delicious. I've been spending most of every day lying lazily in the sun and, well, I've had a lot of time to think. This isn't very easy to say, but I have to do it. Though I'm very fond of you, I really don't think we should get married. I think it's better to accept it now than when it's too late and I honestly don't think it would work between us. We're just too different.'

Tony blinked. Then he read the letter again. She was dropping him. Dumping him. Telling him where to get off. It had never happened to him before in a relationship which had got this far and he didn't like the feeling. But at the same time, a slow sensation of relief warmed him from head to toe. He was off the hook.

He didn't tell anyone how he really felt, of course. He wasn't daft. He could see there was more mileage – and free pints in The Bull – in being the wronged party.

'Ironic, isn't it?' Tony's grandad and his uncle Phil were having a well-earned pint together at the end of a long day of harvesting and hauling grain at Brookfield. 'Tony's had his fun and games with the lasses and never been bothered at ending a friendship before. This time, the boot's on the other foot.'

'The way he tells it, he could see it coming,' said Phil. 'It sounds pretty mutual. Even so, the letter must've been a shock.'

Dan tapped his pipe and relit it.

'Still,' he concluded, 'better to see your mistake before it's too late than after. At least the lad won't be in such a hurry next time.'

It was a good job that his grandfather couldn't see Tony at that precise moment.

'Is that Pat?' he was saying into the phone. 'This is Tony Archer. You know, from Ambridge. Remember me?'

'Oh, I remember you all right.' Her Welsh accent seemed more pronounced on the phone. 'What are you doing phoning me at this time of night?'

'Well, it's a bit of a coincidence really.' He'd rehearsed what he was going to say so many times that he should be word-perfect by now.

Word-perfect but still, he hoped, casual. 'I'm thinking of coming over to a farm sale at Monmouth and – well, you're just a stone's throw from there, aren't you?'

'Depends how powerful your throw is,' she laughed. 'Or your car, on these mountain roads.'

'Oh, I'm sure that won't be a problem,' said Tony. 'So, can I come and see you or not?'

Haydn was only too happy to agree to do the milking for the couple of days that Tony would be away, though Tony omitted to mention that part of the reason – well, let's be honest, the entire reason – for his trip was the desire to see his niece.

He set off in great high spirits one Friday in mid-August. The harvest, thankfully, had gone according to plan: the barley was cut and stored and the winter wheat was still a couple of days off ripening. It had all fitted in perfectly.

As he buzzed down the country roads in his sports car, with Abba's 'Waterloo' belting out of the eight-track, Tony had never felt more optimistic. He'd seen Mary when she'd got back from her holiday and had smiled inwardly at how shifty she'd seemed. She'd offered him the ring back but he'd said magnanimously that she could keep it. Her shoulders were peeling and he thought she'd put on weight – all those 'delicious' meals, probably.

'No hard feelings, then?' she'd said, sounding, he thought, rather disappointed. What did she expect, to find him pining away?

'None at all,' he'd replied. 'I'm sure it'll all work out for the best.'

When he got to Wales after a brief dalliance at the farm sale – he thought he'd better put in an appearance and get a catalogue in case Pat asked him about it – he was captivated. The countryside around Ambridge was lovely enough, but it seemed twee and tame compared with the grandeur of the mountains and the gentle sweep of the valleys.

Pat laughed as he struggled for the words to express the awe he felt for the landscape.

'It's just – stunning,' he panted weakly the next day, when they'd climbed to the summit of the Brecon Beacons, nearly 3000 feet up.

Pat turned so the wind was behind them and pointed.

'Look, the Malverns,' she said. 'If I'd brought my binoculars, I could probably see Willow Farm.'

But Tony knew that wasn't good enough. He didn't want Pat over here and himself in Ambridge. But with all this beauty around her, with her family close by and doing a job she loved, he didn't see why she would ever want to move. And yet he didn't much fancy life back in Ambridge without her. He'd got to get her over there somehow.

·9·

Comings and Goings

He had no idea, though, that Haydn would do it for him – and do it so rapidly. Barely a month after Tony had visited Pat in Wales, her uncle slipped a disc grappling with a heavy tractor wheel – and Pat came to look after him. Tony was in the pub, debating the merits of Aston Villa with his Uncle Tom, when she turned up unexpectedly.

'What on earth are you doing here?' he cried delightedly, wheeling round in response to her greeting. 'I mean – it's great to see you!'

'Steady on or you'll be slipping a disc as well,' she laughed. 'Hello, Mr Forrest.'

Tony's uncle Tom mumbled something in response and drank up swiftly. He spent enough of his time playing gooseberry to Jennifer and Gordon Armstrong up at the Country Park – Gordon was proving persistent – to want to do it in his lunch hour as well. He muttered a hasty goodbye and left them to it.

'You've really come to look after Haydn?' asked Tony. He couldn't get over her hair, which managed to shine even in the gloom of the pub, and those eyes of hers which always seemed to be teasing him. 'I didn't think you'd be able to get away. I've laid on Granny Perkins.'

'And that's been more like a trial by ordeal from what I've heard.' Pat helped herself to a couple of his crisps. 'I won't be mollycoddling him like she's done. Just make sure he gets three square meals a day and keep his spirits up.'

'And what about my spirits?'

She looked at him levelly, munching.

'Oh, I daresay I can lend a hand with them while I'm here. I expect you need cheering up,' she added, 'now that your engagement's all off.'

'I'll say,' said Tony. He'd told Pat all about how things had turned out with Mary when he'd gone to see her in Wales. 'I've been really down in the dumps. But I think that's more to do with not seeing you.'

'Well, you're going to be seeing plenty of me from now on.' She smiled smugly. 'I've given in my notice. I can stay for as long as I'm needed.'

That, thought Tony, could be a very long time indeed.

After that, everything happened rather quickly. When her ministrations to Haydn were done, Pat seemed to find plenty of time during the day to come over to Willow Farm to help out. Tony forbore telling her that Haydn didn't play anything like as active a role in the running of the farm. He was enjoying having her around too much.

The great thing about Pat, as far as Tony was concerned, was that she was prepared to muck in and get her hands dirty. He couldn't help but compare her with Mary. She had liked the idea of marrying a farmer, but it was a modern, executive sort of farmer she wanted, one who ran his business from the farm office and only ventured outdoors to instruct the men. On autumn days Tony would often go out into the yard to find Pat there scraping it and hosing it down, her overalls spattered with slurry. When Tony offered to help her, she wouldn't hear of it, and when he said that she smelled of cattle, she took it as a compliment, not a complaint, which was how it was meant. Far from making a good farmer's wife, Tony quickly realized that Pat would make a jolly good farmer. In fact, they'd make a jolly good team.

Still something held him back. It was only a couple of months since he'd split up with Mary and some misplaced sense of decorum made him feel that it would be unseemly to propose to another girl so soon.

Then one night he and Pat were finishing supper at Willow Farm. She'd cooked him a Welsh hotpot – far superior to Lancashire, she'd told him – and they were discussing Peggy.

Tony's mother hadn't had an easy year. First she'd had to cope with the news of Jennifer and Roger splitting up, then Tony and Mary's engagement had gone sour. Now Ralph had been told he had a heart condition and he'd have to think about giving up the Estate, which was proving too much of a strain. It was hardly any wonder that Peggy had turned to Jack Woolley for support – but he had only complicated things by proposing, which was not what Peggy wanted at all. It had made her feel she had to move out of Grey Gables to Blossom Hill Cottage, which Ralph and Lilian owned. And now, to Tony's horror, she seemed to have fallen sway to a chap called Dave Escott, a salesman who'd been staying at The Bull and whom Tony thought was a bit of a con man.

'You can see it a mile off,' he complained, mashing the last of his potatoes into the gravy. 'He's probably got rich widow-women simpering over him all round the country.'

'Give your mum a bit of credit,' replied Pat. 'She's old enough to look after herself.'

'Funny, that's just what she said when I talked to her about it.' Tony laid down his knife and fork and pushed his plate away. 'That was delicious, Pat.'

'Good,' said Pat, standing up to take his plate. 'But really, Tony, you ought to hear yourself. What gets me is, it's so unfair. Peggy's welcomed me with open arms and I bet she did the same for Mary. You're allowed to do as you like and given the chance to make your own mistakes. But is she? Oh, no.'

She put the plates on the draining-board and moved towards the stove where, Tony knew, a rice pudding was waiting.

'I'm concerned about her, that's all.'

'If she likes him, good luck to her. He's not going to be staying long, is he?'

'I hope not.'

'Oh, you're hopeless.' She banged the rice pudding and two bowls down on the table. 'Has it ever occurred to you that she might be lonely?'

'Lonely? Mum? When she's got all her family around her?'

131

'Are they, though? Jennifer's working hard, Lilian's married, and you . . .'

'Yes?'

'Well, Tony?'

'Hm.' Tony eased a shred of meat from between his teeth. 'Look, I've been meaning to ask you.'

Calmly, Pat fetched a pot of Doris's raspberry jam.

'Go on then.'

'D'you think we ought to cull that cow?'

She burst out laughing.

'What am I going to do with you!'

'What's so funny?'

'You are! I thought . . . I thought you were going to ask me to marry you!'

Tony blinked.

'Marry you!'

She picked up a spoon and began to serve the pudding.

'Yes, Tony. Sorry if I was mistaken.'

'Yeah . . .' said Tony weakly. 'Or – no!'

'No?' The spoon was poised and she was smiling broadly. 'Well, go on then.'

'Erm . . .'

She raised her eyes to the ceiling. The spoon clattered back into the dish.

'Oh, for heaven's sake! If one of us doesn't say it, we'll spend the rest of our lives talking about cows and changing the subject. It's a simple enough question with a simple answer. And if you can't get around to it, I will. So, Tony, will you marry me? What about it, eh?'

The whole thing was typical of Pat – no messing about, no room for misunderstandings – and almost before Tony knew what was happening, he found himself shepherded round for tea with the new vicar, Richard Adamson, to arrange for the banns to be read, and herded into Borchester to hire a morning suit.

'Steady on, Pat, people'll think we've *got* to get married!' he protested when she informed him that she'd decided on 12 December as the wedding date.

'Not getting cold feet, are you?' she chided. 'Anyway, if I left it to you we'd be lucky to get married this side of the year 2000!'

It was a good job there was something for Peggy to look forward to because Ralph and Lilian's news got worse by the week. In the middle of November Ralph went for further tests and the cardiologist was categorical. Ralph needed complete rest if he was to avoid a heart attack. Retirement seemed to be the only option. And that wasn't all.

'Well, I think it's wonderful idea,' Peggy enthused when Lilian took James round to tea at Blossom Hill Cottage and broached the subject. 'Oh, James darling, put that down, there's a good boy.'

Lilian sprang up from her seat and rescued Peggy's bone china shepherdess from James's jammy fingers. She wiped them with a tissue and settled him in front of the fire with his board books.

Peggy smiled indulgently at her little grandson.

'A cruise sounds like a lovely way to get away from it all,' Peggy went on. 'And when you get back, I'm sure Ralph will feel like picking up the reins again, despite what the doctors say.'

'Mum . . .' Lilian sat forward and took Peggy's hand.

Peggy looked down in alarm. Lilian was the least tactile of her children.

'What is it?'

'The cruise . . . it's not just a long holiday. We're taking it to give us time to think. And to give us ideas. About where we might like to settle.'

'To settle?'

'Yes. We're leaving Ambridge, Mum.'

Peggy shook her head. Then she shut her eyes. But nothing could make what Lilian had just said go away.

'You can't be.' Her voice was thin and high. 'Why?'

'Oh, Mum.' Lilian squeezed her fingers. 'You know why. Ralph's under a life sentence if he stays here.'

'That's not true!' cried Peggy. 'Complete rest, the doctor said! Why can't he just retire like everyone else! You can carry on living at the Dower House – or buy somewhere smaller – he can ride and shoot and –'

James looked up, detecting dissonance. He got up and toddled worriedly over to his mother. Lilian took him on her lap.

'It wouldn't work, Mum,' she explained. 'Can you really imagine Ralph sitting around in Ambridge while someone else runs the Estate and not getting involved? Not offering advice or, worse, criticizing their every decision? It'd be fatal. Worse than him running the place himself!'

'But, Lilian, where are you thinking of going?'

'We don't know yet, that's the point.'

'But it's – it's somewhere abroad?'

Lilian shrugged.

'Somewhere warm, certainly. People retire to the sun, don't they, not the frozen steppes.'

'You seem very calm about it, I must say!' Peggy looked at her daughter shrewdly. 'How long have you been planning this?'

'Mum, if you want to know, it's come as a complete shock to me as well.' James leaned against his mother and placed his thumb in his mouth. Lilian stroked his hair. 'But Ralph's my husband. James's father. I have to do what's best for him.'

So, in parallel, as Tony and Pat were drawing up a wedding present list, Ralph and Lilian were planning to put the Estate on the market. As a compromise measure, and to give James a stake in Ambridge in the future, they decided to let the Dower House and to retain 1000 acres, which would be run by the Estate manager, Andrew Sinclair. The rest of the Estate would be split up and sold. The farmhouse at Ambridge Court Farm, which had been Ralph's home before he married, and 1500 acres would form one lot: the other parcel of land would be 1000 acres with shooting rights. As Jack Woolley lost no time in telling Ralph, it was bad luck his dicky heart hadn't been discovered a year earlier, when good agricultural land had been changing hands for £900 an acre. But Ralph wasn't greedy – he could afford not to be. Even in late 1974, at the more realistic price of between £500 and £600 an acre, the sale would net him over a million after tax.

'And in conclusion, ladies and gentlemen, I'd like to say a special word of thanks to Gerry Goodway, my best man, for finally getting me to the church on time, to Mum, of course, to Haydn, for all he's done . . . but, most of all, to Pat, for having the sense – some might say the courage – to agree to be my wife.'

'I thought you agreed to be her husband – that's how I heard it!' heckled Walter from the floor. He had obviously forgotten his avowed intention never to attend another wedding and had delighted some guests and dismayed others by snapping away with his old box Brownie. 'We know who'll be wearing the trousers!'

'Be that as it may, Pat promised in church to obey, don't forget,' Doris reminded him, rapping him on the wrist with her coffee spoon. Walter chuckled wickedly.

'We'll see! If she's got half the spirit of her auntie Gwynnedd, he'll have his hands full!'

Pat's auntie Gwynnedd had turned out to be quite a character and, naturally, had got on with Walter like a rick on fire.

'Well, I think young Tony's struck lucky,' observed Dan. 'He's got himself a partner in Pat in every sense of the word.'

'At least Peggy knows Tony's settled,' remarked Doris. 'He'll be staying put in Ambridge, anyway.'

Dan's eyes followed hers and they both looked over towards Ralph and Lilian. Ralph was looking fitter these days. The doctor had put him on a strict diet and he'd lost a bit of weight. He had a better colour and his breathing was easier. It was Lilian whom the family were worried about.

With Tony's wedding behind them, Christmas and New Year were fast approaching. But with the date for their departure set for the end of January, Lilian regarded the forthcoming festivities with jaded reluctance.

She couldn't help but feel resentful. When she'd married Ralph, and even more when she'd had James, she had felt for the first time in her life, and certainly since Nick, that everything was certain. She was married to a man who adored her and for whom nothing was too much trouble as long as she was happy. If Lilian had asked for an Arab stallion for Christmas, or a house on Mustique, that's what Ralph would have bought her. But it wasn't Ralph's wealth that was important to Lilian. It never had been. Oh, it had been a novelty at first, of course, and it was very nice, after the vagaries of life with her father, to know that Ralph paid a large sum of money into her account every month and never asked to see her cheque stubs. But it was the security in its wider sense that Ralph could offer which had been the appeal. And part of that security had been the certainty that Ralph had put down roots in Ambridge. Now those roots were being tugged up and for the best of reasons – how could she argue with the importance of Ralph's health?

She couldn't argue in public, that was for sure. Going down to the shop to cancel the papers and pay off her account or taking James to choose the spruce tree that Joby Woodford would cut and bring down to the house, she was the cool and collected chatelaine of Ambridge she had always been. Even with her mother and grandmother, not that it fooled them for one minute, she chatted brightly about the tenant the agents had found for the Dower House, and showed them brochures of the cruise liner that would be her home for the early part of the New Year. But one evening just before Christmas she took a boxload of clothes that she couldn't take with her over to Chris's. And as her aunt uncorked a bottle of Beaujolais and Jennifer rooted excitedly through the clothes, Lilian couldn't keep up the pretence any longer.

'I'm dreading going,' she confessed. 'Every time I think about it I feel sick. And it's so ironic. If Nick had asked me to settle in Canada, I'd have gone like a shot. But I was so young. I didn't realize the pull a place can have on you. And I didn't realize, then, how you value your family as you get older.'

Christine poured the wine and Lilian lit up a cigarette. The flame of her lighter flared on the cut-out silver decorations that the children had hung over the mantelpiece. Jennifer draped a red cashmere scarf, which she'd always coveted, round her neck.

'I feel as if we've swapped lives, Lilian,' she said slowly, accepting the glass Chris held out to her. 'I was always the one who was going to get away. You were the stay-at-home. And look at us now.'

Chris passed Lilian her glass.

'Yes, look at us,' she agreed. 'What fine examples of modern womanhood! There's you, Lilian, having to pack up everything in order to stay with your husband. I've kept my marriage together only by putting myself second and giving my husband free rein to go off and do as he likes and when Jennifer tries the up-to-date approach of combining an independent career and motherhood, running herself into the ground in the process, her husband's up and off before you can burn a bra.' She sat back on her heels. 'I don't know what the answer is.'

'It seems to me,' said Jennifer, sipping her wine, 'that you either have to find a man who means what he says about respecting you as an individual and whose ego can cope with your having a life of your own, or you may as well not bother. To be honest, the longer I'm on my own, the more impossible I think it is.'

'It's different for me and Ralph, though,' Lilian pointed out. The lights from the Christmas tree were refracted through the twisted stem of her glass. 'He's from a different generation. And he's not asking me to do anything unreasonable. He expects me to support him – and I want to. I just never thought it would involve me in making such a difficult choice.'

'In my experience, life's either a choice or a compromise,' said Christine tartly. 'And believe me, being able to make a choice, even an uncomfortable one, is far preferable.'

Lilian blew out a ring of smoke.

'Well, thanks, girls, you've made me feel a lot better,' she said sardonically, then, smiling, 'No, actually, you have. I ought to be more positive about it. It's a great opportunity. An adventure. It's not as if Ambridge is the centre of the universe, after all.'

They talked about other things then. About what the children were having for Christmas and about Doris's bout of flu. But when Lilian had gone and Jennifer and Chris were finishing off the wine, they couldn't help but wander back to the subject of Ralph and Lilian.

'Mind you, perhaps we're just jealous because her husband wants her with him,' said Jennifer perceptively. 'By the way, Chris, I should have said earlier. I'll be taking the children to stay at Mum's over Christmas. To give you and Paul some time together.'

'Don't bother.' Chris drained her glass. 'I heard from him today. He's staying in Germany for Christmas. And for New Year too.'

'I see.' Jennifer shared the dregs of the wine bottle between their glasses. She knew that Paul had already missed their wedding anniversary and it was Chris's birthday in a couple of days. It looked as though she'd be lucky to get a card. 'I'm sorry, Chris.'

Chris rubbed at a spilt drop of wine on the table.

'Me too. That's what's so awful. If, after all these years of doing what he wanted and not what I wanted, I lose him anyway, what will it all have been for?'

'You're not going to lose him, Chris.'

Jennifer reached out a hand, but Chris, seeing the touch coming, flinched away. There was no comfort Jennifer could offer her.

'I still love him, you know. I love him so much.'

Somehow they all slogged through the so-called festive season, with Chris miserable about Paul, Jennifer resentful about Roger, who turned up unannounced on Christmas Eve with inappropriate presents for Adam and Debbie, and Lilian, with mounting dread, counting the days until 21 January – the day of their departure.

Christmas itself was a disaster. Ralph and Lilian had decided to throw a big family party on the evening of Boxing Day: Ralph had declared that he wanted their last Christmas in Ambridge to be their happiest. But how could it be? Peggy was thoroughly subdued. Phil and Jill were disappointed that Kenton, who'd gone to sea as a merchant navy cadet in the autumn, would be spending his first Christmas away from home, and as if that wasn't enough, Shula sought refuge from the general gloom with an older man, Eric, she'd met through her business studies course at the Tech.

Phil was still counting the cost of the SVD which had struck at the Hollowtree pig unit earlier in the year: what with that and galloping inflation, he wouldn't be sorry, he said, to see the back of 1974. Only Tony and Pat, in their newlywed-induced state of grace, seemed insulated from the general atmosphere, thrilled by the prospect of going over to mains drains and the arrival at Willow Farm of 100 free-range hens.

When she'd first been told of their departure, Peggy had accused Lilian of letting Ralph set a date that was too close to give her time to come to terms with it. But as January dragged on in its dreary way, Lilian wished they could be going sooner, even though there was lots to do. She had to arrange terms with Chris for her to take over the stables and the new indoor riding school. She had to get a list of all their ports of call and PO box addresses photocopied at the Estate office for distribution round the family. And, a full three days before they were due to leave, she had to start saying her goodbyes.

'I've hardly had a chance to get to know you!' Pat said, hugging her. 'But I am sorry to see you go.'

Lilian bit her lip.

'You'll keep an eye on Mum, won't you?' she asked. 'She's the one I'm most worried about.'

'Of course. You're not to fret.'

Lilian nodded bravely. She looked around the untidy farmyard, the silage face that needed tidying and the barrowload of muck that Pat had stopped forking to talk to her.

'Do you think I'm doing the right thing, Pat?' she asked. 'Would you do it for Tony?'

'Gosh, that's a difficult one.' Pat rubbed a roughened hand across her forehead. 'I suppose I think that in a relationship you should be able to do what you want, provided it's reasonable and it doesn't hurt the other person. But of course that applies to them, too.'

Lilian flexed her fingers in their leather gloves and pulled the belt of her coat tighter. Pat didn't seem to notice the wind that was whistling round the side of the dairy.

'It's hard to imagine.' Pat had got absorbed in the question and, rather than talking to Lilian, seemed to be thinking out loud. 'But if Tony came to me with some plan that seemed crazy and against everything we'd ever done or planned, like – oh, I don't know, let's pick something ridiculous, going organic, say, or growing pineapples or something – well, we'd have to talk it through, and if he could convince me, I'd have to go along with it. In the end you have to trust them, don't you? And if you love them, you want what's best for them – because in the end, that's what's best for you.'

'You're very sure of things, aren't you, Pat?' Lilian didn't know whether to admire or be amused by her new sister-in-law's directness. She wondered how Tony would cope with such plain-speaking.

'I find it helps,' said Pat simply. 'Life's complicated enough without people not saying what they mean.'

Lilian thought a lot about what Pat had said when the day of their departure finally dawned. Dirty snow lay on the ground and the sky was pure white – more to come, as Uncle Tom said cheerily. Peggy and Jennifer were going to be in attendance all day, but the arrangement was that the rest of the family should drop round to the Dower House during the morning, if they were able, to say their final goodbyes.

But, in the event, no one felt up to saying anything of any great significance. Instead the women had an alarming tendency to dissolve into tears and the men made small talk about the forthcoming Young Farmers' quiz and an outbreak of sheep-worrying in the district. They tut-tutted about feed prices and high wage settlements, wondered how much longer Edward Heath could hang on as leader of the Conservatives and whether there was any truth in the speculation that if he did step down, a woman – Margaret Thatcher – might put herself forward to replace him.

Lilian found it excruciating. She had taken leave of her family, she felt, days ago and that morning she had gone out early to say her most important farewell. Saddling up Ebony in the chill dawn, she had ridden him for the last time over Heydon Berrow, where she had ridden with Nick. She had paused to look down over Ambridge.

A cockerel called raucously and, one by one, the lights came on in cottage windows and milking parlours. Ebony stamped and whinnied and Lilian leaned forward to lay her face against his neck.

'I'll miss you, boy,' she whispered. 'More than anything.'

Nothing had ever been as difficult as boxing him up again and making herself walk out of the stables without looking back. After that, saying goodbye to her relatives seemed easy – and unimportant. Lilian had never in her life been so glad to hear anything as the horn of the taxi that was to take them to the station.

'Time to go now, James!'

But Peggy swooped down on her grandson where he'd been playing with the new tractor he'd been given to distract him from all the adult anxiety and hugged him tight.

'I'll carry him!' she said, her voice muffled against James's neck. Lilian unhooked her fingers from under his arms.

'I'd rather you didn't, Mum.'

'It's time for them to go.' Jennifer put her arm round her mother's shoulders as Peggy allowed her own arms to be emptied of James.

'He's big enough to walk on your own now, aren't you, you young rascal,' Ralph chipped in cheerily. Peggy shot him a look of undisguised hatred. All this was his fault and he hadn't even got the grace to be contrite about it! She swallowed hard.

'Bye-bye, then, James,' she said. James looked back, bemused. 'Send me a postcard, won't you, Lilian?'

'Lots of them.'

Lilian felt her mother's arms close around her and felt her swallow a sob. For herself, she had never felt less like crying. She was way past all that. The taxi sounded its horn again.

'We must go,' prompted Ralph.

'Mum . . . please . . .' Lilian pulled away. Peggy's face was pink with the effort of holding back her tears.

'Sorry.' Peggy sniffed. 'Goodbye, darling.' Ralph approached and she kissed him formally on both cheeks. 'Take care of them both, won't you, Ralph?'

Lilian and Jennifer hugged each other tight.

'Best of luck, Lilian.'

'You too.'

Then Lilian picked up her vanity case, Ralph picked up James, and in what seemed like a second they were gone. Peggy stood stock still until the taxi had scrunched off down the drive. Then she sank into a chair. Jennifer looked at her apprehensively.

'It's all right, dear,' Peggy croaked. The tears were rolling down her cheeks. 'I'm not going to cry. I've been very good, you've got to admit that.'

'You were splendid.' Jennifer came and perched on the arm of her mother's chair. 'I knew you would be.'

'Yes, I think your father would have been proud of me.' Peggy blew her nose.

'Of course he would.'

'And in the end, Jennifer, I've got you and Tony here still. Two out of three children isn't bad.'

'Exactly! And two out of three grandchildren. And who knows, Pat and Tony might be presenting you with another before too long.'

'You might have another yourself,' said Peggy, rallying bravely.

'Mum, it'd have to be the immaculate conception!'

'You never know, Jennifer. You're still young. You shouldn't write yourself off.'

'Oh, come on, Mum, who am I going to meet in Ambridge?'

'Well, what about this Mr Barnet, who's bought part of the Estate?' Peggy wiped her eyes. 'Dear me, this hanky's sopping. Or the other fellow, what was his name?'

'Aldridge,' said Jennifer, rather too quickly. 'Brian Aldridge.'

'There you are, see, that's two possibilities already.'

'Mum, if I know my luck they'll be happily married or crusty old bachelors.'

But she knew they weren't – in one case at least. She'd made sure to find that out from Ralph before he left. Brian Aldridge was thirty-two, single and wealthy – he had to be, if he could afford to take on 1500 acres and a farmhouse that needed complete renovation. She hadn't bothered asking about Mr Barnet after that.

·10·

Mixed Feelings

It was all very well her mother talking about Jennifer finding romance with the new owner of the Estate; it was all very well Jennifer fantasizing about it. The reality, as so often in life, turned out to be very different – initially, at least.

'Would Friday night suit you? For supper? Seven o'clock?'

Carol, John Tregorran's wife, had taken time off from her market garden to have lunch with Jack Woolley. On her way to the Ladies' she'd cornered Jennifer in her office and Jennifer didn't see how she would be able to refuse.

'That sounds very nice,' she said feebly. 'I'll have to make arrangements for the children, of course . . .'

'Christine will have them for you, I'm sure!' Carol was the sort of woman who never let practicalities get in the way of her plans. 'I'm glad I caught you, anyway, Jennifer. Now I must get back to Jack. My coffee will be going cold!'

She swished out of the office, leaving behind her a waft of Chanel No. 5 which argued with the scent of the hyacinths on Jennifer's desk. Jennifer sank down behind her typewriter. There was something about Carol Tregorran's efficiency – as flawless as her appearance – that made her feel exceptionally tired. The last thing she wanted after working for Mr Woolley all week was to spend Friday night having supper with him – and she couldn't work out why either of them had been been invited. Unless . . .

'We're there as cover!' she fumed to Christine when she got home. She was still living at Wynfords with Chris. Early in the New Year, Paul had left Germany for another job, but since it was on an oilfield near Carmarthen, he wasn't at home much more than before. Still, Christine seemed happier merely to know he was in the British Isles again and Jennifer, who was still reluctantly separated from Roger, didn't feel she was exactly in a position to criticize anyone else's living arrangements.

'Cover for what?' Christine sat at the dining table, surrounded by the accounts from the stables.

'For the fact that there's something going on between Carol and Brian Aldridge! You know they've been seen in the pub together!'

'Well, that hardly proves anything. He'd been to see her glasshouses, hadn't he?' Christine squinted at a receipt and jotted down a figure. 'Anyway, The Bull's the last place they'd go if they wanted an illicit affair!'

'That's what's so brazen about it. They think that if they see each other out in the open, in front of other people, no one'll suspect. Oh, it's clever all right.'

'Jennifer, this is all sounding like something out of one of your novels,' said Christine mildly. 'I think you've been overdoing it.'

Jennifer picked up a horseshoe that Christine was using as a paperweight and waved it about to illustrate her point.

'Well, it makes me mad! There's Carol getting the sympathy vote for struggling bravely on while her jolly nice husband is flogging antiques and sweating away on the lecture circuit in America to keep her in the style to which she's accustomed and this is how she carries on behind his back!'

'Not jealous, are we?' asked Chris with a smile. She'd given up on her accounts now. She knew what Jennifer was like when she got going. 'I mean, I can see that you might have had your eye on Brian Aldridge for yourself. And please! Give me back that horseshoe. You're making me nervous.'

It came as no surprise to Jennifer when she arrived at Carol and John's house, Manor Court, on Friday to find Brian Aldridge already there. As she congratulated herself on her writer's intuition, Carol told her shamelessly that he'd arrived at five past six, asking if there was anything he could do to help, and had found her in her dressing-gown.

'Now do go and talk to him, Jennifer,' Carol urged, pouring her a sherry. 'Jack can help me in the kitchen.'

Jennifer went through into the sitting room, a mulish expression on her face. Brian Aldridge leapt to his feet at once. He was tall, with grey-green eyes and straight brown hair parted to reveal a high fore-head. And he had a moustache. Jennifer usually liked men with moustaches – she and Chris never missed Peter Wyngarde in *Jason King* – but she wasn't going to let that sway her. She sat down primly as far away from Brian as possible and arranged her Laura Ashley skirt around her. As they exchanged the usual banalities about the weather and the sherry she couldn't help noticing his well-cut tweed suit and silk tie. Hand-made shirt, too. She sighed inwardly. Good-looking, eligible, rich – and obviously fancied himself as a ladykiller. The worst possible combination.

'This is . . . er . . . a lovely place Carol's got,' he said when the stumbling conversation had finally tripped itself up and come to a stop.

'She and John have made it very nice.' Jennifer pointedly underlined the 'John'.

'Yes, of course.' He sipped his sherry. 'He's in America, I understand.'

'For the moment,' said Jennifer coldly. 'They're very devoted, you know. Very.'

'I'm sure you're right,' he smiled. 'I hear he'll be home in a week or two.' There was a pause while he tossed a salted peanut into his mouth, then he grinned at her. 'Did you think I was trying to break up a happy marriage?'

Jennifer was totally thrown.

'Of course not!'

'Oh, please say you did!'

'Pardon?'

He looked at her sideways.

'Because if you didn't regard me as a bounder chasing Carol Tregorran, I'd have to think of another reason for the way you're treating me. The icy glare . . . the disdainful glance . . . I feel like a worm you want to trample underfoot.'

Underfoot? At that moment, Jennifer would have liked to be underground. She had never been so embarrassed in all her life. And in all her life she had never known anyone read her actions or her motives so clearly. She looked at him furtively. He was studying her.

'I'm sorry,' she said, trying to laugh off her severely rattled composure. 'It's just . . . people were wondering if . . .'

'Well, it isn't true,' he said firmly. 'I'm new to the village and Carol's been very friendly.'

'We're all friendly really,' said Jennifer in what sounded even to her like a pathetically apologetic tone.

'Even you?'

He obviously wasn't going to let her get away with it that easily.

'I . . . I think so.'

'Good.' He got to his feet and came to stand close by her chair. His aftershave was fresh and citric. 'In that case . . .' Jennifer looked up, nonplussed. 'Let me fill your glass up for you,' he offered silkily. 'Dry, wasn't it?'

And so, after the worst possible beginning, Jennifer and Brian began to see each other after all – just as Carol Tregorran had planned when she'd invited them round. He took Jennifer for meals at restaurants she'd never discovered in thirty years of living in the area: somewhere miles out in the country which served only fondue and a place at the back of Felpersham Crown Court that specialized in waffles. He was interested in her writing: she was still working on her thriller and he cheered her up when she got despondent because her plot had too many loose ends and not enough red herrings. And with endless patience, he taught her to play golf.

All the while, he was busy settling into his new farm. He'd made special arrangements to get on to the land to sow his spring crops well before he'd taken over on Lady Day, and by the middle of July he was harvesting the rape that had blazed in May in blocks of chrome yellow. Local opinion was admiring. He knew his stuff, he wasn't afraid to innovate, and he was the sort of chap who got on with things. Like the renovation of the farmhouse, which had a team of builders working on it while Brian, with help from Ned Larkin's widow, Mabel, as housekeeper, camped in the only two habitable rooms.

It was an incredibly hot summer with hardly any rain during June, July or August – not that the farmers were complaining. The grain was coming in off the combines without any need for drying and anything which would save them money, after the last few years of inflation and high feed and fuel prices, was welcome.

The summer days were long, with azure skies and heat that hung over the cornfields from early in the morning till late at night. In her longed-for lunch hours at Grey Gables, after the stifling heat of her tiny office, Jennifer walked by the lake or revised her novel in the shade of the horse chestnuts. But she often found herself rolling her pencil absentmindedly on the page and staring into space. She knew she should have been happy that Brian was paying her so much attention, but she felt troubled. She felt a hypocrite. After the fuss she'd made when she'd thought Brian was paying attention to Carol, a married woman, she had to acknowledge that her own position was hardly clear-cut. She was still not even officially separated from Roger. And though she had pretty well given up any hope of a reconciliation, she still felt she belonged to him.

When Jennifer thought back to that long, hot summer in later years, every shimmering hour seemed to blur into one. She and Brian spent an unbelievably hot day at the Royal Show, dazzled by the sun glinting off the machinery stands and sustained only by constant cool drinks in the Members' Enclosure. Kenton came home on leave and brought Shula a grass skirt from Tahiti. Jill was worried that his leave would be spoilt by having to help with the harvest: Phil's farm worker, Jethro, had fallen from the loft over the calf pens and broken his leg. (Phil was more worried that Mike Tucker, who ran his dairy unit and was the union rep, would persuade Jethro to claim compensation.) The disreputable Joe Grundy, who had clung on at Grange Farm, held a pop festival in a flagrant breach of his tenancy agreement, and Peggy, who now worked part-time at the Estate office and part-time at Grey Gables, had to take him to task. The village fête was a great success, but entries for the Flower and Produce Show were woefully meagre owing to the drought. Uncle Tom despaired of his runner beans, and even Jack Woolley's chrysanthemums, raised under glass by Higgs, his rather peculiar chauffeur-cum-handyman, failed to reach their usual mop-headed glory.

But just when Jennifer, opening her curtains every morning to another sky of cloudless blue, was thinking that life could go on like this for ever, a cloud came in sight. Roger got in touch.

He said it wasn't something he wanted to talk about over the phone: he asked her to meet him in London. Jennifer agreed. If he came to the village, everyone would have to know, whereas she could invent an excuse to go to London. She told her mother, who was having the children, that she had a meeting with her publisher. That way, she calculated, she could meet Roger and digest what he had to say to her in private.

She knew, deep down she knew, that it couldn't be good news. But even on the Paddington train, with the prickly upholstery needling the backs of her legs and the sun beating down on the passing fields, she couldn't help but hope.

She'd agreed to meet him in a pub in Notting Hill. The book dealer he was working for had premises off Kensington Church Street and he had appointments there all morning with foreign book-buyers.

Jennifer arrived early. Having been brought up in one, she was too used to pubs to feel self-conscious about drinking alone, so she ordered a glass of wine and found a table beneath an ornately etched mirror from where she could watch the door.

She saw Roger before he saw her – before he even knew she was there. He hadn't changed at all. It was all the same – his height, his thick, dark hair, the impatient tapping of his foot as he waited to be served. Busy, impatient Roger, always wanting to be somewhere else, always thinking someone else was having a better time, making more money, having more fun. He turned with his drink and saw her straight away. He smiled awkwardly as he approached the table, and Jennifer saw that he was changed after all. His hair was long all over, so he could sweep his hands through it Byronically, which he did often and to great effect. His eyes were kinder than she remembered them and he had lost weight. His voice was still the same though, and always would be, she imagined: devilishly deep, like chocolate poured over silk.

He kissed her briefly on the cheek and sat down beside her, a circumspect distance away. He was wearing a biscuit-coloured linen suit and Jennifer could have sat there and nibbled it right off him.

Her reaction to him horrified her. She knew she was still fond of him but she'd thought that all the butterflies she'd ever felt for Roger had folded their wings and died – or at least were pinned in some display case along with the other relics of her past mistakes – like the four-leafed clover Paddy had given her and Adam's tiny wrist tag from the hospital. But now they batted about in her stomach, desperate for Roger to drop his net and capture them once and for all.

'Are you hungry?' he asked. 'The food's not bad here.'

She shook her head. What, eat and crush those beautiful iridescent wings? Hope bounced up again, along with the butterflies. Could she have been wrong about the reason for his wanting to meet her?

He took a sip of his beer and swallowed harder than he need have done, as if he had an obstruction in his throat. His pride, perhaps? He swivelled his beer glass on the table for a moment, then turned towards her.

'I suppose I might as well come straight out with it. I want a divorce, Jennifer. We've been apart for almost two years now, and with your consent . . . are you all right?'

The colour must have leached right out of her face because he actually put out a hand as if he thought she was going to topple over. But she sat stock still while the shock ricocheted all through her body, from her brain to her heart and back again. Rationally, she'd known this was what the meeting must be about, but even till the last few seconds she'd been hoping, emotionally – irrationally – for something very different.

'Why – why now?' she asked in a tiny voice.

'Well, because – surely you must have realized . . . There's some-one else.'

She must be stupid. Really, really stupid. Because it had never occurred to her at all.

'If he'd left me for someone else in the first place, it wouldn't have been so bad!' she sobbed to her mother when she got back to Ambridge. She'd had to explain about her subterfuge and her meeting with Roger: although she'd planned to keep the news to herself, it was too huge and too dreadful for her to contain. 'It would have been awful, of course, but just one massive blow and it would have been over. But this way – oh, Mum!'

'Jennifer, dear, I'm so sorry.'

Peggy pulled another handful of tissues from the box and handed them to her daughter. Even she hadn't realized how attached Jennifer still was to Roger and how much she'd been hoping for a reconciliation.

'I know it's hard, love, but you have to look on it as a fresh start. A clean break. Surely that's better than the sort of . . . limbo you've been living in for the past couple of years.'

'But I'm not ready!' cried Jennifer. 'He wants us to divorce straight away and I need time! I've got to get used to the idea!'

'You can drag it out for as long as you like, Jennifer. That's your prerogative,' said Peggy sadly. 'But if he's decided what he wants, it won't make any difference to Roger's feelings – except to build more resentment. Of course he's hurt you – more than he probably realizes – but believe me, love, if you go on like this, you'll end up hurting yourself more.'

Jennifer snuffled and laid her head exhaustedly on her mother's shoulder.

'It was just – such a shock, Mum. Until he opened his mouth I honestly thought we might have another chance.'

'There's nothing worse than one person caring when the other simply doesn't – or not in the same way.' Peggy had had plenty of time to reflect on this imbalance in relation to Jack Woolley's attentions to her. 'But Roger can't get back what he doesn't feel any more, love. And you certainly can't make him.'

'I know. I know. That's exactly what I thought when he left me. And things had been so bad I was glad in a way to see him go. But life on your own – well, that's not much fun either, Mum.'

'No, it isn't,' agreed Peggy. 'But you're not on your own. You've got your family all round you, a lovely home with Chris. You've got a lot more support than most young women in your situation.'

'I know. I'm so ungrateful.'

Jennifer laid the backs of her hands against her hot, puffy eyes.

'No,' her mother soothed. 'You're just feeling low. And I think you're forgetting something.'

'What?'

'Brian Aldridge. He phoned the office for you today. He wants you to go over and see the progress they've made with the building work on the farmhouse. You'll enjoy that, won't you?'

It wasn't that Jennifer didn't like Brian. She did, a lot. But what she didn't like was the way she felt her family were pushing her on to him. She couldn't deny, as her mother said, that her relatives did offer her a tremendous amount of practical support. But when it came to supporting her emotionally, their preferred route seemed to be to try to find her another husband. And she wasn't even free yet of the one she'd got! She knew, though it had never been said – not to her at least – that the family considered she'd been lucky, as an unmarried mother, to find Roger to take her on. They must have been turning cartwheels, Jennifer thought bitterly, when Brian hove into view – rich, eligible, public-school-educated Brian, so confident of his own position in society that Jennifer's chequered past – two children, now, by two different fathers, didn't seem to bother him at all.

Jennifer wasn't sure herself why she wasn't biting his hand off. Of course, she was still muddled about her feelings for Roger, but it wasn't just that. Maybe it was the rebel in her. Maybe she felt it was all a bit too schematic, too neat and tidy. After all, she'd never conformed with her family's expectations before – why start now? Brian was very nice, there was no doubt about it. He was good-looking, intelligent, articulate and he made her laugh. But there was also something almost antiseptic about him. He was, for Jennifer, a bit too conformist. And a bit too . . . unfeeling? She tried to push the notion away but there was a bit of her that thought she was merely part of his five-year plan. Brian had bought his rolling acres and he needed a wife to complete the picture, like one of those Gainsborough portraits. He'd be buying a gun dog next and wanting her to wear a straw bonnet and building a folly in the grounds. Far from being grateful for being plucked off the scrap heap, Jennifer felt obscurely as if she was the one being used.

Nonetheless, she accepted Brian's invitation to go round to Home Farm – the new name he'd given the place – to see what had been done. For the second time in a few days she experienced a feeling of breathless shock – though this time much more pleasant than the previous one.

When she'd last looked inside Ambridge Court, as it then was, she'd been out for a walk with the children. It had been empty for over two years and house-martins wheeled under the eaves. Jennifer, Adam and Debbie had peered in through the cobwebbed kitchen window. There'd been an ancient settee in the middle of the room and a table covered with newspapers. The tractor drivers used the place to eat their sandwiches when they were up on this part of the farm and, from the shadowy scurryings, they obviously shared it with various species of wildlife. Debbie, who was in an annoyingly girlish phase, which manifested itself in 'twirly' skirts and a passion for lipstick, had wanted to go in and 'tidy up', but Jennifer had muttered darkly about creepy-crawlies and Debbie had swiftly tugged her away back to the path. Now, thanks to Brian's architect and liberal doses of his cheque book, the place was transformed.

'I had a bit of trouble with the builder from time to time,' he confessed, opening a bottle of Sancerre. 'Wanted to knock down walls here and put in archways there and I don't know what.'

Jennifer shuddered. 'Adobe walls and concealed lighting, don't tell me.'

'That's the sort of thing.' Brian extracted the cork and sniffed it. He poured the wine. 'He couldn't understand that I wanted to preserve the character of the place.'

'You've certainly done that. I bet you're pleased.'

'Pleased that *you* like it.' Brian handed her a glass of wine and chinked his own against it. 'Cheers. Shall we go through?'

He led her into the sitting room. The house was elegantly Georgian. The huge sash windows beckoned the evening sun, which was dipping down across the cornfields. He'd had the original Adam fireplace with its honeysuckle work cleaned up and the cracks mended. Above it was a beautiful gilt mirror with pilasters. To one side of the fireplace was a low Chesterfield sofa, and in front of it – a daringly modern touch – a glass-topped coffee table.

'I know, I know,' Brian said, following her eyes. 'The coffee table does rather yell "bachelor pad". The woman from Underwoods who did the curtains talked me into it. But at least I haven't got leather sofas and shag-pile carpets.'

'It's lovely, Brian.' Jennifer settled herself in the corner of the sofa. Brian sat beside her.

'So, what have you been doing with yourself?' he began. 'It's a long time since I saw you.'

'Oh, this and that,' replied Jennifer. There didn't seem any point in not telling him: she'd told all her family now, even Tony and Granny Perkins who were about as modern in their outlook as each other. So she said: 'I went to see Roger in London.'

'Oh,' he said. He picked a bit of fluff off his sock. He was waiting for her to say something else, but she didn't, so he added, 'How is he?'

'Fine,' said Jennifer briefly. 'And so is the woman he's moved in with.'

'Ah.'

'A redhead,' said Jennifer, as if it made any difference. 'Francesca. He wants to marry her. Sounds glamorous, doesn't she?'

Brian pulled a face.

'If you go for redheads, perhaps,' he replied. 'Where are they shacked up?'

Jennifer pushed her fingers into the puckered dimples of the upholstery.

'Her flat in North Acton,' she said sadly.

'North Acton?' Brian exclaimed. 'Definitely not glamorous.'

'Don't you think so?'

Brian grinned.

'Have you ever been there? It's mostly industrial estates and fly-overs. The flat's probably got subsidence and the air quality's terrible.'

'Really?'

'Oh, Jennifer, you do worry your head about some silly things,' said Brian. 'Let me top your glass up.'

She warmed to him that evening, she really did. He was so . . . sensible. Where Jennifer got carried away with wild imaginings, Brian looked at the facts, and for the first time in her life, she could see what a useful characteristic this could be. As Jennifer sipped her wine and listened to Brian talk about cropping ratios she could quite see why her family were so keen to push them together. And she had to acknowledge that part of her resistance was simply her natural perversity against doing what she was told. Some would say she was perverse, full stop: look at the way she'd behaved over Paddy Redmond. But she'd been younger then. With her twenties behind her, spent bringing up two children in a variety of imperfect conditions and scrabbling around doing what work she could, Jennifer could see that perhaps it was time she bowed to the inevitable. Perhaps it was time she acknowledged that her mother was right and that Brian would be a good match for her. After all, Jennifer had chosen the previous two men in her life and they hadn't been a wild success – why not let her family have the satisfaction of choosing the third? They'd be choosing Brian on the basis of his obvious attributes – his wealth and status – but Jennifer would always have the satisfaction of knowing that she had recognized in him something deeper and more important. Brian was the sort of man who would let her be herself. He wouldn't be threatened by her columns in the *Echo* or her involvement with the children, simply because he wouldn't notice. He was too self-confidently self-absorbed to let anything Jennifer did bother him.

By the end of the evening, despite what she'd thought only a few days previously, Jennifer had begun to convince herself that Brian Aldridge might, after all, be her saving grace.

'When are you going to have a house-warming?' She paused on the doorstep as she was leaving. The night was beautiful, still warm beneath a clear sky sprinkled with stars.

'I don't know that I will.'

A powerful waft of jasmine reached them. Jennifer waved her arm airily. She'd had at least half the bottle and it was a long time since her spaghetti hoops with the children.

'You can't have a place like this and not give it a real send-off! That would be criminal.'

'Hm . . . I suppose so,' he acknowledged reluctantly. 'Well, all right. As long as you promise to help me organize it.'

The party was a great success. The date Brian had chosen in October coincided with Dan's birthday, but the family contrived to keep it a secret from him, so when he thought he was in for a quiet evening at Glebe Cottage he found himself taken out and surrounded by friends and family.

'And at someone else's expense!' as Phil pointed out. 'Mind you, Brian can afford it!'

Certainly, everyone agreed, no expense had been spared on doing the place up. But, as Brian had to concede, it was the feminine touches Jennifer had provided that made all the difference.

'Cushions,' he confided to Pat and Tony. 'That's the secret, apparently. Would never have occurred to me.'

'It's lovely,' said Pat. 'You've given me dozens of ideas for our place.'

'Here, hang on,' protested Tony. 'We haven't got that sort of money.'

'No, and you'll soon be having another mouth to feed,' admonished Brian. Pat was expecting a baby early in the New Year.

'And he's talking about upping the cow numbers,' put in Pat. 'Wants us to work up to seventy.'

Brian pulled a face.

'Sounds like hard work. I'm glad I'm not tied to a cow's tail.'

'Walter! No more!'

They turned round to see Doris covering her glass with her hand. Walter hovered over her with a bottle of his lethal elderberry wine. He'd taken a bottle to a party at the vicarage earlier in the year and Doris had got quite tiddly on it.

'Go on, Doris! Let your hair down! After all, it is your old man's birthday!'

'Let my hair down? I'll be falling down if I have any more.' It was true. Doris, who hardly ever drank, already had a slightly glazed look.

'Come on, Uncle Walter, pick on someone your own size.' Jill led him away gently, signalling with a raised eyebrow to Phil that it might be time to take his parents home. 'Let's see if Aunt Laura's still here.'

'Not Laura,' squeaked Walter pitifully. 'She's already told me once this evening about her h'elm tree protection campaign.'

'It's serious, Uncle Walter,' chided Jill. 'Something like six million trees have died from Dutch elm disease.'

'That's as mebbe,' growled Walter, 'but I'd rather get Dutch elm disease meself than listen to all that again.'

John Tregorran – now back from America – stepped manfully into the breach to sidetrack Walter, and Jill returned to help Doris unsteadily to the door.

'Your family are quite something,' said Brian as he helped himself to a smoked salmon pinwheel from the tray Jennifer was carrying past.

'You've noticed, have you?' she smiled.

She was enjoying herself. It was rather nice playing hostess to Brian's guests in this beautiful house, and it had been fun planning the party, suggesting little touches that Brian wouldn't have thought of. It had been fun, too, preparing for it earlier, finding her way around the kitchen and laying out the buffet table. And when everyone had gone, it was nice to sink down with Brian on the sofa among the crumpled napkins and the quiche crumbs with a final glass of wine and Frank Sinatra on the record player and reflect on how well the evening had gone.

'I think everyone enjoyed themselves,' she ventured. She kicked off her shoes and flexed her feet.

'You must take a lot of the credit.'

'Me?' said Jennifer bashfully.

'I spent the whole evening,' said Brian, pretending to be peeved, 'being congratulated on things *you'd* done. All those "little feminine touches" that – apparently – make such a difference.'

'We aim to please,' said Jennifer flippantly.

'And succeed.' He wasn't flippant in his reply. He looked at her as he spoke, then leant across to kiss her. And that was when Jennifer knew with absolute certainty that she would marry him.

·11·

Taken by Surprise

But first he had to ask her. Jennifer knew that if she were a truly liberated woman she should be able to ask him herself – but then if she were a truly liberated woman, she wouldn't need a man anyway. She knew that in the end it was Pat who'd proposed to Tony, but she wasn't Pat – and Brian certainly wasn't like her brother.

Autumn advanced slowly, as if the heat of summer couldn't bear – or couldn't be bothered – to drag itself away. Jays and squirrels, though, were busy burying acorns: they weren't fooled by the still-warm sunshine. Little by little the view from Jennifer's office window changed. The horse chestnuts began to look bedraggled, their crowns a patchwork of yellowy-brown. In the woods, curled leaves whirled to the ground, aided by the wing-beats of woodpigeons searching for beechmast. And as the overwintering birds arrived, so too did an affidavit from Roger's solicitor.

Jennifer received it the same morning she went to Brookfield to deliver Phil and Jill an anniversary card. Jill had just got back from the village and was unpacking her shopping.

'Eighteen years!' Jennifer exclaimed. 'How've you done it, Jill?'

'Lord knows!' Jill rolled her eyes. 'When I think back . . . the first time I saw Phil tail-docking weaners I nearly ran away there and then.'

'I'll never forget you telling me,' remembered Jennifer, 'when I was expecting Adam, how daunted you were by the prospect of fitting into Ambridge.'

'Oh, I told Phil! On practically our first date I told him I could never marry a farmer and I could never live in the country. And look at me now.'

Jennifer looked at her in the kindly warmth of her kitchen, surrounded by bags of flour, dried fruit and mixed peel. Next week it would be Stir-up Sunday, the traditional time to make the Christmas cake and pudding.

'How do you think I'd do as a farmer's wife, Jill?' she asked abruptly.

'Brian's? Has he asked you?' Jill almost dropped a box of icing sugar in her excitement.

Jennifer explained that he hadn't – and she explained, sadly, about the affidavit.

'You mustn't blame yourself.' Jill put the kettle on for coffee. Phil would be in for his soon. 'Of course you're sorry about what's past and what didn't work out. But if I've learnt one thing, Jennifer, it's that life moves on. I mean, Phil thought his life was all mapped out for him with Grace, but it wasn't to be. It seemed like the end of everything for him. But for me, it was just the start.'

Jennifer nodded, but she still felt sad. She couldn't help feeling that Phil and Jill were the lucky ones, to have found each other in the first place and, all these years on, still to be finding things to like in each other. They always presented such a united front. Phil had the farm, while Jill had the children and her interests in the village – but they still had enough in common to have a marriage as well. It wasn't one of those partnerships that had degenerated into something more approaching a business arrangement. And when Jennifer looked around her, apart from Gran and Grandad, of course, whose happiness was legendary, Phil and Jill did seem the exception rather than the rule.

As Jill clattered about with the coffee things, Jennifer went through the gloomy inventory of her immediate family. Ralph and Lilian had spent the summer cruising the Greek islands but they were no nearer finding anywhere they could call home and Lilian was getting increasingly fretful. Since their father had died, Peggy had had a worrying tendency to idealize her own marriage, which Jennifer knew *she* couldn't have stuck out, and since Peggy had turned down his marriage proposal, the only anniversary Jack Woolley had to celebrate these days was that of his divorce.

As for Chris and Paul, their problems continued. He was going to be moved from the Welsh oilfield to a desk job in London and Chris was reluctant to move with him. Jennifer knew some people couldn't understand it, but she could sympathize with Chris's position only too well. Say she pulled up her roots in Ambridge, gave up the stables and moved to Surrey or wherever, and then after six months Paul was on the move, or working away again – Chris would be stuck there without any of the support she could rely on in Ambridge, or would have to move again, hoiking Peter out of school. No, Jennifer thought Chris was doing the right thing. Of all of them, only Pat and Tony seemed really happy – Jennifer had to grant them that – but they hadn't been married a year yet. They were still in the honeymoon phase and with a baby to look forward to.

The kitchen door crashed back and Phil came in, cursing. Someone had left a gate open and the sheep had got into the lane. He'd left Jethro and Neil rounding them up but he'd have to get back out and help them.

'Have your coffee now you're here,' soothed Jill. 'Jennifer's brought us a card.'

'Hm? Oh, that's nice.' Phil eased his boots off. 'And what's your news on that score?'

'Phil!' Jill warned.

'None,' said Jennifer tightly. 'Brian hasn't asked me to marry him and despite my liberated, bohemian reputation, I haven't asked him either!'

• • •

And so Christmas came, bringing with it, as well as the final flocks of redwing and fieldfares, more winter visitors in the shape of Ralph and Lilian. To Lilian's relief, they'd finally decided to settle in Guernsey, where some friends were on the look-out for a house for them. Paul, who felt more like a visitor than an inhabitant of Ambridge these days, came home too. He had good news as well: he'd done a deal with his boss to enable him to work from home three days a week. The family could stay in Ambridge: Chris could keep her husband and her horses.

All Peggy's children were in Ambridge for Christmas and she couldn't have been happier. She invited them all round to Blossom Hill Cottage on Boxing Day, though everyone protested it would be too much work – and, of course, Brian was invited as well. He even had the task of collecting Granny Perkins and giving her a lift up there for the evening: she was having afternoon tea with Walter.

'If Brian survives a car ride with Granny P, you'll have to marry him, won't she, eh, Ralph?' Tony, surrounded by Quality Street wrappers, put his feet up on the discarded Monopoly board. It still seemed odd to him that Ralph, who'd once been his boss, was now his brother-in-law.

'I like Brian.' Ralph was speaking as a farmer. 'Increasing the rape acreage. Growing sugar beet. Seems to have all the right ideas. And the drive to make them work.' He sipped his low-calorie ginger ale. Lilian was very strict about his diet. 'He mustn't get too carried away though. Always a temptation for a go-ahead chap, to expand and get too big. You'll have to keep an eye on him, Jennifer. Make sure he keeps a sense of proportion.'

'Mum, is there some orange juice in the kitchen?' Jennifer stood up abruptly.

Ralph pulled a 'what did I say?' face at an equally baffled Tony as Peggy followed Jennifer out.

'She always was over-sensitive.' Tony unwrapped another toffee. 'Just one more of these, Ralph, and then let's get out and have a walk. See exactly what Brian's up to on your land.'

In the kitchen, Peggy found Jennifer staring out of the window into the fast-fading afternoon. She didn't have to say anything.

'It was the way they were talking about Brian,' Jennifer burst out. 'As if it were all fixed. All decided.'

'And isn't it?'

'Well, in a way it is. I know it, you know it. We all know it. But it's sort of – sort of being taken for granted. After all, he still hasn't got round to asking me.'

She had hoped for it on Christmas Eve, when he'd invited her over to Home Farm. But though they'd lain cosily on the sofa in front of the fire, and he'd given her a beautifully wrapped box which could only be jewellery (a matching pendant and earrings, as it turned out), still nothing was said. Jennifer was beginning to get desperate. Brian wasn't a shy sort of man, he was direct and to the point – goodness knew, she'd heard him telling off his workers! They were getting on better and better, there was no one else on his side and her divorce was chugging relentlessly through the system. So why didn't he just get on with it?

New Year's Eve – another rite of passage – arrived. Phil and Jill were hosting the usual family party and Jennifer didn't see how she and Brian could get past midnight without getting engaged. But just before the party started, Pat went into labour two weeks early and just as Big Ben boomed in the New Year, Tony rang from the hospital to say he was the proud father of a son – the first great-grandson who would carry on the Archer name. Seconds later, Uncle Tom led the Ambridge bell-ringers in ringing in the New Year on the church bells which, as a parting gift, Ralph had paid to have rehung.

'We could make it a double celebration if Brian put his mind to it,' Jennifer thought morosely, filling her glass with water at the tap. Everyone else was drinking champagne but she wasn't in the mood. Still Brian said nothing. New Year's Day came and went. Still nothing. And then, next day, just when Jennifer's nerves were positively jangling, he finally did it.

He'd taken her in to see Pat and the baby – to be called John Daniel, what else? – and then they'd gone for a walk up by Leader's Wood. It was cold and murky. The rooks were holding a parliament, squawking loudly in the trees. Before dusk fell they would disperse to their own nests.

'You're very fond of the country, aren't you, Jennifer?' Brian tucked her arm through his.

'Who isn't?' Jennifer was beginning to resent any question that wasn't the one she wanted to hear.

'A lot of people like living in London,' he said reasonably.

'The only good thing about London is the down train from Paddington,' was her sour reply.

He stopped walking. Rooks circled dizzily overhead.

'You really think that? I mean you're the only person in Ambridge who would look at home in a . . . a Chelsea boutique.'

'Brian . . .' She couldn't see the point of this conversation. 'Is there some purpose behind all this analysis of my character?'

'Perhaps.' He was smiling. 'You see, I always think there's nothing worse than someone who's always wishing they were somewhere else. They're the very devil to live with.'

'I expect they are,' she said quietly. Even then she didn't realize what he was getting at. In fact, she was thinking about Roger: that was just what she'd always felt about him.

'Still,' Brian went on cheerily, 'if you're happy here, that's all right. It's the only thing that's been bothering me.' He squeezed her fingers with his free hand. 'Jenny, I think we ought to get married. Don't you?'

• • •

'Imagine, Peggy,' said Doris when they met after church the following Sunday. 'The New Year's only a few days old and already you've got a new grandson and a new son-in-law!'

'I haven't got over it yet!' Peggy was clearly thrilled. 'And nor has Jennifer. She was completely taken by surprise.'

'She must have had some inkling, surely . . .' Doris put a hand to her hat. It was a wicked wind.

'Only because you and everyone else kept dropping hints the size of manhole covers.' Dan had joined them now, after a word with the vicar.

'That's just it,' smiled Peggy. 'She'd spent so long waiting for it, when it happened it practically knocked her off her feet!'

Jennifer felt her feet didn't touch the ground much again between then and 29 May, which was the date she and Brian had set for the wedding. There was so much to do. It wasn't a case, like her wedding to Roger, of her father's permission being asked and letting her mother organize everything. She and Brian were independent adults: this was their wedding and they would be doing most of the organization themselves. Jennifer spent more and more time at Home Farm. She took to keeping a spare set of clothes there to save her rushing back to Wynfords late at night: Paul was having to stay up in London for a project he was working on and Chris was happy to babysit. In March, Brian took her to Paris and in April, to the family's astonishment, he bought her a pre-wedding present of six Jacob sheep.

'D'you think he's trying to turn her into another Pat?' Jill asked Phil when she heard.

'Jennifer?' Shula, who would be eighteen in August, put down the horsey magazine she was reading. 'She's always been terrified of animals. Anyway, why should she bother? If I was marrying someone as rich as Brian, I'd put my feet up all day and eat chocolates by the pound.'

'You've got to find him first.' Phil finished signing a cheque to the Inland Revenue and looked for the envelope.

'And what's wrong with Bill?' enquired Shula.

Shula's latest beau, Bill Morris, was the son of a wealthy farmer. A bit too wealthy for Phil's liking: on his first visit to Brookfield, Bill had looked pityingly at the milking parlour and wondered aloud how Phil coped with such an antiquated set-up: his father had a rotary parlour for his 200-strong herd. Jill liked him, but then he did bring her flowers and compliment her on her cooking. The art of going out with a girl these days, Phil reflected, seemed to be to get her mother on your side.

Shula was turning out to be something of a trial to her parents. Kenton had set his heart on a career as a naval meteorological officer when he was twelve and nothing would deflect him from it. Jill had finally resigned herself to seeing him only on his extended leaves, and with David away at boarding school, that left just the girls. Elizabeth, just nine, was still happily occupied with ballet and Barbie dolls, which left plenty of time for Phil and Jill to agonize over Shula – time they needed.

Two years ago, she'd been seen by the showjumper Anne Moore, who'd said she might have the makings of a professional horse-woman. Shula had instantly started talking about leaving school and becoming Horsewoman of the Year, but Phil had dug in his heels. He'd insisted that Shula do a business studies course 'just to fall back on', but the following year her wishes had held sway and she'd enrolled for a horse management diploma. But now that she was starting to look for work, she was having to face some hard truths. There was no point in pretending: she didn't quite have the edge to make it as a competitive rider. The only alternative was to teach riding, but there was no vacancy at the stables with Chris who, much as she might have liked to, couldn't afford to create a job just for Shula. And all the other stables in the area were the same: family-run concerns with their own niece or daughter or cousin being groomed for any position which might come up. It looked as though Shula might be falling back on her secretarial skills rather sooner than she'd intended, which was not at all.

'Haven't you got a younger brother?' Shula demanded of Brian at the reception following the small register office ceremony. 'Dad's going to drive Bill away, I know he is, and then where shall I be?'

'Can't oblige, sorry.' Brian was rather nonplussed by her directness. 'Only got a sister. She's over there, look.'

'That's no good to me,' sulked Shula. 'Honestly, I think Jennifer might have vetted you a bit more carefully before she married you. Or Ralph before he sold to you for that matter.'

Brian excused himself and found Jennifer.

'I think your cousin's taken a dislike to me,' he said.

'Shula? Take no notice, she's just being a teenager.'

'Well, she makes me glad I'm grown up.' Brian raised his glass at Tony, who was digging into the food, somehow managing to balance a full glass on a loaded plate. He pulled Jennifer towards him and looped his arms round her waist. 'And there's nothing more grown up than being married.'

'We're going to be all right, aren't we, Brian?' Some of Jennifer's old vulnerability surfaced again, the bit of her that simply couldn't believe it when things turned out right, the bit of her that remembered from childhood Granny P's favourite sayings: 'Up like a rocket, down like a stick' and 'Every silver lining has a cloud'.

'Of course we are,' he promised. 'I'm going to look after you. And the children. Stop worrying.'

Jennifer smiled and bit her lip at the same time. It all seemed much too good to be true.

'Happy now?' asked Brian.

It wasn't really a question. He didn't seem to need, or expect, an answer. It wasn't a statement, either: more of an order. She hardly dared believe it but maybe this really was it: happy ever after.

When they got back from their honeymoon, a week spent in Brian's old stamping ground of Cambridgeshire, with rather more farm visits than Jennifer had anticipated thrown in, she went round to Wynfords one day to collect the last of the children's things from Chris. Though she and Paul had been among the select few invited to the register office, he hadn't after all been able to get back for the wedding.

'Poor Paul, having to work on a Saturday!' Doris had exclaimed to Dan when Peggy had phoned to tell her. She had followed him out into the garden at Glebe Cottage where he was digging the vegetable patch.

'What do you mean, poor Paul!' Dan's fork churned the dense soil, rich with manure from Brookfield. 'Farmers have to work every day of the week.' He stooped and pushed the soil away from a handful of new potatoes. 'How about these for lunch, Doris, with a tin of salmon, I thought, some peas and a drop of parsley sauce?'

'That's right, give me my orders!' grumbled Doris affectionately. 'Sometimes I can quite see why Chris thinks living apart from her husband is a good idea!'

But, as she told Jennifer, Chris wouldn't have agreed. The deal he'd done at New Year, spending part of the week in Ambridge and part in London, had seemed like the perfect solution. But it hadn't lasted long.

'He's had to go back to staying up in London much more,' Chris explained to Jennifer as they piled Adam's train set into a box. 'Working at home was a nightmare. His boss's secretary was on the phone every five minutes, Paul would shoo me away and nine times out of ten the upshot would be Paul packing his bag and leaping on the next train.'

'Oh, Chris, I'm sorry.' Jennifer uncoupled a length of track. 'I had no idea. I was so caught up with the wedding –'

Chris shook her head impatiently.

'It's not your problem. It's Peter I feel sorry for. Having to tell him his dad isn't going to be able to give him the bowling practice he promised or go fishing with him after all.' She dropped a couple of carriages into the box with a clatter. 'I feel so guilty about Peter. We adopted him to give him a normal family life, not all this disruption.'

Jennifer moved the arm of the tiny signalman she was holding up and down, up and down.

'I shouldn't worry about that, Chris. I mean, what's "normal" these days? Adam's had two different fathers already, neither of them his natural father. And now he's being completely hostile to Brian. Hates Brian touching me, won't reply to anything he says. Yet they got on brilliantly before.'

Chris grinned.

'And you thought marriage was going to be the answer to all your problems.'

'And the start of a few hundred more,' said Jennifer wryly. 'Come on, let's get this lot into the car. Perhaps Adam'll cheer up when he's got his beloved train set back.'

Adam did cheer up, transparently, when his birthday approached and Brian promised him a cricket set. On the day, there was a party in the garden at Home Farm for twenty of his schoolfriends, with Brian supervising the games and the whole family looking on.

'Jennifer settled at last!' breathed Peggy to Doris. 'She looks so happy. I daren't believe it.'

'I wish I could say the same for Chris.'

Both of their heads swivelled to where Chris was standing, watching the boys play pass the parcel. Her arms were folded defensively across her chest and her mouth was a thin, straight line. In the bright sunshine she looked somehow . . . faded.

'Paul?' hazarded Peggy.

'He's never at home,' said Doris in a stage whisper. The music had stopped and a boy with an alarming crew-cut was scrabbling at the newspaper-covered parcel.

'Perhaps they need a holiday,' suggested Peggy. 'Get away from London *and* Ambridge. Together.'

And so, a few days later, when Lilian rang with the great good news that their house in Guernsey would be ready earlier than they expected, at the end of August, Chris was one of the first people Peggy thought of.

'I didn't commit you to anything,' she said. She'd gone up to the stables specially to find Chris. 'But if you're interested . . .'

'Paul's always on about going there . . .' mused Chris, obviously tempted. 'It would be lovely.'

'Well, go on, then,' urged Peggy. 'Give him a ring in London.'

Chris was doubtful. She'd rung Paul once in the middle of closing a business deal and he'd complained that the hiatus had given the customer an advantage. But this was important. She'd been nagging him to fix a holiday for weeks: with all the weekends he'd had to work, he was certainly owed the time off. It would give her and Peter something to look forward to – and Paul, as well, for that matter.

'Do you know, it might just work!' she exclaimed. 'I'll ring. He can only say no.'

Peggy followed her into the little office, gloomy after the dazzle of the concrete yard. She looked around idly as Chris dialled, at the dusty rosettes and lesson timetables that were pinned to the walls. Chris smiled excitedly.

'They're putting me through,' she said. Peggy thought she looked better already: some of the anxiety and tiredness had lifted from her face. 'Hello, I'd like to speak to Mr Johnson please . . . it's his wife.' There was a pause while the voice at the other end of the phone twittered something. When Chris spoke again, her voice was completely different, less certain. 'What? But he couldn't . . . I see. Thank you. No, there's no message. Goodbye.'

She replaced the receiver carefully, as if trying not to detonate a bomb.

'Well?' queried Peggy.

'He's not there,' said Chris, clearly too stunned to tell her sister-in-law anything but the truth. 'He told them he'd be working at home today.'

·12·

A Learning Curve

It was obviously time for the family to start worrying properly about Chris. Since Paul had started working away again, there'd been a sort of generalized concern, but now there was evidence of – of what? Deceit? Or merely a misunderstanding?

'Chris maintains it was the office's fault,' Peggy told Doris the following week. She'd made a point of checking with Chris what had happened: she'd felt she had to. She didn't want to pry, but since she'd been there, unfortunately, when the call was made . . . It was really all very embarrassing.

'How does she work that out?' Doris, displeased at having to hear all this second-hand, and having to hear it at all, poured Peggy another glass of her home-made lemonade and replaced the little net cover, weighted with beads, over the jug. Peggy took a grateful sip. This summer was proving just as hot as last year's: there was already talk of empty reservoirs and water rationing. She was glad of the shade of Glebe Cottage's apple tree.

'They assumed "home" meant Ambridge,' Peggy explained, 'when really Paul had meant the flat in London. And he *was* there, but there must have been a fault with the phone because when Chris tried, there was no answer.'

'And that's his story, is it?' Doris sniffed.

'It's always possible.'

'Possible, maybe. But is it probable?' Doris shifted to a more comfortable position in her deckchair. 'After all, Peggy, we all know that it wouldn't be the first time he's been up to mischief.'

Doris was well aware that Chris would have been mortified if

171

she'd thought her family knew as much as they did about Paul's past indiscretions. But this was Ambridge, for goodness' sake, where a lie could be halfway round the village before truth had got its boots on. How on earth could anyone hope to keep anything quiet?

Even before Paul and Christine had been married, Dan had been told at market, if you please, that Paul's car had been seen outside his secretary's house in Borchester late at night. And then – years ago, now – Phil had told his dad that Paul seemed in danger of taking up again with a childhood sweetheart, Marianne Peters, whom he'd bumped into in Paris while Phil and Paul had been on a short trip there. On both occasions, of course, Dan had told Doris, both times prefaced with the words, 'Now you're not to worry, love, but . . .' How could she help but worry, as she'd flared at him at the time. Christine was her only daughter. Having brought her into the world and raised her, Doris's only remaining function *was* to worry about her.

But she'd kept her worries to herself, grateful for the knowledge because, if Chris did choose to confide in her – if Chris even knew what was going on – then Doris would be prepared. If Christine asked her advice she would give it, though she knew that it might not necessarily be what Christine wanted to hear. Doris valued Christine's happiness above all, but she was of the generation that still believed marriage was for life, especially where a child was involved, and that a woman's happiness proceeded from her marriage. She would have advised Chris to stick with Paul, to work at things and to make the best of it.

Over the years Chris had come to her mother for advice about lots of things – the stables, Peter's potty-training, Paul's frequent changes of direction in his work, but she had never spoken a word about Paul and another woman. Doris had respected her privacy and she'd never stirred the pot. But she knew from what wasn't said that Chris had known all about the Marianne Peters episode, and she suffered for her. And subsequently, every time Chris came to her bright-eyed and told her about Paul's latest scheme or job offer, Doris suffered a bit more. She knew that Chris was doing exactly what Doris would have advised – trying to make her marriage work. The only trouble was that making a marriage work took two willing participants – and Paul very often seemed to be pulling in the opposite direction.

For Chris, after the fateful phone call, it all unfolded with a queasy sense of déjà vu. She went back over the past few months and it wasn't hard to convince herself. The phone calls at home. Paul's quick dashes off to London – not for work, as he'd claimed, but to see *her*, whoever she was – someone he worked with, presumably. And, tellingly, the refusal to plan anything with Chris, like a holiday, for instance. So hurtful now that she knew the reason – so that he could keep himself available for his girlfriend.

She knew he wouldn't tell her about it voluntarily. It had taken her months, and the arrival of Marianne Peters in Ambridge, to extract a confession from him last time. But sadly, though it was a game she'd never wanted to play, she now knew the rules of engagement. She had to watch and wait. And at a moment she chose, she would confront him about it.

A couple of weeks later, at the end of July, Paul turned up un-expectedly at home one Thursday evening. Chris was hot and tired. The school holidays had begun and she'd had a stream of pupils all day, interrupted by constant phone calls from helpers at the village fête, which she was involved in organizing. How much room did the Hollerton Silver Band need and would they be bringing music stands? Was any one person providing sacks for the sack race or was everyone meant to bring a handful from their own barn? Sid Perks had found a mysterious – and uncannily unforeseen – rip in Mrs Perkins's fortune-telling tent and she was demanding a new one by tomorrow. By the time she got home, Chris had had enough. She didn't care whether the fête went ahead or not: the church roof could fall in for all she cared. Then Paul arrived back.

'Why don't we drop everything and have a weekend away?' she asked him, washing her hands at the kitchen sink before starting to make the supper.

'You'd miss the village fête.'

'So? I'd much rather be with you and Peter. A break would do us good.'

Maybe, she thought, if they got away, she might find the moment to quiz Paul about what was really going on.

'The thing is . . .' He fiddled with the controls on the cooker. 'I shan't be here at the weekend.'

'What?'

There was some conference, he said, he had to attend. With some overseas bigwigs. On a Saturday. In the summer.

How credulous does he think I am? thought Chris, insulted. She fetched a cooked chicken from the fridge and began hacking it to pieces. She wanted to lay into Paul then and there and tell him what she knew, for she had long gone beyond merely suspecting. But she realized she was too tired and overwrought to challenge him about it now. Anyway, to Paul's obvious relief, the phone rang. It was her mother. She'd just checked the contributions for the bottle stall. They were mostly pickled onions and mustard. Did Chris think it mattered? With supreme self-control, Chris told her not to worry, people were just glad to win a prize.

Peter, who'd been over at Home Farm with Adam, was delighted when he got home to find his father there. After supper they played football in the garden. Chris watched them as she washed up. Paul was a good father, when he was around. It was a pity he wasn't a better husband.

As Peter went up to bed, the phone rang again: another query about the fête. Paul made packing gestures at Chris and disappeared upstairs, too. When Chris had finished making soothing noises about the plant stall, whose offerings would be severely depleted owing to the drought, she wandered out into the garden and took a deep breath. The air was still and sticky and provided no relief. At the bottom of the garden, swifts raced over a new-cut cornfield, hoovering up the insects that had been disturbed. Under the eaves, house-martins scrambled in and out of their mud nests, bedding down for the night. The scent of stocks and nicotiana mingled in the dusk. Perhaps there was no point in waiting to challenge Paul.

Perhaps she'd never feel calm and rational about it. Why didn't she just get on with it?

Reinvigorated now that the confrontation was finally going to happen, she strode up the stairs and into their bedroom. Paul was folding a shirt.

'I'm sorry, but I've had enough,' she said. 'I can't take any more of your evading and misleading. What's her name?'

He clicked his tongue impatiently.

'What? Chris, all I want to do is finish my packing.'

She snatched a tie out of his hand. She could have throttled him with it.

'When you've answered my question.'

He said nothing.

'Come on,' she ordered. 'I know there's someone. Who is she?'

When he told her, it was such a cliché, she almost wanted to laugh. He was having an affair with a secretary from work. Not his own secretary, though. Typically of Paul, over-ambitious, arrogant, he didn't have the sense, as her dad would have put it, to dirty his own doorstep. She was his boss's PA.

'Is it serious? That's all I'm concerned about.'

And suddenly, it mattered very much that he said no.

'I don't know.' He sank down on the bed. 'That's the stupid part of it. One minute it seems like the most important thing in the world. And the next – well, it comes a rather poor second to what we have here. But don't ask me any more just now. Please.'

Chris felt sick. She thought she'd been prepared for this. But what did they say about not asking questions to which you might not like the answer? She realized that she hadn't actually thought beyond challenging Paul and getting an affirmative answer to her suspicions. What she'd forgotten – and she kicked herself now – was that getting an admission out of him wasn't the end of it. It was just the start.

He went to London. She couldn't see how she could stop him and she couldn't see the point. This other woman – Brenda – was organizing the conference, which he maintained was genuinely happening. Chris could, he said, phone the office and check if she liked. And he said that he'd always intended to use it as an opportunity to work out what he wanted.

'You mean, which of us?' It was Friday evening and Chris had driven him to the station. 'So I just have to wait for my future to be decided. Thanks very much.'

'Chris, it's not like that!'

'You're telling me it's not.' She pulled into a space in the car park and snatched at the handbrake. 'Never mind the future, we've got a past. Doesn't that count for anything? And we've got Peter, in case you'd forgotten.'

'Of course I hadn't. I love Peter –'

'It's just me you don't.'

'I do. I do love you. It's just – it's different with her.'

'I bet it is.'

She realized, despite her new-found bravado, that she wasn't in a terrifically strong position. She was the tried, the trusted. All she could offer Paul was more of the same, more of what he already knew, whereas Brenda was something fresh and exciting, and Chris understood her husband. She knew how easily he could find himself enthralled by the thrill of the new.

But maybe her cynicism, born of bitter experience and her present hurt, was making her too jaundiced about Paul because the very next day he surprised her.

The fête was in full swing: Silver Band playing, stallholders shouting their attractions, coconut shy clattering, entrants in the terrier race yapping. Chris had a pounding headache and the muscles of her jaw felt like two giant gobstoppers in her cheeks. All night, it seemed, she'd lain awake, facing the giddying prospect that this time Paul might actually leave. Now she was light-headed with exhaustion. But she was one of the fête organizers, and organize she must. She was busy leading Lucy Perks, Sid and Polly's little daughter, up and down on a pony, when Paul wandered over, looking hot, bothered and ludicrously out of place in his city clothes.

'Can we go home?' he asked abruptly. 'I need a cup of tea and not too much company.'

You're not the only one, she thought. He'd obviously made his decision but she couldn't read from his closed face which way it had gone.

'I'll ask Shula to take over,' was all she said.

He was serious about the tea, for sure. As soon as they got in, having driven home in silence, he filled the kettle noisily and placed it on the stove. He even managed to light the gas by himself. Then he began looking vaguely in the cupboards.

'It's here,' she said impatiently, reaching a canister from a shelf. Didn't that just say everything? She'd thought they had a marriage, but he didn't even know where she kept the tea any more.

'I didn't go to the conference,' he said finally, when she'd got out the cups and saucers and taken the teapot from its place by the toaster. She assumed he was capable of working out that the milk was in the fridge.

'Oh, Paul.' It had fallen to Chris to sort out Marianne Peters in the end. Was she going to have to do it this time as well? 'You are in a mess, aren't you? Up to your ears in trouble with me and now you've upset her as well.'

'I may not see her again,' he said quietly. 'At least not for some time.'

Chris let out a sigh. She didn't know whether it was relief or resignation. He still hadn't said he'd broken things off completely.

'I've arranged to go to our North Sea oil headquarters in Aberdeen in the next few days,' he explained. 'I should have gone before but I kept putting it off.'

To keep his trysts with Brenda, Chris thought resentfully. She'd been so damn understanding, sympathizing with his having to work so hard, defending him to her family. And all the while he'd been taking her for a fool.

'So you're escaping from both of us?'

'No. I want you to come with me. Peter too.'

'Where's this leading us?' asked Chris warily.

'Back together again, I hope.'

The kettle started to squeal and puff behind him.

'Kettle's boiling,' he said, shooting her an appeasing glance.

'Yes,' said Chris, turning off the gas. 'And I've a good mind to boil your head in it.'

But she managed to resist the temptation and, a couple of days later, they all set off for Scotland. Paul had a day or so's work in Aberdeen and then, they'd decided, they'd travel about, play it by ear. Peter was thrilled: he'd read *Rob Roy* and *Ivanhoe* in his Children's Classics series and wanted to see proper Scottish lochs and castles for himself. He hoped to catch a glimpse of the Loch Ness monster and do some fishing. He wanted to go to Lower Largo to see where the 'real' Robinson Crusoe, the sailor Alexander Selkirk, came from. He wanted lots of things that they were not, in the end, able to do. Instead they had to come home because there was a crisis at Brookfield.

Jill had been looking tired and lethargic for weeks: in fact, Doris had been hard pushed to know how to divide her worrying between her and Chris. Nothing anyone said could persuade Jill to go to the doctor and she'd become increasingly snappy when anyone had suggested it. Then, while Chris and Paul were away, she'd collapsed in the bathroom the night before Shula's eighteenth birthday party, and had been whipped into Borchester General in a coma. The doctors said it was a thyroid deficiency – myxoedema – but complicated by a kidney infection, which made the position very grave. The next few days, they said, would be critical. Poor Phil – in the middle of harvest – was spending day and night at the hospital, and poor Shula, who blamed herself for the stress of the party arrangements and for not forcing her mother to get medical help, was hardly in a position to cover for Chris at the stables as she'd promised to do. Doris, of course, was beside herself about both Jill and Phil as the shadow of Grace seemed to hover over him again.

So, having heard all this over the phone, Chris and Paul bundled poor Peter into the car again for the monumental drive. They tore back to Borsetshire, barely stopping, and raced to the hospital, only to find that Jill was out of danger, Shula was coping at Brookfield and Doris was gradually returning to a state of calm. It didn't look as though they'd be needed after all.

'Let's go away again,' said Chris impulsively when they finally reached home. It was nearly ten and they'd been back all of half an hour. Peter had gone to bed without a bath, dead beat, but Chris didn't feel remotely tired. Back in Ambridge she felt agitated, wound up. She felt as if she might suffocate even though Paul was going round the house flinging open the windows.

'All the way back to Scotland? You must be mad.'

The flower borders Chris had planted were still smelling sweet and their scent oozed inside on the humid air. Chris gulped a breath. Their time away had been useless. She and Paul had had no chance to be together, let alone to talk about everything that had precipitated the Scottish trip in the first place.

'The West Country, then,' she said desperately. 'Lyme Regis, Charmouth . . . we'd get in somewhere.'

'There's no need.' Paul stood calmly at the French windows and spoke into the darkness outside. He breathed appreciatively. 'Mmm. Silence, stillness, the scent of the flowers . . .'

'Stocks,' said Christine automatically.

'I don't want to work in London any longer,' he said calmly. He still had his back to her. 'Whatever happens, I've finished with that job, that place, that . . .' – he wouldn't or couldn't say 'woman' – 'that flat . . . everything about the place.' He turned towards her and she could see that he meant it. 'I've finished with it, Chris.'

Chris waited to feel something. Relief, at least, or a rush of love? She should surely want to burst into happy tears, or to hug him close? She felt absolutely nothing. Her heart was beating fast and she felt slightly sick, but that was all. Then she realized what it was. Despite the physical agitation, she felt utterly weary. She'd been through all this before. She knew that though Paul said everything was finished, her work was just starting. She had to rebuild her trust in him all over again. She would have to face the family and explain that Paul was giving up his job, and smile through the cooings of how nice it would be for her to have him around more, and how he must have finally come to his senses and realized he couldn't live without her, hah-hah. And try to believe it wouldn't happen again.

If Chris had known, of course, how much the family had already inferred, or if her pride had allowed her to tell them the truth, she would have saved herself a huge amount of effort and gained a huge amount of support. But what had always been most important to her was her dignity. Almost worse than the hurt of Paul's betrayal was the humiliation she knew she would have felt if it had all had to come out.

Only her father, wise as ever, suspected something was up. Or at least, he was the only person who actually said anything.

'A bit sudden, wasn't it, this change of heart?' he asked her. It was September and they were out collecting blackberries before the song-thrushes and blackbirds got to them.

'You know Paul. Never been one to hang around.' She pulled a bright cluster of berries from a branch.

'What are you going to do for money? You'll be the sole bread-winner after the end of the month.'

'Oh, Paul'll find something. He always does.'

She wished she really felt as confident. To say Paul had had a chequered career was an understatement: his CV read like a suicide note. And firms these days, hit by inflation, were laying people off, not taking them on.

'You've had your share of worries with him, haven't you, love?'

Christine was silent. She couldn't betray Paul, even to the person who, with her mother, cared about her most in the world. Dan put his arm round her and squeezed her against him.

'Any time you want a chat, Chris . . .'

'Thanks, Dad. But it's all right. We'll survive.'

But as she rode out in the burnished September mornings, Chris considered her family and her place in it. Look at her parents, secure and happy in their marriage after almost fifty-five years. Look at Phil and Jill. Jill was out of hospital now, pledging to give up some of her outside commitments and conserve her energy, while Phil remonstrated with himself for spending too much time on the farm and not enough in the farmhouse. Their children were growing up fast: Kenton and Shula eighteen, David doing his A-levels, Elizabeth ten next birthday. Then there was Peggy, on her own admittedly, but with her rosy memories of her marriage and with all three of her children happily settled, two of them in Ambridge. Tony and Pat were still blissfully happy, working Willow Farm together, and Jennifer, Chris felt sure, was settled for life with Brian. Even the teething troubles with Adam had worked themselves out – he'd been scared, he finally admitted, that Brian would go off and leave them, like Roger had done. By contrast, what had Chris got to look back on as she and Paul approached their twentieth wedding anniversary? A marriage that had been blighted by Paul's unreliability at work and in his personal life. She'd 'won', she supposed, the battle with Brenda, but what were the spoils? Life with a man who'd started out as a loving husband and companion and was now someone whom she couldn't much respect any more.

She couldn't help but compare herself with Jennifer. In some ways they'd seemed to have the perfect set-up when they were living together at Wynfords. They'd had their children, their work, their family and friends. Paul's absences – and his arrival home – had seemed less important then. But Roger had wanted a divorce, Jennifer had had to accede, and now look at her. Newly settled with the wealthiest farmer in the district, a father for her children and someone who seemingly adored her.

What am I saying? thought Chris to herself, as she galloped up Heydon Berrow, pushing the horse and herself to their limits, forcing herself to think the unthinkable. That I'd have preferred it if Paul had gone off with Brenda? When it had seemed a possibility, she'd been terrified. And she knew then that it was all too late for her and Paul. If they'd been going to part, they should have done it years ago. Now they were linked for life. As they'd promised each other nearly twenty years ago: for better, for worse.

She wasn't really the best person to have to listen, then, when she trotted back into the yard to find Shula there, glumly shining up a saddle and all too ready to unburden herself about the agonies of being young and in love.

Shula had been round Europe in the summer with Michele, an intrepid New Zealander who'd turned up at Brookfield with the sheep-shearers. She'd thrown Bill Morris over some time before because he was 'too full of himself', and while she was away had fallen heavily for a Spaniard called, inevitably, Pedro.

'You've no idea, Auntie Chris,' she breathed dreamily as Chris rubbed down her horse. 'We sat on the beach at midnight and he told me I was beautiful and he'd never met anyone like me.'

'Really?' said Chris kindly, thinking, 'until the next plane-load of tourists flew in'.

'He said he'd write. I'm thinking of signing up for an evening class, then I can write back in Spanish.'

'Another language would always come in useful,' Chris equivocated, hoping she was saying the right things.

'Oh, there's no point pretending.' Shula suddenly flung down her bit of rag. Chris's horse stamped in surprise. 'I know I'll never hear from him again.'

'There, boy, it's all right.' Chris restrained the horse's jerking head. 'You might.'

'No. Anyway, what's the point. I'd just like – oh, I don't know. My life's such a mess. I don't know what to do for a job, I can't meet anyone who's right for me . . .'

'Oh dear, you are in a bad way.'

Chris smiled inwardly. All this adolescent angst. She supposed she'd be going through it with Peter soon. And she was still going through it with Paul.

'I just want to meet someone who's worthy of me, Auntie Chris. I don't want to throw myself away on someone who doesn't appreciate me. I mean, we're all special, aren't we? I may not have made it to Montreal with the Olympic equestrian team this year, and I'm never going to. But I'm still worth something. I think so anyway.'

Shula's words replayed in Chris's head all day as she shouted instructions to pupils and led a small group out for a hack along the leaf-strewn lanes.

Paul didn't truly appreciate her. Perhaps he never had. But she'd let him get away with it because she hadn't known or expected any better. And much as Jennifer's present situation seemed perfect,

Chris knew that she'd had her confidence severely knocked by Roger. He'd made her doubt herself as a wife, a mother, a writer, everything. And yet Jennifer was fifteen years younger than Chris – practically a different generation. She'd grown up in the free-thinking, free-living 1960s. She'd been the family rebel, but she was still, eventually, influenced by her need to be approved of and given a place, a status in life, by a man.

It was only young women like Shula – at eighteen, thirteen years younger again than Jennifer – who really knew where they were going. Shula wouldn't have called herself a feminist. She still wanted a relationship – and why not? Even Chris had to admit that though she'd had some of the worst times of her life with Paul, she'd also had some of the best times. But Shula would make sure that any relationship she entered into was an equal one, where her needs counted for just as much and her voice was heard.

It might be too late for her, but Chris was glad, very glad, that her niece's generation, and Peter's generation, wouldn't be repeating the mistakes of the past.

·13·

Discoveries

'What exactly does Shula think she's playing at?' fumed Phil. He moved along the milking parlour, bending to remove the teat cups from a cow that had finished.

Jill followed between the rumps of cows and foaming jars of milk, watching where she put her feet.

'I don't suppose she posed for the photograph,' she said mildly. 'Else she wouldn't have looked so startled.'

' "Hunting on the Dole"!' From his pocket, Phil took out a copy of the *Borchester Echo* and waved it at Jill. Under a banner headline, they'd printed a huge photograph of Shula soaring over a fence on her favourite horse, Mister Jones.

'It's not bad of her, though, is it?' said Jill proudly. The cows turned and looked at the photograph too, with their conker-coloured eyes. 'Do you think we could get a print?'

'A print? Never mind that, how does it make *me* look?' Phil stuffed the paper back in his pocket. 'I'm going to be sworn in as a JP in a few weeks, don't forget.'

'I know, dear,' soothed Jill, adding, 'I'm sure she didn't do it on purpose.'

'I'm not sure of anything any more.' Phil squirted disinfectant over a cow's udder. 'The only time she speaks to me is to make some facetious comment about my appearance or to ask me for a loan. Well, she needn't think I'll be paying her hunt subscription after this!'

Jill shook her head wearily as she walked back to the house. There'd been friction between Shula and Phil ever since she'd got to know Simon Parker, the new editor of the *Echo*. One week Shula had

185

been bemoaning the lack of a man in her life, the next it had been 'Simon says this' and 'Simon thinks that'. Jennifer knew him already, from the 'Country Notes' column she wrote for the paper, and she'd given Jill the low-down. He was thirty-three, keenly ambitious, devilishly handsome and – well, devilish full stop, really. When they'd first met, Shula had told him about how the committee wouldn't allow a Youth Club in Ambridge village hall. Newly promoted, freed from the tyranny of writing 'Scouting Notes by Woodsmoke' and subbing down the purple prose of local WI secretaries, Simon had seized on the story. 'The Village That Forgot Its Young', he headlined the article, and quoted 'bubbly blonde farmer's daughter Shula Archer' at length.

That had started Phil worrying that Simon was after Shula, and Jill was sure that he was, so she couldn't understand why he'd now gone ahead and printed the hunting story, which could only cause her embarrassment. It wasn't Shula's fault that so few jobs came up in Borchester. She'd only claimed the dole for a bit: she was intending to fill in as Phil's farm secretary in the weeks before Christmas when he planned to catch up with his paperwork. Jill couldn't help wishing that Shula could find a proper job, though, to help reconcile her to the fact that the career she'd dreamed of all of her life, working with horses, just wasn't going to materialize.

Shula bought her copy of the paper in Borchester, from the blind man by the market cross, and when she opened it in Underwoods cafeteria – she might as well treat herself if no one else was going to – she almost choked on her coffee. She scrambled back into her coat, collected her parcels – she'd been doing some early Christmas shopping – and went straight to confront Simon.

'How dare you?' she demanded. 'A feature piece about the hunt, you told me.'

'It's come out rather well, hasn't it?' It was a quiet day for him now the paper was out and he was loafing about the office on his own.

'I thought we were friends!' Her voice wobbled with indignation. 'My dad's going to go spare!'

'Shula, Shula.' He got up and came towards her with a cynical smile. 'Don't get so excited. It'll be lining cat-litter trays all over Borsetshire tomorrow. I thought you'd see the joke.'

He put out a hand towards her but she backed away.

'Joke? What joke?'

He perched on a nearby desk and looked at her winningly.

'Let me buy you lunch to make up for it. The Feathers? A steaming bowl of their home-made soup and some French bread? And a ginger wine to go with it?'

Shula gave in. She couldn't imagine ever doing anything but give in to Simon. Women never did, which was why he was so unbearable and so attractive all at once. Shula wondered why she found his arrogance quite so compelling. Perhaps it was because her dad was just too nice.

Her father was nice to her about the hunting story in the end, and he was nice when she started as his farm secretary and made a bit of a muddle of the wage packets, and he was even nicer when Mr Rodway, of Rodway and Watson, Estate Agents, rang and offered her the job she'd applied for.

'You're glad to get rid of me!' she accused him as he poured her a celebratory sherry. Shula didn't think the job of office junior was much to celebrate but her father wasn't having any of it.

'It's a very sound start,' he beamed. 'You could be on the way to a proper career.'

Yes, thought Shula miserably, and not the one I'd envisaged.

She hated Rodway's at first. She hated the routine and being stuck in an office and having to remember the sweeteners for Mr Rodway's coffee. She hated not being able to phone her friends when she wanted and she really hated having to get up at seven thirty every day. Most of all she hated not being able to walk out of the Brookfield yard and down the track across the fields to say hello to the sheep, or to see if she could catch sight of the woodpeckers digging out grubs from the dead elms.

But knowing Simon helped. She had to phone him quite legitimately sometimes about planning permissions and listed buildings and he always made her laugh. He'd often come and whisk her out from under Mr Rodway's nose and take her to lunch, from which she came back flushed and giggling and quite incapable of decoding her wobbly shorthand outlines. The afternoons didn't seem to drag so much after lunch with Simon.

By the time the spring came, she felt confident enough to call him her boyfriend, even though he was desperately unreliable, always being late and breaking dates. Still, Shula understood. Deadlines, leads, contacts: a breaking news story was no respecter of arrangements. Considering this was what her dad always said about a calving cow, it was a pity he couldn't be a bit more understanding.

All Phil wanted to understand was what Shula saw in Simon. To his mind, she was mad. To think she'd thrown over Charles Hodgeson, member of the Hunt and chairman of the Borchester Young Conservatives, for that inky blighter Parker – frankly, Phil despaired. Jill listened loyally to Phil's tirades about Shula's waywardness but she kept her own counsel. She wasn't particularly thrilled about Shula's choice either, though not for the same reasons as Phil. Jill could detect something different in her daughter. Shula was on edge all the time, as if she were playing a part. She was trying to be the witty, brittle character she thought Simon wanted. But underneath it all, Jill felt Shula had lost her heart to Simon; she just hoped he'd keep it in one piece.

May arrived, in all its giddy glory.

'Can't *you* have a word with Shula?' Phil beseeched Jennifer. She'd come to talk to Jill about the village celebrations for the Queen's Silver Jubilee and had found Phil in the house, waiting for a phone call. Jennifer, who was expecting a baby in September, finished pouring herself a cup of tea.

'To do what?'

'To put her off Parker.'

'But I like him,' she said, dunking one of Jill's chocolate chip cookies in her cup. 'He's intelligent. He's a good deal more interesting than the Charles Hodgesons of this world.'

'That's your opinion,' snorted Phil.

'Yes, it is,' confirmed Jennifer, 'and quite honestly, it's not my business to put Shula off Simon Parker or anyone else.'

Phil grimaced. He remembered now. Pregnancy did make women unbelievably stubborn.

'Well, at least don't encourage her,' he conceded.

'It's no good, Phil,' Jennifer asserted through a chocolatey mouthful. 'Shula's got to be allowed to make her own mistakes. I was, and look at me now.'

That was another thing. And it wasn't just because of her pregnancy. Since she'd married Brian, Jennifer did seem to have become incredibly smug. Tony was always saying so, and now Phil could see why.

'Well, if you won't help, all I can do is keep my fingers crossed,' he said. 'I just feel I don't want Shula to get involved with Simon Parker. Now or at any time.'

It was almost a month later, 21 June – the summer solstice: the longest day and the shortest night. It was dark, even so, when Shula got home from an evening out with Simon. Jill was out too, at a WI skittles evening, and Phil was alone in the sitting room listening to a Mahler symphony. Shula flopped down languidly on the sofa. She looked a bit odd, Phil thought, bright-eyed and suspiciously rosy. Parker had probably been plying her with drink.

'Mmm,' she sighed. 'I've had a lovely evening.'

'Good,' said Phil, and then grudgingly: 'Did you do anything special?'

'Hmm? No, not really.' She yawned and trailed the fingers of one hand up and down her arm. 'We went to a meeting of the Netherbourne Angry Residents Association.'

'The what?'

'That was what Simon called them. They're driving each other up the village maypole.'

At least, that was how the evening had started. Simon had had to cover it for the paper. Then they'd gone for a drink at The Crown and then, driving back past Netherbourne Woods, Simon had suddenly stopped the car.

'D'you know what I've always wanted to do?' he asked. Shula shook her head. 'Make love to a beautiful girl in the middle of a huge cornfield on a warm summer's evening.'

And that was how, on the rug from the boot of the car, Shula had let him make love to her. Not in the middle of the cornfield – the NFU would have had something to say about people who tramped into the middle of a crop, and she was a farmer's daughter after all – but at the edge, under the lacy elderflowers, beside the ears of wheat.

• • •

'I don't know what you want me to do about it.'

'I just thought . . .' began Jennifer.

'As long as he does his job, it's none of my concern who Simon Parker sees,' Jack Woolley asserted. 'Now come on, Jennifer, try one of these. You're eating for two, you know.'

Jennifer didn't need any persuading to help herself to a miniature raspberry *mille feuille* from the plate her boss was offering her. Grey Gables's new chef Jean-Paul really was a find.

She wasn't sure what had prompted her to bring up the subject of Shula and Simon with Jack, except a slightly guilty feeling of having been rather dismissive of Phil's concerns. Jack did own the *Echo*, after all: if Simon needed bringing in line, he was the man to do it.

'It's just that he's so much older than Shula and so much more – well, experienced. I know Phil and Jill are worried.'

Jill had told her that Shula and Simon were seeing more and more of each other, and that Shula was getting home later and later. Jennifer privately thought they were lucky she was coming home at all, but she hadn't wanted to put that thought into Jill's head.

'I'm sorry, Jennifer.' Jack sprayed her with crumbs as he spoke. 'I didn't quiz him about his moral standards when he took the job. I mean, if he had any, he wouldn't be a journalist, would he?' Chuckling at his own observation, he wiped a blob of cream from his moustache. 'Anyway, if they're having fun, what does it matter?'

Jennifer wondered if Shula was on the pill, and if Jill had thought of this. Jack was busily tucking into a mini-éclair.

'I'd better get back to work, I think, Mr Woolley.'

Jack looked at his watch.

'Goodness me, yes. I've got Paul Johnson coming by in a bit. Says he's got something he wants to discuss with me urgently.'

Jennifer knew why. She'd heard about it from Doris. It was another of Paul's crazy ideas, although this one sounded crazier than all the others put together. He wanted to see Jack, her gran had told her, to ask if he'd go in with him on a site on the River Am at Grey Gables. He wanted to start a fish farm. Trout. Honestly, poor Chris. Was there no end to it?

There was no end to it for Phil, certainly, where Simon Parker was concerned. Or at least no end to his habit, as Phil saw it, of defaming him or his family in print.

'Look at this! "Farmers are the fat cats of society"!' In the yard at Brookfield, Phil thrust the latest edition of the *Echo*, and the article with Simon's offending byline, under Shula's nose. 'Say what you like, the whole thing is a deliberate attack on me!'

Shula had been perfectly happy until then. The previous evening she'd had a wonderful time with Simon at his flat in Borchester. This morning, ravenously hungry for some reason, she'd got up early and gone out mushrooming in the sharp September air.

'Did you see this vicious article he wrote?' her father demanded.

Shula examined the pleated underside of a mushroom.

'No . . . I mean, I glanced at it. Look, Dad, I think he just wants to be lively and to . . . I don't know . . . make things jump.'

'Jump!' exploded Phil. 'He'll jump when he finds a cartload of slurry dumped outside his office!'

Jethro lumbered up with some lugubrious question about a hedge and Shula was saved from a full-scale argument, but she knew it had only postponed the inevitable. Her father and Simon were bound to meet before long, and Phil wasn't in the mood to let things lie.

A couple of days later it was the Harvest Supper. Shula was torn.

She hated the thought of spending an evening without Simon, but if he came along, he'd have to see her father. In the end, it wasn't much of a struggle. She was so weak-willed where Simon was concerned. And weak-kneed, she conceded, as they walked hand-in-hand down to the village for the festivities.

He was wearing his old denim shirt, her favourite. The sleeves were rolled back and where his skin brushed hers she kept getting tiny tingling shocks which seemed to jump-start her heart. It was all very well her dad going on about Simon having no conscience and the morals of a wild mink: her dad couldn't see how gorgeous he was.

'Can't you write something nice about farmers?' she pleaded.

He shot her a sideways look.

'What, and lose my integrity?'

That would be nothing, Shula thought, compared with what she'd lost to Simon. They walked on in silence for a bit.

'Hmm. I'll have to see,' he pondered. 'Perhaps I can manage a faint note of sympathy for the struggling pig industry.'

Shula felt cheered. Her dad had only been saying at breakfast what a bad year they'd had with the pigs.

'Come on,' she said, pulling him towards the village hall. 'We'll miss the community singing.'

'Hah! It's the ritual sacrifice I'm worried about,' he retorted, dragging behind. 'With your Aunt Laura as the arch-druidess.'

'She won't even be there,' Shula reassured him. 'She's had to go into hospital for tests.' Laura had badly burnt her hand and it was possible she might need a skin graft. 'Freddie Danby's organizing it all.'

Colonel Danby, an old soldier of limited means, was Aunt Laura's lodger. Simon's face brightened.

'I was expecting bread and cheese. Does he do a good curry?'

'That's all he does do. Poor Aunt Laura's tastebuds will need a skin graft soon. Oh, hello, Dad.'

They all arrived at the village hall together. Phil had driven Jill down in the Land Rover with the back seat full of puddings.

'Evening, Simon,' said Phil frostily.

'Dad, perhaps you could show Simon where to get a drink,' she suggested. 'I promised Mum I'd give her a hand in the kitchen.'

She didn't see much of Simon after that. He seemed to fall in with Joe Grundy and his sons Alf and Eddie, knocking back vast quantities of scrumpy and making up rude words to Uncle Tom's party piece, 'The Village Pump'.

After supper was over, though, as she helped clear the tables, she saw Simon and her father deep in conversation. She didn't dare to go over, not even to warn Simon to go easy on the Grundys' cider. Instead she hid in the kitchen, peeping out occasionally from under the roller shutter and listening to her Auntie Chris droning on about Paul's plans for the fishery, which was now up and running and stocked with 20,000 seven-inch trout. It all sounded very dodgy, especially as Paul had gaily handed in his notice at the agricultural machinery place where he'd been working and the only money they had to live on until the trout grew big enough to sell was Auntie Chris's earnings from the stables. But at least it took Shula's mind off what Simon and her dad might be discussing.

She wouldn't have believed it, but Phil was, in fact, giving Simon some well-meaning advice.

'I . . . er . . . I'd be careful how much of that you drink if I were you,' he cautioned as Simon refilled his glass.

'It's very pleasant. They call it scrumpy, I believe.'

'In some places.' Phil had heard it called far worse things.

'And locally made,' enthused Simon. 'It might make a feature.'

'Surely not,' said Phil acidly. 'An article that doesn't knock farmers?'

'Oh.' said Simon. 'I think I know what you're getting at.'

'Tell me,' Phil enquired, sensing an advantage, 'what exactly is a fat cat? Apart from an overfed tabby?'

He was gratified to see Simon was sweating slightly, although that could just have been the drink.

'Well . . .' Simon replied guardedly, 'a fat cat is someone who's sleek and . . . prosperous . . . and . . . doing pretty well for himself.'

Phil straightened the salt and pepper pots on the cloth.

'I see.'

'Look . . . if you're talking about last week's *Echo*,' Simon went on, 'I didn't mean . . . that is . . . the thing is, there was nothing personal.'

Was this the person whose typewriter dripped venom? Who fought fearlessly for the freedom of the press? Phil had never heard him so apologetic or, for that matter, so incoherent.

'Are you sure you're all right?' he asked.

Simon shooed away his concern.

'I'm fine.' He leant forward – or rather, lurched forward. Phil shrank back. 'Actually, Shula's going to ask you something . . . concerning the two of us.'

Hit by lightning, Phil sat forward again.

'What was that?'

'She's worried you might put your foot down . . .' Simon burbled. 'Refuse to give your approval . . . because you don't like me very much.'

Phil was struck dumb. Surely not. Impossible. Shula couldn't be thinking of *marrying* the man?

The trestle table rocked as Simon leaned on it to get up.

'Excuse me . . . can you tell me where . . .' he said worriedly. He was still sweating but he'd gone terribly pale.

'Oh, down at the end, but – wait a minute.'

But Simon was gone, pushing his way through the crowd with his hand over his mouth.

Phil sat back and blinked, trying to take in what he'd been told. He and Jill were going to have to box clever over this one. When Shula set her mind on something she could be very stubborn indeed. There was no question about how Simon had managed to persuade her – she was clearly besotted – but what were his motives? He was thirty-three, he'd avoided marriage for this long and suddenly . . . A cold dread coated Phil. Surely Simon didn't intend to try and get his hands on Brookfield?

When they got home, Phil told Jill his suspicions. Shula was out in the yard with Simon. The taxi she'd rung to take him back to Borchester had just arrived and she was giving the driver instructions to see him right up to the flat.

'Shh. Now be careful what you say,' warned Phil as they heard the taxi pull away.

'Me? You're always the one . . .' Jill began.

Phil shushed her as Shula came in.

'I hope Simon's all right,' she fretted. 'It was a bit rotten of you, Dad, sitting watching him drink all that cider.'

'I can't stop *you* drinking,' protested Phil. 'I don't see how I'm supposed to stop *him*. Er . . . Shula . . .' There was no point in waiting. He didn't see how he'd sleep a wink if he didn't get the truth out of her tonight. 'Simon said something to me, just before he turned green.'

'Phil –' cautioned Jill.

'We might as well know the worst,' he told her. 'I mean, find out what's going on.' He turned to Shula. 'He said you wanted to . . . ask our consent to something. You were worried about our reaction.'

'Oh . . . oh yes.' Shula looked down at the floor.

She looked so vulnerable that all Phil's resolve melted. What could they do? She was crazy about the wretched man. He obviously made her happy. However much fuss he and Jill made, she wouldn't take any notice, and it might turn her against them for life.

'I don't know why you should be afraid of speaking out,' he said kindly. 'If you and he . . . well, it's your life.'

'You don't mind? Oh, Dad.'

She threw herself at him and gave him an enormous hug, which Phil returned. Over Shula's head, he gave Jill a helpless look.

'Oh, Shula,' said Jill, already smelling the orange blossom, 'all we want is your happiness.'

Shula beamed electrically at her mother.

'It would only be for ten days.'

'*What?*' asked Phil.

'And there'd be a whole group of us!' She turned back to Phil and hugged him again. 'Oh, Dad, thanks for being so super about it!'

After all that, it turned out that she'd only wanted to ask for permission to go skiing in Austria.

Phil's worst fears might not have been realized, but there was still plenty for him to fret about. Slippery slopes, for a start . . .

'She's told us she'll be sharing with this Penelope girl,' soothed Jill reasonably, as he worried out loud the following evening. 'Are you saying you think she's a liar?'

'No, of course not, but you know how it is!'

Jill pushed her needle through her tapestry and out again.

'Do I?'

Phil rubbed his forehead impatiently.

'All the *après-ski* and schnapps and sneaking along corridors at midnight! I can't imagine Simon taking no for an answer! And she might just be besotted enough to give in to him!'

Poor Phil. He wasn't to know that his concerns for his daughter's honour were purely academic.

'And then where does that leave her,' he continued, pacing the sitting room, 'if, God forbid, she's serious about him? A man like Simon's not going to buy the cow if he's already drinking the milk, is he?'

'Phil!' Jill wrinkled her nose. 'That's a bit crude!'

'Well, I'm sorry, Jill, but all she'll get out of this skiing trip is a reputation and a broken heart.'

'So, Shula's off in January,' Jill told Jennifer when she and Christine went to visit her a couple of days later in hospital. She'd just given birth to a daughter, Katherine Victoria, to be known as Kate.

'We'll have to give her something towards her spending money.' Having displayed the baby to her admirers, Jennifer laid her back in her crib. 'For looking after Adam and Debbie the other night.'

Jennifer had gone into labour during the evening and Shula had been called on to put the children to bed at Home Farm.

'She enjoyed doing it,' said Jill. 'Phil said she seemed very maternal. Which worried him even more!'

Christine smiled to herself. Barely a year ago, she'd been telling herself that Shula was different. Now it seemed that she was going to be a slave to emotion and biology, just like the rest of them. A year ago, she'd felt at rock bottom with Paul after the shock and pain of his affair. But as the hurt had receded and slowly, slowly, the habit, then the affection and then the trust had come back, she'd decided that she and Paul were meant to be together. Now he had his new enterprise at the fish farm, he was the old Paul again, the Paul she'd married – ambitious, optimistic and charismatic.

Paul and his fish farm! When he'd first told her back in the summer that he wanted to quit the safe, if dull, job he'd found in Borchester and set up on his own, raising trout for the table, she'd wanted to laugh out loud. Not because the idea was so ridiculous – Paul reckoned he'd make 100 per cent profit in the next fortnight when he sold the trout he'd bought in August – but out of sheer relief. He'd spent a couple of weeks being so preoccupied and furtive that she'd been briefly convinced that he'd started seeing Brenda – or someone – again. When it transpired that he hadn't, Chris had felt triumphant. She began to feel as if she need never worry again. He was wayward, he'd strayed in the past, but he was cured of all that. And even if Paul's interest did wander, she truly believed he'd always come home. He needed the security. He needed her.

The baby whimpered and Jennifer shot to soothe her. Chris watched wryly as Jennifer picked Kate up again and placed her against her shoulder. The modern world had changed a lot of things but some, clearly, were going to take longer than others.

·14·

Endurance

Kate's arrival had some surprising repercussions. Brian had been fascinated by Jennifer's pregnancy in a scientific, farmerish sort of way, but few expected his interest to outlast the birth. They were wrong. He turned out to be a doting father, carrying Kate around the sugar beet and the sheep pens and explaining to her why the ewes had different colours on their backs (the rams were in with them) and the importance of detecting foot-rot. Jennifer was so delighted that she quite forgave him his recent jibes about her bottom sliding down her legs and applied herself to her post-natal exercises with a new determination. Visits to Home Farm turned Pat very broody, but Tony told her firmly that another baby was out of the question until they were settled at Bridge Farm on the Estate, which they were to take over as tenants next Lady Day. And Shula continued to be surprisingly maternal with the baby, which did nothing to assuage Phil's concern over her proposed ten days in a ski-lodge with Simon.

Christine smiled and observed it all. She could well remember her own passionate longing for a baby and she was grateful that it had passed. Now, she couldn't imagine why she had ever thought she needed a baby when, after all, she had Paul.

She looked down indulgently as she stood over him with his breakfast tray. It was the end of October and he'd been up in London the day before. He'd got back late, tired and frazzled, and though he'd asked her to wake him at his usual time she'd decided to let him sleep in. He'd been working what seemed like twenty-five hours a day since he'd set up the fish farm and Chris thought he was due a break.

Endurance

He was lying on his back, snoring slightly, or as he would insist if she challenged him, breathing heavily. Chris eased the tray on to the bedside table, then leaned down and kissed his half-open mouth. He smiled in his sleep.

'Is that you, darling?'

'Who else?'

Chris went to draw the curtains. Paul raised himself up on his elbow, yawning and scratching his head. Then he saw the clock.

'It's practically afternoon! Why didn't you wake me?'

Chris motioned him to sit forward while she propped a pillow on its end behind him. Then she plonked the tray on his lap, pushed his legs over and sat on the edge of the bed.

'Because you needed your sleep, that's why.'

He was bare-chested and still, Chris thought, heart-stoppingly handsome. She wanted nothing more than to snuggle in beside him, but he was tetchily tapping the shell of his egg and pointing out that of his two helpers at the fish farm, Jim Oakley was away and Percy Jordan wouldn't be in till mid-morning.

Heigh-ho, thought Chris, I can't win. I give him the mistress treatment and he wants me to behave like a nagging wife.

'Slow down!' she chided. 'You're entitled to take it easy sometimes.'

Paul, who was slurping coffee, chomping toast and spooning in egg like a man possessed, shot her a look as the phone shrilled beside them.

'See? They're chasing me up.'

Coffee slopped on to the saucer as he crashed down his cup but Christine reached the receiver first. It was probably for her, anyway.

But it was Percy Jordan. He wanted to speak to Paul. He sounded in a dreadful state.

'What a mess!'

They'd rushed to the fish farm and, as Percy had dolefully promised them, it was a terrible sight. Thousands and thousands of dead trout, slithery not silvery, the iridescence bloated out of their scales, flabby and already starting to smell.

Paul had taken charge straight away, instructing Percy to drain the water out of the tanks and then get rid of the fish, but Christine knew from his face that this was not just serious, it was a disaster – and though, over the next few days, she denied it to Paul time after time, she knew it was all his fault. Not because he'd been sitting in bed eating soft-boiled eggs that morning but because he'd rushed into this fish farming business – he'd been under-capitalized and he'd cut corners. He'd cut the corner, for example, that would have provided a stand-by pump to switch on automatically when the other one, the filters choked with autumn leaves, had failed. And, crucially, he'd cut the corner that would have insured them against the loss.

'It's really bad luck.' Tony, who'd come up that morning intending to have a go at Paul for pinching Percy Jordan, his relief milker, from him, was feeling both guilty and grateful. If ever there was a lesson for him and Pat about not over-reaching themselves when they got to Bridge Farm, this was it.

Christine stuffed her hands in her pockets and said nothing. She could see her mother's tight-drawn look when she'd told her about Paul's latest venture.

'Does he have to leave his job?' Doris had worried. 'Couldn't he do this fish farming part time till it's established? It puts such a pressure on you, Chris, when you have to be the only breadwinner.'

And, as ever, Chris had defended Paul. Said he wanted to do it whole-heartedly or not at all. Said he'd done all his research. Said he'd found the site: a couple of disused tanks at Grey Gables, where Jack Woolley had once thought of running a sporting fishery. And then, to prove to the family her belief in her husband, she'd sold the paddock behind their house to Phil, to enable Paul to buy in the 20,000 trout that would be fattened up to half a pound weight and sold to the catering trade. The 20,000 dead, useless, stinking trout that would now, along with all Paul's hopes, have to be thrown away.

'I really am sorry, Chris.' She blinked as she tried to concentrate on what Tony was saying. 'If there's anything Pat or I can do...'

Christine screwed up her eyes and looked at the sky. She badly didn't want to cry in front of Tony. When she and Paul had driven hell-for-leather over to the fishery, it had been a perfect autumn day. The sky had been a hesitant blue with a faint marbling of cloud and the sun had lain on the ploughed fields' curves. In the hour or so they had been there, though, grey clouds had swelled on the horizon and a freshening wind hissed in the trees. There would be rain again before long.

Paul approached them over the muddied grass.

'Come to gloat, have you?' He spoke sharply to Tony.

'Paul,' chided Chris. 'Tony was just offering to help.'

'It's a bit late for that,' said Paul shortly. 'Oh, by the way, you can have Percy Jordan as often as you like now. It looks as though my famous fish farm has gone out of business for good.'

• • •

'Oh, well, that's marvellous! All our problems solved in one fell swoop! Step forward St Dan of Ambridge, the patriarch with the golden cheque book.'

'Paul! Stop it!'

Paul raked savagely at some leaves. He was building a bonfire. November the fifth was approaching and they had promised Peter fireworks in the garden. As Paul said bitterly, life must go on. 'You can't see it, can you?' He stopped work abruptly. 'I've got a creditors' meeting arranged for Thursday, during which I'm planning to abase myself, grovel and ask for one year's grace to pay them back, but is that enough for your family? No, they have to patronize me to the end. They're as good as telling me not to bother sorting things out. Why should I when your doting dad and dear brother will do it for me?'

Chris had just taken a phone call from her father and had rushed out into the garden to tell Paul about it. Dan had, he thought, come up with the perfect solution. He'd talked at length to Phil. They'd taken advice from the accountant and the bank manager. What they were proposing was that Ambridge Farmers Limited buy the stables for Christine.

'I don't know what's got into you!' she cried. 'I wish I'd never told you!'

She had charged out from the house without a coat, and felt the still afternoon air enter her lungs, cool and medicinal as menthol.

'I don't know why you bothered,' said Paul coldly. 'I mean, think about it, Chris. They're not doing it for me, are they? This is all about you.'

He threw down the rake and marched off towards the house. Chris heard the front door bang and the car motor start.

'Mum?'

Peter appeared round the side of the house: he'd been out on his bike with Adam. Damn. He must have heard it all.

Chris opened her arms and he came towards her. In private, he was still enough of a child not to be ashamed to show her affection. He slid his arms round her waist and put his head on her shoulder.

'Mum,' he said, 'will you tell me what's going on? Are you and Dad getting a divorce?'

At least she could answer that one honestly.

'No,' she said softly. 'Dad's just got some problems with the business, that's all.'

'Oh, that,' said Peter, pulling away and looking up at her. 'They've all been talking about it at school. They're saying he's gone bust.'

'And what do you say to that?'

'I tell them they don't know my dad. He'll find a way out of it somehow.'

Chris smiled.

'You're right. I'm sure he will.'

But it seemed that Paul's usual ability to emerge from a crisis shaken but not stirred had deserted him this time. Jack Woolley spoke up for him at the creditors' meeting and waived the rent on the hatchery tanks, but not everyone had Jack's belief in Paul, or perhaps not Jack's deep pockets. To a man, they opted for getting their money sooner rather than later, and Paul had only two options. He could let them make him bankrupt or he could bankrupt himself. He chose the latter. Even at the end, he liked to believe he had some control over his fate.

'So,' said Chris brightly to Jennifer when she called round a few days later, 'there's some good news. The Official Receiver's been this morning and we can keep the house for the moment. The fact that we remortgaged it has turned it into a liability, not an asset, which is rather lucky really. And we can keep the car because we said I need it for my business. Paul's bank account's been frozen, of course, and they've made us install a pre-pay electricity meter –'

'Oh, Chris.' If she hadn't been holding Kate, who'd fallen asleep halfway through her feed, Jennifer would have leapt up and hugged her. Chris noted the instinctive movement and was grateful that she hadn't. She'd get through this, she thought, as long as no one touched her, or was too kind. She bought time, and strength, by pouring them each another cup of tea.

'Still, at least Paul's given up spouting on about Dad's idea of buying the stables.'

Jennifer stirred sugar into her cup with her free hand.

'He's come round to seeing that it's a good idea?'

'Come on, Jennifer, you know Paul better than that. Even if he did, he'd never admit it. No, I think he's just decided he can't fight on all fronts at once.'

The truth of it was that all the fight seemed to have gone out of Paul. All their married life Chris had marvelled at – and often resented – how he'd emerge smiling from the things he'd put her through, things that had left her battered and weary. Sometimes it had seemed to her that he actually gained energy from these setbacks: he'd seemed to pick himself up and start again with a new vigour. Not this time. Out-manoeuvred and out of control, he lurked at home. He wouldn't face the family. He refused to go to Kate's christening at the end of November and Chris found the letters of apology he'd written to his creditors, which she'd thought to be a good sign, stamped and thrown in the bin.

Afterwards, Chris reproached herself. This was not the Paul she knew and she should have seen the signs, maybe even got him to go to the doctor. But busy running the stables, and planning to own the stables, busy keeping the fridge filled and Peter's homework checked, she let Paul get on with it, waiting for the day when, mysteriously reinvigorated, he'd bound through the door saying he'd met up in

Borchester with an old pal who'd offered him a job. It didn't happen. Instead, he disappeared.

When Chris came in from an afternoon's Christmas shopping, there was a note on the kitchen table. In it, Paul had written that he needed to go away 'to think'. He'd taken the car, and Chris inched through the next couple of days expecting, if not his return, then at least a phone call. None came. She would have to tell the police.

She knew what they'd be thinking. That Paul and Chris had had a row. That he'd been depressed about the loss of his business, suicidal even. That, given the circumstances, she should have reported his disappearance straight away. Most of all, that she should have seen the signs.

When the phone rang a couple of days later and it was a cheery sergeant from Borchester Police, she felt quite jubilant. Surely he wouldn't sound so jolly if anything was wrong? But what the sergeant had to say didn't make Chris feel very jolly. They'd found the car in London – not abandoned, as she'd dreaded, but sold. Sold – and it was still on HP. And in Chris's name.

· · ·

'Right, that's it.' Brian, who'd been driven inside by the sheeting rain, lifted the coffee pot hopefully and, finding it empty, looked appealingly at Jennifer. 'I've held back because I'm hardly close family, but I can't let well-meaning amateurs like your grandad bumble about any longer.' He investigated the biscuit tin where he had more luck and emerged with a couple of pieces of Jennifer's almond shortbread. 'Does Chris still expect him to come back when the money runs out?'

'I'm not sure.' Jennifer put the kettle on to boil. 'Don't you?'

Brian crunched his biscuit. 'I don't think it's very likely.'

'It might be no bad thing.' Jennifer stooped to finish loading the washing machine with Kate's little vests and stretch suits. 'In some ways I think Chris would be happier if she knew he'd gone for good.'

Brian leaned against the dresser, making the cups rattle.

'There's a bankruptcy hearing outstanding against him, don't forget. That's not going to go away.'

'They can't have it if he's not here.'

'No, but they'll adjourn it. They might adjourn it half a dozen times, but every time it's going to be reported in the *Echo*. Every time it's another slap in the face for Chris.'

Jennifer twirled the washer to the right setting and switched it on. 'Oh, I see what you mean.'

'And in the end,' concluded Brian, brushing crumbs from his sweater, 'they'll issue a warrant for his arrest. That's why, whatever Chris says, we've got to find Paul and make him face his responsibilities. I don't suppose you know if he took his passport?'

And so, at last, Brian, cosmopolitan Brian, someone who actually knew how the world worked, who'd actually been to London within living memory, who knew about airport police and Interpol, swung into action. And it wasn't long before he had a result.

It was the night of the Christmas concert at Peter's school. Since Paul had disappeared, Chris and Peter had been staying at Home Farm and Jennifer, Chris and Phil had been to hear Peter perform.

'Didn't he sing beautifully, Phil?' Chris asked when they got back, shooing Peter up to bed with a kiss.

'Are you all full of the spirit of Christmas?' Brian appeared from the farm office where he'd spent a pleasant evening with his machinery magazines and a tumbler of whisky.

'We shall be when I get this bottle open,' called Jennifer from the kitchen. 'How was your evening, Brian?'

'I'll go and fix us some sandwiches,' offered Chris, as Jennifer came in waving a bottle of Beaujolais and four glasses.

'There's a joint of roast beef in the fridge, Chris,' suggested Brian, who'd been nibbling the burnt bits all night. 'Beef and chutney, everyone?'

Phil murmured his approval and Chris left them to it.

'Thank goodness she's gone.' Brian accepted a glass of wine from his wife. 'I was wondering how I'd get rid of her.' He took a long swig. 'I've had some news about Paul.'

Brian's sweet-talking of the airport police had borne fruit. Despite it being a busy time of year, and Johnson being a common name, they had traced a Mr Paul Johnson, travelling on the correct passport number, who'd flown out to Hamburg on 10 December. He was staying at a hotel in the centre of town.

'Germany?' gasped Jennifer. 'What's he gone there for?'

'We've got to stop him doing this to her!' Phil managed to mute his voice but he couldn't play down his fury. 'There's going to be no end to it. It's going to be one shock after another and there's a limit to what one person can stand.'

But Chris was stronger than they had given her credit for. When Phil told her, as gently as possible, what Brian had found out, she turned a ghastly putty colour and went straight upstairs, where Jennifer followed her and insisted she took a couple of the sleeping pills the doctor had given her. But the next morning she told Jennifer in confidence that she'd decided what she must do. She was going to fly out to Paul and see if he'd come home.

'You must help me do it by myself,' she pleaded. 'If I tell Phil, or Mum and Dad, they'll insist on coming with me and – I can't explain, it's just something I want to do alone.'

Jennifer told her that it wasn't a confidence she could keep, but that she'd back Chris up in front of the family. They didn't like it but, somehow, doggedly, Chris got her way and on 20 December, the day before her birthday, she flew out to Hamburg where Paul had agreed to meet her at his hotel.

'He says he can hold his head up over there, get his confidence back.' Chris told her mother exhaustedly when she returned two days later. 'He's got a job and somewhere to live. He says he'll send money back when he can.'

This was all way beyond Doris's comprehension, but perhaps the mysteries of Chris's marriage always had been.

'What about the bankruptcy?' she questioned.

'Oh, he knows there'll be a hearing. And he'll come back for it. He's not trying to run away, Mum.'

Doris looked at her daughter. Was this going to be a repeat of every other Paul-inspired crisis she'd had to live through?

'Chris, love, it hurts me to ask you this, but…'

Christine managed a twitch of a smile. It was so long since she'd smiled spontaneously she'd almost forgotten how to do it.

'I know what you're going to say. Did I fall for his patter all over again?' Chris pressed the palms of her hands against her tired eyes, then looked straight at her mother. 'No, I didn't. I thought I'd reached the end, you know, Mum, when I found the note telling me he'd gone away. Then I thought I'd reached it when I heard he'd sold the car, and again when I found out he was in Germany. But talking to him, Mum, in this cheap hotel, and him prattling on as if what he'd done was perfectly normal and acceptable, that was what finished it for me. I just don't want to know any more.'

Doris reached out and took her daughter's hands. She squeezed them tight. The end of a marriage was no cause for celebration, but Doris felt nothing but relief.

'Chris, you've done everything you could for him. If that's really what you're feeling, perhaps this separation will be for the best.'

Doris went on holding her hands and looking at Chris, her own eyes full of tears. Chris could feel her engagement ring, the big ruby and diamond that she'd been so proud of, digging into her finger. She didn't wear it very often: it was totally impractical with the horses. But it was still hard to believe that one day she might take it off for good.

She thought back to that awful meeting with Paul in the hotel breakfast room, with the waitress laying tables for the next day, the little pats of butter and the catering packs of jam. It wasn't exactly a scene set for big dramatic gestures, but in the end, Chris hadn't needed to make any.

At times like this, people often said something had snapped inside them but it hadn't been like that for Chris. More reluctant, more painful for being so long drawn out, something inside her, held together only by hope, had finally tugged apart. Not her heart: that was far too fanciful. It was, perhaps, she thought, her spirit.

·15·

Starting Afresh

Christine did the best she could. At Christmas she put on the bravest of faces for Peter, and in the New Year threw herself into work at the riding school. She moved to the farmhouse at the stables. She made marmalade and cushion covers and tried not to mind that she hadn't heard another word from Paul. Despite what she'd told her mother, it was one thing to say she didn't care for Paul any more and another thing entirely not to feel it. She couldn't confide in the family. They'd all written Paul off, and were relieved to think she had, too. To her surprise, she found that the only person she *could* talk to about it was George Barford.

She'd hardly known him before. His arrival in the village as Jack Woolley's gamekeeper some four years earlier had scarcely touched her. She'd heard bits of gossip in that time. How he'd started out in the police force back home in Yorkshire. About a messy separation from his wife which had sent him to the bottle, and a son, Terry, who was a bit of a layabout. But she'd had too many problems of her own to pay attention to his. Anyway, he was living with Nora McAuley, who'd divorced Greg Salt and reverted to her maiden name.

He took to calling in on Chris during the day. He was her nearest neighbour, for a start, and he was always out and about checking on the pheasants. He often brought her something: one time a sack of logs, then some early primroses. He'd hang his thornproof on the back of the door, ease his boots off and sit at the kitchen table, eating Doris's gingerbread and listening.

'I know it sounds crazy, but I still loved Paul, even when everything was going wrong. If anything, I loved him *more* because when he was

209

down, he needed me. And however much I say I don't care for him, I know I still do, even now.'

George cupped his big, red hands round his mug of tea.

'I dunno why you're so surprised,' he said. 'You can't turn feelings on, so why should you be able to turn them off?'

'Because he's behaved so badly,' explained Chris. 'It makes me feel like some kind of masochist.'

'Rubbish,' said George. 'It's habit, that's all it is. After – what – twenty years or more, it's hard to fathom not feeling *something* – whether it's for him or anyone else. It's just that at the moment you can't imagine it not being him.'

Paul continued to stay out of touch and out of reach. When the April date set for the bankruptcy hearing came and went with no sign of him, a new date had to be set and a new summons issued.

'I can't think why you thought he'd come,' said Phil, more harshly than he meant to, when he went over to see Chris at the riding school. Paul did exasperate him so, and Chris's craven belief in him – still!

'I couldn't believe he wouldn't. Not this time.'

Christine rubbed tiredly at a piece of tack. Phil wished she could rub Paul out of her life as easily.

'He can't just lie low in Hamburg and pretend they don't exist! I'll have to go and see him.'

'It wouldn't do any good!'

'At least let me try,' implored Phil. 'You've done so well, Chris. You've picked yourself up and made a new start. Don't let him drag you down.'

Chris heaved a huge sigh and Phil sensed her weakening.

'If you won't let me go over there, at least let me write to him,' he urged. 'This whole thing has gone on for far too long. Give me his address and I'll get you off the hook.'

Christine never knew what Phil put in the letter but it must have been pretty extreme – threats of burying Paul at low-water mark, perhaps, Brian speculated cheerily to Jennifer. Whatever it was, a contrite Paul wrote back, promising faithfully to return to England for the next hearing, which had been set for mid-May.

'Well, I'm pleased for your sake,' George told Christine. It was St George's day, Phil's birthday, and Chris was getting ready to go to Brookfield for supper. 'But for heaven's sake, stop fiddling with your hair. It looks very nice.'

'D'you think so? Mum raves about this Amanda but she always sends me out looking as if I've been to the poodle parlour.'

'Will you women never learn to take a compliment when it's meant? It looks very nice, I'm telling you.'

Christine put down her comb.

'All right, I believe you. Now, I'm really sorry, George, but I've got to throw you out. Peter and I are due at Brookfield in ten minutes and he's probably up a tree somewhere.'

George lumbered to his feet and pulled on his ex-army surplus jerkin.

'That reminds me – I said I'd take him fishing when I've a spare hour,' he said.

'Oh, you didn't. He'll hold you to it, you know. He never forgets.'

'I don't want him to. I'm owed a bit of time off. Now you enjoy your evening.'

Christine did. Things were starting to straighten out at last. Paul was coming back to face the music, Peter seemed to have adapted to their new life, the riding school was doing well . . . They were having coffee and Jill, too, was just complimenting Chris on her hair, when Uncle Tom's truck pulled up in the yard.

'It's a bit late for him,' said Phil, going to the door. 'He and Auntie Pru are usually tucked up with their cocoa by nine.'

But Tom had some news – news that couldn't wait till morning.

'You won't believe this,' he said. 'And it'll interest you, as well, Christine. Nora McAuley's run off with some feller she works with at the canning factory! She's walked out on George!'

· · ·

'No. No . . . it's not true.'

Her father came and sat beside her. He put his arm round her.

'I'm sorry, Chris, it is.' And then, as she began to cry, 'Get her a brandy, Phil, she's as white as a sheet.'

Christine heard Phil rummaging about in the sideboard. She knew he wouldn't find any brandy – she'd drunk the last of it when Paul hadn't turned up to the previous bankruptcy hearing. Now he wouldn't be at the next one either.

'Tell me what happened,' she whispered, as Phil approached with a tot of whisky. Of course, there was a half bottle of whisky that someone had given George for Christmas and he'd passed on to her because he was teetotal these days. 'Please, just tell me.'

'Have a sip of this first.'

Christine did as she was told – she sometimes felt she'd spent all her life obeying other people's instructions – and felt hot dryness, rather than liquid, go down her throat. Then Phil perched on the coffee table in front of her, his knees touching hers, and told her what they knew, which wasn't much. Just that Paul had been on the auto-bahn just outside Hamburg when his car had gone out of control. There was no other vehicle involved and no one else was injured. Just Paul, who'd been killed outright.

It was the answer to the family's prayers, Chris thought bitterly, as she undressed that night, when Phil and her father had finally gone. She'd refused to go to Glebe Cottage, or to Brookfield. She didn't think she could absorb any more of her family's pity, especially when she knew they must be thinking that it was the best thing that could have happened. No one had mentioned the bankruptcy, but it was obvious that all that would be dropped. And as for the untidy business of Chris living in England and Paul in Germany – two years separation with consent, or five years without, as grounds for divorce – well, that was removed as well. All gone in a moment's misjudge-ment on a motorway. The sun in his eyes, or having to brake too suddenly.

They said he'd died instantly. What was that supposed to mean? Even if he'd felt no pain, what about the panic in the seconds when he knew the car was out of control? What about knowing that he was leaving behind business affairs that were a total mess, and even if he didn't spare her a thought, a fatherless twelve-year-old boy? For days Chris had been dreading seeing Paul again at the bankruptcy hearing, terrified that even now he might be able to persuade her to give him another chance. It wouldn't happen now, and she felt cheated. She'd never, ever know if she'd have been able to resist him. Another decision taken for her.

She pulled on her nightdress and scrambled into bed: the stables farmhouse wasn't the warmest house on earth, even in May. She lay there, stiff and shivering. It was a long time since Paul had held her in this bed. It was a long time since anyone had held her, anyone who wasn't family.

Christine Johnson, widow. She tried the dismal word out in her mind, imagined writing it on forms – there'd be lots of forms to fill in over the next few days, she felt sure. Chris felt the sobs start to shake in her throat. In the morning she'd have to tell Peter, who'd been whisked straight from school to Home Farm, that his father had been killed. She lay on her back and let the tears stream into her ears and soak her hair. She'd have to be strong for him, and then she'd have to be strong for herself.

It was a terrible time for Chris. She'd picked herself up once already this year: that had been hard enough, and it wouldn't be any easier a second time. She told Peter the next day. He seemed to take it all in his stride: he'd seen more of Phil than Paul over the years – how could he grieve for someone he barely knew? The day after, Christine and her father flew to Germany, where the inquest recorded death by misadventure. They asked her if she wanted to bring the body home but there didn't seem any point. Paul's parents were long dead and he'd entirely lost touch with his sister, Sally, who was running a stud farm in Wiltshire. And what would be the point of bringing Paul back to Ambridge, a place he'd only ever wanted to get away from? It was no more appropriate as his final resting place than Newmarket, where they'd once lived briefly, or the oil rig off the Welsh coast where he'd worked, or the offices of Arnolds Agricultural Machinery in

Borchester, which he'd been so keen to leave to set up the fish farm. Paul hadn't lasted long anywhere. Arguably, he'd had some of his happiest times working in Germany, in the years when he'd been selling horseboxes over there. That was where he'd died and, Chris felt, that was where he should stay. With the help of the British Consul, she arranged a funeral in a tiny whitewashed church in a village near where he'd died, then Paul was laid to rest in a corner of the cemetery. Nearby, a white lilac was just breaking into blossom and a blue tit chirruped from one of its bouncing boughs.

Dan stood a little way off as Christine said her final goodbye to the husband who, in his opinion, had caused her nothing but heartache. When she finally stood up, he went over to her, his hat in his hands.

'Ready?' he asked gently.

She nodded and took his arm.

Dan took one last look at the grave and eased her away. They couldn't put the headstone up yet: the ground needed to settle, but Chris had ordered a simple one. It was going to say: 'In Loving Memory of Paul Johnson, 1930–1978. Always remembered by his wife Christine.'

Looking down from the plane on the way home, as they crossed the coast and headed for Birmingham, Chris studied the minute farms and microscopic sheep of the South Downs, wrapped round with roads like strips of wire. She couldn't relate what she saw to real people with real lives, and when she got back to Ambridge, even though everything was life-size, it still felt unreal. People either avoided her with their eyes on the ground, or they talked loudly at her about what was happening in the village as if Paul had never existed. She learnt that Shula's journalist boyfriend, Simon Parker, the editor of the *Echo*, had left for a job in Fleet Street, leaving Shula broken-hearted. Jennifer's au pair, Eva Lenz, from Stuttgart, was settling in well, apparently, but the solar-heated swimming pool that they were installing at Home Farm had been victim to several tiresome delays. Joe Grundy, the Estate's most troublesome tenant, had recovered from his bad bout of flu, but was going to have his whole herd slaughtered through brucellosis. On top of which, his favourite ferret, Turk, had been found dead in a trap, and Joe had been heard to say he didn't care about anything any more.

Christine knew how he felt. No one could accuse her of idealizing her time with Paul. When Phil had lost Grace, he'd had nothing but happy memories, but her memories of Paul were very mixed. In the past six months she'd hated him for what he'd put her through, but she'd still wanted to see him again. She'd wanted to prove to herself that it was all over between them and she'd wanted Paul to face up to the bankruptcy proceedings so that a line could be drawn under that, too. Now, though in one way everything was indisputably over, it still felt unfinished. She'd never had the chance to make her peace with him, or even a truce, and she'd not been able to say goodbye.

George understood. He came round practically every day and brewed endless pots of tea while she talked or cried or sometimes just sat silent. He took Peter out round the pheasant pens to give her some time to herself and helped him with his algebra, which was way beyond her. He didn't crowd her and he didn't ask anything of her. He was sensitive to how protective her family were: he kept saying, as he fixed a dripping tap or changed a fuse, that he didn't want to tread on any toes.

The family noticed, all the same. As the weeks went on, Doris had to put up with Walter speculating about Christine's 'h'admirer' and Dan heard from Jethro that George had enlisted Christine's help in choosing a dress for his daughter Karen's birthday.

At the end of July, there was a huddled conversation at Brookfield after lunch one Sunday which Jill, coming in with the coffee, said was nothing short of insensitive.

'If she likes his company and he's good for her, where on earth's the harm in it?' she demanded. 'After all she's been through, I can't believe you begrudge her a bit of innocent pleasure.'

'Is it innocent, though, love?' Dan poked his pipe with a matchstick. 'We don't know what sort of a man George Barford is . . .'

'But Dan, we do.' Doris accepted her coffee from a stony-faced

Jill. 'I'm sorry to say he's an ex-alcoholic, who lived openly with a woman –'

'Go on, say it, who's no better than she should be! I don't believe I'm hearing this!'

'Jill, we're only thinking of Christine,' pleaded Phil as Jill banged the coffee pot down and shoved the cream jug rudely towards her mother-in-law. 'Lord knows, she's made one big mistake in her life –'

'You're not thinking of Chris, you're thinking of the Archers and their famous place in the village,' retorted Jill. 'Honestly, sometimes I think it's a miracle anyone's ever been allowed to marry into this family!'

If Jill had seen Christine first, she might have warned her that the family were on the warpath, but as it happened, Chris sought Phil out, hoping to buy some hay. When they'd shaken on the deal, Phil enquired, politely he thought, if she'd been seeing much of George lately, and Chris went up like a rocket.

'Look.' Chris folded her arms. 'George has been a tremendous help to me over the past couple of months. I don't care what you and a lot of other people may think about him. I value his friendship.'

'I'm only saying this for your own good,' replied Phil weakly, singed by the force of her anger. 'Remember the sort of man he is.'

'I *know* the sort of man he is,' stormed Chris. 'Kind and sympathetic and understanding. I won't have anyone running him down, not even you, Phil. I'm old enough to choose my own friends and I'd be glad if you'd bear that in mind.'

Having said her piece, she turned and walked off, shaking, to the car. But as she started the engine, she couldn't help smiling to herself. She couldn't remember when she'd last torn Phil off a strip like that – not since they were kids, probably. It didn't half feel good. It had been a long time in coming, but perhaps she really was starting to make her own decisions and tell people what she thought of them. Perhaps, at long last, she had stopped caring what people thought. She put the car into gear with a neat flick of the wrist. After all, when you've been at rock bottom and people have written you off, what have you got to lose?

Starting Afresh

The car bumped down the track. In the rear-view mirror, Chris could see Phil standing there looking puzzled, like a child who's dropped his ice cream, staring for a moment at the empty cornet before the tears begin.

Poor Phil. The idyll of his marriage to Jill had rendered him such an innocent. He really had no idea of what life was like outside his own cosy little Eden.

·16·

Temptation

' "Farewell happy fields
Where joy forever dwells: hail horrors, hail
Infernal world . . ." '

'Shula?'

It was a blowsy April day and they'd scuttled gratefully into The Feathers. Shula chewed, wincing, on the slice of lemon she'd fished from her gin and tonic. Her new friend, Caroline Bone, a cordon bleu cook who'd come to Ambridge to work at The Bull, but had swiftly been appropriated by Jack Woolley to help him at Grey Gables, was looking at her worriedly.

'*Paradise Lost, Book One,*' Shula explained. 'One of my A-level set books if I decide to enrol at the Tech. They gave me a crib sheet.'

'It'd be worth getting some A-levels. If that's what Mr Rodway says.'

'Would it?' Shula dropped the lemon rind into an ashtray. 'It's going to take for ever. Two years for my A-levels. Four years to become a chartered surveyor. I'll be – that can't be right – twenty-eight by the time it's all over.'

'And a fully qualified estate agent.'

'Then I've actually got to do the job. Farm sales. Measuring up. Dry rot. Woodworm.'

'Shula,' said Caroline gently. 'If you're going to stay in Borchester, you've got to do something. "Nor love thy life, nor hate; But what thou liv'st, Live well." I think that's it.'

'Sorry?'

'*Paradise Lost, Book Nine*, if I remember rightly.'

'Since when were you a secret student of Milton?'

219

'I'm not.' Caroline smiled, and you could see the similarity to the ancestral portraits at Netherbourne Hall, to the flat-chested Tudors and the Edwardian society beauties. Caroline was from a very good family: Lord Netherbourne was her uncle. 'We had this mad nanny once,' she went on. 'Only ever spoke in quotations. Some of them just seem to have stuck.'

Getting stuck was just what Shula dreaded. This time last year, she'd been planning her round-the-world trip with her new boyfriend, Nick Wearing, who'd come to work at Brookfield before going to college. It had been Nick who'd finally snapped her out of her gloom over the departed Simon Parker. He'd jollied her into going on Young Farmers' treasure hunts and picnics. And he'd said he'd go with her when Shula got the idea of travelling overland to visit Michele, the New Zealander who'd come sheep shearing at Brookfield a couple of years previously. Shula's parents had hardly been thrilled, especially her father, who didn't seem to acknowledge that there was a world outside Brookfield, still less that anyone might want to see it for themselves, but in the end, as on so many previous occasions, Shula's potent combination of pleading and pouting had achieved the desired result. Phil even advanced her some money for her twenty-first, which she'd now be celebrating while she was away.

'Just think . . .' she'd enthused over breakfast one day. 'Instead of a barn dance here at Brookfield, I could be spending my birthday on the beach in Bali.'

'Or struck down with amoebic dysentery, or working for white slavers,' offered David helpfully, as Jill turned pale.

But Shula just thumped him and there was not much her mother could do, apart from tuck a couple of packets of Shula's favourite custard creams in her rucksack and tell her not to let Nick out of her sight.

She was gone almost six months. At first it had all worked out brilliantly, travelling through eastern Europe and Turkey on the train, then flying to Calcutta, where they'd intended to part company so that Nick could fly back to England and start his course. But they were having far too good a time. They'd met up with other back-packers in various youth hostels and cheap hotels and had promised to meet some of them in Thailand, to marvel at the temples and loll on the sands in Phuket. So Shula and Nick had travelled on – but Nick, it seemed, couldn't stop travelling, and before long he caught a flight to Australia, leaving Shula to share a room with another girl, a former PE teacher from Liverpool.

It was in Bangkok that reality intruded in its usual messy way. They returned to their room one day to find the flimsy lock forced and everything gone: passports, tickets and money. Shocked and frightened, the girls had to report to the indifferent police and the implacable consul: then Shula had the horrible job of phoning Brookfield to tell them she'd have to come home.

She'd arrived back in November, amazed by the lack of daylight and the lack of colour in the pinched winter countryside. She'd been thin and brown and, by this time, blasé about her adventures.

'We were just unlucky,' she told Neil and Jethro in the pub, blowing a perfect smoke-ring. 'I'd do it all again tomorrow.'

Neil, admiring, cadged a roll-up off Jethro and attempted a smoke-ring himself, but ended up coughing and picking tobacco out of his teeth.

'I bet the Young Conservatives have missed you,' he said.

'The YCs? If they think I'm going back to ringing doorbells when I'm more used to the sound of temple bells, they've got another think coming,' retorted Shula caustically.

Crushed, Neil stubbed out his unwanted cigarette. He'd spent the entire time she'd been away missing Shula. The two postcards she'd sent him were taped to his wardrobe mirror and the sour-smelling leather wallet she'd brought him back was now his most treasured possession.

Shula stubbed out her own cigarette. (Her parents had been appalled that she'd taken up smoking: David had told them to be grateful she hadn't come back smoking cheroots.) To tell the truth, though, smoking didn't seem as sophisticated back in England. Perhaps she'd give the rest of her duty-free allowance to Jethro.

Rodway and Watson hadn't got a job for her straight away. When they'd agreed to her travelling plans, they'd offered to hold her job open for her, but, arriving home when the market was traditionally quiet, they announced that she'd have to wait till the spring. Shula filled her days with long walks and bar work in The Bull, but having time on her hands just made readjusting more difficult. She thought of taking off again but she had no money and no travelling companion. Instead she took over the nursing of an orphan lamb whom she named Qwerty. His mother had died and he spent his first couple of days of life in the bottom oven of the Aga. Shula would take him out to give him his feed, and sit him on a hot-water bottle on her lap, stroking the bony head. She would remember the staring flocks of goats on dirt tracks in Turkey and the wandering cattle that would regularly stop buses in India. Then, when Qwerty was resting, she'd have to get out her postcards and photographs in case she'd imagined it all.

Finally, at the end of March, Mr Rodway had phoned to say that the market was picking up again and they'd have her back if she wanted. But there was to be no more 'gallivanting', he warned. If Shula came back, she must apply herself seriously to the noble calling – not to say the practice – of estate agency. Hence the A-levels and the chartered surveyors' exams – and Shula's looming depression.

• • •

'Brian? Brian, is that you?'

Jennifer thrust Kate's half-dressed doll back at her daughter and hurried into the kitchen. Brian was standing there unsteadily, beaming.

'Jenny my love,' he greeted her. 'You're the light of my life, d'you know that?'

'Don't you "Jenny my love" me.' She could smell pub on him from five feet away. 'Where on earth have you been? I've been worried sick.'

'Sorry, darling.' Brian stepped forward to embrace her and she wrinkled her nose. 'I popped into The Feathers at lunch time –'

'Brian, it's gone six o'clock!'

'Is it really? Good heavens!'

'What have you been doing all afternoon?' Jennifer broke away and started to fill the kettle. Coffee was called for. Black.

'I was telling you, but you interrupted.' His voice rose with the injustice of it all. 'I popped into The Feathers and who should be there but Shula. And Caroline.'

'So?'

'Well, Shula was a bit down in the dumps, so I thought I'd take her out to lunch to cheer her up. Caroline had to get back. Pity . . . Anyway, we didn't go till The Feathers had closed –'

Jennifer slammed a pottery mug down on the work surface and turned on the kitchen spotlights as Brian, squinting, pulled out a chair.

'I don't think I need to hear any more, thank you, Brian. If you want to idle away your hours in the pub with young women . . .'

'Oh, come on, now, Jenny, that's not fair!' wheedled Brian. 'What about all the hours you spend with old Tregorran in The Goat and Nightgown?'

'Don't be ridiculous. John and I only used to go there when we were doing that course of lectures because it's round the corner from the Tech. Now we've got the landscape survey up and running, I'm far too busy to go sitting in pubs.'

'And far too busy to cook your husband's lunch,' said Brian mournfully. 'You can't blame me, Jenny. Look at what you left me yesterday. A bit of soup . . .'

'Home-made vichyssoise?'

'All right, it's still only soup. And a bit of cheese flan.'

'Brie and walnut quiche, if you don't mind.'

'I had rump steak today.' Brian smacked his lips. 'It was delicious.'

'Good,' said Jennifer briskly, 'because you're having cold ham and a baked potato for supper.' Brian squeaked a protest but she went on. 'I told you all about it. The landscape survey team's meeting at Bridge Farm tonight. We're going to discuss boundaries.'

The proposed landscape survey of Ambridge had arisen out of a course of local history lectures which Jennifer and John Tregorran had attended. The lectures had covered history, natural history, town and country planning and archive sources, and their purpose was to teach amateurs how to carry out a full survey of their parish, discovering how it had developed through the ages. John had been the initiator, but Jennifer had found his enthusiasm catching, and they'd soon gathered together a band of volunteers – Colonel Danby and Laura in the forefront, with Pat, Caroline and Shula rather less willing conscripts. From the start, Brian had been scathing about what he termed Jennifer's 'scrabbling about in hedge-bottoms'. John's wife Carol was similarly uninvolved, but then she had other concerns. At the market garden, her orchards needed grubbing up and the continuing oil shortage was giving her problems heating her greenhouses. But Jennifer had thrown herself into the survey: she needed a new project now that Eva, the au pair, took Kate off her hands for a large part of the day, and she needed something to cheer herself up. She'd spent the autumn and winter shuttling backwards and forwards to Guernsey, where Ralph had suffered a succession of heart attacks before succumbing to a final one in January. Jennifer had seen how narrow Lilian's life was there: bridge evenings at the yacht club and a frightening amount of gin. She was determined that the same thing wouldn't happen to her.

'It'll never happen to you because I'm not twenty years older than you with a dicky heart,' Brian had reasoned one winter's evening as they sat by the fire.

'Maybe, but I don't want to turn into a bored little girl like my sister,' Jennifer had replied.

'Bored little girl – Lilian?' spluttered Brian. 'Merry widow, more like! She owns the Estate, remember, she's sitting on a fortune –'

'Brian! She's had an awful time nursing Ralph!' Jennifer protested.

'And now she's going to make up for it. Who can blame her?' Brian flipped through one of his farming magazines.

'Well, I don't want to wait that long. I want something that'll stretch me and keep me active now.'

'I can think of something.' Brian shifted on the sofa. 'Come and sit by me and I'll show you.'

'Oh, Brian, honestly. I'm talking about mental stimulation.'

'So was I. Don't you want to see a picture of the combine I'm thinking of buying?'

Jennifer tutted impatiently.

'Exactly. I rest my case.'

Pretending offence, Brian spread himself out again and put his feet on the coffee table.

'You don't fool me. All this intellectual intensity's just a smoke-screen. I know the real attraction. The dashing John Tregorran.'

'What?' laughed Jennifer. John was a good-looking man for his age, but that was still fifteen years older than Jennifer.

'I bet he's forgotten more about Harold Pinter than I ever knew.' Brian selected another machinery catalogue. 'I don't suppose you'd like to pour me a whisky and soda, would you, darling?'

Brian could be flippant about John Tregorran, but there were some in the village who took a dim view of Jennifer's spending so much time in his company. Doris was one.

'The minute I heard about those talks they were going to, I was worried. Dan will tell you.' Doris rubbed at the eagle supporting the church lectern. It was her week for the brasses. 'I mean, Jill, do you think Jennifer's being wise?'

Jill repositioned a sprig of mahonia in the pedestal arrangement she was doing, then stood back and considered it, along with Jennifer's predicament.

'It's not as if they're doing this survey on their own,' she soothed. 'Freddie Danby's involved. Surely he'll keep them on the straight and narrow?'

'You're not saying they've wandered off it before?'

Jill cursed her choice of words. And in church.

'Of course not, Mum. They share a common interest, that's all. And it does sound interesting. Jennifer was telling me they can discover which fields were ancient common land by looking at the banks and hedgerows.'

With a tut of contempt, Doris twirled her duster over the eagle's straining neck.

225

'Jennifer can be so headstrong,' she said. 'And she's such a romantic. Adam's the proof of that. It's really not a very good combination.'

Jennifer would have been touched to hear Jill's loyal defence. As time progressed, she would need her defenders more and more. Throughout the spring the landscape survey team walked the village, looking for sunken lanes and old field markings, and as far as Jennifer was concerned, she and John were merely fellow-enthusiasts. She knew people were talking, she knew Brian's comments were becoming more and more pointed, but still she insisted that there was nothing more between her and John than an interest in the past.

'Going in for another spot of time travel with Rip Van Tregorran?' Brian would ask nastily as she donned her wellies. 'Another little ramble back to Anglo-Saxon times?'

And Jennifer would spit back that if what he really wanted was a nice middle-class wife with a horsey headscarf and no interests of her own, he'd married the wrong person, he should have realized that by now. And in the meantime, he'd jolly well have to babysit Kate because Eva, who was to be married to Ambridge's policeman, James Coverdale, had gone to see the vicar about the hymns.

That April must have felt like the cruellest month for some of the villagers of Ambridge. Brian stomped about the farm supervising the cultivations and the late-lambing flock. Carol Tregorran, efficient and remote, busied herself replanting her orchards and arranging for Nelson Gabriel, who was setting up a wine bar in Borchester, to sell some of her and John's Manor Court wine. Throughout it all, Jennifer continued to type up the survey's findings, to wash shards of pottery and fragments of glass, and to display them in her studio, which had once been furnished with her spinning wheel and rugs made from the fleeces of her Jacobs, but which was now the nerve-centre for the survey team.

Then, at the beginning of May, John invited her to take a walk with him. He wanted, he said, to look at Leader's Wood on Brian's land, which he thought might be a relic of some ancient woodland.

It was one of those spring days full of promise. A boisterous sun dodged in and out of the clouds so that the landscape was brightly illuminated one minute and cast in shadow the next. Up in Leader's Wood, the leaves were a vivid green, and bluebells competed for space on the woodland floor with pungent wild garlic.

John seemed very excited.

'Wild garlic and bluebells side by side – often an indication that a wood dates back to medieval times!' he enthused. 'And – oh, look, Jennifer!'

Jennifer followed the direction of his pointing finger.

'That tree – the small graceful one – that, my girl, is a small-leaved lime.'

'Really?' Jennifer couldn't quite see the significance.

'A native lime,' John explained. 'Not the rude Continental type. Aren't you lucky having it on Home Farm?'

'Thrilled.'

'You know – ' John had been struck by a sudden thought. 'A wood this old would be worth a study all of its own – wildlife, flowers, insects . . .' He sighed deeply. 'I hope it lasts for ever. I hope there are always woods like this.'

Jennifer looked at him. Dear John. He took it all so seriously.

'You needn't sound so sombre!' she teased, hoping to lighten his mood.

All around them leaves shivered in the wind. He was looking at her fixedly. Jennifer shivered herself.

'Look,' she said, rubbing her bare arms, 'would you like to come back for a coffee? I told Brian I wouldn't be long.'

He gave her a wan smile. 'I told Carol that too.'

He looked away from her, up into the canopy of trees. Jennifer looked round awkwardly. She felt rather self-conscious, standing here alone with him in the filtered light.

'John?' she probed. 'Are you all right?'

He spread his hands in a silent gesture.

'I'm sorry, I was just thinking. All the things we're capable of doing in our lifetime and how little most of us actually do.'

'Oh, John.' He sometimes got these melancholy moods, she knew. Withdrew into himself. It intrigued her. Brian was always so direct.

'You ought to keep on with your writing,' he said suddenly. And then: 'Would you like an idea?'

'I don't know.' Jennifer was taken aback. 'What is it?'

'Well,' he began. 'It's about a man in early middle age. Married for some years. He has a good marriage – very good – only he has this rather . . . dreamy side to his nature.'

Still she didn't realize what he was trying to tell her.

'He just has this . . . discontent,' John went on. 'He ought to be fulfilled but there's a dull ache. All the time.'

Slowly it dawned on her what he was saying. She didn't need him to add, when he did:

'Well, d'you think you could make something of it, Jenny, my love?'

Jennifer froze. She didn't want any of this. She wasn't John's 'love'! And only Brian called her 'Jenny'!

How could she have been so stupid? Everyone in the village had known John had a crush on her. Everyone had known she was in too deep. They'd tried to tell her but she'd told them they were wrong. Or worse, she'd known they weren't, but she'd been secretly flattered and thought she was in control. Well, perhaps it was about time she was.

'No, John,' she said, trying to be composed. 'It's really not my kind of story.'

He started to say something in reply but Jennifer didn't want to hear it. She just wanted to get home to Brian, who'd seen what was coming and had tried to warn her. Instead she'd picked fights with him and made him eat cold suppers and left him minding the children.

Composure didn't matter any more. She could hear John shouting after her but she didn't look back. She didn't even stop running until she could see the farmhouse.

Even then, they might have got away with it: the gossip about John and Jennifer might have been no more substantial than thistledown. It might merely have been marked down by those in the know as Ambridge's first case of the male mid-life crisis, an affliction which, according to the papers, had the nation by the throat. But Jennifer panicked. Appalled by her own insensitivity, she told Brian what had happened, and she told her family. Even then, it might have remained off-limits, as the Archers closed ranks. But John panicked too. The next day, he left abruptly for America, where a friend of his needed help in organizing antique fairs. For the customers of the shop and the drinkers in the snug at The Bull, open season had been declared on their quarry.

'Well, anyone could see it coming. Listen to me, I sound like your grandmother.'

'Don't, Caroline. Gran hasn't stopped going on about it. Poor Jennifer.' Shula drained her glass of Muscadet and placed it back on the bar of The Bull, pulling a face. 'That was horrible. The sooner Nelson opens his wine bar the better.'

'Middle of the month, I heard.' Caroline shifted on her bar stool and re-crossed her long legs. In her short white skirt and navy T-shirt she looked more South of France than South Borsetshire. A couple of farm hands, supping pints in a corner, muttered behind their fists. 'And he's asked Eddie Grundy to be waiter-cum-bouncer.'

'Eddie? All he knows about is scrumpy!' Shula despaired. 'I was hoping Nelson's was going to become the "in" place. Where you could go and meet people.'

'You mean men,' said Caroline shrewdly, cowing the farm hands with a steady stare.

'Well, of course.' Shula picked up a Shires beer-mat and spun it on the bar. 'I mean, I did catch Auntie Chris's bouquet!'

'I think it's lovely. She's made a new man of George,' said Caroline fondly.

George and Christine had overcome both the disapproval of the family and the initial reluctance of the church to marry at St Stephen's. Chris had worn a dress of cream lace and old gold satin; George had worn a smart suit and a beaming smile. They had set up home at the stables and George was enjoying his new post as shooting manager at Grey Gables.

'I know,' agreed Shula. 'And I'm really pleased for her. She'd had such a rotten time. But,' she went on, 'right now, I'm more concerned about me. When am I going to meet someone decent?'

'You've got all those estate agents to choose from!' protested Caroline. 'Better than me at Grey Gables – Higgs and Jean-Paul!' She chortled at the thought and the farm hands looked over longingly.

'Estate agents are such a bloodless lot.' Shula spun her beer-mat with extra venom. 'You never hear about any crimes of passion committed by estate agents, do you?'

'What about *on* them? When my brother was buying his flat in London –'

'You know what I mean, Caroline,' Shula interrupted her, and stopped her mat-spinning activities for a moment to make a serious point. 'There's no romance in their soul. You wouldn't have found Desdemona or Anna Karenina training as a chartered surveyor.'

'Perhaps they should've. Could have saved them from a nasty end.'

'All I want is a *happy* end,' pleaded Shula. 'Walking off into the sunset hand in hand.'

'Ah.' Caroline smiled. '"They hand in hand with wandering steps and slow, through Eden took their solitary way".'

'That's it!' cried Shula, waving her beer-mat excitedly. 'A loving companion to stroll through life with me.'

Caroline looked at her wryly.

'You're going to have to pay more attention in your English class. That's from right at the end. When Adam and Eve have fallen from grace. When she's been tempted.'

'Oh, dear. Like Jennifer.'

'Well, not really. Jennifer didn't fall, exactly, did she?'

'She sort of stumbled,' said Shula. 'And I bet Brian won't let her forget it in a hurry.' She threw down the beer-mat with a sigh. 'Oh, Caroline, I don't know. If marriage isn't the answer and I'm fed up on my own, what else am I going to do?'

'I don't think even Milton would have had an answer to that,' smiled Caroline. 'Try this one. Have we got time for another drink before last orders?'

·17·

Losses and Gains

It was a still Sunday evening in late October. All the family – well, all the family who could fit into the tiny sitting room at Glebe Cottage – had been invited there for tea. No particular reason, Dan had told Jill in issuing the invitation, just that Doris, who'd been suffering from headaches, was feeling a bit better and fancied playing hostess instead of being waited on for a change. Jill had said that she and Phil would be delighted to come, as long as Doris let her bring a cake, but that she couldn't speak for the children.

'I'm afraid they live their own lives, Dad,' she'd said.

Dan had smiled and said that Doris would understand.

'But she'd like to see Shula,' he added. 'If she's not busy on Sunday. Shula was always her favourite, you know.'

So Shula had gone, secretly pleased to have been singled out – always a novelty when you were a twin – and now she stood in the garden, shaking out the tablecloth into the dark and listening to a pair of tawny owls hunting along the edge of the orchard. Nearby she could see the hump of the church tower and the lit windows. Her grandad and Uncle Tom had gone to Evensong, where her father was playing the organ. Uncle George, with Peter and David, had taken a walk round the pheasants: the shooting season was about to start and George was twitchy about poachers. Only the women were left: Doris was resting while her mum and her Auntie Chris were dealing with the washing-up.

Mark had been invited, though he wasn't family: Doris liked him. Everyone liked her new boyfriend, Shula often thought, perhaps more than she did herself. She didn't like asking Mark to family gatherings.

There were too many implications, or expectations. And if he came to Sunday tea with her family, then she might be expected to go to tea with his parents, Reg and Bunty Hebden, who lived on an 'executive' estate on the other side of Borchester, where on Sundays all the gardens had freshly striped lawns and the gutters foamed with suds from gleaming cars.

Shula gave the cloth a final flap. She was tempted to drape it over her head and sneak into the kitchen, pretending to be the Wandering White Lady of Loxley Barrett, whose ghostly existence had been discovered by Jennifer's historical landscape survey. But she mustn't. She must try to grow up and be sensible, especially now she was going out with Mark, who was a solicitor and a very sensible person indeed.

When she went in, her mother was just brewing up a fresh pot of tea.

'She was much more like herself today, wasn't she?' Auntie Chris was saying of Doris. 'Especially when we were all sitting round together.'

Shula put the folded cloth down.

'Go and ask your gran if she'd like a cup, will you, Shula?' her mother said, tucking the pot under its cosy. 'She's in the front room with her feet up.'

Shula went out into the tiny hall, made tinier by the ornaments that bristled from the walls: horse brasses and warming pans and hunting horns. She tiptoed into the parlour, as Gran still called it, and peeped over the back of her gran's chair. Her head had lolled to one side. She must be fast asleep.

Shula moved round and crouched in front of her. She touched her hand.

'Gran?' she said. Then, 'Gran . . .'

Shula went with Auntie Chris to the church. Her mother had called the doctor, and then there'd be an ambulance and everything, and no one wanted Grandad to walk back to the cottage and find all that going on.

So they waited outside in the evening air, which had got suddenly colder: Shula couldn't stop shivering. Inside, they were singing the last hymn.

'I think I'll go in,' said Chris suddenly. 'Wait at the back. By the vestry. I'll be able to get hold of Phil then – and Dad.'

Perhaps it hadn't quite sunk in yet with Auntie Chris. She still seemed to be able to think normally, to decide on things and do them. Shula felt as if her head had become detached from her body.

'Thanks for coming with me, Shula.' Her aunt squeezed her arm.

'That's all right,' said Shula tightly.

'She must have died very peacefully.'

'Yes.'

And Shula had found her. Shula had touched her hand.

'Come on.' Chris linked their arms. 'It's nearly over. They won't be long now.'

She pulled Shula with her round the side of the church, their feet, miles away, crunching on the gravel. The singing swirled around them and soared overhead. Shula wondered if the owls could hear it.

'So be it Lord; Thy throne shall never
Like earth's proud empires pass away;
Thy kingdom stands, and grows for ever
Till all Thy creatures own Thy sway.'

The village shouldn't have been shocked by Doris Archer's death. She was eighty years old: she and Dan were just a year off celebrating their diamond wedding anniversary. But everyone in the village seemed to take her loss personally. Everyone knew her and had come into contact with her. At Brookfield, Jethro wept openly: his wife, Lizzie, had died of a stroke a month earlier and Doris had been deeply upset. He said he could remember Mrs Archer's kindness to Lizzie when he'd first come to work at Brookfield, giving her bottled plums and curtains for the cottage that went with the job. Even Joe Grundy went to Glebe Cottage to pay his respects. Doris, he said darkly, had done his late wife Susan innumerable favours and she'd always had a kind word for the lads, Alf and Eddie, when they were small – which was more than you could say for most people in Ambridge.

The funeral was the following Thursday. A tentative sun washed the windows of St Stephen's as the packed congregation sang Doris's favourite, Psalm 121: 'I will lift up mine eyes unto the hills'. There was sadness at the graveside but, as the coffin was lowered into the earth with just the family gathered round, a sense of calmness too. Dan stood at the grave, head bent, tears pouring down his cheeks, but when Chris went to support him, he said he was only crying for the happiness he and Doris had shared and his disbelief that one man could be so lucky.

'They were so happy together! Still! It seems so unfair!' Shula sobbed into Mark's hanky. She'd agreed to go out for a drink with him on the night of the funeral – her mother had said it would do her good – but when he'd drawn up outside The Fox at Edgeley, she hadn't wanted to get out of the car.

'I know, I know.' He drew her awkwardly towards him.

'And I keep trying to remember what was the last thing I said to her,' gulped Shula, 'and whether I was looking bored when she was telling us at tea about the WI's cross-stitch competition . . .'

Mark pushed a damp hank of hair off her face and kissed her temple.

'Shula, you loved your gran very much and she knew it. And she loved you.'

Shula just wailed louder until Mark drove her home. Hearing them come in, Jill tutted and hugged the pair of them. Then she made them a pot of tea and sent them into the sitting room and told Phil not to disturb them on any account.

Shula went to work the next day, although Mr Rodway had told her she didn't have to. She'd decided it would be better to be occupied. On the way home, she called at Glebe Cottage to see if her grandad wanted a lift down to the farm: he'd refused to leave the cottage but he'd agreed to come to Brookfield for his meals. He was standing out in the dusk in his old tweed jacket. Shula gave him a hug.

'He's down there all right,' he said. 'Charlie Fox. Just been through the far end of the orchard and startled a pheasant.'

'I heard it,' said Shula: the pheasant had puttered up from the undergrowth as she'd come round the side of the house. She exhaled a deep breath. 'It's lovely out here. It's always been my favourite garden. I remember how we used to come and pick the apples from that old tree just inside the hedge. The one that collapsed seven or eight years ago and was all hollow in the middle.'

Dan nodded, remembering.

'They were red and shiny and just like sugar lumps.' Shula smiled at the memory. 'It used to produce so many.'

'Dying trees often do.'

'Yes,' said Shula cautiously, wondering if this was safe ground. 'I'd heard that.'

Dan looked out over the darkening garden. He nodded his head slightly, then turned to her.

'Anyway, for what it's worth,' he said, 'I think your gran made the right choice. It's what I'd like, as well, to know the place is going to be looked after.'

'How do you mean, Grandad?' Shula felt slightly nervous. She'd never had to deal with anyone bereaved before. She knew they could go a bit funny.

'It's going to be yours, love,' he explained. 'Glebe Cottage. Your gran's passed it on to me, for my lifetime, and after that it goes to you.'

Doris's thinking had been simple. Her own children and Peggy were settled. Of the grandchildren, Jennifer and Lilian were well provided for. Tony, however many problems he might have had recently – Pat had had a difficult breech birth with their daughter, Helen, and now there was mastitis in the herd – would one day inherit The Bull. Kenton had made himself a career, and David would eventually live at Brookfield. Elizabeth was still young, but Shula – Doris had wanted to know that Shula would always have a home in Ambridge, so she had given her hers.

'Oh, Grandad.' Shula was near to tears. 'I don't know what to say.'

'Just live here and love the place like she did,' said Dan simply. 'That's all she'd ask.'

On a filthy night a month later, Shula's Metro bounced to a halt at Brookfield. November rain, driven by the wind, punched her in the face as she ran across the yard. Breathless and cursing, she practically fell in through the kitchen door.

'Mum? Dad?'

They weren't expecting her back this early: they were probably in the sitting room, and hadn't heard the door over the sound of the TV. She shuddered out of her coat and kicked off her ruined shoes. She hoped her parents were still up. She wanted to talk to someone.

The hall was in darkness but from the living room she could hear the plangent sound of a guitar concerto playing low. She suddenly remembered that David was supposed to be spending the evening at home with his girlfriend Jackie Woodstock. She prayed she wasn't going to find them slobbering over each another. She didn't think she could stand it. Especially not right now.

Hesitantly she pushed open the door, poised to creep away, but David was stretched out on the sofa on his own, in the light of the standard lamp, cradling a can of beer. Earlier in the week he'd come off the four-wheeled farm bike Phil and Jill had given him for his twenty-first birthday and his bruises were all the colours of the rainbow. Jackie was supposed to have been ministering to him tonight, feeding him chocolate raisins and trying not to cuddle up against his sore side.

'What happened to Jackie?' Shula asked, after David had explained that their parents had gone to bed.

'She went home,' he answered curtly. 'Or perhaps she didn't. I don't know.'

Shula stirred the glowing ashes and put another log on the fire. She sat back on her haunches to see if it would catch. David took a final swig of beer and squeezed the empty can malevolently.

'What's the matter?' Shula asked.

236

'Nothing,' said David unconvincingly. Adding straight away, 'She's packed me in.'

'Oh.' said Shula. 'Oh.'

Her mum would be relieved. She thought Jackie was too 'fast', laughed too loudly and drank too much. It made Shula smile. Just as Phil's protective antennae twitched whenever a male under thirty or, indeed, in Simon Parker's case, over thirty, looked in Shula's direction, Jill tightened her apron strings against any girl who might be interested in David. David had noticed it too, and had complained to Shula. 'You'd better get used to it,' she'd laughed, knowing by now that her parents couldn't help it. 'Why d'you think Kenton joined the Navy?'

But none of that helped David with the way he must be feeling this evening. He'd been going out with Jackie since the summer – a long time for him – and Shula suspected that he'd been truly smitten.

'I'm sorry,' she said, and she was sorry for him, though not sorry that she wouldn't have to put up with Jackie's matiness whenever they met in Nelson's wine bar or her constant threat to take Shula out shopping and show her where she bought her clothes. Ann Summers parties, probably, Shula and Caroline had decided.

'I'm sorry, too, as a matter of fact.' That was about as close as you'd get to an admission of feelings from David. 'But that's how it goes.'

'Did you have a row?' Shula asked sympathetically. She could imagine Jackie's wild dark curls taking on a life of their own during a row, each of them hurling their own accusations.

'No. She's not really that sort of girl.'

No. She was the sort of girl who expected to get her own way. Her self-made father, Clive, who owned a couple of gravel quarries in the county, had taught her that. She wouldn't have given David the chance to get a word in, poor thing.

'Oh, well,' said Shula, thinking of her own evening, 'as long as she didn't tell you that you were shallow, spoilt, self-centred, unfeeling and wonder what she'd ever found attractive in you . . .'

She leaned back on her outstretched arms and looked into the fire.

'What are you talking about?'

'That's what Mark told me. We've both been dumped, David.'

She'd met Mark just over six months ago, only a week after her despairing conversation with Caroline in The Bull about the lack of eligible men in the area. She supposed it only went to prove the sort of things that her gran and Mrs Perkins had always said about how, if you lived to be a hundred, you never knew what was round the corner, although Shula had always felt that if you were a hundred years old, you must have a pretty good idea.

Anyway, she'd turned up at Hordern's Farm one May morning that scintillated with light. It was a deceased estate on which they'd had an offer and she'd expected to meet Mr Holden, from Spencer and Holden's, there because of a dispute about boundaries and drainage rights. He was bringing the deeds and they'd got to walk the farm. When she pulled up, however, there was a young chap lounging against the bonnet of his car, squinting into the sun, which was ricocheting off the barn wall. He introduced himself as Mark Hebden.

Shula scrambled into her wellies and surreptitiously checked her reflection in her wing mirror. He wasn't just dishy for a solicitor, he was dishy full stop. He had on a bright white shirt and a navy suit and a navy and white spotted tie. He had black, curly hair and cool grey-green eyes. Shula found her hands were shaking and she gripped her clipboard.

'Right, then,' he said. 'Shall we make a start?'

By the time they'd finished, it was nearly lunch time, and she'd followed him back to Borchester, memorizing the number plate of his car and making up silly phrases out of the letters, in which the words 'Mark', 'marry', 'dishy' and 'divine' seemed to keep recurring. He'd already asked her to join him for lunch at The Feathers. He had that grave, formal manner that solicitors seem unable to shake off even out of the office, and he made sure to ask if she wanted ice and lemon in her drink before the barman had had a chance to. They sat at a window table with Shula stuffing bits of bread and cheese in her mouth when she thought he wasn't looking – she was absolutely starving – and trying to find out more about him and look alluring all at the same time. When he looked at his watch and said he must get back to the office, she found herself gabbling that he must come to supper some time, hah-hah, in fact, why not tonight? And to her astonishment, horror and delight, he'd said that he'd love to. She'd had to ring and warn her mum, but she could sense when they met that Jill liked Mark straight away, and even her father wasn't as openly hostile as usual.

So they'd started going out, and Mark had helped with the hay-making and taken her up in a hot-air balloon for her birthday, and Neil had bitten his nails and looked morose. And though Mark was maddening – so organized, so punctual – he was certainly the nicest boyfriend Shula had ever had – too nice, sometimes. He'd been so sweet when Gran died, putting up with Shula's moods and buying her silly presents to cheer her up. And now it was November and they'd split up, and all because of the hunt saboteurs.

Shula hadn't been out hunting on the day it happened: it was a midweek meet and she'd had to give up her half day because dopey Jane, the office junior, was off sick. But Caroline had been there and had told Shula all about it.

They'd had a pretty poor day's sport altogether, rather stop-start. The hounds had changed scent twice on the far side of Loxley Woods when this couple, a man and a woman, all duffel coats and good deeds, had appeared, shouting and waving placards. Some of the horses had panicked, and some of the Hunt had started shouting back. Gerald Pargetter, from Lower Loxley Hall, who was Master of Foxhounds, had seen them off with some pretty choice language apparently, but there'd been a scuffle, and the woman had let off some spray paint on a fence-post, frightening the horses some more. Finally, Jim Coverdale had come plodding along in his Panda car and had carted the couple off and charged them with causing criminal damage and a breach of the peace.

Shula would probably have thought no more about it: the Hunt had never been bothered by saboteurs before. She had never, in truth, thought much about hunting: she did it because she loved horses and the countryside, and the three seemed to go together. She'd seen the carnage a fox could cause in a hen-house or a field of sheep, but she didn't hunt because she felt vindictive towards them. It was simply that foxes were part of the food chain – but with no natural predators, they had to be kept down somehow. In the end, she hunted because it was part of living in the country. All the people she knew did it: even Jennifer, who was pretty 'green', had taken Adam and Debbie to a children's meet. As far as Shula was concerned, it was as much part of her as her preferring sheep to pigs and autumn to spring. She'd never even discussed it with Mark – not till the night she got dumped, anyway.

They'd been to their favourite Italian place and Shula was just deciding between caramelized oranges and *zuppa inglese* when Mark said he'd taken on some new clients.

'It's a chap and his wife. Name of Jarrett. They were staging a protest about blood sports. It was your local bobby that made the arrest.'

'Those two!' Shula snapped shut her menu. 'Caroline told me there'd been some saboteurs trying to upset things.'

'They were the ones that were upset.' Mark hadn't even looked at the menu. Shula knew he didn't need to. He'd have cheese and biscuits. He always did. 'Bruised ribs, swollen hand . . . It sounds to me as though they were deliberately knocked over by some of the people on horseback.'

'Good!' said Shula, and went on as Mark goggled at her, 'It's a pity they weren't trampled as well. Types like that make me sick . . . spoiling everybody's day!'

'They're not *types*.' Mark had switched into his cold, professional voice, which Shula had heard him use in court. 'They're two earnest, if somewhat eccentric, people who've had a very nasty experience.'

'Which serves them absolutely right, as far as I'm concerned!'

And which led Mark neatly into his decisive summing up: that Shula was callous, self-centred and . . . oh, well, what was the point of going through it all. They were finished, that's all there was to it.

Except that she missed him. Dreadfully. He'd been so annoying when she'd been going out with him, so disciplined about getting back to the office on time after lunch, so punctilious about ushering her into the car, that Shula had sometimes wanted to laugh. He took everything so seriously.

'I expect you'll make it up with Mark, won't you?' said her father kindly one Sunday morning soon after they'd split up. 'You do seem a bit upset about it.'

Shula was in the depths of gloom. She'd spent the previous evening playing Monopoly with Brian, Jennifer and Mrs P at Home Farm, then going to the late-night horror film with David. Twenty-two, and the best she could find to do on a Saturday night was playing Monopoly with old-age pensioners, then going to the cinema with her brother!

'I'm upset about the kind of person he's turned out to be,' she began. 'Going on about his innocent clients when it's obvious they're a couple of criminal lunatics who had that paint in their hands the whole time –'

'Shula,' said Phil, wagging the Sunday paper at her, 'that's enough. I'm on the bench on Wednesday and I don't want you to talk to me about the case.'

'"Borchester high-class mafia"! "Socially accepted amateurs"! Who does he think he is?'

Phil was waving another paper, this time the *Borchester Echo*.

Mark's clients, the Jarretts, it reported, had been found guilty by Borchester Magistrates' Court of causing a breach of the peace, and Mrs Jarrett had been found guilty of criminal damage for spraying a fence-post. But Mark Hebden, their solicitor, according to the *Echo*, was not taking the decision lying down. He intended, he said, to appeal, to prove that justice could be done and that the right to protest should not be taken away from the citizens of Borsetshire.

'What a load of pompous twaddle!' said Caroline, placing Nelson's dog-eared copy of the *Echo* back on the bar. The wine bar had been decorated in 1920s speakeasy style, but Nelson had drawn the line at providing the *Herald Tribune* for his customers to read. 'I used to think Mark was okay. You're better off without him.'

'I suppose so.'

Christmas was coming and Shula didn't relish the thought of spending it on her own. It was always nice to be going out with someone at Christmas.

'You're not defending him, are you?'

'He's only doing his job,' said Shula in a small voice.

'I suppose you tried telling your father that?'

'There's no talking to Dad. He's been to see Mark and demanded an apology. And, just in case Mark was thinking of making things up with me, he's banned him from Brookfield.'

'Really?' Caroline popped a pretzel in her mouth. 'If only the Hebdens would get involved. It'd be like the Montagus and the Capulets.'

'I don't want to have to knock myself out with a sleeping potion to get Mark to go out with me again,' brooded Shula. 'And that's if I get the chance. Auntie Peggy told Mum she saw him the other day with that vile Jackie Woodstock.'

Disheartened, Shula slogged on towards Christmas. She missed not being able to tell Mark about the awfulness of the office party, just the six of them in the back room with warm white wine and Mr Rodway's Bing Crosby tapes. When she got home in the evenings, the kitchen table was covered with mince pies and hams with scored rinds like honeycomb. Her mother said she could stick her finger in the brandy butter but Shula wasn't hungry: the Jarretts' appeal was going to be heard on New Year's Eve and she couldn't possibly feel festive until she knew the outcome.

On the day of the appeal, she couldn't stop herself from sneaking into the public gallery at Felpersham Crown Court. Mark looked nervous, but he'd obviously briefed the defending barrister very thoroughly. The barrister asked the court to consider how much of the affray PC Coverdale, whose evidence had been so damning before, had actually seen. And he emphasized again that the fence-post would never have got sprayed had Mrs Jarrett not been knocked to the ground when someone (Gerald Pargetter, everyone knew) had ridden straight at her and caused her to press the nozzle of the spray canister as she fell.

After the verdict was announced in favour of the Jarretts, Shula raced to find Mark outside the robing room.

'You were brilliant!' she cried, somehow resisting the urge to kiss him in full view of a group of barristers. 'And you got the verdict you wanted. Dad'll have to forgive you now!'

'I don't know about that. Just the opposite, I'd have thought.'

'Oh, Mark, I don't think so. Dad has a great respect for the law.'

'Which is why he handed out the verdict he did at the Magistrates' Court. If you think he's going to be pleased it's been overturned –'

'Never mind all that!' Shula didn't want to get bogged down in legalities. 'You are coming tonight, aren't you? To the party at Brookfield, I mean?'

She was desperate to have him there. Christmas had been such a wash-out: she had to at least see the New Year in with him. Then, maybe, with everything starting anew, so could they.

'I'd like to, but –'

'Oh, Mark, just say yes.'

So he came, but best of all, he had the foresight to ring her father up beforehand to apologize for what he'd said in the paper so there would be no awkwardness during the evening. Phil, though quietly seething at the way the appeal had gone, had got the apology he'd asked for, so when Mark turned up, he had no option but to tell him he was looking well and graciously offer him a drink. Shula clung to his arm. She'd scooped up her hair at the side with a sparkly clip, and was wearing the new red dress she'd bought in Felpersham that morning, after court.

'Mark's mad about her,' Jennifer hissed to Jill. 'You can see it in his eyes.'

'D'you think so?'

'He's been looking at her everywhere she goes! You must have noticed it, Jill!'

Jill looked around for Shula and Mark to confirm it, but they were nowhere to be seen. They must have gone for a dance. She stood by the buffet table and nibbled a stick of celery.

What a year 1980 had been. Doris's death, and Ralph's, and David's twenty-first and Dan's eighty-fifth . . . The landscape survey, and Tony getting tetanus, and then Pat announcing she was pregnant for the third time . . . Colonel Danby proposing to Laura and being turned down, Eva marrying Jim Coverdale, and Shula meeting Mark . . . Jill smiled as Phil, burdened with a bottle of wine in each hand, approached. David had finished at Agricultural College and he was working full-time alongside his father at Brookfield now. All year they'd been reorganizing the farm. They'd set up new sheep-handling yards and bought 300 ewes for Lakey Hill. Then they'd sold the beef cattle to Brian, drained thirty acres of land and applied for a potato quota.

'Want a top-up?'

Jill shook her head.

'No thanks, love.'

Gently she took the bottles from him and placed them on the table. Quite a year. And twenty-five of them since the death of Grace.

'How about a dance? We can just fit one in before midnight.'

'Us? That'll give the children something to laugh about.'

'Let them.' She took his hand. 'I think I'm entitled to a dance with my favourite man.'

On the landing, with the party humming below them, Mark and Shula were sitting on the window seat. Shula had drawn the curtain back. The night was still and clear. It was Mark who'd suggested they come up here, but he'd gone awfully quiet.

'You look a bit funny,' said Shula. 'You're not going to say it's not going to work out, are you? I mean, I know my dad's a bit cross with you still, but that doesn't mean we can't go out together, does it?'

'No.' Mark's voice sounded as if his collar was too tight. 'Shula . . . I wanted to ask you something.'

Shula tilted her head expectantly.

244

'Would you like to marry me?'

Shula blinked.

'Marry you? You mean – get married?'

'Yes.' Mark was breathing more easily now but he seemed to have passed all his breathing difficulties on to Shula.

'It's a bit of a surprise,' she said weakly. 'I mean, I wasn't expecting it . . . but . . .' She smiled through the suddenness of it all. 'Yes, yes, I will!'

Ever cautious, Mark had to make sure.

'You will marry me?'

'Yes, if you want to.' Shula was laughing now. She hugged him tight. 'Yes, definitely. Oh, let's go and tell everyone. Get Dad to open the champagne!'

From downstairs, the bongs of Big Ben were accompanied by cheers and the bells of St Stephen's began to peal in the New Year.

'I think he might have done that already.' Mark leaned forward and kissed her. 'Happy New Year, Shula. Lots of them.'

·18·

Inevitabilities

'Robin Catchpole, *Borchester Echo*.'

Shula took the outstretched hand, shook it and returned it to its owner. Even though he was hopelessly attractive, with dark hair that curled on, and inside, his collar, and a sweet face like a Renaissance painting, she was Mark's fiancée, after all.

'So what's your contribution to all this erudition?' he asked.

'Well,' replied Shula, 'I helped Jennifer with her survey. And,' – indicating the display board nearby – 'these are my grandmother's old photographs.'

Robin pulled a tragic face.

'Not another Archer!' he exclaimed. 'Is this whole village run by The Firm? I might as well be in Palermo.'

'I suppose there are quite a few of us,' Shula apologized. 'Just don't get Joe Grundy on the subject.'

It was the night of the Landscape Survey Exhibition in Jennifer's studio. For the past week the team had been busy with scissors and sticky tape, mounting the exhibits and writing identification cards. Tonight, Jennifer had provided the food, Brian the wine, and judging by the turn-out from the village and the presence of a reporter from the *Borchester Echo*, the evening might be judged a success. Except, possibly, by Jennifer herself.

'She looks proper washed out,' Mrs P muttered to Walter from their pole position near the buffet table.

'I suppose she's tired from h'organizing this little lot,' speculated Walter. He gestured round the room with a sweep of his arm, which took in the walls plastered with photographs culled from Doris's old albums and the display tables showing fragments of glass, lumps of pottery and the odd coin, said to be Roman. 'Not to mention *this* little lot.' He helped himself to his fifth miniature asparagus quiche.

'Huh,' snorted Mrs P. 'The fact that she keeps watching the door waiting for John Tregorran to arrive has nothing to do with it, I suppose. And if you don't lay off them pastries, Mr Gabriel, you'll be paying for it by midnight.'

'Doh . . .' Walter, whose hand was hovering over a plate of vol-au-vents, withdrew it reluctantly.

Mrs P sipped her cream sherry. She had a very good idea why Jennifer was looking so drained, and it was nothing to do with preparing for the exhibition. Jennifer wasn't afraid of a bit of hard work, something which Mrs P maintained she'd inherited from the Perkins side of the family. The things that exhausted Jennifer were always emotional.

Her granddaughter's year had started badly, Mrs P reflected, when Paddy Redmond had turned up in the village. Supposedly on his way to a farm manager's job in Ulster, he'd decided, so he'd had the nerve to tell Tom Forrest in the pub, to look up a few 'old friends'. And to stir up a lot of old memories, as Mrs P had remarked darkly to Dan. Mrs P (to her frustration) didn't know the ins and outs of it, but, though Brian had tried to get rid of him, Paddy had eventually cornered Jennifer on the village green. Adam had been with her and Jennifer had been terrified he'd try and talk to the boy and tell him everything. Luckily, Paddy's curiosity about his son had seemed to be satisfied merely by seeing him, but Jennifer had got home in such a state that Brian had had to leave young David, who was helping him during lambing, and come in to comfort her. As a result, a load of lambs had been mismothered and three had died, but to his credit, Brian hadn't even made a fuss. And at the end of the week, his generosity had been repaid. Paddy left the village without further contact and Adam was able to go back to Sherborne, where he was at boarding school, completely unaware that he had almost met his father.

And then, thought Mrs P, covering her glass as Tony offered her a refill, when Jennifer was starting to relax, Carol Tregorran had announced that John was due back from America at the beginning of February, just in time for the Landscape Survey Exhibition.

Mrs P shook her head, especially permed by Amanda for the occasion. What was it about Peggy's girls? There was Lilian, when she visited Ambridge, spending all her time drinking in Nelson's wine bar and Jennifer behaving like a teenager with someone else's husband. Only Tony, who had been so spoilt as a baby and whom Mrs P had confidently predicted would turn out to be trouble, had turned out all right, working his socks off at Bridge Farm and about to become a father for the third time.

Mrs P glanced across the room. Jennifer had joined a group around that young reporter chappie. She ought to be safe enough there. If Mrs P knew anything, he'd got his eye on Caroline . . .

'It's a very creditable effort,' Robin was saying. As the only good-looking and eligible male in the room (though Walter would have taken issue with the claim), he was now surrounded by a bevy of Ambridge women: Shula, Jennifer and the gigantically pregnant Pat. 'Some really nice pieces. Those sketches by – who was it? – Caroline someone-or-other . . . Very pretty.'

'Ye-es,' agreed Jennifer. She hadn't felt very well-disposed towards Caroline earlier in the evening, when Brian had explained at great length and with great mirth how, when the three of them had gone up in his Cessna to photograph the deserted village of Ambridge Superior, Caroline had had to take over the camera when Jennifer had come over all queasy.

'All the photos bar one came out – she was brilliant!' Brian had crowed. 'All perfect except for one of the back of my head!'

Caroline had laughed and quipped back: 'Well, it is your best side, Brian,' and Brian had chortled merrily as he refilled her glass.

However, Jennifer decided that, for publicity purposes, and mindful of the *Echo*'s readership, she should wax a little more magnanimous.

'Caroline's a very talented artist. Her sketches have really added to the atmosphere of the exhibition,' she added, and was gratified when Robin looped it down in shorthand.

'And what a stunner! And then there's Shula here and yourself, and Pat, of course,' he added gallantly. 'And you've all worked on the survey. Such talent!'

Jennifer wasn't sure in what sense he was using the word, but she smiled anyway. All that wine on an empty stomach was making her feel quite light-headed. And still no sign of John.

'I don't suppose you've thought of putting all the material you've collected out in book form, have you?' Robin went on. 'I don't honestly think it would attract a mainstream publisher, but a little local outfit might be interested – even if it was only as a vanity publication . . .'

Suddenly it made sense. All those hours in the Public Record Office and the County Archives, the dank evenings in Joe Grundy's cellar, which was part of an old ruined chapel from Ambridge Superior, the pages of data on water tables and Roman roads and classic ridge and furrow . . .

'Robin, that's a brilliant idea!' she enthused. 'I'd never even thought of it.'

'I'll go one better,' Robin went on. 'Why don't I mention it to our proprietor, Jack Woolley?'

• • •

'Listen to this, Shula.' Clarrie Larkin read from the newspaper she was holding. ' "They are over the moon," said Lady Sarah. "It struck me they were in love just before Christmas. There was an extra sparkle in her eye and I thought a wedding would be on the cards." ' Clarrie sighed extravagantly. 'Prince Charles and Lady Diana engaged! Isn't it lovely!'

'Mmm,' agreed Shula. She was in rather a hurry. She'd only popped into Underwoods for a birth congratulations card for Pat and Tony – it was another boy, Thomas – but Clarrie had trapped her by the news-stand. Shula glanced at the front pages. Every one of them carried the same photograph: Lady Diana looking up at the camera from under her eyelashes with Prince Charles's hand, like the future, heavy on her shoulder. In the corner of one portrait, a close-up of the ring was inset: a huge sapphire encircled with diamonds. Shula looked down at her own engagement ring: three opals in a Victorian setting which had been passed down through Mark's family. They'd set the date for 26 September and, having told Dan they had no intention of making him leave Glebe Cottage, were buying a terraced cottage in Penny Hassett.

'How's Eddie?' she asked. Clarrie had been going out with Eddie, Joe Grundy's younger son, since the previous year, much to Jethro's disgust. 'Has he recovered now?' There'd been a nasty incident in the milking parlour at Grange Farm a few weeks back, when Eddie, and a few of the cows, had received electric shocks thanks to a short circuit in the power supply.

'Oh, he's fine,' said Clarrie sadly, folding her paper. 'Treated me to a Chinese and chips last night. I had a choice. It was either that or a darts match down The Cat and Fiddle.'

'And what about his recording career?'

Clarrie sniffed. 'Nelson Gabriel's supposed to be helping him with that. But in return, Eddie's promised to bottle up all this herbal shampoo that Nelson's flogging. The turkey shed's full of it, and it's yours truly who's doing most of the work. Still . . . you chosen your wedding dress yet, Shula?'

'I can't see anything I like. I think Mum will end up making it.'

'I'm sure it'll be beautiful,' sighed Clarrie enviously. 'Getting married . . . And in the same year as a royal wedding. It's bound to be lucky for you.'

'I hope so.' Shula hadn't felt very lucky at the weekend when she'd had to go to Sunday lunch with Mark's parents and Bunty had quizzed her about her prospects at Rodway's and whether, when they had children, she'd be prepared to give up her career.

'Hello, girls!' Robin Catchpole's head suddenly popped up over a display of early Easter bunnies. Shula smiled despite herself. She kept bumping into Robin in Nelson's wine bar. He was always teasing her about how, once she was married, she'd have to spend her lunch times queuing in the greengrocer's, so she should enjoy them while she could. 'Catching up on the gossip?'

'He's a card, isn't he?' Clarrie whispered as Robin wove his way round to join them. 'Eddie says he's got a roving eye. But you're all right. You're engaged.'

'Yes,' said Shula. 'I am, aren't I?'

And no one will let me forget it, she thought.

As the months progressed, Shula felt as though she was being propelled towards her wedding by some external force, broadly benign, but not at all interested in what she was feeling.

'If it's like this for me, what must it be like for them?' she demanded of Caroline, meaning the Royal Couple, as they were now referred to. Their faces appeared on toffee tins and tea towels. The papers, television and even the radio crackled with speculation about the dress, the honeymoon destination and the seating arrangements in St Paul's. By comparison, the plans for Shula's wedding were remarkably simple. She should have felt grateful: at least she didn't have to curtsey to her future mother-in-law, though she suspected Bunty would rather have liked it.

But all through that sultry, rather disappointing summer, she felt the pressure build. At the end of July, there was a public holiday when Prince Charles and Lady Diana were married. The villagers of Ambridge had sent a telegram of congratulation. Dan and Walter recalled the Queen's Coronation and her Silver Jubilee: the younger generation smiled at the human touch of the helium balloons attached to the going-away carriage by Prince Andrew. But when Neil, passing Shula in the yard the following morning, said blithely, 'You're next!', she fled indoors without the eggs she'd gone out to collect, leaving her father and mother looking at each other in bewilderment over her empty place at breakfast.

From then on, Shula often thought afterwards, it was only a matter of time. She went to church with Mark and both sets of parents to hear the banns read. She and Mark started marriage preparation classes and chose the hymns. They drew up a wedding present list. Shula wanted a Meissen dinner service and a silk carpet. Mark wanted a power saw.

Inevitabilities

She was seeing less of Robin Catchpole now: she felt she had to. He'd invited her over one night to the flat at Nightingale Farm he shared with Neil; he'd cooked her supper and told her that he loved her. For days afterwards he'd laid siege to Rodway's with flowers and absurd, florid poems he'd written. But Shula had avoided him. Seeing him aroused feelings and raised doubts she didn't want to confront.

She tried to fight it because she knew how much everyone was looking forward to the wedding and the effort they'd put into the preparations. It seemed that, like so many other things in life, it would be easier to go through with it than get out of it. When her mother questioned her, she maintained stiffly that she was all right, it was just nerves, and she avoided Caroline, from whom she didn't think she could hide her feelings. She thought she was doing a pretty good job of hiding them from Mark, too, but he wasn't insensitive. When he took her out to Grey Gables for her birthday, she almost got away with it, but Jack Woolley, trying to be kind, sent over champagne. It made her weepy at the best of times: when Mark raised his glass and said 'To us!' she burst into tears and he had to hustle her out to the car. There she cried hotly into his shoulder and he suggested that they postpone the wedding. She shook her head violently.

'No!'

'I'm not saying we won't ever get married, but we haven't got to do it now. We can give ourselves another six months to get the house straight, calm you down. What's the rush?'

But Shula knew she couldn't stand the waiting any longer. If she didn't go through with it next month, maybe she never would. So things were patched up – again – but it was like bandaging a cut with a plaster whose stickiness had already worn off.

Just a few days later, Shula and Mark were doing some decorating at the cottage. They'd been spending most of their evenings there, painting the downstairs magnolia, and their bedroom Wedgwood blue, and glossing the skirting boards and the French doors into the garden. Shula was just knocking in a nail for one of Caroline's sketches, which she'd given them as an engagement present, when Mark came into the room.

'Try and hit it square,' he said helpfully, standing right behind her.

'I am,' said Shula, giving it another bash. 'Ow!'

'Why won't you let me do it?'

She'd dented the plaster now, but Mark wasn't even cross. He was amused, which was worse. And Shula just flipped. She turned on him and accused him of being patronizing and impatient, and he snapped back that she'd try the patience of a saint, dithering like she had been over the wedding, which, for God's sake, affected his future as well as hers, and then jumping down his throat because he offered to help her bang a nail in straight.

'I don't think you understand what you're saying half the time,' he accused.

'I'm sorry,' she said coldly. But she was.

'What do you want from me, Shula?' he demanded. 'Well? Do you know?'

Shula lowered the hammer carefully and placed it on the mantel-piece. Caroline's drawing was propped against the wall. It was of the tower of St Stephen's, where the bells would ring out for their wedding, with white trumpets of convulvulus in the foreground.

'It's not going to work, is it?' she said quietly.

'I don't know.' Mark scuffed the bare floorboards with the toe of his shoe. They were having the carpets fitted on Friday. 'It's not for lack of wanting it to.'

'I know,' said Shula. 'I've tried.'

'I really didn't think it would ever come to this.'

'I know.' She began to cry. 'Oh, Mark, I'm sorry. So very, very sorry!'

Jill poured Peggy another cup of tea. Summer – or at least, sunshine – had arrived at last. From the other side of the orchard came the thrum of the combine as it chopped its way through the winter wheat. To and fro in the yard came the trailers of slippery grain to be poured into the pit in a slither of gold. Later, there'd be the bales to stack under the eaves of the Dutch barn and earnest conversations between Phil and David about moisture content and tonnage per acre. Every year the same: the worry about the weather and the spare parts that were out of stock, and this year, Brian's furious account of day-trippers who'd left behind a picnic chair that had caught in his combine and clogged it for half a day.

'So the wedding's definitely off?' Peggy refused another piece of Jill's banana bread, delicious as it was.

Jill sighed and sat back in her deckchair.

'This is the first chance I've had to sit down since Shula told us,' she said. 'I've been on the phone for two days solid undoing everything.'

'Oh, Jill, what a shame.'

'Yes, it is, but not if it's what she wants.'

Peggy looked round the garden, the flower borders humming with bees and the bent apple tree.

'Do they ever know what they want, though?' she brooded. 'Take Jennifer . . .'

'Oh, yes, Jennifer.'

Jill had already heard from Martha Woodford (Radio Ambridge as David called her) about a disastrous dinner party at Home Farm. John Tregorran had ticked Brian off about deep ploughing some classic ridge and furrow, and Brian had barked back about literary types who knew nothing about the countryside making themselves and everyone around them look ridiculous. According to Martha, by the time Jennifer had served the soup, John had got his jacket on to go home and Brian was saying John was lucky he hadn't booted him through the window.

'All she can say in defence of her friendship with John is that he provides an extra dimension to her life.' Peggy stirred her tea and took a sip. 'That's all very well, I told her, but what if Brian decides he needs an extra dimension to his life? She wouldn't like that one bit.'

'No,' sighed Jill. It all seemed very complicated. She hadn't had Shula's doubts before she'd married Phil: she hadn't experienced Jennifer's lack of fulfilment since.

'The thing with Jennifer,' Peggy concluded, 'is that she tries things out. Teaching. Writing. Paddy. Roger. Brian. What she doesn't seem to realize is that you don't just try marriage out – you stick with it.'

'Yes,' said Jill. 'I think that's what Shula realized. Just in time.'

• • •

Jennifer poured Brian's coffee in silence. At the other end of the table was the pile of book proofs that John Tregorran had brought over earlier. He'd said that he thought it would be better all round if he handed responsibility for checking them over to her: there was really no need for them to collaborate any more. Jennifer slid Brian's cup across the table and he looked up from the letter he was reading.

'Farmers' co-operative in Penny Hassett,' he informed her. 'Want to know if I'm still interested in going in with them for the sugar-beet equipment.'

'Really?' Jennifer tried to sound interested. Out of the corner of her eye she could see John's writing on the top sheet of the proofs, his tidy italic script. She tried again. 'I thought you'd decided you'd got too big an acreage to do that.'

'Hm.' Brian twisted his mouth in thought. 'They're good blokes. It might be worth keeping them sweet. I'll write back straight away and explain the position.'

Jennifer strained to see what the page of proofs was about. Ah, John's piece on the Borsetshire dialect in Shakespeare. She'd thought it was so brilliant when she'd first read it.

'Phil's gone in with them,' Brian mused, 'for his potatoes. Had to put in a couple of thou, but for that he gets the use of the planter and lifter, storage – and marketing, of course.'

Jennifer stood up and began to clear the table.

'Hey, I haven't finished!' Brian sawed himself off another lump of Stilton. 'What are you doing this afternoon?'

Jennifer opened the dishwasher.

'I was going to rework my piece on the deserted village of Ambridge for the *Echo*,' she said coolly. 'But it sounds as though you'll be using the decent typewriter.'

256

'It does belong to the farm,' Brian pointed out reasonably. 'You'll just have to use your trusty portable.'

Jennifer clattered plates and glasses into the racks. That was the thing with Brian, he was so irritatingly reasonable. When she'd told him about Shula's broken engagement, all he'd said was that he'd never thought it would last. In his opinion, Mark was too sensible and Shula too flighty. Jennifer had looked at him in case he was being sarcastic. But the irony of his remark seemed totally to have escaped him. Perhaps it was just as well.

·19·

Liberation

'Women's Studies?' Jethro Larkin sounded puzzled – but then, he often did. 'What's that when it's at home?'

Tony took a bitter sip of his pint. That was the point: Pat wasn't at home. She was off on her course at the Tech, which was why he'd had to seek refuge – and his supper – in The Bull.

'Women's Studies,' mused Jethro. Tony wished he'd kept his mouth shut. 'Bakin', I suppose. And mendin' and the like.'

Tony slammed his tankard back on the bar. There was no point in trying to get Jethro to understand about consciousness-raising. This was the man whose daughter had married Eddie Grundy.

'Yes, Jethro,' he replied. 'That's the sort of thing.' And then, determined to deflect the conversation, he asked, 'You put the tup in with the ewes yet at Brookfield?'

As Jethro maundered mildly on about harnesses and crayons and what he'd said to Master Phil that morning, requiring only grunts in response, Tony found himself able to think his own thoughts.

It was over a year now since Pat had started behaving, well, oddly. It had all started with her CND kick – sympathizing with all those strange women protesting against the Cruise missiles at Greenham Common, and going to a Peace Service for Nagasaki in Borchester with the vicar, Richard Adamson, and his wife Dorothy. They'd had coloured lanterns, apparently, and had floated little paper boats on the Am.

'Didn't they get soggy and sink?' Tony had demanded prosaically, to sighs from Pat.

'I can remember, just after I met you,' she'd retorted, 'you telling me how you'd have liked to have been in Hyde Park when Mick Jagger released all those butterflies for Brian Jones.'

'Pat, that was years ago!' he'd exclaimed. 'You grow out of things like that.'

'Do you?' she'd said hollowly.

And then she'd had to go and see to Tommy, who was eighteen months old and still cutting his back teeth and producing horrendous nappies in the process. And Tony had hunted around for the paper so he could look at 'The Gambols' before he went to do the afternoon milking, only to remember that Pat had switched to the *Guardian* because, she said, it was the only newspaper that took women seriously. But there weren't any cartoons in the *Guardian* – not ones Tony could understand. To cheer himself up he'd had a can of lager instead.

'So,' said Jethro ponderously, cutting across his thoughts. 'How's your calving going?'

Tony replied mechanically – about the problems with Sybil, who'd got milk fever, and how there were so many heifer calves he wished he'd gone for the AI from the bull which promised to throw them with good feet, which would come in useful in the parlour later on. But he was still thinking about Pat, and when things had started to change and, more importantly, why.

He wondered sometimes if, in a way, it had all begun five years ago with their move to Bridge Farm. They'd thought of it as a new start, and a brilliant opportunity, their own free-standing tenancy with no partnership agreements to worry about. But nothing about the move had been straightforward. There'd been all the difficulty over moving dates, and that fraught time when the Tuckers were living with them because they'd had to get out of their cottage before Tony and Pat were out of Willow Farm. Betty had been pregnant with Roy, and Pat had been broody, but Tony had said no way till they were settled at the new place. And Mike had got on Pat's nerves with his loud opinions and the way he belittled Betty, not to mention his Country and Western music, which they'd had to endure till all hours. Still, Pat and Tony had finally moved on Lady Day, milking their seventy cows in the second-hand herringbone parlour Tony had installed.

In the September Pat had told him she was pregnant and he'd been thrilled. He knew she was secretly hoping for a girl, and when Helen arrived the following April, everything should have been perfect. But she'd been a breech baby, a long, hard, distressing birth for Pat, and as a result the baby's hips were dislocated, which meant she'd have to spend months in a plaster cast. Pat sank really low. She fussed over Helen at the expense of John and suddenly, in the summer, announced that she was taking both children to Wales for a change of scene. Tony, who'd come to rely on her help on the farm less and less, had encouraged her to go. He got Percy Jordan in to do the afternoon milking, and Gerry Goodway to help with the harvest.

He'd soldiered on, driving the tractor and trailer alongside the combine, baling the straw, drying off the cows. But he was only human. And when a new milk recorder, Libby Jones, arrived to take samples, and to flirt while she did it, he couldn't see the harm in asking her in for a cup of tea. Next thing he knew she was dropping by whenever she was in the area, doing the washing-up and emptying the kitchen bin. As a thank you, he'd invited her to the cricket club dance. Where was the harm in it? She knew full well he was married, but that only prompted a lecture from Jennifer, which made Tony stick out his bottom lip defiantly and determine to do what he liked.

Who knows what would have happened if Pat hadn't come back? But in the middle of September she returned and told him crisply that she was going to keep an eye on him from now on. How did she *know*? Jennifer swore she hadn't said a word – and life went on as before. Of course, the magic of their early married life was gone: they each had a twenty-four-hour-a-day job, seven days a week, running a farm and caring for two small children. It was enough to contend with when things were going well, let alone when they weren't. And they did have some bad luck. There was a bad outbreak of mastitis, then suspected foot and mouth – and Tony's own tetanus which he'd contracted from a rusty nail. No sooner had he recovered than Pat found she was pregnant again with Tommy – just after she'd given all the old baby clothes to Betty Tucker for her second.

So there it was. A five-year catalogue of, if not exactly disasters, then difficulties. Hard work for small rewards and few pleasures in life except, for Tony, a pint or two at the end of a long day, and for

Pat . . . the children, he supposed. Wasn't that where women were supposed to find their fulfilment? She certainly didn't seem to find it in him any more, judging from the amount of time she'd started spending off the farm and on these courses in Borchester.

Jethro was clearing his throat meaningfully and pulling at a thread on his ancient green cardigan. Tony realized it was his round. He produced a pound note from his pocket and waved it at Sid, who was busy at the other end of the bar.

'Still, you got summat to look forward to,' Jethro pronounced. 'Miss Shula tells me you're going to the ball.'

'Oh, that.'

Somehow they'd been conned into forking out twenty quid a ticket for a do in aid of the Borchester Hospital League of Friends. *And* it was fancy dress.

'Fancy dress, I hear,' echoed Jethro, as if demonstrating psychic powers. 'I daresay Pat's looking forward to getting dressed up pretty.'

Tony grunted. If he knew anything, Pat would make him go as a nuclear warhead while she went as a peace candle. He really couldn't wait.

'Miss Shula's going with Nigel Pargetter,' chortled Jethro. 'He's a card, that one!'

'Walking disaster area, more like. I'm surprised Phil lets him near the place. Pint and a half of Shires, please, Sid,' Tony added as the landlord approached.

'Oy!' said Jethro. 'Who said I was only having a half?'

Tony and Sid exchanged glances.

'You only ever drink halves after nine o'clock,' said Sid.

'Well, I'm living dangerously tonight. I ain't got far to walk.'

Tony fished in his pocket for some change. Jethro Larkin living dangerously. That was all he needed.

'Nigel, put me down! Put me down this minute!'

Pat's shrieks topped with Nigel's baboon noises carried over the thump of the disco. Tony was not amused.

'Honestly, Shula, your boyfriend ought to be locked up.'

Shula poured herself another glass of champagne.

'Gorillas know a thing or two. That's the way to treat 'em, Tony. Bundle 'em over your shoulder and away you go.'

'He's an oaf,' ranted Tony. 'A degenerate oaf. He ought to grow up.'

'Poof!' giggled Shula. 'And furthermore, piffle! Ooh, look, you've gone all streaky!'

'Yes, well, if your boyfriend hadn't sprayed champagne all over me . . .'

Tony had been worried from the start about his Superman costume. Quite apart from the unfavourable comments he could see his puny pectorals attracting when compared with the real thing, Pat had dyed a white T-shirt red – a process he never trusted – and had made his Superman motif out of crêpe paper. A dousing in champagne had turned the T-shirt a marbled pink and made the crêpe paper curl at the edges. He'd suspected some sort of irony in Pat's suggestions for costumes anyway – she'd come as Little Bo Peep – and now his worst fears had been realized. In the absence of Pat, rashly attempting to jive with Nigel, he turned on Shula.

'I don't know what gets into you, I really don't. There's Mark, a nice, reliable, responsible sort of bloke . . .'

'Oh, shut up,' smiled Shula. 'Where's the rest of that champagne, or did Nigel waste it all on you?'

Tony allowed himself to be pacified with another drink, sulkily watching the dancing. Shula leaned against a pillar and adjusted the spangly bra top of her harem girl costume. She wished Tony hadn't reminded her about Mark, especially as he was here with his new fiancée – yes, fiancée – Sarah Locke, whose father just happened to be a partner in Locke and Martin, another local firm of solicitors. Shula had had a dance with Mark earlier because you had to be civilized about these things, though she didn't feel very civilized when she saw Mark kissing Sarah during 'Jealous Guy', which had always been one of their songs – at least, while Robin Catchpole had been around. Still, she'd jilted Mark, if not quite at the altar, then as good as, and now he had Sarah and she had . . . A gorilla's paw grabbed her round the waist and she squealed. Pat followed, laughing. She looked happier than Shula had seen her look for years.

'Do something with him, Shula, before he gets us all thrown out,' she pleaded.

'She's not as frightening as she looks,' confided Nigel, who always professed himself terrified of Pat, 'but she can't jive.'

'I can.' Shula pinned on her cheerful face again and grabbed Nigel's paw. 'Come on, let's show these boring old farmers how it's done!'

'I don't think I'll go to church this morning, Phil. I rather fancy a little lie-in and getting the lunch ready at a leisurely pace.'

It was the morning after the ball. Phil, who'd just come in from milking, and had brought Jill up a cup of tea, looked concerned.

'Jill? Are you feeling all right?'

'I'm fine. Just tired.'

Phil sat on the side of the bed.

'Lying awake half the night worrying about Shula, I suppose. I can't say I blame you when she's out with that buffoon.'

'Baboon, Phil, he was dressed as a baboon.'

'You know what I mean. Nigel's not exactly a good influence, is he? It was only a couple of weeks ago he rode straight across my young barley with the Hunt . . .'

'He was lucky he didn't come off.'

'Standing up in the stirrups and waving his riding crop, it would have been his own fault.' Phil clattered his cup back in its saucer as a new thought struck him. 'He's not coming to lunch, is he?'

'I don't think so, dear.'

'Good. I had enough of him at supper the other night, treading sprouts into the carpet.'

'That was an accident, Phil,' said Jill quickly. She couldn't help it. She liked Nigel. 'It could have happened to anybody.'

'Maybe. But I notice it only actually happened to him.'

Jill snuggled down under the covers and sighed. She certainly wasn't going to tell Phil that she'd been awake since three, dozing off and on, waiting for the sound of the back door, or the fridge door, or anything that would have told her Shula was safely home. And how she hadn't heard any of them. And how, after Phil had gone out to do the milking, she'd got up and gone to the window, and there Shula had been, picking her way across the yard in her harem costume. Jill had shot downstairs to let her in and make her a hot drink, and had learnt that Nigel had insisted on driving her home past Netherbourne Woods, where he'd insisted there would be bluebells.

'In November?' Jill had asked.

'You know Nigel when he gets an idea in his head,' Shula had shrugged. 'And there weren't any, of course, and after about an hour of traipsing round in the cold, we went back to the car, and we both had a little snooze, and then I woke up, and Nigel was still snoring, so I left him there.' She smiled fondly. 'He looked so peaceful. For once.'

Jill shook her head, amused. Phil didn't approve of Nigel, she knew, and he was perhaps a little high spirited, but she was just pleased to see Shula enjoying herself. It was over two years since her cancelled wedding to Mark, and it wasn't easy for her, still having to do business with him and see him around Borchester. And now he'd gone and got himself engaged again. It really was a good thing that Shula had Nigel to distract her.

Even Phil would have had to concede that life was never dull with Nigel around. Many was the time during that winter when he came in at twilight after a dank day walking the crops, or doing a bit of fencing with David, to find Nigel in the kitchen. Jill would be plying him with tea and Dundee cake and laughing while he regaled her with some story or other. They'd often hardly notice Phil come in. He'd get himself a cup from the dresser and join them at the table while Nigel explained that he'd had German measles as a child and when he'd got back to school they'd done subtraction and after that, well, he'd never really got the hang of maths . . . Jill would tut sympathetically and pour more tea and Phil would keep his own counsel, remembering that this was the scion of a noble family whose ancestors could be traced back to the sixteenth century. Lead piping and bad roads, he concluded, really did have a lot to answer for. After a bit, Shula would appear in a scrap of a frock that barely covered the essentials and after a fluster of goodbyes, they would roar off merrily into the night.

It was a source of some amazement to Phil, judging by the amount of time Nigel spent at Brookfield during the day, to learn that he did actually have a job. When, however, he found out what it was, his amazement was somewhat diminished because it was the only sort of job that someone as bird-brained as Nigel could possibly get. Nigel's job was selling swimming pools and, as he frequently said, you wouldn't have thought it would be difficult with all the wealthy farmers in the area adding to the grain and butter mountains and banking their subsidy cheques. But Jennifer and Brian already had a pool, and Phil, despite Shula's pleas, had no intention of buying one. Every other week, it seemed, Nigel's boss told him that if he hadn't sold a pool by the end of the month he'd be sacked, but even when he did manage to clinch a sale, somehow Nigel's high spirits got in the way of success. A deal with Jack Woolley was looking good when Nigel and friends foolishly celebrated prematurely at Grey Gables, doing the conga round the East Wing and mixing cocktails in Jack's precious Chrysanthemum Society Challenge Cup. Needless to say, the next day the deal was off.

But Phil had to admit that Nigel had style. One night he'd whisked Shula off to dinner in London – the Connaught, if you please – and Phil had come down first thing to find the papers, hot off the presses in Fleet Street, on the breakfast table. Sometimes – a lot of the time – though, Nigel's good intentions rebounded on him. Early in the New Year he cooked Shula lunch at Lower Loxley, the decaying Jacobean mansion where the Pargetters had lived since 1702. Duck with Cumberland sauce. A nice gesture. A pity, then, that he'd managed to use two bottles of port in the sauce – and not just any old port – two bottles of Taylor's '50 from Gerald Pargetter's cellar.

'It's so nice in here, isn't it?' said Nigel the next evening, after he'd been invited to supper at Brookfield and they were all drinking coffee in front of the fire. 'The log fire and the comfy chairs. That huge settee. And the central heating.'

Shula looked at him and looked at her mother. When Nigel's father had found out about the port, he'd thrown him out – and not just out of the house. He'd even gone prowling round the grounds and had thrown his son out of the garden shed where he'd curled up on a bit of sacking. Nigel had had to go and stay at his friend Tim Beecham's flat. Tim never washed anything, just threw it down on the floor and bought another one. He was a trainee accountant and should have known better but he just said he was contributing to the GNP.

'Look, I don't think . . .' Phil deftly anticipated what was coming. 'We're right in the middle of lambing, Nigel,' he explained. 'You wouldn't get much rest here.'

'Oh, that wouldn't matter, Mr Archer,' said Nigel quickly. 'I'm used to that.'

'Oh, Dad, please let him stay!' Shula grabbed her father's hand. 'I don't suppose you've ever spent the night on the floor of a filthy flat in an ex-Army sleeping bag with your head in an old ashtray, have you? Well, have you?'

Phil looked helplessly at Jill, who shrugged happily.

'If you don't mind the sofa, Nigel, you're welcome to stay for tonight,' she smiled. 'More coffee, Phil?'

There was something about Nigel, Phil had to acknowledge wearily the next day after Nigel had eaten more than his fair share of sausages and pinched the last slice of toast at breakfast. He had all the women in the family on his side. Even Peggy, who'd thought he was a wastrel of the first order, had warmed to him when he'd found her cat, Sammy, who'd gone missing after a fire at Blossom Hill Cottage. Pat, for all her feminist principles and her cant about the oppression of the masses, in which the Pargetters must surely have played a part to have been rewarded with that great house, had allowed herself to be wooed with out-of-season strawberries and apologies for Nigel's behaviour to Tony at the fancy dress ball. Jill and Shula seemed to be potty about him. Only Elizabeth, home for the weekend from her boarding school, gave Phil some cause for hope when she proclaimed crisply:

'He's a total idiot.' Then added, 'But a very nice one.'

'You ought to try it, Shula. Are you sure you won't come along?'

Shula shook her head.

'Is that straight now?' she puffed.

'Hang on . . . up a tiny bit on the right . . . down a bit . . . OK.'

Pat made a pencil mark on the wall for the screw holes of the brackets and Shula lowered the shelf to the floor. Pat had turned the box-room at Bridge Farm into a study. She'd painted the walls yellow, stripped an old table for use as a desk and now wanted shelves in an alcove. Shula didn't mind helping with the shelves, but she certainly didn't want to get roped in to Women's Studies classes at the Tech with Pat and her CND friend, Rose.

'I'm surprised you haven't got Helen putting up these shelves for you,' she remarked, as Pat selected the right bit for the drill. Rose, not one for stereotyping, had given Helen a tool-kit for her birthday. Helen and John had promptly taken off all the door handles with it, trapping Tommy in his bedroom.

'Do you know what your kids have done now?' Tony had boomed.

'*My* kids, huh? Must be something pretty bad.' Pat had lifted her head from a pile of invoices. 'Do you know how much we've spent on nitrogen this spring? It's astronomical.'

And so from Helen and John's misdemeanours they'd got into a discussion about the farm and how they were going to pay their way if, as was threatened, quotas were put on milk to curb over-production.

'Tony's confiscated the tool-kit,' Pat explained to Shula now. 'He got it in the neck from Joe Grundy in the pub. His fragile male ego couldn't stand it.'

'Right.' Shula watched as Pat attacked the wall.

'I hear there was a bit of confusion over bedrooms in your house, too,' Pat said wryly when the terrible grinding noise had stopped.

'Don't remind me.' Shula passed her a rawlplug. Nigel was

currently banned from Brookfield. When they'd got back from a ball in the early hours rather the worse for wear, Shula had forbidden him to drive home. Instead, she'd fetched some blankets and pillows and tucked him up on the sofa.

'You are good to me, Shulie,' he'd murmured confusedly.

'I know,' she said fondly, kissing the top of his head. 'Now you go straight off to sleep and I'll see you in the morning.'

She wasn't to know that Nigel would rouse himself after she'd gone and, thinking it too good an opportunity to miss, had crept upstairs – straight into Phil and Jill's bedroom.

'Were you . . . were you looking for the bathroom, Nigel?' Jill had quick-thinkingly improvised, as Shula had arrived in her parents' room, wondering what all the noise was.

'The bathroom. Yes, that's right. That's what I was looking for.' Nigel had stood there with his bedspread clutched round him, looking like a refugee from Pompeii. 'Hello, Shula.'

'Hello, Nigel,' she'd said weakly. The fool! How could he!

'Your boyfriend just tried to climb into my bed,' said her father stonily.

'Phil, he was looking for the bathroom!' her mother chided.

'Sorry, Shula,' said Nigel unnecessarily. 'I thought this was the bathroom.'

'It's half past three,' thundered Phil.

'Oh dear,' gulped Shula. 'I mean, sorry, Dad. Come on, Nigel.'

Shula still came over all hot and cold when she thought about it. She usually managed to explain away Nigel's behaviour but this incident had been beyond even her powers of invention. Next morning, her father had told her in terms that left no room for doubt that Nigel was no longer welcome overnight at Brookfield. Even the combined charms of Jill and Shula could not sway him and Nigel's offer to muck out the pigs with a teaspoon to show how sorry he was hadn't gone down well either.

Leaning against Pat's lemon-coloured wall, looking down at a pile of books with titles like *Empowerment: Utopia or Male Myth?*, Shula sighed. Nigel was a poppet, but he really was a liability half the time.

He'd been so good for her over the winter. He'd 'taken her out of herself', as her gran would have said. But now the spring was here, he'd hung up his gorilla suit till the cold weather came again, and though she knew he'd offer her an enticing summer of picnics by the Am and days at the races, the prospect somehow made her feel tired.

'Another rawlplug, please, Shula.'

Pat had been busy with her drill and there were now nine neat holes in the plaster. Pat didn't seem tired. Anything but. She'd had her hair cut and it really suited her. And she'd started wearing eye make-up. Obviously that was acceptable in Women's Studies.

'Pat,' began Shula, 'do you ever wish you hadn't got married? I mean, do you think single people have more fun?'

Pat, who was selecting screws, looked at her sharply.

'What have people been saying?'

'Nothing. Nothing.' Shula was a bit taken aback.

'Peggy hasn't been saying anything, then? About my evening classes?'

'No, honestly. I was just thinking about me and Nigel, that's all. And how different my life would have been if I'd married Mark.'

Pat gave her a wry look.

'I wouldn't be in too much of a hurry to get married, Shula. You know what it says on the T-shirts: "It starts when you sink into his arms and it ends with your arms in the sink."'

'Yes, I know. I know all that, but . . .' Shula tailed off.

How could she explain to Pat, who had to persuade Tony to babysit every time she went out, and who had to get her mother-in-law in to cook the kids' tea because Tony said it wasn't his job, that she'd have liked nothing better than to be tied to a house and a baby and how all the hectic evenings with Nigel just seemed pointless?

She told Pat it was nothing, she was just being silly, and they went on to talk about the NSPCC Fashion Show that was going to be held at Grey Gables and how excited Jack Woolley was because the Duke of Westminster would be there, and how he was badgering Nigel to get the pool, which he'd finally ordered, finished on time.

And Pat made her a cup of tea and she did a floor puzzle with

Tommy, who'd just woken up from his nap, and then she went back to the office and there was a note on her desk from Mr Rodway. He'd got to go to London, he said, could she take over two measuring-up jobs for him? One in Edgeley and one in Penny Hassett. Shula glanced briefly at the addresses. Elm View, Edgeley and . . . 10 Middle Cottages, Penny Hassett. Mark's cottage. Their old cottage.

Of course. Sarah Locke wouldn't want to live there. It would be far too modest for her. She'd want somewhere smarter – on a new estate, perhaps, where she could entertain Mark's colleagues with the fondue set they'd doubtless be given as a wedding present and she could park her sporty Fiesta next to Mark's BMW on the drive.

Shula got up from her desk and went to the Ladies'. Too sad to cry, she leaned her face against the metal of the roller-towel holder and closed her eyes. Oh, God. Why had she ever let Mark go?

·20·

A Parting of the Ways

'There's no two ways about it, Dad.' David eased the back of his neck with his hand. 'To stay within quota, we're going to have to reduce the size of the herd.'

Phil chewed his lip unhappily. It was nearly nine and they'd been poring over the figures in the farm office since supper. The introduction of milk quotas to tackle the problem of the overflowing 'milk lake' in Europe meant that farmers would have to produce less milk or pay a penalty. They could try and cut the cows' output by feeding them less, of course, but the difference would be minimal. Brookfield's animals were top-class beasts, bred to produce a fat milk cheque, and Phil realized that David was only articulating what he'd known all along. Something like fifteen of their 110-strong herd would have to be culled. They'd lose money on them in the short term because the market in dairy cattle was non-existent, but in the medium term there would be the reduction in the cost of their feed, and in the long term, the prospect of coming in on quota, or even under it.

Automatically, Phil reached out and felt the coffee pot. It was still vaguely warm and he poured the dregs into his cup.

'Not a very cheerful prospect, is it?' he said.

So much was said these days about farms being like factories. Dan mourned the fact that the cows had numbers now, not names, but Phil, David and Graham the cowman still knew them all individually. They knew that number 56 had a weak bag, that 79 was a kicker and that 105 was unsteady on her feet. It was always the same half dozen who were first at the gate to be brought in for milking and the same little groups that grazed together. To send fifteen of them to the abattoir to become meat pies and beefburgers before the end of their working lives felt unnatural, somehow. It would feel like murder.

'Haven't you finished yet? It's the news in a minute.'

Jill poked her head round the door.

'I won't be long, love. Is Shula in?'

'Not yet.' Jill looked thoughtful. 'Nigel popped round earlier.'

'Nigel? But he knew she was measuring up Mark's cottage tonight, surely?'

'Yes. That's what was worrying him.'

'Oh, for goodness' sake!' David helped himself to the last biscuit and chomped on it viciously. 'I wish that's all I had to worry about.'

'He's very fond of Shula.' Jill, as always, came to Nigel's defence.

'And he thinks she's still fond of Mark?' asked Phil shrewdly.

'He didn't put it quite like that.' Jill stacked their cups on the tray. 'What he actually said was that he thinks she still loves him.'

'Oh Mark! I'd forgotten!'

Shula stepped out into the sweet-smelling dusk and looked round her. Puzzled, Mark stood behind her on the cottage's back doorstep.

'What?'

'The forget-me-nots! Just look at them!'

Mark grinned awkwardly.

'That's a bit of a contradiction, isn't it? But then I'd forgotten they were your favourites.'

Shula moved, entranced, towards the fuzzy sea of blue.

'When they grow all over like this they are.'

'They have taken over a bit.'

Mark followed her as she stood on the lawn and craned her neck up to look at the back wall of the house and what she could see of the roof. A pair of turtle doves called from the horse chestnut at the bottom of the garden.

'It all looks quite presentable,' Shula concluded. From what she could see, it did, though she should have got out here earlier. It had been just too tempting to linger inside, to see what Mark had done to the place and to criticize inwardly any touches she felt might be Sarah's. 'And we had a surveyor's report when you moved in.'

'Exactly,' said Mark. 'And I don't see what I could have done to the roof or the walls. I haven't been here that long.'

Shula stepped a pace further back. She crossed her arms over her chest and sighed.

'It's a dear litle cottage, isn't it? It's a pity . . .'

She stopped. Mark said nothing. The turtle doves gurgled away.

Then he asked tentatively: 'Fancy a glass of wine? I've got a bottle chilling in the fridge.'

'I'd love one,' said Shula quickly. 'If you're sure.'

'It's half past eleven,' said Nigel. 'She's been in there for four hours.' Caroline looked at him sympathetically. She'd driven over to Penny Hassett to give Charlie, her old English sheepdog, a good run over his favourite bit of country and, coming back to her car, had found Nigel sitting on a waymarker outside Mark's cottage. That had been nearly three hours ago. She'd suggested they go for a drink in the local pub, The Griffin's Head, but after closing time, Nigel had insisted on coming back to see if Shula's car was still there. Unfortunately, it was, and he had embarked on the second stage of his vigil.

'Oh, Nigel,' she said, as Charlie began to whine. 'Don't cry. You're upsetting Charlie.'

'I'm not,' insisted Nigel. 'A bit of hay fever I think.' He patted Charlie's summer-cropped coat. 'There, there, Charlie. I'm all right really.'

'I'll give you a lift home, shall I?' urged Caroline. 'You don't want to wait out here.'

Nigel looked up at her tragically. Charlie looked up at her as well – two pairs of sad brown eyes.

'No,' he said. 'I don't want to wait any longer.'

'Oh, Nigel.' Caroline put a hand on his arm. 'I don't know what to say.'

'There's nothing you can say, is there?' he replied stiffly. 'It's as I said to Mrs Archer earlier. She still loves him, Caroline. She still loves him.'

Shula wished she knew what she felt. Her feelings were so muddled that she couldn't disentangle one from another and increasingly she felt enmeshed by them.

Nothing had happened between her and Mark the evening she had measured up the cottage. Shula hadn't blurted out that she still cared for him, he hadn't pledged to throw over Sarah and marry her instead. She'd gone into the office the next day and given Jane the house details to type up: she'd have to go back in the daylight and take photographs of the exterior. When it went on the market, there was a lot of initial interest and a swift offer: a young couple, buying it for their first home, just as she and Mark had intended. At that point Shula decided she'd had enough. She handed the sale over to a colleague: the last thing she wanted was to be in on the negotiations about carpets and curtains. After all, it wasn't her cottage any more. Why should the outcome affect her?

She found that she couldn't take any interest in the usual summer goings-on in the village, either. The Grey Gables charity fashion show came and went, with the unexpected appearance of another aristocratic guest – Princess Margaret, no less, who was the NSPCC's patron. A fawning Jack Woolley had nearly fallen in the newly constructed swimming pool when the Duke of Westminster had led her over, and Caroline was furious because he now wanted to move her to a box-room and rename her old suite of rooms, where the Princess had powdered her nose, the Royal Garden Suite, so he could let it to gullible Americans.

But even with the fashion show behind them, there was still the fête and the Flower and Produce Show for the village to look forward to. An appeal had been launched for funds for the church organ. Uncle Tom was doing a sponsored slim, incensed by Eddie Grundy's taunts of 'Fatman Forrest', and Nigel had offered to do a parachute jump. Phil, grudgingly impressed, had conceded that Nigel could stay overnight at Brookfield again: Shula, however, knew the truth. Mark had joined the Borsetshire Buzzards, a skydiving team. The jump was simply a terrified Nigel's way of proving himself to be just as macho.

But Shula, it seemed, wasn't the only woman in Ambridge who was torn between two men. Gossip went round that Pat, fearless, feminist, independent Pat, had been spotted in a dark corner of The Feathers beside a man with tousled dark hair and a donkey jacket, who apparently was called Roger and was her lecturer from the Women's Studies course.

'It seems funny to me to have a man giving talks on Women's Studies,' Peggy remarked. She hadn't heard the gossip, but she knew with a mother's instinct that she was being called upon rather too often to babysit at Bridge Farm and that Tony looked thoroughly miserable. 'I wonder why this Roger's interested,' she added pointedly.

'He's interested in all sorts of politics,' Pat had replied shortly. 'Can you see if the kids' fish fingers are done, please, Peggy?'

The full extent of Roger's political interests became evident when Pat offered a load of books and pamphlets to the village fête.

'Saussure, Lacan, Althusser – who are these people?' demanded Jennifer, who, as one of Ambridge's few intellectuals, might have been expected to know.

'Search me,' Shula had shrugged. She was setting up a kiddies' corner at one end of the bookstall. 'Is that how you pronounce them?'

'If I don't know, I can't see anyone else in Ambridge knowing.' Jennifer delved in the box again.

'Ah! I know who that is!' Shula put down *The Secret of Spiggy Holes* in which she had been engrossed.

'Not terribly subtle is it?' Jennifer tossed the book on to the pile. 'Even Uncle Walter would recognize a bearded gentleman plonked in front of a large hammer and sickle. I wouldn't mind,' she continued, 'but if that's Pat's political leaning these days, how come she's demanded a special sale or return deal and a share of the profits?'

In the end, they didn't have to worry because Richard Adamson, the vicar, had a word with Pat and told her didn't think her literature was suitable for a church fête. Pat was incandescent, accusing him of having no interest in the wider world.

'Roger told me this would happen,' she fumed. 'It's victimization. The only surprise is that I'm surprised.'

Then she'd loaded the books back into the Land Rover and had driven off, leaving Tony to drag the children round the donkey rides and the coconut shy under the sympathetic eye of the crowd.

Tony didn't know what to make of Pat's behaviour. Well, in truth he had a very good idea what to make of it, especially when whispers about Roger reached him, but he didn't want to make anything of it. He didn't *want* to believe that Pat could be seeing someone else, and if she was, he didn't want to believe it was serious. But, as he thought to himself the following week, gloomily opening another can of lager – Pat was out 'at her class' and the kids had finally gone to bed – if she wouldn't talk to him about it, how could he know for sure, and even if he did know, what was he going to do? He'd been married to Pat for ten years and if he knew one thing about her it was that nothing he said could ever make her change her mind. He had no choice but to let things run their course.

As Tony watched and waited, summer blossomed all around. Cow parsley frothed in the ditches, the corn turned from green to gold, and on still afternoons you could hear the skylarks calling. At Brookfield the tractors buzzed in and out of the yard, carting first silage, then hay. Tony watched the glossy sides of the cows plump in pregnancy, looking forward to the time when they would start to dry off, and ease the burden of twice-daily milking on top of the work in the fields. Brian's role was less hands-on but he was still busy, giving the men their orders and making sure that the machinery was maintained in preparation for harvest. With an acreage the size of his to be cut in a fortnight, you couldn't afford to take chances – the weather itself was quite enough risk for most farmers to bear.

By contrast, work at Rodway's was quiet for Shula. The end of the school term was approaching and people were thinking about their summer holidays, not selling houses. Nigel tried to entice her out. There was always someone having a Pimms party or a crowd going punting but Shula fobbed him off. The sale of Mark's cottage in Penny Hassett was proceeding, though his wedding to Sarah had been postponed from July to September because Mr Locke had been called to Washington on business. It made Shula's agony worse. It was just longer to wait, unable to say what she felt. And September was *their* month – the month when she and Mark would have been married . . .

One night at the beginning of July, Nigel phoned. There was a party in Borchester, he said. There would be pink champagne and dancing till dawn. Shula pleaded tiredness, but she felt guilty. She wasn't being fair to Nigel. Perhaps she should finish with him. She knew only too well what it felt like to be keen on someone who didn't seem to notice your existence. Maybe she should put him out of his misery.

'Not tonight, Nigel, honestly,' she said. 'I'm sorry. Apart from anything else, I've promised I'll meet Caroline from the train. She's coming back from London.'

Normally he'd try to get her to change her mind, but this time he just said, 'Yes, I see,' in a tiny voice and she felt so rotten that she relented. Nigel bucked up at once.

'We'll leave early,' he promised. 'We won't keep Caroline waiting. Oh, Shula, thanks. We'll have a lovely time.'

Shula had hated the party, which had been full of Young Conservatives dancing to 'Y.M.C.A.', and by the time they came out, cutting it fine to meet Caroline, she was anxious and cross. And then Nigel couldn't find his car.

'I'm positive I parked it here earlier today,' he declared. He'd picked her up in a taxi. 'Absolutely positive. Right here.'

'On this double yellow line?'

'Yes. Well, hereabouts.'

Shula supported herself against a lamp-post. She felt exhausted. And she hadn't even been drinking.

'Of course! Look!'

'That's not your car.'

Nigel was dragging her towards to a clapped-out old sports car parked nearby.

'No, but it's Tim Beecham's, isn't it? It's a joke. He's taken mine and hidden it somewhere.'

'Why?'

'You know Tim. Anything for a laugh.' Nigel fumbled with his keys. 'We'll take his. One of my keys fits it exactly. We used to pinch each other's cars all the time.'

'The keys are in the ignition,' said Shula coldly. Why, oh why hadn't she just stayed at home and watched the highlights of play at Wimbledon? She had a bet on with David that Navratilova would win for the fifth time: David said she should be disqualified to give everyone else a chance. 'I expect you'll find the door unlocked.'

Weary as she was, she did at least have the sense, after Nigel had reversed the old crate into a lamp-post, to make him swap seats and let her drive. When the flashing blue lights had come up behind them on the Borchester bypass, her first thought had been to slow down to let them past: then she realized that the police car was flashing its lights at her. They were being chased and when the police pulled them over she found out why. It wasn't Tim's car at all. They'd stolen a complete stranger's.

Even before her parents, the person she phoned from the police station was Mark. It was one in the morning and she'd nearly cried when, yawning, he'd picked up the phone. She'd tried not to think about whether Sarah was in bed beside him as she'd spluttered out her tearful story, but he'd just told her to keep calm, he was on his way. It was only when he'd arrived that Shula had finally collapsed in tears, clinging on to him and blubbing that she was sorry, so sorry. She didn't know what she was apologizing for – it could have been so many things – but Mark had gently wiped her eyes. He'd had a chat with the arresting officer and the custody sergeant and then, bit by bit, he'd extracted their story from them.

'Tim Beecham didn't help,' he frowned when he'd heard it all. 'The police have checked with him and he said he'd never heard of you in his life.'

'What?' squeaked Shula.

'A little Beecham joke,' Mark explained quickly. 'Then he said he might have heard of you, Nigel, but he wouldn't lend you his car if you were the last man on earth.'

'Well, thank you, Tim,' said Nigel, disgusted.

'The trouble is,' said Mark mildly, 'that Tim doesn't have a sports car.'

'But I've driven it!'

Nigel jumped up and thumped the tatty interview room table.

'Not for over a year you haven't.' Mark looked at his notes. 'He sold it in July 1983.'

Shula let out a groan and Nigel dropped back into his seat.

'So he has. I forgot.'

'His wasn't the same model either,' Mark continued remorselessly. 'Different year and a different colour. So all that about thinking it was Tim's car didn't go down very well.'

Shula put her head in her hands.

'So what happens now?' she asked plaintively.

'Basically, they're going to charge you both with taking and driving away.'

'If they're charging me,' cried Nigel, 'why don't they let Shula go?'

'Joint enterprise.' Mark was packing away his papers. 'They say you were in it together. Still, you'll get bail. No problem.'

When Shula went to see Mark at his office the next day, he wasn't much more forthcoming. Their case was to be given a preliminary hearing at the Magistrates' Court the following day and Mark was to represent them both.

'How could I have been so stupid!' Shula slumped wearily in her chair. Mark maintained a tactful silence. 'Letting Nigel talk me into it! It was only because I was so tired and fed up!'

'Don't worry.' Mark screwed the top back on his fountain pen while Shula shot a poisonous glance at the silver-framed photograph of Sarah on the bookcase behind him. 'As long as Nigel behaves himself in court tomorrow, it'll all be forgotten by the weekend.'

But of course Nigel, or rather his parents, Gerald and Julia, couldn't let it go. They announced before the hearing that they didn't think Nigel would get a fair trial at Borchester Magistrates' Court and that, grateful though they were for all Mark had done so far, they wanted to engage what they charmingly called 'a professional' to defend him. Despite Mark's protests, Nigel insisted that he wanted to opt for trial by jury, which meant that the hearing would be adjourned, giving the Pargetters time to engage a top London barrister, Sir Michael Sturdy, who'd been at school with Gerald. In court, the Pargetters got their way and the final hearing date was set for 23 August.

'What do I do now?' wailed Shula afterwards. 'That's six weeks away!'

'You carry on as normal,' counselled Mark. 'I should take a holiday if I were you. But first let me tell you how we're going to play it when we get to the Crown Court.'

Now that the stakes had been raised, as Mark put it, he was quite clear that there was a very different case to be made out against Shula from the one against Nigel. Though she felt a bit of a heel for letting Nigel take the blame, it was true, when Mark put it like that, that the whole escapade had been Nigel's idea. Far from being a willing accomplice, she had tried to exercise restraint and was only driving, not because she had any intent wilfully to deprive the owner of the car of his property, but because she'd thought Nigel was over the limit. The way Mark told it, Shula was in fact a model citizen: the consequences of the taking and driving away (TDA, as he called it) would have been much worse had she not been involved. Shula felt quite breathless at his skill in turning things round and she remembered how Mark in solicitor mode had always impressed her. That was how she'd made up her mind about him in the first place, really – when he'd defended those hunt saboteurs. And at least this time her dad and Mark were on the same side.

His idea about a holiday was a good one, too. She needed to get away somewhere – away from the black looks her father had been giving her and her mother's puzzled concern when she refused to take Nigel's phone calls. Shula considered her options – where she could go at short notice and with no money – and the only thing she could come up with was to visit Lilian in Guernsey.

It was the middle of harvest: her dad and David were working from dawn till dusk. Her mother had to be on standby to tear off to the machinery dealer for spares for the combine and to provide endless flasks of tea and stacks of sandwiches. There was no one to take Shula to the airport. And then Mark offered.

As they stood near the departure gate among hordes of travellers, Shula regarded him gratefully. He looked so solid in his dark suit among the crowds of holidaymakers, most of whom, it seemed, had dressed in anticipation of rushing straight from their plane to the beach.

'Are you sure you've got everything?' he asked.

'Um . . .' Shula patted her pockets in a panic. 'Where's my boarding pass?'

'There. Stuck to your ticket.'

'Oh, yes. Well, thanks for the lift, Mark. And for waiting to see me go.'

'My pleasure.' Near them, a small child fell flat on the polished floor and began to wail. 'Goodbye then, Shula.'

Shula leaned forward and kissed his smooth cheek. The child was picked up by her mother and given a cuddle. Shula smiled briefly at her and even more briefly at Mark. She really didn't want to go.

'Bye, Mark. I'll see you when I get back.'

Reluctantly, she started to walk away but he caught her arm.

'Shula. Before you go – there's something I ought to tell you.'

'Yes?' she breathed.

'Last night I went to see Sarah. We had a bit of a chat. And we – well, we decided to call it off.'

The PA system blared over their heads.

'This is the last call for passengers on British Midland Flight BD1591 to Guernsey. Last call for British Midland Flight BD1591 now boarding at Gate 6.'

'You'd better go,' he said.

'But . . .' Shula couldn't take it in. 'Oh, Mark. I'm so sorry.'

'Go on,' he urged. 'You don't want to miss your plane, do you?'

It was Shula's birthday while she was away. Nigel sent her a dozen red roses and a silly but lovey-dovey card. She didn't hear from Mark.

She mooched around at Lilian's in the morning and, in the after-noon, borrowed a horse for a hack round the lanes. It was another day of brilliant sunshine. It was the hottest summer for years – almost a drought. The horse was a placid old thing, always stopping to pull up dandelions by the roadside, and Shula did nothing to restrain him. She had too much else to think about, like the staggering news Mark had told her at the airport. She'd been so stunned, too stunned to say anything, and now she was kicking herself. Why, when she'd had the perfect opportunity, hadn't she told him how much she still felt for him, and asked him if he didn't think they should give it another go? But he'd pushed her gently towards the departure gate.

'Anyway, not your problem. Off you go and enjoy yourself, or you'll miss your plane,' he'd chided.

Enjoy herself? Didn't he realize that she hadn't enjoyed anything, not even with Nigel, since she and Mark had split up?

Well, she'd missed one chance but she wasn't going to let it happen again. When she got back, and once they'd got the court case out of the way, she'd sit Mark down and tell him exactly how she felt. He might not want to do anything about it – and this might not be the right time – he'd got to get over Sarah first. But at least she'd have told him. Then it would be up to him.

'Tony?'

'Over here!'

Tony heard Pat's footsteps approach across the yard to where he'd tethered a cow in a loose box. He checked the syringe before stoop-ing to inject the antibiotic.

'Peggy and I were going to have a cuppa –' Pat stopped and winced when she saw what he was doing. 'Oh dear,' she said. 'Foul in the foot?'

The cow bellowed and tugged at her rope as the needle went through the skin.

'OK, old girl, OK,' soothed Tony. 'Yup. I thought she was lame when I dried her off yesterday.'

'Poor thing.' Pat came round and held the cow's head. 'Ouch. The size of that injection.'

'The price of these antibiotics,' countered Tony. He straightened and patted the cow. 'There now, girl, all done. I left her up here in case it went away of its own accord,' he added. 'Sometimes a hard dry floor helps.'

'Not this time, though.'

'No.' Tony gathered together the empty antibiotic bottle, the syringe and its paper and plastic wrapper: the last thing he wanted was the animal laming itself in another foot by stepping on something sharp. He glanced at Pat and tried to think of something uncontroversial to say. There didn't seem to be much between them that didn't lead to arguments these days. Then he remembered that Pat and Peggy had been to court to hear the verdict on Shula and Nigel's trial.

'So, how did it go?'

'Depends. Nigel was fined £200 with £200 costs. Shula got off,' Pat explained. 'Nigel's usually so . . . pink. It was strange to see him that pale.'

Tony snorted and went to the tap to fill a bucket for the cow.

'He ought to be locked up.'

'That's what I thought originally,' conceded Pat. 'You know how I feel about drunk drivers and everything. But I did feel sorry for him today.'

Tony trudged back with the bucket. So Pat was capable of feeling sorry for Nigel. She didn't seem very sorry for him, leaving him babysitting with a supper of leftovers while she went off to some talk or other and then on for a drink with 'people' from her course.

'Are you out tonight?' he asked casually as the cow swivelled its billiard-ball eyes and lowered its head to drink.

'Tony, I did tell you!' Pat flared. 'It's the book fair at the Tech!'

'Oh, right,' said Tony mildly. 'No, that's fine. And you're helping, are you?'

'I promised I'd do a couple of hours on the stall, yes. Is it a problem?'

'No, no, you do what you like,' said Tony. 'Rose'll be there, I suppose, and Jan?'

'Yes,' said Pat guardedly. 'What are you getting at?'

'And Roger, of course.'

'Roger?'

'Oh, come on, Pat, you know him better than I do.'

'What?'

It didn't suddenly come over him. He didn't suddenly snap. It wasn't a red mist in front of his eyes and a desire to strangle her. He just turned to her, there in the loose box, with the sun sliding in through the doorway and the cow slurping her water and asked what he should have asked her months ago.

'Don't you think it's time you told me just *how much* better?'

'Oh, go on, Mark, my treat.'

It was the evening of the trial and they'd come to Nelson's wine bar – where else? – to celebrate.

'Shula, really, I've got a lot of work on at the moment –'

'You've just stopped me from being sent to Holloway. Or at least having to paint the old people's bungalows or something!' Shula protested. 'You can surely let me buy you a drink!'

'Yes, but not –'

'We'll have a bottle of champagne, please, Nelson, and two glasses,' Shula began, then, seeing Nelson look downcast, 'Oh, all right, then, three.'

Nelson smiled smugly – there was someone who knew his way round the legal system, as Mark often remarked – and went to fetch their drinks.

Shula pulled Mark over to a corner table. The relief at having put the trial behind her was a great bubble that nothing could burst.

'Did you see Sir Michael's face when the verdict was handed down?' she exclaimed. 'His eyebrows were shooting up and down so much I thought they'd fall off. I'm sorry Nigel was clobbered, of course, but you must admit Sir Michael was funny.'

'Mm.'

Nelson brought their drinks over and opened the bottle with aplomb. He chinked his glass against theirs.

'Congratulations, Shula,' he said. 'Another triumph for British justice.'

'You'd know all about that, Nelson,' said Mark crisply. 'I hear they're talking about having another go at extraditing Ronnie Biggs.'

'I can't think what you mean,' Nelson said with dignity. 'Now if you'll excuse me, I have a party of bank managers to attend to.'

'The old crook.' Mark swigged his champagne as Nelson wove his way elegantly back to the bar.

'Oh, who cares? Who am I to judge?' replied Shula gaily. 'As long as the champagne's all right, what does it matter? Here, have an olive.'

She reached for the dish but Mark put out his hand.

'Shula, I've got something to tell you.'

Shula half turned in her seat. She'd worn a grey linen dress for court, to look demure, but for this evening she'd put on white jeans, a T-shirt and her butter-coloured jacket, which she knew Mark liked.

'Every time I see you these days you say that. What is it this time?'

Please God, not that his wedding to Sarah Locke was on again. Or that while she'd been on holiday he'd started seeing that appalling Jackie Woodstock again, or had fallen for David's girlfriend Sophie, a vapid fashion student who only ever talked about unstructured jackets and silkscreen prints? Not when Shula, once she'd had another drink, had planned to tell him what she'd decided in Guernsey she must say? That she'd been beastly to him, but she still loved him and if he'd give her another chance she wanted to try again?

Mark sipped his champagne. For someone who hadn't wanted to drink he was getting through it faster than she was. He put his glass down and took her hands.

Shula blinked. Perhaps he felt the same. Perhaps they'd both come to the same realization at the same time?

'The thing is – it's come about rather suddenly – I'm going to Hong Kong.'

Hong Kong?

'There's a case coming up and they need an assistant. It's commercial, rather complicated –'

Hong Kong? Was he that desperate to get away from her? *Hong Kong?* And she'd hoped –

She'd lost him once. And now she was losing him again.

• • •

'I just want you to talk to me, Pat.'

'Tony, I've got to go, I'll be late. Did you put some petrol in the car?'

'I don't believe this!' Tony followed her out into the yard. 'I'm trying to have a serious talk about us, about our marriage, and all you can think of is getting off to your blasted book fair! And we all know why!'

'Are you going to look in on that lame cow again, or do you want me to do it?'

'What, in your best jeans and a pair of sandals? Don't be stupid.'

'I'm quite happy to. I'd rather do that than stand here with you haranguing me about your fevered imaginings.'

'Hah!' They'd reached the car now and Tony banged his hand down on the roof. It was still hot from the sun. 'Imaginings? I'm hearing from half the village that you and this – Roger – have been seen drinking in The Feathers.'

'And that's a crime, is it?'

'No, but –'

'We were talking, Tony. You know, conversation, ideas. The sort of thing civilized adults who have interests in common get up to in the evenings.'

Tony leaned his elbows on the roof of the car and put his head in his hands.

'I thought we had interests in common, Pat. Like three kids and 150 acres.' He raised his head and looked at her. 'Like wondering how we're going to survive under these quotas when our income will be £5000 down and our input costs are going up all the time –'

Pat said nothing, just fiddled with the car keys.

'Well? Hm?'

'I'm sorry, Tony,' she said abruptly. 'I can't talk about it now.'

'Sorry?'

She got into the car and turned on the ignition. The driver's window was wound down and Tony leaned in.

'What do you mean, you're sorry?'

Pat looked straight ahead. She put the car into gear and released the handbrake.

'Pat, talk to me!'

Then she drove off.

Next day, Tony had to go round to Brookfield. He'd promised to go through Phil's herd with him: Phil wanted his opinion on the cows he was intending to cull. He was there when Shula came into the kitchen: Phil had already explained she was off work with a migraine. Tony thought she looked terrible. As bad as he did, probably: he'd lain awake for hours waiting for Pat and when she'd finally come in, she'd woken him from a deep sleep and he couldn't get off again. Anyway, Shula had started fiddling with the toaster, complaining that it wouldn't work, that the bread wouldn't stay down, and getting in a right tizzy about it. Jill had just suggested tactfully that he and Phil take their coffee through to the office when Shula had burst into floods of tears and had started blubbering something about Mark going to Hong Kong and not loving her and how she'd never see him again. Phil had raised his eyebrows at Jill and Jill, holding a heaving Shula, had signalled back incomprehension. Phil had gestured to Tony that they should leave them to it, and they'd crept out with their coffees into the yard.

'What was all that about?' asked Tony.

'I haven't the first idea,' Phil confessed. 'She was meeting Mark in Nelson's last night. I think she was hoping for a reconciliation.'

'Ah.'

The pubs and bars of Borchester had obviously been seething with intrigue last night. Mark and Shula. Pat and Roger. Assignations. Intimations. Decisions.

In silence, the two men drank their coffee and watched the swallows swirl in the sky. They'd soon be off to Africa, thought Tony.

And Mark was off to Hong Kong. Where would Pat be this winter, he wondered. Where would any of them be, with quotas and the Common Market slicing into their income? And what, Tony wondered, could he do about any of it?

·21·

Fighting Back

'Lovely cup of coffee, Pat. If I'm allowed to say that.' Martin Lambert, the new assistant vet, had heard all about how fierce Pat could be if she thought she was being patronized.

'It'll take more than a cup of coffee to revive me, the shock I've had.' Tony traced his finger through some spilt milk on the table.

Martin had come round to do some PDs – pregnancy diagnoses – only to find that several of the cows had not held. In previous years Tony had had a 100 per cent success rate with AI.

'You're sure it isn't too much nitrogen?' queried Pat, refilling Martin's cup. 'I've heard that can cause mineral deficiencies.'

'We've already had a problem with staggers,' Tony chipped in. 'Had to put them on high-magnesium cake.'

Martin shook his head.

'I think it's simpler than that. I don't suppose you fed them much cake in the summer?'

'Wasn't much point, was there,' said Tony bitterly, 'when our quota was based on ninety-one per cent of last year's yield.'

'Cake's expensive,' added Pat. 'And they were milking well enough, despite the drought.'

'But that's their training,' reasoned Martin. 'They were milking off their backs.'

Pat glanced guiltily at Tony. In the past, when she'd been more closely involved with the herd, she'd often been the one to notice if the cows were losing condition. She almost wished he'd point this out, even in front of Martin. Then she could feel got at, which would justify why she wanted to spend more and more time away from the farm. But Tony was so careful with her these days – over-polite, so as not to inflame her. It was a clever tactic, but it didn't change how she felt.

'This mineral deficiency,' Tony was saying. 'Can't you do a blood test to check? Or give them an injection to improve their condition?'

As Martin explained the options, Pat looked at her husband. His overalls were splattered with dried mud and the collar of his shirt was frayed. Her fault, she supposed. She should have mended it, like a good wife – or at least bought him a new one. Two of his knuckles were newly grazed – her fault too, probably. She knew she wasn't concentrating on things and supposed he wasn't either. It made you careless. The bald patch at the back of his head was definitely bigger. That was certainly her fault.

Two months further on – October, with the cultivations to do and now all this worry about the cows – and Pat was no nearer to making a decision about what she wanted out of life. Her classes at the Tech had started up again in earnest and Tony had backed off from any further confrontation. He'd meekly got Peggy in to help with the kids when at the last minute Pat had got a place on a conference in Carmarthen about 'Women as Economic Units'. Even on Saturday evening, when she'd gone to meet the others and had spent all night, fascinated, listening to Roger talk about the culture of patriarchy, Tony hadn't said a word. And when she'd come back late, having had to stop the car in the lane to have a good weep about it all, and had spent the night in the spare room, he'd never even questioned her.

The stupid thing was, there was nothing going between her and Roger. They weren't having an affair, not in the sexual sense of the word, or any other, really. He was too busy arguing with his ex-wife over access to his two small daughters and planning his new course of lectures: 'Women – A Caged Species'. They were friends, that was all. He asked Pat's opinion and was interested in her replies. He was intrigued, he said, by her mind and how her ideas had been shaped by her confined Welsh upbringing. He was always telling her how he admired the working partnership she'd achieved with Tony. If only he knew what a treadmill it was. Cooking the breakfast, getting the kids to school, doing the shopping, dealing with the feed and seed reps, keeping the records, bucket-feeding the calves: in the middle of it all, and particularly since she'd had Tommy, she'd forgotten that she had a mind for anyone to be interested in. Although, she had to admit, she'd have liked Roger to find her physically irresistible as well, she realized that this was just a hangover from her previous, pathetic, female desire to please. She tried not to think about what it would be like to be kissed by Roger and to tangle her fingers in his hair and she managed to overlook the fact that her gratitude for his interest was just another kind of enslavement.

Shula, who, with Jill and Peggy, was frequently called on to babysit at Bridge Farm, found it terribly depressing. The children were unsettled – John and Helen rebellious and cheeky, Tommy clingy and refusing to be put to bed.

'Oh, Mum, isn't it awful? I didn't think it would be like this,' she told Jill one night when she got back. This time it was Tony's turn to go off to a conference – though he hadn't told Pat where, or what about – but Pat had still insisted, in a slightly hysterical tone, Shula had thought when she'd asked her to babysit, that she had to get out to her class. 'You know how people talk – splitting up – having an affair – they make it sound so easy – light-hearted almost.'

'Let's hope it won't come to that,' said Jill swiftly, stirring the cocoa. 'All marriages have their bad patches.'

'Not like this,' insisted Shula. 'Not with everybody so miserable. What's the point of it?'

Jill looked at her daughter sharply and resolved not to let Shula babysit for Pat again if she could help it. Shula was in a funny state of mind herself, and had been since Mark had gone to Hong Kong. Shula had been to the airport to see him off. He'd invited her over for a holiday and had promised he'd come back, but that was all he'd promised. Nevertheless, Shula had finished with Nigel. Phil had enjoyed at least half an hour's quiet exultation before Elizabeth, who'd managed to get herself expelled from her boarding school and was completing her A-levels at the Tech, had come skipping into the kitchen to announce that Nigel was taking her out to Nelson's that evening and she'd made him promise to wear his gorilla suit. Shula didn't even mind. The new vet, Martin, had taken her out a couple of times, but she wasn't very bothered. She seemed, Jill thought, to have put her life on hold until Mark came back – and, like Pat, Jill suddenly realized as she poured the cocoa into mugs, Mark was someone else who perhaps didn't know what he wanted out of life.

• • •

'Organic farming? That old "muck and magic" thing?'

Brian strode around the echoing shed, checking the ventilation. He was planning to loose-house some beef cattle there and feed them silage all year round – a much more efficient way, to his mind, of using grass than letting them graze at will. More controllable. And much more profitable.

'There's more to it than that, Brian, and you know it.' Tony followed at his heels.

'And this was what your conference was about?' smiled Brian. 'With the knit-your-own lentils lot?'

Tony could have thumped him. Brian always seemed so smug and lately he'd seemed more pleased with himself than ever.

'Brian, I came to sound you out because I respect your opinion. You might at least take me seriously.'

'Sorry, old chap.' Brian stopped and folded his arms across his quilted chest. 'I'm listening.'

'Well, the trouble is,' began Tony, 'farming's been taken over lock, stock and barrel by the chemical industry.'

'That's a slight exaggeration.'

'No, it isn't,' insisted Tony. 'Look at the fortune they spend on glossy adverts. What chance has the farmer got to choose a sensible system?'

'Oh, come on, farmers won't buy anything if they can't see some benefit,' protested Brian.

'The only benefit is to the chemical company profits. Look at me,' Tony went on, 'spending thousands on fertilizers and sprays just to produce huge surpluses. Pumping antibiotics and hormones into the cows to keep them producing more milk to throw away.'

'This is Pat's influence, isn't it?' asked Brian. 'It must be. And those radical feminist friends of hers.'

'It's got nothing to do with Pat. If you want to know, I haven't even discussed it with her yet.'

'Thought you'd have a dark secret of your own?' quipped Brian before he could stop himself. Then, 'Sorry, mate.'

Tony braced his shoulders.

'Look, I know the whole village has been talking about the state of my marriage all summer. It just seems to me that we've gone way off track. The whole farming industry, I mean. And I think organics could be the way to redress the balance. Not just for the farm, but for me and Pat too.'

'So, how are you, Pat?'

Shula hardly needed to ask. Pat had great panda-like circles under her eyes and her face looked thinner. She'd been behaving very oddly lately. Jennifer had caught her walking the dog by the river when it was practically dark and one Sunday evening she'd even been to church.

Pat shifted her bag of shopping from one hand to the other.

'Oh, you know, Shula. Just putting one foot in front of the other.'

'Hm. Actually I do know.'

She'd had a postcard from Mark that morning. Not even a letter. Just a picture of Stanley Market, wittering on about silk shirts and the view over the harbour from the cable car. Hardly the sort of communication that spoke of a man with a broken heart, missing her madly. Maybe, Shula thought, Pat's friend Rose was right. As long as you had your family, your work, your friends – what were men for? Mind you, Pat had been going to two years of lectures on the subject and she still didn't seem too sure.

'I'll have to go,' Pat apologized. 'I promised Tony I wouldn't be long.'

Shula watched her trudge off towards the car, tugging Tommy with her. If that was what marriage did to you, maybe Shula was better off without it. She thought about it, standing there with her letter to Mark, which she'd brought down to the post, in her hand. In it, she'd chattered on about what had been happening in the village. About how Nigel had taken Elizabeth to a ball at Heybury Hall. About how Uncle Walter's back, which he'd hurt falling out of his hammock, was on the mend, and how Martin had given him a budgie to cheer him up. She was especially pleased with the mention of Martin. Casual, but effective. Mark was a lawyer, after all. He was sure to pick up on it.

'You look tired,' Tony greeted Pat when she got back.

'Thanks.' She parked Tommy in front of the children's programmes on the television and started to put away the shopping. Washing powder. Cornflakes.

'It's just that – we can't go on like this for ever, Pat.'

Cheese. Pickle.

'Like what?'

She'd already told him to give her time to think about this organics idea.

'Like two complete strangers who happen to live under the same roof. For God's sake, I've been patient enough, haven't I?'

Pat put the jar of peanut butter she was holding down on the work surface.

'Yes. Yes, you have.'

On Saturday, she'd phoned Roger and asked him to meet her. Just the two of them. And she'd told him that she couldn't do this any more and that she wouldn't be coming back to his lectures either. He'd been puzzled and surprised, but then he didn't know how she felt about him. Really.

'Well?'

Pat sank into a chair. She could feel her knees starting to go.

'I was going to tell you this anyway, as soon as I'd had a bit more time to think.'

'Yes?'

'It's about the farm, that's all.'

'What do you mean, that's all?'

'Listen,' pleaded Pat. 'I know you're serious about this organic idea. I've read all the stuff you gave me and I agree with you. If you think we can get out of chemicals, I think we should go ahead and do it.'

'We? You're sure about that, Pat?'

She nodded, till she could swallow the lump in her throat and speak.

'Yes. If you want to go organic, then I'm with you. All the way.'

• • •

'Brian? *Brian*?' squeaked Shula.

'That's all there is to tell,' shrugged Caroline. 'I said I'd come back to Ambridge on one condition. That we stopped seeing each other.'

'Brian! I don't believe it!'

'So you keep saying.' Amused, Caroline topped up Shula's glass. It was a warm evening at the beginning of June. Outside, through the open French windows – Caroline had insisted on being restored to her rightful place in the Royal Garden Suite – Higgs was cutting the grass with his ride-on mower. The smell of it filled the room.

'But Brian!' squeaked Shula again. 'Those awful clothes he wears! Those little gold chains on his shoes!'

'Just because he's a sort of relation, you don't see him as a human being.' Caroline sipped her wine. 'He's a very attractive man.'

'Is he?'

'Yes.'

'Oh.' Shula considered. 'Well, if you say so. But when did you – I mean, how did it start?'

Caroline tucked her legs underneath her on the sofa. It had all started, she explained, at Grey Gables a couple of Christmases ago. MrWoolley had been throwing a cocktail party. She'd been recovering from another failed romance – the one with Alan Fraser. 'International man of mystery', Brian had called him – and Caroline had certainly been mystified when, after courting her intensely for almost a year, Alan had disappeared off to the Middle East and never come back. What she remembered most clearly about Brian that evening was that he'd made her laugh. He'd phoned her up the following week and asked her out to lunch. They'd had a few lunches together in the New Year but she could see the way things were going. Her morality was very complex but there were two basic precepts – she didn't do one-night stands and she didn't have anything to do with married men. So she refused Brian the next couple of times he called, and he quickly got the message.

But then last autumn, it had happened all over again. It was Paul Chubb who'd broken her heart this time, a friend of her brother's and a pilot in the Fleet Air Arm. She'd really thought he was the one. But one minute he was whisking her off to Walberswick for the weekend and pledging undying love, the next he came back from an exercise and announced he was getting engaged to someone called Philippa. This time she'd met up with Brian at the Hunt Ball. He'd sympathized. And though she tried very hard not to let him, he'd made her smile. And so they'd started to see each other again.

She'd sometimes thought that all they had in common – apart from sex, of course – was food. Brian took her all over the county to little places he'd found, where they could get mussels or perfect Beef Wellington or *îles flottantes*. When she'd asked about Jennifer, he'd always shrugged it off.

'She has everything she wants,' he'd say. 'Forget about her. Now, come on, eat up your profiteroles.'

But Caroline couldn't forget about Jennifer, especially not when she had to help at an Open Day at Home Farm, and there was Jennifer knocking herself out to make it a success and Brian being so nasty to her about romanticizing the countryside and making him look a fool in the process. Caroline had seen another side to him then, the arrogant side that she'd always known was there and that was sometimes sort of attractive. But that day, stuck behind the tea urn with Mrs Perkins, it had been ghastly, and as soon as she could, she got away, told Mr Woolley that her friend Sally was ill and had taken off for London. Brian had tracked her down and had started talking about leaving Jennifer, then about leaving the village and all sorts of nonsense. He wouldn't listen till she practically pushed him out on to the pavement and told him she didn't want to see him again, ever, even if she had to leave Ambridge to do it.

In the heat of the moment, she hadn't seen how they could live in the same village and pretend nothing had happened between them, but then, when she got back, she'd bumped into Brian on the village green. He'd been charming and witty, as usual, and Jennifer had come out of the shop and joined them and said that Caroline must come to dinner, and Brian had agreed. It was a revelatory moment for Caroline because she realized at once just how easy it was for him to behave normally with her, and it occurred to her that he'd probably had quite a lot of practice in deception. And after he'd given Jennifer such a hard time over poor old John Tregorran, who'd probably only wanted someone to discuss poetry with.

'Anyway,' concluded Caroline. 'It's all over now.'

'Brian . . .' muttered Shula weakly.

'Shula! For heaven's sake, stop saying "Brian"!' scolded Caroline. 'Come on, snap out of it. Tell me about you and Martin. Or you and Mark.'

'There's nothing to tell,' said Shula sadly. 'I had a big row with Martin and we've given each other the boot. He says I'm still in love with Mark.'

'That's perceptive of him. Even Nigel spotted that.'

'What am I going to do, Caroline?'

'Mark will be home soon. Then you'll have a chance to get things sorted out.'

'Not till the beginning of September,' brooded Shula. 'Three whole months away.'

'Oh, honestly!' Caroline looked exasperated. There was nothing like ending an affair for making you see things clearly. 'If you can't wait that long, there's only one thing for it. Go and see him yourself!'

• • •

'There – there she is, look!' Jill waved madly as Shula, pushing her loaded trolley, emerged from Customs.

'All right, she's seen us, she's coming!' Phil ducked to avoid Jill's flailing arm. 'She looks tired, doesn't she?'

'It's been a long flight. She's very brown, though.' Jill ran forward to hug her daughter. 'Hello, darling. How was it?'

'Oh . . . fine,' said Shula vaguely.

'Hong Kong as lively as they say?' Phil didn't like the look of Shula at all. She looked very fragile, somehow. He hoped she wasn't coming down with something.

'And how's Mark?' Jill added.

There was a long pause before Shula spoke. She seemed to be having trouble connecting with anything they said.

'Mark . . . oh, he was fine, as well. Sends you his love. Seems to be doing very well out there.'

'I'm sure he is,' said Phil.

'He's brown too,' said Shula. 'It suits him.'

'Did he . . . say anything about coming back?' queried Jill tentatively.

'Um . . .' Shula looked around. 'Look, I think I'll just go and wash my hands. I feel a bit dirty.'

'Yes, of course,' urged Jill. 'And are you hungry? Would you like to stop somewhere for supper?'

'No, thanks.' Shula shook her head. 'Let's get home. I just want to see my own room again.'

'Oh, Phil,' whispered Jill as Shula trailed off in search of the Ladies'. 'It obviously hasn't worked out with Mark. Look at her. She's walking as though she's fifty. Oh, Phil. What a shame!'

·22·

The End of an Era

'On Lakey Hill,' Shula told Caroline dreamily, 'with the sun shining down and Brian's combines whirring away in the distance.'

'Very romantic,' said Caroline wryly. 'Did Mark go down on one knee among the sheep droppings?'

'Not quite,' admitted Shula. 'But after he'd asked me and I'd said yes we did both sort of – well, lie down for a little bit.'

Caroline hugged her friend.

'I'm just delighted for you,' she smiled. 'I know you're right for each other.'

'It took us long enough to find out,' sighed Shula. 'Thank you for listening to me, Caroline. I don't know how you've put up with me all these months.'

'No, nor do I,' reflected Caroline.

'I'll make it up to you,' Shula promised. 'I'll get Mark to have a think. See if we can't find you someone nice among his friends.'

'Don't you dare! I am not going out with anyone from the Borsetshire Buzzcocks!'

'Buzzards,' corrected Shula. 'Anyway, Mark's given up skydiving now.' She poured Caroline another glass of elderflower cordial, made from Doris's old recipe. 'But you are looking for a boyfriend? I mean, you're not seeing Brian again?'

'No, I am not! However much he pesters me!'

Shula nodded sagely. She felt much wiser than she had a year ago, and it couldn't all be down to the sapphire and diamond ring on her finger. It was more to do, she thought, with seeing other people's marriages under pressure – Pat and Tony, Jennifer and Brian – and watching how they struggled through. Not that anything like that would happen to her and Mark, of course. As Caroline had said, they were right for each other. If they weren't sure of it now, they never would be. They'd be together for ever. No question about it.

'Look at her! I've never seen her so happy. Oh, Phil, isn't it lovely?'

Phil nodded through a mouthful of smoked salmon. Jill had wanted to hold Shula and Mark's reception at Brookfield, naturally, but after last time, when the marquee had had to be cancelled and the top tier of the wedding cake re-iced with robins and eaten at Christmas, Phil had thought it better not to tempt fate. So they'd booked Netherbourne Hall, which was just as well, since the photographer had let them down at the last minute and Caroline had said she'd draft in someone called Patrick who – typical Caroline – turned out to be Patrick Lichfield. At least, Phil reflected, he must feel at home in the Long Gallery, snapping away under the twinkling chandeliers.

'Are you enjoying yourself, Jethro?' Elizabeth, in pale blue satin, designed by David's girlfriend Sophie, flitted past with a glass of champagne in each hand.

'Very much, ta,' Jethro replied, tactfully not mentioning that he had thought his salmon a bit off. It certainly didn't taste like the stuff he usually had in sandwiches for his Sunday tea.

'How are you, Mr Archer?' Nigel materialized at Phil's elbow. He was also carrying two glasses of champagne. Phil began to wonder if he was seeing double. 'I thought you did your bit awfully well, if you don't mind me saying so.'

'What, walking Shula down the aisle?'

'It can't have been easy. I'm not sure I could have walked in such a straight line.'

Phil said nothing. He hadn't been able to believe it when Mark and Shula had announced they'd chosen Nigel as best man and Phil's worst fears had been realized in the vestry when Nigel had taken for ever to sign his name.

'I suppose he came rather late to joined-up writing,' Phil had hissed to Jill. She quelled him with a look before taking Reginald Hebden's arm for their procession down the aisle. Phil offered his arm to Mark's mother, Bunty, who'd spent the entire service in tears.

'I know Shula will look after him,' he said comfortingly.

Bunty sniffed.

'They're not with you for long, are they?' she mourned.

Four years longer than they might have been, thought Phil, but said nothing.

'One minute they're playing football and reading *Look and Learn*,' Bunty continued, as Mark helped Shula to arrange the train of her dress, 'and the next – well . . .'

The days of *Look and Learn* seemed an awfully long time ago to Phil. They'd lived at Hollowtree then. Elizabeth hadn't even been born. When he'd come in from the farm, Shula would run to meet him, her blonde pigtails bouncing on her checked school dress. He'd pick her up and swing her in the air then, though she was too big for it really, carry her into the kitchen, stepping over the boys' Meccano, to see the biscuits she'd helped Jill bake or the embroidery on a bit of Aertex she'd laboured over at school.

He could never admit it, but there was no doubt about it. Shula was his favourite child.

When she'd come back from Hong Kong in the summer so disconsolate, he could have cried for her. She'd done a lot of crying herself, he knew, up in her room. She spent a lot of time with Caroline at Grey Gables, telling her the details, he supposed, of what he and Jill had heard only in controlled amounts. How Mark had been the perfect host. How they'd done the sights and she'd met his colleagues and his friends at the tennis club. How they'd gone to the beach and the floating restaurant but how, obviously, nothing had been said in the way of a commitment, still less a proposal.

Phil had resigned himself to months of Shula's moody silences punctuated with Elizabeth's chatter about Nigel's new career as an ice-cream salesman under the name of Mr Snowy. But then one August evening when he came in from doing the milking, Jill had greeted him excitedly. Mark had phoned. He was flying home the next day and he wanted Shula to meet him at Heathrow.

Jill had paced the kitchen all the following afternoon. The Flower and Produce Show was looming and she was supposed to be thinking up jam recipes. There was a rumour that Auntie Pru was going to enter a jar of rose petal, which sounded like a winner on novelty alone.

'Where do you think they are?' she demanded when Phil charged through the kitchen to ring the machinery firm about a new belt for the combine: they'd just made a start on the wheat in Blacklands when it had snapped. 'Mark's plane was due in at one.'

'Jill, I really –' Phil had begun.

Then the back door had opened and Shula and Mark, looking rather pink, had trooped in.

'Shula, darling! Mark! How lovely to see you!'

Jill hugged Mark while Shula stood by, beaming.

'Yes, good to see you, Mark. Now if you'll excuse me –' Phil sidled towards the office.

'Oh, Dad, don't go!' Shula seized his arm. 'Mark and I have got something to tell you! And I think you're going to be really pleased!'

'Raspberry sauce and cornets! My poor car!' Mark and Shula had somehow managed to negotiate their way from the reception, peering through a windscreen daubed with shaving foam – or, keeping to Nigel's theme, perhaps cream – but had had to stop Shula's car in the lane by Netherbourne Hall to scrape off the worst of the damage. 'I dread to think what he's put in the cases.'

'Hundreds and thousands, probably.' Mark chucked a handful of soggy cornets into the hedge. 'It's Mr Snowy's revenge. Still, you only get married once.'

'I don't know why,' laughed Shula. 'I could do it every Saturday. Why doesn't anyone tell you how much fun it is?'

'I don't think I'd want to go through it all again.' Mark sounded heartfelt. He wiped his hands on a pile of tissues. 'It's the next two weeks I'm looking forward to.'

They were going to Scotland for their honeymoon, to Melrose on the Tweed. Mark wanted to have a go at salmon-fishing.

'Look,' he went on, 'I'm sorry about my mother, howling like that.'

'She didn't howl,' said Shula fairly. 'She just . . . sobbed.'

'It's not that she doesn't like you,' explained Mark. 'She couldn't get her hat on right this morning. It upset her a bit. Things were rather fraught at our house.'

'Poor Mark.'

Shula came round the car. She slid her hands under the jacket of his new grey suit and kissed him.

'Mmm. I think I'm going to like being married. I do love you, Shula.'

'I love you too.' She snuggled in closer. The light was fading over the tidy September fields, the earth already turned and sown in readiness for another year. Mark stroked her cheek. 'How were things at Brookfield?'

'Hm? Oh, this morning?' She smiled. 'Dad and David were more worried about a cow with milk fever than the wedding.' She sighed and looked over Mark's shoulder at the splashy berries in the hedge, bright blood-red. 'I couldn't help thinking about Gran.'

'Whatever for?' He pulled away slightly and looked at her.

'Just how she'd have loved to have been there today. She loved a good wedding.'

'Your grandad had a word with me at the reception. Told me I'd got to look after you or he'd be after me.'

'Bless him. He and Gran were married for nearly sixty years. It's an awfully long time.'

'Well,' Mark looked at his watch. 'We've been married six and a half hours. I suppose it's a start.'

• • •

'Mind you don't go too fast down here, love.'

'Sorry, Grandad.'

'There's a nasty bend at the bottom of the lane.'

'I *know* that, Grandad.'

Reluctantly, Elizabeth let the speedometer drop back to forty. When she'd offered to run her grandad home after her father's birthday tea she hadn't anticipated it taking the rest of the afternoon. She'd finished with Nigel soon after Mark and Shula's wedding, and she'd recently started going out with Tim Beecham. He was taking her out for *her* birthday treat tonight and she wanted to wash her hair. Her grandfather was wittering on about how he'd forgotten to tell her father something but he couldn't remember what it was.

'Tell him what a good driver I am,' suggested Elizabeth. 'And how I need my own car.'

She'd been hoping to get one for her birthday but Phil was cunningly blackmailing her into working harder for her A-levels by saying he'd 'think about it' when her results came through.

'That wasn't it,' fretted Dan. 'Now, what was I going to tell him?'

'Tell him to behave himself at my party,' insisted Elizabeth, changing down to take a bend. 'I want him and Mum out of the barn and tucked up in bed by five past midnight.'

The party was the following Saturday. Its theme was gold and she'd even managed to persuade her parents to fork out for a live band – Lelulu's – as well as a disco. If her Dad was too stingy to buy her a car, Elizabeth reasoned, it was the least he could do. After all, Shula was off his hands now – she and Mark had been married six months and were well and truly settled in their flat in the Old Wool Market in Borchester. Dan had offered to move to Brookfield so that they could have Glebe Cottage, but Shula wouldn't hear of it, and Elizabeth was pleased. It was useful to have somewhere to crash in Borchester and Mark could always be persuaded to cook her an omelette when she turned up starving in the early hours, after a night at Rags disco.

'Nineteen's a lovely age,' mused Dan. 'Doris was nineteen when we started courting.'

Here we go, thought Elizabeth, Lakey Hill, Midsummer's Eve bonfire, sprigs of St John's wort and all for the seven millionth time. But she didn't say anything because she loved her grandfather really, and it must be miserable to be nearly ninety with joints so stiff you had to turn your whole body round just to look behind you and feet that were sore and ears that needed syringing every few months. Instead, she thought about the black boob tube she would be wearing tonight. She hoped Tim wouldn't try to put cream down her cleavage again. He'd ruined her red dress doing that.

'Elizabeth! Slow down!'

'Grandad! I can't go any slower!'

'Stop the car!'

'What?'

'Over there, look,' tutted her grandfather impatiently. 'Well, stop the car! Don't just drive past!'

Elizabeth pulled the car in to the side of the road and her grandad began to struggle out, pointing a trembly finger over the hawthorn hedge towards a nearby field.

'You can't leave a sheep on its back, can you now?'

Elizabeth looked across. The rest of the flock munched on, unconcerned, while one poor animal was comically upturned in a dip in the field, waving its legs like a beetle on its back.

Dan was half out of the car now, hauling himself out of his seat by leaning on the open door. Elizabeth lurched across and grabbed at his overcoat.

'There's nothing we can do! Why don't we go back to Brookfield and get David. Or we'll phone him from Glebe Cottage, we're nearly there now . . .'

But Dan was out of the car, tucking the ends of his muffler into his coat.

'I'm going to see to that sheep. Are you coming or not?'

Elizabeth thumped the steering wheel in frustration.

'Grandad, you've been going on all afternoon about how your shoulder was hurting, you surely can't . . .'

Dan was already walking away from her towards the field gate.

Swearing under her breath, Elizabeth clambered out and slammed the door. No wonder her father and David were so stubborn, it was in the blood. She caught Dan up as he tussled with the gate.

'Here, let me do it.' She released the catch. 'And you're to let me turn the sheep, all right? Honestly. We shouldn't be doing this at all. You've got your best shoes on.'

Dan grunted, but she could tell he was pleased he'd got his way because he let her take his arm and they made their way across the bumpy grass. All around, sheep raised their heads and looked at them, chewing. A couple came up to Dan and butted his pockets in search of sheep nuts, but for once he took no notice. All he was interested in was the sheep that was in trouble. The stupid animal, bloated with spring grass, had obviously caught its foot in a rabbit hole or something, slipped and couldn't right itself.

'OK.' Elizabeth squatted down, tucked her scarf out of the way, and eased her arms under the animal's back. 'Now you tell me if I'm doing it right. I'm going to try and flip her over away from me.'

'That's the way,' her grandfather urged. 'Just give her a bit of encouragement. There, girl, Elizabeth's got you,' he advised the sheep.

Elizabeth grabbed hold of a couple of hanks of greasy wool and braced her arms. She heaved and strained and tried to push but the sheep was a ton weight. She didn't seem to be able to get her arms far enough underneath to get any leverage and her feet kept slipping from under her.

'Stupid thing's so heavy,' she puffed. 'No, Grandad, don't! I didn't mean you to –'

Dan was bending down to see if he could help. One minute he was squatting beside her, the next, he seemed to lose his footing and with a little moan he was down on the grass beside the sheep.

'Grandad?' Elizabeth found herself pinned between her grandfather and the sheep. Sobbing, she struggled to her feet and stepped over him. She crouched down and touched his face. He was a funny colour. 'Oh, my God. Grandad?'

'This was his favourite time of year. You'd be walking down the lane and there'd be Dan, leaning over a gate, watching all the lambs and rabbits jumping about the field, and the trees in blossom.'

Phil patted Uncle Tom on the shoulder. He'd taken the news very hard.

'I shall miss him. I don't like to think how much.' Tom's voice quavered.

Phil rubbed his forehead. Since it had happened, he'd called the doctor, who'd said it was a heart attack, informed the undertaker and had been to Borchester to get the death certificate, but it still seemed unreal.

'I'll never be able to come up here without thinking of him,' he said.

They were standing on Lakey Hill. The bracken was uncurling and bright blue speedwell was snaking through the grass. Chiffchaffs, arrived for the summer, darted in and out of a patch of brambles, building their nests, and the sheep moved as if mesmerized, cropping the turf.

'Mind, he had a good life and a long one.' Tom tried to sound positive. 'Eighty-nine years of age.'

'It's amazing to think of the changes in farming he went through,' concurred Phil. 'He and Mum started with a few cows and chickens.'

He couldn't help smiling at the thought. Dan had been a tenant of the Estate to start with, but he'd scraped together enough to buy Brookfield when the Squire had had to sell up, and by the time he'd passed it on to Phil, he'd doubled its acreage. Phil had expanded even more: he and David were now farming over 400 acres and, since Neil had left to set up on his own, with the same labour – one man and a cowman – that Dan had employed when the farm was a quarter the size. That was mechanization for you. That was the price of combine harvesters and computerized cattle feeding, and if one thing was certain it was that there was more change to come. David was talking about wanting to introduce flat-rate feeding for the cows; Phil was resisting in exactly the same way, he knew in moments of insight, that his dad had resisted his attempts to keep the cows off the kale with an electric fence back in the 1950s, or try potatoes or oil seed rape in the 1960s.

'A few cows . . .' Tom echoed. 'Those days are gone, eh, Phil?'

'I'm afraid so,' replied Phil. He could still see his dad in the old stable, harnessing Blossom and Boxer, the shire horses, or doing the farm accounts at the kitchen table under the light of the gas jets. And his mother would come in with the eggs, which still had to be washed by hand, followed by Chris with a basket of windfalls from the orchard. Jack and Peggy had been at the smallholding in those days, Tony just born. And Phil had been Mr Fairbrother's farm manager, building up a herd of pedigree Herefords and courting Grace. 'Yes, Uncle Tom,' he agreed. 'Gone for good.'

• • •

'More mulled wine, anyone?'

As Mark circulated, refilling glasses, Jill looked round the sitting room at Glebe Cottage. Shula and Mark had got rid of some of the furniture and they'd freshened the paint and had new curtains made. But enough reminders of Dan and Doris remained for their presence still to be felt, this first Christmas without either of them.

'Jill?' Mark hovered with a steaming jug which was giving off odours of cloves, cinnamon and brandy. 'It's Nelson's recipe from the wine bar.'

'All the more reason to say no!' Jill covered her glass. 'I shall be sliding under the table when we sit down to lunch.'

'Jolly good. It's about time you had Christmas day off for once in your life.' Shula, her face flushed from the stove, offered her a plate of bacon-wrapped prunes.

Jill took one and smiled at her daughter. Shula and Mark's move to Glebe Cottage had been one of the happier outcomes of Dan's death, as was the money he'd left outright to Christine and to Tony. It was Phil, unfortunately, as executor, who'd had to deal with the thorny issue of capital gains tax on Dan's share of the farm, and which totted up to an astonishing £50,000. Phil had struggled with the figures all year and had eventually decided that the only option was to sell some land – something no farmer ever liked to do. Fifty acres plus thirty acres at Meadow Farm were currently on the market and due to be auctioned in January, but the sale had already caused unpleasantness in the village with people worrying about the risk of speculative building. Phil had borne the problem, and the gossip, in his usual stoical way, but Jill knew it had severely interrupted both his work on the farm and his grieving for his father.

Still, thought Jill, watching out of the corner of her eye as Mark and Elizabeth fought over Handel's *Messiah* versus Madonna by the stereo, it hadn't been a wholly bad year. There was David and Sophie's engagement, for one thing. Jill had had reservations about Sophie's suitability to start with but, as Phil said, if David didn't know his own mind by now it was a pity, and they had, after all, been going out for over two years. So a date had been set for the summer and Sophie was starting to talk about Vivienne Westwood-inspired organza for the dress, and David spent the whole time looking proud of her and pleased with himself. Jill wondered what sort of farmer's wife Sophie would make, but then farmers' wives came in all shapes and sizes these days. It might be a very good thing that Sophie intended to follow her own career: if Phil could be persuaded, Jill herself was keen to branch out with her own farm diversification into bed and breakfast for tourists. Jill was sad that David wouldn't be with them today: he was having Christmas lunch with Sophie's parents, but she realized only too well that, having dedicated her life to bringing up her children, her next challenge was to let them go.

'Mum! Have you seen their Christmas card from Nigel! It's even glossier than the one he sent to Brookfield!'

Elizabeth, in velvet trousers and a silver shirt that didn't leave much to the imagination, bounced over. After two seasons as Mr Snowy, Nigel had finally been pensioned off – sent back to the polar wastes as he put it – and his father had decided once and for all to put a stop to his son's career in sales. He'd rung up Nigel's Uncle Lindsey, who worked in the City, and had bullied him into giving the boy a job. To everyone's amazement, Nigel was doing terribly well. He had a different pair of braces for every day of the week and was considering buying a Porsche – 'Vulgar, I know, but it's the done thing,' he'd explained apologetically when he was last back for the weekend. Elizabeth was astounded at his new-found career-mindedness, but it was a sign of the times. They were all capitalists now. Even she had got herself a regular job in the Classified Sales Department of the *Echo* and was hoping it would give her a start in journalism.

Sanity had prevailed and the chords of the *Messiah* soared through the room. Phil was standing by the mantelpiece, talking to the new doctor, Matthew Thoroughgood. He'd called in with Caroline and they'd been invited to stay for lunch. It looked as though Caroline had a new admirer there. She deserved it, Jill thought. From what she could gather, hearing one side of the story from Shula and the other from Peggy, Jennifer had found out in the autumn that Caroline had had an affair with Brian and had confronted both of them about it. Brian had blustered and said that Caroline only looked on him as a sort of father figure – a shoulder to cry on when her romances went wrong. ('Great!' Caroline had complained to Shula. 'Makes me sound like some dreadful neurotic!') Caroline had been more truthful. Faced by a furious Jennifer, she couldn't bring herself to lie, but Brian, in his usual winning way, had calmed Jenny down. He'd promised they'd do more things together and promised to involve her more in the farm. He'd even talked about them going organic, like Pat and Tony, who were making a big success of it, and to prove he was serious, he'd bought her a new pair of Hunter wellies.

'If that's all it takes, I'm surprised more farmers don't have affairs,' David had said cynically, though not in front of Sophie, who took a purist line on these matters.

Jill took a sip of her drink and reached for a cashew nut. Any longer and she'd take root in this chair! But Shula had forbidden her from entering the kitchen: she and Caroline were clattering about in there quite happily. Mark was collecting the empty glasses and Elizabeth was curled up in corner of the sofa chuckling over a book of cartoons he'd been given. Phil and Matthew were still hogging the fire. Jill decided to join them.

'Good heavens! What are you two doing?' she said in alarm as she approached.

'Matthew thought he might be able to mend Dad's clock.' Phil turned to her with a smile.

Dan's old carriage clock had inexplicably gone wrong soon after he'd died. What with one thing and another, the move to the cottage and her new job as agent for the Estate, though she was still employed by Rodway's, Shula hadn't got round to getting it repaired.

'Do be careful, Matthew,' Jill urged as he fiddled with an intricate bit of the mechanism with a pair of tweezers he'd produced from his pocket. Trust a doctor, never off duty . . . She squeezed Phil's arm anxiously as Matthew concentrated, then held up the clock in triumph. It was ticking.

'If you could bring the greens in, please, Caroline?'

Shula's footsteps crossed the tiny hall.

'Come here, Shula,' called Jill, 'and listen.'

'What is it?' Shula came in, carrying the gravy. 'I'm about to serve up the turkey, you know.'

Phil took the sauceboat from her hands and put it on a side table.

'Listen,' he said. 'Just listen. This'll remind you of your grandad.'

Shula took the clock and held it to her ear.

'It's working!' she exclaimed. 'Mark, the clock's working again!'

Mark came over and put his arm round her.

'Happy now?' he asked, fondly. 'She's been fretting about that clock,' he added to Jill.

Shula lowered the clock and looked at it. It had been a present to Dan from the Squire to mark his sixty-fifth birthday: the clock face was gold and etched with a cherub blowing a trumpet. She turned to her parents.

'It's stupid, isn't it?' she said self-consciously. 'Looking for signs in things. But it did seem significant, somehow. Grandad suddenly wasn't with us any more and the clock suddenly stopped too. But now it's working again – well, it's as if Grandad's given us permission to live here, Mark and me, and be happy here, and – well, just to carry on. All of us.'

'Oh, Shula,' said Jill, 'I hope so.'

'Of course we will,' Phil confirmed. 'We owe it to Mum and Dad. We wouldn't be here without them.'

'Look, you lot.' Elizabeth pushed her way in between Mark and

313

Shula. 'Are we eating today or not? Some of us have got places to go, people to see later on.'

'Oh, Elizabeth, trust you,' smiled Jill.

'What? What have I said now?'

'Nothing,' smiled Shula. 'Just stopped us getting all sentimental, that's all.'

Elizabeth groaned.

'That's the trouble with this family, always harking back to the past. We've got a future as well, you know.'

'Yes, Elizabeth,' smiled her mother. 'With you around, none of us need be in any doubt about that.'